# THE GHOSTS OF CRAVEN MANOR

# MANOR

Written by Joseph Daniels

Dear reader

This is not a simple story you hold in your hands, but rather an interactive time travelling adventure in which you choose what happens next.

To play this game you will require a single dice, or two if you have them, and some paper.

Firstly, please turn to the back of the book and copy the statistics onto one of your sheets of paper. You do not need to write them as shown. This layout is merely a suggestion. You can also, if you wish to, scan or photocopy the statistics so you do not have to write everything down. Do not read the rules yet, because they are only there as a point of reference, and will be explained to you individually, throughout your adventure, as and when you need to know them.

All you need to know right now is that your name is Dave Ingram, you are engaged to a woman called Liz, and you have just recently bought a house called Craven Manor together.

Now please **turn to 1** and begin your adventure.

## 1

"So I just need you to sign there... And there...And you're done. Here are your keys. I hope you'll both be happy in your new home."

No sooner has the estate agent left the café, when you turn to your fiancée and share a look of excitement before embracing her with a passionate kiss.

"Oh Dave this is so great," she says, "our own house."

"I know," you say, "and what a bargain."

"Well the agent did say that the last owners died there. That kind of thing generally brings down the price. I still think we should have asked for details about that."

"Why, Liz? So we could scare ourselves into not buying the place? What we don't know won't hurt us."

"I suppose you're right," she says. "Anyway, I need the toilet. Be back in a bit."

After Liz has left, you are considering ordering something else to eat, when your thoughts are interrupted by the sound of crying. You turn to see that a little boy has dropped his ice cream on the floor. To this you snigger, and then quickly turn your face away from the boy's mother before she sees. It's not that you really care what people think, but you can never tell how they are going to react, especially stressed mothers. Even something as simple as a snigger could cause a scene, and given the great day you are already having, you don't want to ruin it.

Looking towards the menu again, you are interrupted for a second time. This time it is by a young waitress who is being harassed by a couple of drunks. 'There really should be a law about people drinking in the day', you think to yourself, 'although it wouldn't matter if there was. People would still do it, and you can bet the police wouldn't even bat an eyelid if they saw them'. You consider for a moment coming to the young girl's aid and then stop yourself. 'I'd probably only make matters worse and besides its part of the job that she chose.'

It is not long after this that Liz returns and sits down.

"What time have you got?" you ask.

Liz looks to her watch.

"Two, thirty."

"And what time's the removal van meant to be showing up at the house?"

"About Four-ish."

"Then we're going to have a bit of time to kill. What do you say to getting out of here soon and having a look around town?"

"I suppose so," she says. "I noticed a jewellery shop on the way in."

"I was actually more interested in the book shop next door to it," you say.

"Well we're probably only going to have time to look in one. Which should we go to?"

If you choose to look in the bookshop **turn to 44**
If you choose to look in the jewellery shop **turn to 159**

## 2

(74 x3)

Now inside the house, you only have a limited amount of time before the butcher returns, so you must pick where you intend to search, quickly.

If you search his bedroom **turn to 468**
If you search his kitchen **turn to 36**
If you search the store room **turn to 97**
If you search the living room **turn to 500**

## 3

With your chest pounding and your legs feeling like jelly, you eventually make it across the ledge to another window on the far side of the house. Luckily the window isn't particularly secure, so you find it easy enough to apply force and pull it open. Then once there's a wide enough gap, you stumble through into the corridor on the other side. As you land on your hands and knees, you notice that you are not far from where Ruth shot her father, which would mean your amulet is also nearby. You know if you could just get to it, you could either attempt to undo all of this, or return to your own time, so you get to your feet and race straight over. It's only when you reach Ruth's father's body that you suddenly realise that you are no longer being chased, and a sudden dread comes over you. Where is Ruth? You assumed she was following you, but what if she knew you'd come back here. Unfortunately by the time you have come to this realisation, it is too late, because out from her hiding place she steps, with her gun pointing in your direction.

Ruth is about to shoot you, when Peter, who it turns out is not dead after all, leaps out from the shadows, grabs her and wrestles the gun from her hand, sending it sliding over to you. You immediately pick it up and point it at Ruth, but see that you do not have a clear shot. If you attempt to shoot Ruth while she is wrestling with Peter.

**Roll one die**

If you roll 1-2 **turn to 459**
If you roll 3-5 **turn to 105**
If you roll 6 **turn to 285**

If you would rather attempt to distract her so Peter can overcome her, you could try shouting something that may get her attention. **If you know what to shout, replace the letters in the word with the numbers below and then turn to the number in question. Be sure to make a note of this passage just in case you get lost.**

| A | B | C | D | E | G | H | I | M | N |
|---|---|---|---|---|---|---|---|---|---|
| 6 | 2 | 2 | 5 | 0 | 4 | 3 | 3 | 0 | 7 |
| **O** | **P** | **Q** | **R** | **S** | **T** | **U** | **V** | **W** | **Y** |
| 9 | 6 | 0 | 4 | 1 | 5 | 8 | 7 | 1 | 0 |

4

When you can't give any proof that you have evidence against him, the butcher takes you by surprise and forces you to the ground, before picking up a rock to crack your skull open.

**Roll two dice**

**You may add up to 2TTP to ensure your roll is higher**

If you roll 10 or over you manage to move out of the way in time **turn to 457**

If you roll less, you are not quick enough and the rock comes down hard on your skull. Unfortunately because you are in no position to do so, you will be unable to reverse time and avoid this terrible fate, so I'm afraid your journey ends here.

<h1 style="text-align:center">5</h1>

As you step inside the workshop, you are surprised to find that it looks exactly the same as it did back in the 1800s, with Ruth's father, Nicholas Craven, carving something at his work bench. At first you think you have somehow travelled back in time, but looking back through the door, you see that the rest of the house is unchanged.

"Greetings Mr Ingram," he says. "I've been expecting you."

"You have," you say, confused.

"Just give me a few moments and I'll be right with you."

It is only now that you realise you can understand what he is saying.

"How come..."

"You can understand me when the language of all the other ghosts in the house is distorted? That is a good question," he says as he turns round to face you, "almost as good as: Why does this room appear the same as it did in the past? The answer to both questions is quite simple. I am not a ghost. You see the doorway you just stepped through is a portal, one which bridges the house in your time to my workshop in 1905."

"But that's impossible," you say. "You are dead in 1905. You died during the Craven Manor Massacre."

"That is because I do not come from the 1905 in your timeline," Nicholas explains, "but rather an alternate one, in which my family and I were not murdered. You see the doorway you stepped through is more than just a time portal; it is the doorway to another reality. I created it specifically so we could have this conversation at this very moment in time."

"How is it that you know me?" you ask.

"I must be careful with what I say, because any divergence in what happened could cause a chain of events that may indeed prevent my reality from ever becoming."

"In English?"

"If I tell you your own future you may do something different that could result in my world disappearing. I can only tell you what you told me to say. Suffixed to say that the reason my family and I survived that night in this house, is because you saved us all. I will not say how, but after you did so, you told me about this specific conversation we had had, and how it helped you in saving us. It was after this that I began constructing this doorway, so we might have this conversation. Anyway for you to understand what really happened that night, you will need a particular item. That item can be found in the miscellaneous room upstairs, you know, the one that is padlocked. You told me that the combination is **349**. You should go now, the portal is unstable and I fear if you do not leave in time, you may be stuck in my reality forever. Good luck and God bless."

Quickly you step back through the door and moments later, Nicholas Craven disappears as the workshop transforms from being a clean brightly lit room, to a dark, dismal area filled with cobwebs.

You now return to the house **turn to 13**
**Mark down the Display Room as complete, as you will have no need to revisit this place.**

6

You return to the present to find that it is once again light outside. The man in black is gone and the doors are no longer sealed. You immediately go to your fiancée in the living room to hear her speak in that strange distorted language that you have yet to understand.

*T462v motr anrute awont. Becalpe ognikate anever amorfe gsredrume behte apotse aylbissops anehte adnaf oytitnediv asihd orevocside adluoch muoyt osoo81f metale mehte onik bemite ayma bota akcabe olevarti gote ayawe bag ednife owohemosh adluoch buoyt ofik. okcalbi onig aname asihte ehtiwe alaeds ethgims mewt awohk anom paedim anaf meme asevige aylneddush belbissoph asif asihte atahte agniwonky. ayenruoje aruoye anog aneesh mevahs oyame muoyt asgnihte mehte arofe buoyt ayvneg bin? otin asawe awohk. hemite ahguorhte adellevarte mevahs muoyt bosh."*

You can now search parts of the house you didn't before and go out into the town. Bear in mind that you can also time travel at any point if you have a date to travel to. You cannot return to a period you have already been to before unless otherwise specified.

From now on the only requirements to time jump are for you to be present in the house when you do, as the energies surrounding the house are needed to make the jump. However this is only when making the jump from the present. From those other times, you can jump from anywhere, but when travelling back to the present you will always return to the house.

You can now continue to explore the house **turn to 13**
Or explore the town **turn to 444**

**7**

(449 (Via study and ballroom) 220 (Via ballroom) 423 (Via toilets)

You run to the garden door as fast as you can, only to find much to your horror, that it is magically sealed shut. You consider quickly turning back and trying another route, but before you have a chance, the man in black grabs you and you feel your life force being slowly sapped away. If you are unable to reverse time, I'm afraid your journey ends here.

**8**

(329)

The man continues knocking and then eventually another man answers the door.
"Where is she?" asks the man. "Tell her to come down here now."
"She doesn't want to see you," says the house owner. "Perhaps you should come back when you've sobered up,"
"Tell her to get her ass down here now or I'll come in and drag her out."
"If you take one step into my home, I promise that you will regret it."
It looks like these two men are going to fight.

If you attempt to intervene **turn to 122**
If you continue on to Craven Manor **turn to 446**

**9**

(305)

Opening the cage you brought with you, you release the rat into the kitchen. A few moments pass before the maid notices it, and then runs out of the house screaming:
"Rat! There's a rat!"
Thankful that she did not run into the main house and alert the butler, you use this as your opportunity to sneak inside.

**Turn to 66**

**10**

(240)

"Look, you need to listen to me right now," you say. "You are all in great danger. There is a killer in this house, and he intends to kill you all before the night is out."

"Are you threatening my family?" asks the butler.

"No, I'm not the killer. I'm warning you about someone else."

"Are you saying there's a second person in this house?"

"Yes and they may be killing your family as we speak. We need to go and stop him."

"I'm sorry, but who are you exactly?"

"It's not important who I am. If you don't do as I say, people are going to..."

Suddenly the most blood curdling scream you can imagine, echoes through the house, and the butler turns and runs up the stairs. You realise it is too late, the killing has begun. Your best bet now is to reverse time or else leave the house and return to the present **turn to 13**

**Bear in mind that if you do return to the present that you will not be able to return to this time again and so will have to find some way to deal with the man in black in your own time.**

11

(19)

By shining the torch towards the pond, you catch sight of a statue in the centre; an angel with its hands held out before it, and in one of those hands appears to be a shiny blue object. What it might be, you have no idea, but you have a feeling it could be something useful.

If you wish to wade through the water to get to the statue **turn to 441**

Or you can use Future Knowledge F8

Otherwise you can return to the house **turn to 13**

**If you return to the house, mark down the number of this passage as a shortcut for The Pond. When visiting here you will be able to come to this shortcut instead of the original number written on your navigation list.**

12

((476) After using Future knowledge D1 (490) Not using Future Knowledge D1)

Exploring the living room, you find something written on a note pad. It seems to be the address of a local storage building.

**Add CMIP N. This will give you access to building C/1800s Town (The Storage Building.)**

If you explore further into the house **turn to 317**
If you leave **turn to 408**

13

CRAVEN MANOR NAVIGATION LIST
(MODERN DAY)

Below is a list of rooms you can explore anytime throughout your adventure. You can go to any one of these rooms as many times as you like, but you must be sure to keep note of the shortcuts when they are given to you. These will allow you to return to the passage you were on before you left the room,  so you can return there without having to go back over things you have already done. You will also be told if a room has been completed, when this happens you should make a note that you do not need to return there. This can be for two reasons. One, to ensure you don't keep going back to rooms that have already been fully explored, and two, to avoid ruining the illusion that your actions in each room have consequences.

If this is your first time here, after checking three rooms, not including locked doors, you must **turn to 288**

**Ground Floor**

Kitchen **turn to 262**
Dining Room **turn to 182**
Ballroom **turn to 145**
Cellar **turn to 58**
Storeroom **turn to 368**
Library **turn to 292**
Storeroom Two **turn to 233**
Study **turn to 168**
Conservatory **turn to 402**

**Garden**

Pond **turn to 19**
Shed **turn to 230**
Gazebo **turn to 120**

**Upstairs**

Storeroom Three **turn to 343**
Bedroom One **turn to 135**
Bedroom Two **turn to 43**
Miscellaneous Room One **turn to 258**
Miscellaneous Room Two **turn to 184**
Attic **turn to 326**
Bedroom Three **turn to 438**
Bedroom Four **turn to 158**
Bedroom Five **turn to 309**
Bathroom **turn to 365**
Display Room **turn to 332**

(You cannot visit the following areas until you are told they are available to you)

Go to Town **turn to 444**
Go to 1800s Town **turn to 488**

## 14
((476) After using Future knowledge P (490) Not using Future Knowledge P)

Walking back through the shop, you pass the taxidermist while he is serving a customer.
"Thanks for your help," you say. "But I should really be going."
"You're not staying?" he says disappointedly, "but we were just getting started."
"It's all right; I think you've given me everything I need."
"Well, if you're sure."
He looks like he wants to try harder to get you to stay, but is so busy with the customer, he decides to let you go. You leave and walk further up the road **turn to 317**

## 15
(358)
You decide to keep up the pretence a while longer, and find yourself being led on a tour of Gil's home, which eventually brings you to his display room.
"And this is where I keep my most valuable treasures," he says, as he leads you through a room full of glass cabinets holding all kinds of precious items.
"Is this where you intend to hold your event?" you ask.
"Oh no," he says. "I'm going to be preparing the dining room for that. After all, it's more useful to be nearer the kitchen."

11

"With all your treasures on display like this, does it never worry you that someone may break in and steal something?" you ask.

"What, these trinkets? No. They may look nice but these are the least valuable items I own. The more precious items are locked away in the safe, which only I..."

Gil is suddenly cut short as the lights go out in the room, leaving you in complete darkness. (FK: A1+20)

"Oh no," says Gil disappointedly. "The electricity has blown again. Don't worry; I'm sure Kenworth is already on his way to replace the fuse."

"I don't think that's what this is," you tell Gil. "I think this might be the first signs of a robbery in progress."

"A robbery," he says in disbelief. "Don't be so ridiculous. I've never been robbed in my entire life."

"There's a first time for everything," you say.

If you have a gun and choose to prepare an ambush for the men coming in **turn to 456**

Otherwise you have no choice but to wait and see what happens next **turn to 282**

## 16
((90 x3) If you were syringed (490 x3) If you collapsed)

You awake to find yourself tied down to a table. Your head is splitting, your vision is completely blurred, and for some reason you cannot move a single muscle in your body. As you feel a wave of panic come over you, a figure steps out of the shadows.

"Ah, you're awake," says the taxidermist. "I imagine you are confused right now, probably wondering why you can't move. It is because of the concoction that I dosed you with. You see it not only contained a powerful sedative, but also a paralytic. It will ensure that you are unable to move during the operation. I hate squirmers."

You can already guess what this operation is going to entail. He intends to cut you open, take out your insides and then fill you with sawdust and put you back together, just like he's done with his stuffed animals.

"Now, where is that scalpel?" the taxidermist says. "I know I left it round here somewhere. Damn, I need that scalpel! An artist can't be expected to finish his work without his favourite paintbrush. I must have left it in the house. Don't go anywhere until I return. That's a joke by the way, as I know there's no possible way you can go anywhere."

After he has left, you try to will your body to move, but no matter how hard you try, you can't even wiggle your left toe. It is only when you hear whimpers coming from your left, that you turn your eyes and notice the girl tied up in the chair next to you, probably due to receive the same treatment.

((FK: B9 part 1 of 3 -49) Note that you need to find all parts to get the right sum to add or subtract when the time comes to use the future knowledge)

Soon the taxidermist will return, so unless you can rewind time your adventure is over.

## 17
### (499)

To climb the trellis is going to take both caution and agility.

**Make a note that the trellis has six sections then roll a single dice.**

**For each time you roll 4-6 you progress one section up the Trellis.**

**If you roll a 3, nothing happens.**

**If you roll a 2, you lose your grip and fall to the section below.**

**If you roll a 1 on sections 1-4, you fall to the bottom and must start again.**

**If you roll a 1 on section 5 or 6 of the Trellis, you fall and break your back and must reverse time to undo your mistake.**

If you make it to the top in less than 10 throws, you make it in through the window and come into the house **turn to 100**

If you do not make it in time, screams are heard, signalling that the killings have begun. Your best bet is now to reverse time or return to the present **turn to 13**
**Bear in mind that if you do that, you will not be able to return to this time again and so will have to find some way to deal with the man in black in your own time.**

## 18

Checking under the bed you find several boxes filled with shoes, and another filled with books. The one filled with books is so heavy that you can barely pull it out. (FK: D4 +99)

You can now either check the wardrobe **turn to 245**
Or check under the grill **turn to 474**

Or return to the house **turn to 418**
**If you have chosen to hide in this room turn to 271**

### 19

The pond is so over canopied by the surrounding trees, that the area is pitch black and you can barely see anything.

You now return to the house **turn to 13**

### 20

Entering the attic, you are met with a very old and musty smell. Several boxes of junk have been left here. You wonder if you might find anything useful, but as you go to have a closer look, two blue translucent figures emerge from the shadows. One is a man and the other a woman, both wearing fairly modern clothing. By your observations these people can't have died that long ago. (FK: F5-49) As they come towards you, the man raises his hand angrily and sends you flying back. Then the woman screams, launching several objects in your direction with the power of her mind. Luckily you are able to dodge each one of these. These are vengeance spirits and will not let you past, so until you can find a way to get rid of them, you cannot return to this room.

You now return to the house **turn to 13**

### 21
(482)

As you leave the antiques store, you find that Ruth is being consoled by Peter.

"It's alright," says Peter. "Whatever it is, you can tell me."

"No, I can't," she says. "It's too..."

"Ruth! Ruth!" you hear a third voice shout.

You then see Ruth's father walking towards them both.

"Mr Craven," Peter says surprised.

"Out of the way," the father says as he pushes Peter to one side. "You've already done enough damage."

"I was only trying to help."

"By encouraging her to sneak away? Look boy, I know you mean well, but do yourself a favour and stay out of this. It is none of your business. Come on Ruth we're going home."

It seems that Ruth is almost catatonic as her father drags her away. Choose who you wish to follow from this point on.

If you follow Ruth and her father **turn to 347**
If you follow Peter **turn to 109**

22

You hand the glasses to the policewoman and she tells you to wait while she checks them for fingerprints. When she returns, she reports her findings.

"The fingerprints on the glasses are a match to some of those on the knife, but there appear to be another set on there too."

**((FK: B4 part 1 of 3 –12) Note that you need to find all parts to get the right sum to add or subtract when the time comes to use the future knowledge)**

You now return to the town **turn to 444**
**When returning to the town, be sure to mark down 188 as a shortcut for future fingerprint checks.**

23

In the maid's quarters you find a very pristinely, clean room with minimal furniture. The only thing of interest is a journal on top of the chest of drawers. You decide to browse through it and find an entry that is of particular interest.

*Jan 20th*

*The usual routine today. I have to confess that I cannot wait for my six weeks leave that is coming up at the end of next month. I've been completely rushed off my feet. I caught that boy with the crooked nose spying on young Ruth again. This time he had climbed the tree directly outside her bedroom window. Cheeky monkey! I chased him off, of course. I didn't tell Nicholas about it because I just knew he'd worry. He's got enough to be thinking about with everything that has been going on.*

**(FK: B6 part 1 of 3 –16) Note that you need to find all parts to get the right sum to add or subtract when the time comes to use the future knowledge)**

Once you have read the journal entry, you return to the house **turn to 418**
**If you have chosen to hide in this room turn to 271**

## 24
### (487)

No sooner have you taken a step towards the carvings, when Ruth's father spins round and catches you.

"Who the devil are you?"

The shock of being caught causes you to stumble back, and you find yourself landing on a sharp saw blade that slices your throat open. As you lie there bleeding to death, you know your only hope is to use the amulet to undo this awful mistake. If you are unable to reverse time, I'm afraid your journey ends here.

## 25

As you draw closer to the cupboard, the scratching grows more intense and then turns into a banging. With every bit of courage you can muster, you pull open the door and then to your horror, something flies out of the cupboard past your head. Your scream is so loud, that moments later you feel embarrassed when you realise it was simply a cat. (FK: F2 +28) Before you can even get a good look at it, the cat shoots round the corner.

You now return to the house **turn to 13**
**Mark down The Dining Room as complete, as you have no reason to return there.**

## 26
### (160)

"Wait a minute," she says. "I know you. Yes it was you. You were the one I spoke to in the garden at the Craven Manor party. You made up a story about being a treasure hunter to convince me that you had been invited to the party."

"What makes you think it was made up?" you ask.

"Oh please. Part of what I do for a living is separating fact from fiction. So I'm not crazy after all."

"Why would you think you were crazy?"

"I saw you later that night," she explains. "I was on my way to use the toilet and I noticed two people standing outside the front door. One was a girl who appeared to be quite distressed, and the other was you. I was intrigued to know what the conversation was about so I moved closer. I didn't hear much, just you telling her that she shouldn't tell people about something that had happened to her because they might think she was crazy. She left soon after that, but you hung around for a while. I watched you for a few moments longer and was considering coming back to the party, when suddenly, you disappeared into thin air."

Upon hearing this you start to panic. How on earth are you going to explain this?

"You saw me disappear?" you say, with a tone suggesting that this is the craziest thing you have ever heard.

"To be honest I wasn't really sure what I saw. Up until seeing you today, I was considering the possibility that I may have imagined you altogether, since no-one else at that party recalled seeing you there, and let's face it, no-one just vanishes like that, but here you are. Interestingly enough, your disappearance that night coincided with another mystery. A guest at the party claimed that he had gone looking for his girlfriend earlier that night, and whilst looking for her, had been attacked by a mysterious stranger who had knocked him unconscious, before absconding with his girlfriend. You wouldn't happen to know anything about that would you?"

"No," you lie.

"Because you can see how a person might think the two events were linked?"

"What are you getting at? Do you think I attacked that man?"

"Are you saying you didn't? Because it does look suspicious that the woman I saw you with outside, matches his girlfriend's description. Look I want to give you the benefit of the doubt here. You saved me from a beating tonight, so I know you're not a bad guy. In fact if I were to hazard a guess, I would say you were possibly rescuing that woman from her abusive boyfriend. Tell me I'm wrong?"

"It was nice to see you again Zoe," you say as you make an attempt to leave.

"If you refuse to talk to me, then I'll have to go to the police with what I know," she threatens, right before she spots a policeman walking down the road. "Oh wait a minute, there's an officer over there. Hey officer! Officer!"

Even though there is nothing she could say to the police that could affect you in the long run, she could force you to have to leave this time earlier than intended, so you need to find some way to rectify this. You can either reverse time to make sure you never saved her from those thugs, or you can tell her the truth.

If you choose to tell her the truth **turn to 216**

**27**

(335)

As you run out of the door, you see the taxidermist coming up the opposite way.

**Roll two dice**

**You may add up to 2TTP to ensure your roll is higher**

**If you roll 10 or over, you manage to outrun him and make it to the exit**

You can now return to the town **turn to 488**

**Mark down Building F as complete, as you will have no need to revisit this place.**

**If you roll less than 10, you must fight the taxidermist.**

**If you need to, you can now consult the rules of Combat at the back of the book. But be sure to make a note of this passage so you can return here after.**

**Fight will last 12 rounds**

**If you beat the taxidermist, you manage to stun him briefly and escape.**

**If at any time you roll a double or over 10, you manage to grab for his knife and are now able to wound him and escape mid battle. (The roll over 10 must be made by the dice alone without TTP added or it does not count)**

If you escape, you return to the town **turn to 488**
**Mark down Building F as complete, as you will have no need to revisit this place.**

## 28
### (464)
"Actually, I've come to buy something," you say.
  "What would you like?" the butcher asks.
  "A leg of lamb," you improvise, "three beef steaks, and a whole chicken."
  "That's a lot of meat. Are you having a party?"
  "A family gathering."
  "Any particular occasion?"

If you wish to continue on with the small talk **turn to 472**
If you try to get him to leave so you can swipe the key **turn to 99**

## 29
### (82)
Removing the mask, you are shocked to see Ruth Craven staring right back at you. The shock of this causes you to draw back, just in time to see Ruth's father coming up behind you, followed by Peter. Ruth's father has a gun held at you.

((FK: B5 part 1 of 3 + 15)(Alternative) Note that you need to find all parts to get the right sum to add or subtract when the time comes to use the future knowledge) Alternative means that if you have this piece of knowledge already you can ignore it)

You can now use Future Knowledge D2
Or **turn to 509**

## 30
### (327)

You are contemplating how you are going to get out of the room, when the door flies open and the man in black swoops in and grabs you. Unless you can reverse time, I'm afraid your adventure ends here.

## 31
### (335)

You are so concerned with escaping that you do not hear the taxidermist return, not until he has stuck a needle in your neck with the same paralytic you were meant to have drunk. From this moment on there is no hope of escape, so you must reverse time or die.

## 32
### (420)

Nothing happens for a long time, so you step inside to see what's going on. It's only when you notice the gust of wind blowing in from the back room, that you decide to check back there and find the open window. It then becomes clear to you what has happened **(FK: D9+19)** The man who came to the door was obviously the person you were looking for, and while you were waiting for him, he used the opportunity to escape and flee. Reeling from this disappointment, you decide to leave.

You now return to the town **turn to 488**
**Mark down Building E as complete, as you will have no need to revisit there.**

## 33
### (73)

Remembering that the stuffy businessman outside is the same man from the pub who said his wallet had been stolen, you go back outside and watch from afar as the young boy shines his shoes. A few moments pass, and then you notice the boy accidentally drop some of his polish onto the man's trousers.

"What do you think you are doing!" the man says, angrily.

"Oh I'm terribly sorry. Allow me to clean that up for you."

"You'd better had."

As you watch, the boy grabs a cloth, and while he is cleaning the stain on the man's trousers with one hand, he reaches into his pocket with the other and removes the man's wallet. He does this with such speed and finesse that the man doesn't even notice.

"There you go sir, all done."

"How much?" the man asks.

"No charge sir," the boy says. "Think of it as my apology for getting polish on your trousers"

"Well I should think so to," the man says unappreciatively before he saunters off down the street.

Once he is gone, you decide to approach the boy

"Shine your shoes sir?" he asks.

"No thank you," you reply, "but I will take that wallet you just stole."

"I have no idea what you are talking about, sir."

"I'll bet you don't. Come on hand it over, or I will have to report you to the police."

"Here it is," the boy says as he hands you the wallet. "Please don't report me to the police. I don't make a habit of stealing, I just felt like he deserved to be taught a lesson."

"Don't worry, I won't say a word."

"Thank you sir," he says. "As a gesture of goodwill I would like to offer you a free shoe shine."

"And have you take this wallet back, not to mention my own? Did you think I was born yesterday?"

"Oh well, you can't blame me for trying."

You reach into the wallet and pull out a handful of coins, which you give to him.

"Here, I believe your last customer forgot to pay you."

"Thank you sir," he says.

You now leave him and decide to look at the full contents of the wallet. Inside you find £50 in cash and a card for a gentleman's club with the word CRANE written on it. You decide to keep both. You now continue up the street.

**Continue to 234**

## 34
(98)

Whether you tried or not to stop it, the kid trips and drops his ice-cream. You are tempted to laugh again, but you stop yourself. As the mother helps the boy to his feet, you notice that his shoelaces are untied. (FK: A +13)

**Turn to 147**

35

*THE BOOK OF GHOST DETERRENTS*

*There are three types of spirits one can encounter from beyond the veil. Vengeance spirits, Manifestation spirits, and Echoes.*

### *Vengeance Spirits*

*These are often murdered victims who died under extraordinary circumstances and have become wicked and cruel over time. Unfortunately there is only one way to deal with a spirit like this and it is to discover the location of the remains of the person, so you can salt and burn their bones.*

**Add CMIP J. This will give you access to the graveyard, where you can go to salt and burn the bones of Vengeance Spirits. To do this you require salt and a lighter.**

### *Manifestation Spirits*

*These are spirits that are created by events and emotions that take on a malicious form of their own. They often appear as a dark figure, black smoke or a monster. They can possess the living and force them to carry out their bidding, or appear temporarily, in a solid form, to carry out their business themselves. Since these are not people, they cannot be destroyed in a conventional way. The only way they can truly be destroyed is to discover the spirit to whom they are connected, and destroy that spirit in the same way you would a vengeance spirit.*

*There are, however, ways to deter a manifestation spirit.*

1. *Striking it with an obsidian blade.*
2. *Using a spirit box to temporarily capture it.*
3. *They also only come out at night, because they are repelled by the daylight.*

### *Echoes*

*These are often friendly spirits carrying on the duties of the person who died before them. They continue on because they have unfinished business. There is no need to deter or destroy these spirits, but they can be dealt with in the same way as a vengeance spirit.*

## 36
### (2)

You are not quite sure why you find yourself searching the butcher's kitchen, because all you are likely to find is left over food, crockery and utensils, but nevertheless you find yourself there. Seeing the leftover stew again, does make you wonder how a man who sells meat for a living could make something so terrible. You are about to leave, when you notice a biscuit jar, and decide to have a look inside. Upon opening it you are glad you did, because inside you find a key with a tag on it saying Workshop. **Congratulations you have just found the elusive Key to the Craven Manor Workshop. You can add this to your inventory.**

If this is the first place you checked **turn to 370.**
If it is the second **turn to 458.**
If it is the third **turn to 417**

## 37

With the wind knocked out of him, the butcher falls back and slumps against a tree. It seems like the fight is over, but as you stop to catch your breath, your opponent goes in for one final attack. As he lunges towards you, you instinctively move out of the way, and watch as he trips and stumbles past you, down a hill, to land deathly still at the bottom. When you see that he is not moving, you go to investigate and find that he has cracked his skull on a rock similar to the one he had tried to end your life with. For a moment you consider if you should help him, but then when you see his eyes roll back, you know it is over. You didn't want it to end like this, but he gave you no other choice.

After taking a few moments to compose yourself, you start to wonder what kind of unintended consequences this could have on the timeline. Would there be an investigation into his death? Would some poor innocent soul be hung for a crime that they did not commit? You consider whether you should hide his body, but then stop yourself. For the butcher to suddenly go missing, would pose more questions than someone finding him dead in the woods. At least this way, there is a chance that people may just assume that he had simply had an unfortunate accident. After all, aside from a few bruises he could have picked up on his fall, there is no evidence to say he had been in a fight.

Accepting the fact that there is nothing more you can do now, you decide to return to the night of the Craven Manor Massacre, hoping that your meddling with the past has resulted in at least one positive outcome.

**Turn to 393**

**38**

(312)

The man seems like a snob, but is still content to drink in this pub. If you are looking for someone, perhaps he may be able to help you.

**If you know who you are looking for, exchange the letters of the person's name for the numbers below and turn to the number in question. There is only one person you can find here. Make sure to make a note of the number above, just in case you end up going to a paragraph that doesn't match up.**

| B | D | E | G | I | L | M | N | O | T |
|---|---|---|---|---|---|---|---|---|---|
| 2 | 0 | 6 | 3 | 9 | 2 | 5 | 9 | 1 | 4 |

Or if you do not wish to talk to him any longer, you can do one of the following.

If you approach the rocker **turn to 115**
Or leave **turn to 277**

**39**

(86 (Via Peter's) 382 x2 (Via Craven Manor))

It takes you a long time before you are able to find Ruth, and by the time you do, you find that she is being consoled by Peter outside the Antiques shop.

"It's alright," says Peter. "Whatever it is, you can tell me."

"No, I can't," she says. "It's too..."

"Ruth! Ruth!" you hear a third voice shout.

You then see her father walking towards the couple.

"Mr Craven," Peter says surprised.

"Out of the way," the father says as he pushes Peter to one side. "You've already done enough damage."

"I was only trying to help."

23

"By encouraging her to sneak away? Look boy, I know you mean well, but do yourself a favour and stay out of this. It is none of your business. Come on Ruth we're going home."

It seems that Ruth is almost catatonic as her father drags her away. Choose who you wish to follow from this point on.

If you follow Ruth and her father **turn to 347**
If you follow Peter **turn to 109**

## 40
(151)

You decide not to take the risk of running up the crates onto the roof, and continue following from the street. Unfortunately, the crowds on the street begin to slow you down, and you see the thief getting further and further away. There is no way you will catch up to him now.

You must now return to the town **turn to 488**
**Mark down Building E as complete, as you will have no need to revisit this place.**

## 41

Remembering the account you made a year ago, you decide to stop in and pick up your winnings. You cannot believe your eyes. The bet you made has won you £300. Not bad. Now what could you use that for?

You can now return to the main gaming area **turn to 289**
Or you can return to the town **turn to 488**
**If you came here via the woman with the pill, then by leaving you give up your attempt to find out more about Reardon and help this woman's husband.**

**Add CMIP T. This will allow you to return to Reardon's Gambling Den just for gambling purposes.**

## 42
(172)

"Would I be able to use your facilities, please," You ask. "I've got a bit of a bladder infection at the moment and I tend to go at a moment's notice."

"Of course," the man says. "It's the third door on the left."

Ducking into the toilets briefly, you are amazed to find how archaic they were back in this time, simply a seat with a big hole that drops directly into the sewers, and boy does it stink in there. You don't wait very long before leaving and making your way towards the manager's quarters on the second floor. Unfortunately the route you must take is in clear view of the manager's desk, but since he is reading a book, you may be able to slip by unnoticed.

**Roll the dice three times and try not to roll a 1.**

**If you do roll a 1, you can retake the roll, but it will cost you 2TTP.**

If you succeed **turn to 106**

If you fail to get past the manager, you make an excuse about getting lost before you leave and return to the town **turn to 488**

**Since you messed up this opportunity, you will not be allowed to try again. Mark down The Hotel as complete.**

43

This is the master bedroom; the same one you were asleep in not too long ago. In the centre is a big double bed, but there appears to be nothing else of interest.

You can now use Future Knowledge F2

Or return to the house **turn to 13**

44

The Bookshop is so crammed with books on the shelves and in piles on the floor, that there is barely room to walk around. While Liz moves off into a corner of the shop to look at books on art and textiles, you are approached by the owner, a small bent over mole of a man with big glasses.

"New in Town?" he asks.

"Yes, my fiancée and I just bought a house here, the old mansion on Blakemore Drive."

"You mean Craven Manor?"

"Yes, that's right. We're moving in today. We're both actually very..."

"You should leave now while you have the chance."

"What?" You say, surprised by his sudden change in tone.

"That house is a place of unspeakable evil. Everyone who has lived there has either died or gone missing."

"Ah, so it's a haunted house? Boy I really did get a good deal. Ghosts free of charge," you chuckle.

Suddenly the man grabs your arm.

"It is no laughing matter. You should heed my warning. You might not have another chance."

"Hey, alright I get it," you say humouring the man. "The house is haunted and we're all going to die. I'll heed your warning," Then under your breath, "you mentalist."

Now feeling uncomfortable in here, you go to join Liz and then leave the shop.

**Turn to 176**

## 45
### (290)

You wait for a little while, expecting that the butler will return with Mr Craven, but instead he returns completely alone.

"I have spoken to the master of the house," the butler says, "and he confirms exactly what I had suspected, that he made no such appointment with you or anyone else from the council. So unless you wish to book an appointment for another time, I must say good day to you sir."

After he closes the door you realise that you must either reverse time and try something else with him, or attempt to sneak in **turn to 320**
If you have exhausted your options, you travel back to the present **turn to 13**

## 46

You hand the diary to the policewoman and she tells you to wait while she checks it for fingerprints. When she returns, she reports her findings.

"The fingerprints on the diary are a match to some of those on the knife, but there appear to be another set on there too."

((FK: B5 part 1 of 3 + 15) Note that you need to find all parts to get the right sum to add or subtract when the time comes to use the future knowledge)

You now return to the town **turn to 444**
When returning to the town, be sure to mark down 188 as a shortcut for future fingerprint checks.

## 47

As you are on your way out of the old peoples' home, you suddenly recall a conversation you had back in the 50s with a business man called Tom.

"This town needs a library, don't you think? All I need to do, is raise £500 and then I can complete the project."

Remembering this, makes you wonder if this might be the way forward. All you have to do is find £500 and travel back to give the guy the money, and then a library will appear when you get back. Unfortunately you cannot travel back to a time you have already been to, but there may be a way of finding another date within the same month.

You now leave and return to the town **turn to 444**
**You can now mark down Building C/Town as complete, as you will have no need to revisit this place.**

## 48
(277 x3)

No sooner have you left the pub, when you are grabbed from behind and pushed up against a wall by two men. You recognise them as the same thugs who you faced in the alley earlier.

"Well look who it is," says one of them, "the hero. I told you you'd regret ever meeting us, and now you're about to find out why. It's time for you to meet our boss."

He then clubs you over the head with a bat and everything goes black. You awake moments later to find yourself in a dimly lit room, tied to a chair. You struggle for a little while trying to break free, but the ropes are too strong. Soon a group of men enter the room, led by a man with a scar on his face, whom you recognise as the ghost from the hotel basement in your time.

"Do you know who I am?" he asks.

"Bob Jenkins," you reply.

"That's right," he replies. "I've been hearing a lot about you from my boys; how you attacked them to rescue that reporter woman. When I heard about what you did, I was impressed. You see there are not a lot of people in this town who would have done what you did. Mainly because they know what would happen to them if they crossed me, but also because not a single one of them has the guts that you do. Now normally I would rip those guts out and play with them, but I think that would be a real waste. Talent like yours is hard to come by, and it just so happens that I am in need of a man with such talents, for a job I intend to carry out tonight; a jewellery theft. If you agree to help me, not only will you get to live, but you'll also be paid your fair share. So what do you think, want to make some real money?"

If you agree to his offer **turn to 125**
Otherwise **turn to 215**

49

You run for the window and climb out carefully onto a ledge. You must make your way carefully round to one of the other windows.

**Roll the die, six times**.

**If you roll a 1, you must roll over 8 on two dice to avoid slipping. If you succeed, you continue with the remainder of your six rolls**

**If you fail the roll, you fall and grab the ledge.**

**To pull yourself back up you must roll a 12 in four rolls. Then you continue the remainder of your six rolls.**

If you make it to the other side **turn to 3**

50

Approaching the headstone of John and Hayley Barnett, you wait until you are sure no-one is watching and dig up their grave, before salting and burning their bones. You only used a few handfuls of salt, so there is still plenty left if you need to do this again.

**Add CMIP B. This affects The Attic.**

You now return to the town **turn to 444**

51

You are considering what precious stone to take, when you have a reaction to a turquoise stone that you just picked up. As you hold it in your hand, it glows and you feel a tingling sensation flow through your body. You are amazed to discover that it is actually a time stone.

You must now increase your maximum TTP by 2 and can bring your current TTP to full. As well as this make a note that you have the following ability:

Forward time

This will allow you to skip one single dice rolls worth of rounds of combat and can be used once per fight with no TTP expense. This is best used when you are currently winning the combat row.

"I'll take this one," you say.
"Ah, I purchased that one in a charity auction six days ago," he says. "I was led to believe that it was magical, although I have yet to see this magic for myself."
"Thank you," you say. "I appreciate this gift."
"In addition to this I would like to offer you membership to my private gentleman's club. If you were ever interested in visiting," he says as he hands you a card. "They will ask for a password at the door. The current password is Crane."

Make a note that you can visit this club at any time whilst in 1954, providing you are not in the middle of any kind of encounter. To go there you simply must turn to 345. Do make a note of where you are at the time though so you can return there.

Congratulations, not only did you save Gil from being murdered, but you also prevented his would be murderer from being sentenced to death.

Add CMIP D. This has affected The Hotel.

Also remove Future knowledge I and H1.

If you do not wish to go to the business club now, you say goodbye to Gil and return to the present turn to 13.

## 52
### (379)

Upon catching you, the butcher looks really angry
"What do you think you're doing sneaking down here like this? Is this any way to treat someone who saved your life, who has been nothing but kind to you."
"I know what you did!" you say.
This flusters him, and you use the opportunity to push one of the hanging pigs at him with a considerable force. As he falls to the floor, you decide to leave the way

you came in and get yourself to safety.  Unfortunately by doing this you have ruined any chance of finding any more evidence against the butcher.

You now return to the town **turn to 488**
**Mark down The Butchers as complete, as you will have no need to revisit this place.**

53

As you enter the entrance hall, you gasp in shock at the sight of the two corpses lying on the floor. One is a woman in her mid-forties, wearing the outfit of a classic Victorian maid, and the other, a young boy no older than twelve. This must be Clara and Jack, you think to yourself. Both appear to have met their fates in very different ways. The maid obviously died from having her throat cut open, and the boy may have been struck with a blunt instrument, given the wound on his head. As you are looking around, hoping to find a possible murder weapon, you notice a few pieces of wood surrounding the boy, and look up to see that part of the banister on the first floor hallway is missing. Perhaps it gave way during a struggle with his attacker and he fell. This makes you wonder if perhaps the wound was caused by the fall.

You return to the house **turn to 418**
**If you have chosen to hide here turn to 271**

54

On your way into the Gambling Den, you bump into a woman who grabs you by the arm.

"Please sir," she says. "I'm sorry to bother you, but I really need your help and I didn't know who to ask."

"What's the problem?" you ask.

"Well it's like this see, my husband owes Ray Reardon money and to pay off that debt he is fighting in the ring. So far he's done alright, but his next opponent is known for already killing the last two people he fought. I begged Reardon not to have him fight, but he won't listen, so the only way I can see to save my husband is to stop the fight myself."

"How?"

"With this," she says as she shows you a red pill. "If he takes this it will not only cause vomiting, but he'll have such bad stomach cramps that he won't be able to fight. All I need is someone to bring it to him."

"And I'm guessing that's what you want me to do?"

"I would take it to him myself, but only other fighters are allowed back there. I thought if I could find a man who would be willing to volunteer to fight, then they could do it for me. Please I am really at my wits end."

If you agree to help the woman **turn to 134**
**Or you can use Future Knowledge E3**
If you can do neither of these things, you apologise and leave her to do one of the following:

If you wish to continue into the Gambling Den **turn to 289**
If you wish to visit Ray Reardon **turn to 504**
If you choose to leave and return to the town **turn to 488**
**Note that if you return to the town you give up your attempt to find out more about Reardon and help this woman's husband.**

**Add CMIP T. This will allow you to return to Reardon's Gambling Den just for gambling purposes.**

55

Remembering that the object is a key, and not wanting to mangle your arm again, you realise that all you need to do is make a device to hook into the hole to pull it up. You will need two objects to do this.

**When you find both objects, mark down the numbers of the rooms you found them in and then take the smaller number away from the larger. The result will be the number you must turn to in order to use them.**

You can now return to the house **turn to 13**

**If you return to the house, mark down the number of this passage as a shortcut for The Kitchen. When visiting here again, you will be able to come to this shortcut instead of the original number written on your navigation list.**

56
(262)

As you lower your hand into the garbage disposal and try to get the silver object, you find that it is out of your reach, so you put your whole forearm in. You have just gotten hold of the object, that feels like an old key with a hole in the top, (FK: C – 207) when to your horror, you hear the motor start and feel the most excruciating pain as rotary blades begin to shred your arm to pieces. You cry out in agony and quickly try to pull your hand out, but it is too late. Your hand is gone, and all that is left is a mangled, bleeding stump. You fall to the ground, feeling that you will soon pass out and die on the kitchen floor. Unless you can reverse time, I'm afraid your journey ends here.

### 57
(90)

Moving further into the house you see several adjoining rooms. You pass a kitchen, a bath room, and a bedroom. You check them one by one, but there doesn't seem to be anything of particular interest. You are considering leaving, when you hear a noise coming from behind a large mirror in the corridor.

If you wish to investigate the noise **turn to 419**
If you decide to leave **turn to 119**

### 58

Approaching the cellar door, you realise it appears to be locked.
If you have a rusty bronze key **turn to 433**
If you have a bronze key **turn to 494**
Otherwise, you return to the house **turn to 13**

### 59
(2 x2)

When you hear the front door of the shop close, signalling the butcher's return, you realise you may have just one more opportunity to search for the evidence you need. If you already have it, you may leave and return to the town **turn to 488**

**If you do this, mark down the Butchers as complete, as you will have no need to revisit this place.**

If not, or you wish to explore further, choose where you will look next.

If you search his bedroom **turn to 468**
If you search his kitchen **turn to 36**
If you search the store room **turn to 97**
If you search the living room **turn to 500**

Returning to the living room, you find your fiancée, who speaks to you in that strange ghostly voice.

*"E5bs degdelwonke gerutufe mesum bote melbaf tebe adluohsh muoyt asif erellike mehte mohwt awonke muoyt afik. atsern mehte mode enach bin ednam osik orelliks mehte oknihth muoyt mohwa meme ollets asid mode bote muoyt adeene min allam. atserk mote aluosh as'relliks aymo atupe mote ayawe orehtonak asid merehts. ayrrowe atons mode enehts, mote atone mesohch brok aredrume mehte apotsh mote belbanul jerewa puoyt afik."*

You can now return to the house **turn to 13**

**61**
**(465)**

As the butcher goes to investigate the door with the broken chain, you seize the opportunity to go through the door he came through, and make your way into the house **turn to 2**

**62**

Stepping foot into the old people's home, you are met by a moody looking carer, who after some explaining, eventually leads you to the lounge where you find Rose Everett watching TV. You recognise her immediately, because despite her grey hair and wrinkles, she still resembles that young woman you saved back in the 50s. As you approach her, you expect that she might not recognise you. For you it was only hours or days ago that you met, but for her it was over 60 years ago. But surprisingly, despite the years gone by, her face lights up when she sees you.

"It's you," she says.

"You recognise me?"

"Of course," she says. "But how can it be? You haven't aged a day. You saved my life that day, you know."

"I was just in the right place at the right time. It's good to see you again, Rose."

"I always suspected that I may see you again. After all, a man who came from out of nowhere has to come from somewhere, or should I say some time."

"You knew?"

"I had a long time to think on the subject."

"Listen Rose," you say, feeling regretful that you have to get straight to business. "I need your help."

"Anything for the man who saved my life," she says understandingly.

"Your granddaughter said that you did some research on the past occupants of the house."

"That's right."

"Would you be able to share some of your findings with me?"

"Well I do recall that the ghosts only started appearing after a murder back in the late 1800s," she begins. "Although I can't remember the details. Unfortunately my daughter threw away all my research because she was worried that I was getting a bit obsessive. I suppose in a way she was right, but that doesn't help you now, does it? If only there was a library in town I would suggest going there to look for some old papers, but unfortunate they never built one, something to do with not having enough funds."

You thank Rose for her help and then leave.

You can now use Future Knowledge G.

Or leave and return to the town **turn to 444**

**You can now mark down Building C/Town as complete, as you will have no need to revisit this place.**

## 63
### (54)

"Alright, I'll help you," you agree. "But I'm afraid I'm going to need a favour first."

"Anything," she says. "Whatever you ask?"

"I'm actually going to be having a meeting with Reardon, myself, shortly. I would like you to follow me up there and wait close by, and about five minutes after I have gone into his office, I want you to yell fire!"

"Fire! Why?"

"It's not important. I just need to know that you'll be willing to do it."

"For you helping my husband, yes of course."

"Thank you."

You then put your plan into action. The meeting goes ahead as before and when the woman yells 'fire,' you are surprised to find that Reardon looks towards an ugly bust of Nelson in the corner of the room. (FK: E4+327). It then seems like he is about to get up and leave, when one of his workers charges into the room.

"It's alright," he says. "It's a false alarm. There isn't a fire. Probably some street urchin playing a practical joke."

Not long after this, your meeting comes to a close and you return to the woman who helped you.

"Did it work?" she asks.

"Like a charm," you reply. "I just need to find a way to get back in there."

"Can't that wait? Remember, you promised to help my husband."

"Of course," you say. "Give me the pill."
She gives you the pill and then you leave her to return to the gambling den.

**Turn to 289**

64

Upon entering his home, the butcher brings you into his bedroom and leaves you to get out of your wet clothes and into one of his dressing gowns, while he starts a fire in the living room. By the time you come to join him, the fire is glowing and he beckons for you to sit in one of his comfy looking arm chairs.

"So any idea why someone would want to attack you?" he asks.

"No," you say, "I've only been here a few hours."

"And what exactly have you been doing in that time?"

"Nothing much," you lie to be safe, "just talking to a few people around town."

"About anything in particular?"

You choose not to answer him.

"Look, your business is your own. I don't mean to pry, but whatever you've been talking to people about has obviously attracted someone's attention; someone who obviously feels that they have cause to harm you. If you want my advice, I would stop what you are doing and get out of this town."

"I'm afraid I can't do that," you say.

"Then you might want to consider finding out who this person is before they come for you again. The chances are it was someone you spoke to today."

You begin to consider all the possibilities, but none of them strike you as more obvious than the next.

"I imagine you must be rather hungry after all that excitement today," the butcher says. "There's some leftover stew if you're interested."

"Yes that would be lovely," you say.

While the butcher goes to heat up the stew, you find yourself looking around the room and noticing that he seems to be quite a man of culture. On the mantel piece there is an abstract sculpture, besides which sits a set of pan pipes, and on the wall are also several works of art, which look to be hand painted by the butcher himself. (FK: A8+10)

"Did you do these paintings?" you ask the butcher as he re-enters with your stew.

"Do you like them?"

"Very much," you say.

"It's one of my many hobbies," he says. "I've always loved creating and making things. I used to work with an inventor in town. Perhaps you know him, Nicholas Craven."

"You mean the father of the Craven family?" you say in disbelief.

"Yes, god rest his soul. We were partners back in the day. Even after our partnership ceased, he still allowed me the use of his workshop for my own projects. He was a good man and a good friend. His daughter was quite lovely too."

"Ruth."

"Did you ever meet her?"

"In a way."

"Right from a young age you could tell she was going to be a beauty. It's a tragedy that so precious a thing could be taken from this world. Anyway that's enough talk of sad things. Enjoy your stew."

You sit back and eat. The meal isn't great, but you eat it to be polite. Then once your clothes are fully dried, you thank the butcher for his hospitality and leave to continue your investigation.

You now return to the town turn to 488

**From this point on you will be allowed to time jump from here back to the house in your time, and from there to this 1800s town.**

## 65

You approach Peter's door and knock. It is not long before he answers.

"Hello?" he says, unsure.

"Hi there," you say. "My name is Dave Ingram; I'm Ruth's cousin."

"Ruth Craven?" he says, surprised. "I didn't know she had any cousins."

"We used to write to each other a lot. She often told me about you in her letters."

"Strange how she never told me about you. I'm guessing that you heard the terrible news?"

"Yes, I was deeply saddened," you say, before coming up with a suitable story. "I've been working abroad for the past year. Where I was, there was no communication with the outside world, so I only found out about her death recently."

"What brings you here now?" Peter asks.

"Well since I got back, nobody has been able to tell me what really happened that night. I know they were all killed, but I just don't understand why or by whom. Since you were probably one of the last people to see her alive, I was hoping you might be able to tell me something. I need some kind of closure."

"I'm not sure if I can help you with that, but I'll try," he says as he holds the door open for you. "Come in"

You accept his invitation and follow him into his dining room where he gestures for you to sit down.

"Can I get you a cup of tea?"

If you take him up on his offer **turn to 529**
If you decline his offer **turn to 192**

## 66
### (9 (Via kitchen) 156 (Via study)

As you step into the entrance hall, you hear a man's voice shouting:

"Crowther!"

"Coming Sir," a second man replies.

You see the house butler make his way past the stairs and onto the corridor leading past the ballroom. You realise your best choice is to follow him to the voice in question, since it is very likely to be Ruth's father. Now that you are inside the house you will have to be extra careful not to be noticed.

**Roll one die and try not to get a 1.**

**If you are unsuccessful, you can use your reverse time ability to roll again as many times as you like, but each time you do this will cost you 2TTP.**

If you succeed in following him quietly **turn to 174**

If you fail and are unable to undo your roll, the butler suspects you of being a burglar and tells you to leave the house. You realise after this that there is no way you will witness the moment in time you wanted to see, and decide to travel back to the present **turn to 13**

## 67

As you enter the pub, your eyes water from the amount of smoke in the air. Amidst the fog, you look around for possible people to question. Most people look drunk or unapproachable, but you do see two who might be able to help you. One is the bar man; a plump bearded man, and the second an attractive woman in a purple dress who looks like she's waiting for someone.

If you talk to the barman **turn to 155**
If you talk to the woman **turn to 178**

Or you can return to the town **turn to 488**

**68**

(304)

Thankfully, you find that you are able to afford a night in the hotel and drive on over there. The manager, a thin, balding man with a raggedy beard, greets you as you enter and gives you your room key. The room is not worth the price you paid for it, but that doesn't bother you, because you are just happy not to be spending the night in that house.

You soon fall asleep, but feel a sense of déjà vu when you awake to find that Liz is not by your side. You assume that it is mere coincidence and that she simply got up to use the toilet, but upon checking, you realise she is not there. You get dressed and go to have a look around the hotel, thinking that you might find her wandering around, but she is nowhere to be seen. By this time you are starting to panic, so you talk to the manager, hoping that he may have seen her.

"Yes, I did see her," he says. "She was acting kind of weird, kind of drowsy and like she was not all there. When I saw her wandering outside, I asked her where she was going and she said she was going home."

"Going home?" You say surprised. "Did you notice if she took the car?"

"No, she left on foot."

"Walking in which direction?"

"North."

"Towards Craven Manor?"

"Yes, that's right."

Hearing this, you run straight to your car and drive on over to your new house, to find the door wide open. Inside you find Liz standing in the hall. Relieved to see her safe, you run over and take her in your arms, closing your eyes as you embrace her.

"Thank god you're okay," you say. "Come on, we need to get out of here. There's something wrong with this house."

You are about to leave, when you notice that Liz doesn't seem to be moving.

"Liz? Come on, we don't have time for this."

As you pull away you hear a sickening, squelching sound, and look down to see the bloody knife in your hand that you have just removed from your fiancée's bleeding stomach. For a moment, she looks at you shocked.

"Dave!" she says, a sound of betrayal in her voice. "Why did you..."

"I didn't," you say. "It wasn't me."

She is about to fall back, but you manage to catch her and then lower her to the ground softly. As she breathes her last breath, you feel your heart breaking all over again.

38

"Why!" you scream into the heavens. "Why send me back if there is nothing I can do to stop this? What more can I do? You have to give me another chance. It can't end like this."

You then close your eyes and concentrate on the café, in the hopes that the day will reverse so you will have another chance to get this right. And as luck would have it, it does.

**Turn to 427**

**Turn to 427**

## 69
### (29)

Remembering what is to come, you stop Ruth's father from making the same mistake twice.

"Stop," you shout as he goes to approach her. "I don't think she's completely unconscious. Peter and I will restrain her. You cover us with the gun."

"Very well," says the father.

As you and Peter approach Ruth, she jumps to her feet and attempts to fight back, but the two of you are more than a match for her and manage to restrain her easily enough.

"Bring her this way," says the father, as he points you towards her bedroom.

You drag her down the corridor, kicking and screaming, and push her inside. Then her father locks the door behind her.

"I must send a telegram to Dr Greenfield," he says. "He's the only one who can help her now."

"What is wrong with her?" you ask.

"What my Ruth suffers from is a multiple personality disorder. Inside her is this other person who sometimes takes control of her and forces her to do unspeakable things."

"Has she always had this?"

"No, the doctor believes it first started after the incident back in 1892, when she was raped in the woods. This started a chain of events, which led to her creating this other personality to protect herself from those who might harm her, myself included. Yes, I too was seen as a threat. You see when her sickness first took hold, I was more concerned about my good family name than I was about her wellbeing, which is why I kept the whole thing secret and made sure she was locked away in her bedroom at all times. For that I am deeply regretful."

"But she got better," says Peter. "She must have, because I saw her several times since, and before today I had seen nothing of any second personality."

"That's because the good Doctor Greenfield helped her to bury that personality deep in her subconscious. It probably would have stayed there too, if something had

39

not brought it out today. Do you have any idea what might have triggered her change?"

"No," says Peter. "It just happened all of a sudden when we were in the store."

"Well whatever it was, I'm not sure Doctor Greenfield will be able to help her in the same way again, not with it coming this far. I hate to say it, but I'm afraid she might need more permanent care."

"You mean put her in the nut house?"

"Peter you saw what she was like. If Ruth is in there she's buried deep, and bringing her back out is going to take some time and medical expertise that we do not have at our disposal. Unless you can think of something else that hasn't already been tried, I'm afraid it may be the only solution."

**(FK: B5 part 3 of 3 +9) (Alternative) Note that you need to find all parts to get the right sum to add or subtract when the time comes to use the future knowledge) Alternative means that if you have this piece of knowledge already you can ignore it)**

If you can think of a final date to travel to, you can go there now, otherwise all you can do is return to your own time in the hopes that your preventing of the Craven Manor Massacre, may have removed the ghosts from your house. If you do go to another date, make a note of the number below so you can return there after your jump.

**Turn to 316**

70

Unfortunately all bets are closed for the night's fight, and the next one is not until the following week, a time that you do not have the coordinates for. You are about to leave when you hear two people talking about the fight.

"So who did you bet on?"

"Who do you think? Billy Bone-Crusher of course. He's won every fight he's ever been in. Every one since he entered the ring back in 97."

"You mean when he fought Jimmy Long Paws. I never saw that one. I heard he knocked him out in the fifth round."

"That's right he did. It was one hell of a fight." (FK: D8 +146)

You can now return to the main Gambling Den page **turn to 289**
Or return to the town **turn to 488**

If you came here via the woman with the pill, then by leaving you give up your attempt to find out more about Reardon and help this woman's husband.

Add CMIP T. This will allow you to return to Reardon's Gambling Den just for gambling purposes.

## 71

You are about to leave the room, when you hear a noise under the bed and look under to find a familiar looking cat staring back at you. It is in fact the same one who scared you down in the dining room. You reach out your hand to it and say in the gentlest voice you can.

"Come on, I'm not going to hurt you."

And then it comes to you, purring. After giving it a stroke, you notice that it is wearing a collar with the name Leo on. The cat looks to be about twelve years old, which means it could have belonged to the previous owners. Not wanting it to get hurt during everything that is to come, you decide to let it out into the garden and shoo it away. Eventually it leaps the wall and disappears into the distance.

You leave and return to the house turn to 13
**Mark down Bedroom Two as complete, as you will have no need to revisit this place.**

## 72
### (228)

"Now our first lot is a precious stone donated by Sir Felix Bentley," the woman continues, as one of the household servants brings out a beautiful turquoise stone. "This stone has been in Sir Bentley's family for several generations."

As the cabinet holding the stone is brought past you, you are very surprised to feel a strange tingling throughout your body. You wonder if this might be something to do with the time travel, like an inner warning system telling you that you should leave, although part of you wonders if it might be something to do with this precious stone.

You are about to move closer to the podium to get a better look, when you overhear a man behind you, who seems to be running around frantically asking several guests the same question.

"Excuse me," he says. "Have you seen the woman I came here with? She said she was visiting the powder room, but I haven't seen her since. This simply isn't like her."

Finally someone speaks up.

"Yes, I think I saw her heading upstairs about five minutes ago."

"Thank you," the man says, right before he leaves the ballroom.

You now feel incredibly torn on where you should go. Even though this precious stone has you intrigued, you know from your own experience that a person wandering off on his or her own in this house is never a good thing.

If you follow the man looking for the woman **turn to 128**
If you stay for the bidding on the diamond **turn to 148**
If you decide to return to your own time **turn to 6**

## 73
### (421)

As you cross the road, you happen to catch sight of a young boy shining shoes out the front of the shop. His current customer is a stuffy businessman in a suit..

"Make sure they have a good sheen to them," the man says as he sits in the chair. "I want people to notice them when I walk in the room."

"With the sheen I give them sir, people will not only notice your shoes, but they will be blinded by them."

"I didn't ask you to talk boy. So if you wouldn't mind, a little more silence from here on out. I would like to read my paper in peace."

What a rude obnoxious prig! You are half tempted to accidentally spill something on the man's shoes as you pass by, but you resist the urge. Instead you ignore them both and enter the shop.

"Hello there," says a bent over man as you enter the store. "Welcome to my shop. Are you here to buy or to sell?"

"To sell, possibly," you say.

"Well let me see what you have."

Below is a listing of what you can sell here and what amount you will receive in return

| | |
|---|---|
| Cigarette Case | £40 |
| Penny Dreadful | £25 |
| Toy train | £70 |
| Antique Vase | £500 |
| Silver Statuette | £500 |

You can now use Future Knowledge W
Or once you have made your sales you can leave and continue on down the street **turn to 234**

## 74

After your recent discovery, you are beginning to wonder what the connection is between the butcher and Ruth Craven. Could he have been the one who attacked her all those years back? If so, why would he kill her and her family? You need answers and the only way you think you are going to get them is to sneak into his house and find more evidence.

If you go in through the shop entrance **turn to 464**
If you look for another way in **turn to 413**

## 75
### (282)

You quickly grab for the gun of the man nearest to you, and attempt to wrestle it from his hand. During the struggle, the gun goes off, hitting the ring leader and starting a chain reaction of gun fire, which ends with you being shot in the stomach. As you fall back, dying from your wound, you notice that both Zoe and Gil are dead, and realise you have failed in more ways than one. Unless you can reverse time, I'm afraid this is the end for you.

## 76
### (329)

On your way across town, you hear a woman cry out and turn round to see that she has been drenched by a carriage driving through a puddle. She doesn't look happy and seems to be shouting at the driver. You realise that the carriage could be just the thing you need to get to Craven Manor quicker, but someone else has decided to take it. (FK: C9+30)

If you jump in anyway **turn to 213** (Note that you will need £2 to pay your fare.)
If you ignore it and try to make your way to Craven Manor on foot **turn to 382**

## 77

The study is very similar to the one in your time. Not a lot has changed, except that there are a few less books maybe, and a smell of stale cigar smoke. As you search the room, you come across a letter on the desk that is addressed to Nicholas Craven. It has already been unsealed so you feel no danger in having a peek. Upon opening it, you read the following:

*Dear Nicholas*

*I have tried asking nicely and have offered you a very generous sum, but for some reason you will not even consider selling me what was mine to begin with anyway. I hate that it has come to this, but I now feel compelled to take drastic action. Unless you reconsider my offer, I will be forced to make life extremely unpleasant for you. This is your final warning.*

*RR*

**(FK: B8 part 3 of 3 +27) Note that you need to find all parts to get the right sum to add or subtract when the time comes to use the future knowledge)**

Taking note of this letter, you now return to the house **turn to 418**
**If you have chosen to hide in this room turn to 271**

## 78

Seeing the tree that was felled by the thunderstorm earlier on, makes you wonder if you can perhaps make use of it to cross the pond and avoid getting wet and muddy. You are fortunate enough to find a big branch that not only reaches over to the statue, but has enough strength to take your weight. Making your way over carefully, you reach the statue and quickly grab the object you came for. It is a carving of some sort, but you decide to take a better look at it once you are safely back on the other side.

**Turn to 88**

## 79

Hannah lives in a self-contained bungalow around the back of a boarding house. You knock on the door and hear a voice shout back to you.
  "No visitors today, thank you."

If you decide to wander round to the back of the house to see if you can find a way to sneak in **turn to 353**
If you continue to knock on her door **turn to 212**
Or you can leave and return to the town **turn to 488**

## 80
(535)
Offering her the cigarette case, she looks confused.

"That's a bit of an expensive gift to give to someone you don't even know, besides what exactly would I do with it, since I don't smoke? No thank you. Please don't come back here."

Unfortunately, unless you are able to reverse time and redo some of your choices in this conversation, you have ruined your opportunity to speak to Hannah.

You now return to the town **turn to 488**
**If you decide to return to the town, mark down Building A/1800s town as complete, as you will have no need to revisit this place.**

## 81
### (503)

As you reach the final rooftop, the thief stops in his tracks and turns around.

"Please, don't kill me," he begs. "Tell Reardon that he'll get his money. I just need more time."

"I have no intentions of killing you." You tell him. "I just came to ask you some questions."

"So Reardon didn't send you after me?"

"No, no-one did."

"Then why were you chasing me?"

"Because you ran away."

"Oh sorry about that," the thief says, calming down. "What did you want to ask me?"

"I'm investigating the Craven Manor Massacre," you tell him.

"So you're with the police?"

"No, not exactly."

"Then what's your interest in it?"

"I'm just a friend of the family looking to avenge their murders."

"Well I can understand that," he says. "Unfortunately I can't help you with any information on the subject because I never knew the family myself, but I do know where you can get some."

"Where?" you ask.

"Reardon's office. Rumour has it that the father of the Cravens had upset Ray over some business deal."

"What kind of business deal?"

"I don't know the details of it, but I can bet he still has evidence of it in his office."

**Add CMIP R. This will give you access to Building G/1800s Town (Reardon's Gambling Den.)**

"How would I get into his office?"

"You could sneak in and have a look for yourself, or you could hire a skilled thief to do it for you," he says with a cocky arrogance.

"And how much would this skilled thief want?" you ask.

"Well I currently owe Reardon £150 and I've already managed to raise £50, so £100 would be a fair amount. What do you say?"

If you have £100 and wish to give it to the thief **turn to 520**

Otherwise, you now return to the town **turn to 488**

**If you return to the town, mark down 520 as a shortcut to bring the thief his £100. When visiting here again, you will be able to come to this shortcut instead of the original number written on your navigation list.**

### 82
(100 x2)

Having disarmed the Killer, you now find yourself in a hand to hand fight.

**If you need to, you can now consult the rules of Combat at the back of the book. But be sure to make a note of this passage so you can return here after.**

**This fight will last 24 rounds.**

If you win the fight, you can now choose to unmask the killer.
If you came in with help **turn to 29**
If you came in alone **turn to 471**

If you fail, unfortunately you are too bruised to move, and the killer reclaims the knife and finishes you off.

### 83

Outside the door of the library you find the body of a tall balding man in a suit. He appears to have been stabbed several times in the chest. By his look you imagine that he must have been the house butler. His hand appears to be clenched round something. As you prise his fingers open, you find a fabric of clothing. You decide to take this with you, as it could be an invaluable clue. (FK: B1-20)

You now return to the house **turn to 418**

If you have chosen to hide in this room turn to 271

## 84
### (340)

Following via the street, you run alongside the thief, as he leaps from roof to roof. Unfortunately you are so busy watching him, that you only see at the last minute, the horse and cart, heading in your direction. This could be a matter of life or death.

**Roll two dice**
**You may add up to 2TTP to ensure your roll is higher**

If you roll 10 or over **turn to 151**
If you roll less, you must either reverse time or accept being trampled to death by the horses.

## 85

"Another ghost nut eh?" the antiques dealer says. "I was into all that when I was younger. I even snuck over to the place once as a dare. I never actually saw anything, but an ear piercing shriek telling me to 'get out,' was enough to scare me for a life time. Having said that though, I have been tempted to go and scavenge the place for valuables I could sell in my shop. It's generally empty and most people who move in, leave within the first few days. If Trevor wasn't so stingy with lending out his metal detector, I bet I could find myself all kinds of hidden treasures in that place." (FK: E6+70)

"Who is Trevor?" you ask.

"Oh, he's the crazy guy who runs the local book shop in town. If you want to know about ghosts, I bet he'd have some good books on the subject."

You can now return to peruse the shop **turn to 284**
Or you can return to the town **turn to 444**

## 86
### (360)

By the time you arrive at Peter's address, you realise he too has already left the house. You continue on to the antiques shop **turn to 39**

## 87
### (272)

"So she says: 'If you were my husband, I'd poison your tea'," says one of the pompous men as you approach. "And in reply to this he says: 'Madam, if you were my wife, I'd drink it.'"

To this they all laugh, and to appear that you are one of the group you laugh with them, even though you haven't the slightest idea what they were talking about.

"So what do you make of the Starling agenda?" one of the men asks you.

If you decide to try and blag an answer **turn to 397**

Or you can use Future Knowledge F

Or if you are not interested in hanging around, you can either approach the girl sat down **turn to 131**

Or you can approach the business man **turn to 301**

## 88

Returning to the other side of the pond, you take out the wooden carving you placed in your pocket and have a closer look at it. It is a blue, wooden, carving of a dog, with a number 9 carved into it. You can now add this to your inventory.

You now return to the house **turn to 13**

**You can mark down The Pond as complete, as you will have no need to revisit this place.**

## 89

**If you have CMIP D, turn to 251 immediately. If you don't have CMIP D yet, then please continue reading.**

The hotel clerk comes to the desk and asks you what you want. If you had been here before it must have been on one of the repeated days, because it seems he doesn't recognise you. You get straight to the point.

"I was wondering if you could tell me anything about Craven Manor."

"Craven Manor," he says. "Why would you want to know about that place? You know that it's haunted right? What people say about the ghosts, it's all true."

"I am aware of that. I'm a paranormal investigator," you lie.

"Really?" The man says. "Interesting, well I don't know much about that house, but if ghosts are what you want, I can tell you that it's not the only haunted place in this town. In fact I have my own ghost in the basement."

If you ask to see the basement **turn to 255**
Otherwise, you now leave and return to the town **turn to 444**
**If you return to the town, mark down 255 as a shortcut for The Hotel Basement. When visiting here again, you will be able to come to this shortcut instead of the original number written on your navigation list.**

## 90
### (475)

"No thank you," you say, refusing the glass of wine.

"Are you sure," he says. "It's quite a rare vintage."

"Yes, I am."

"Very well," he says sounding quite disappointed. "Let's get down to business shall we."

You ask him a whole array of questions, ranging from where he was on the night of the murder to how he knew the Craven family. The answers he gives are similar to those of most people who did not know the family very well. You are about to ask him some questions about himself, when the bell rings at the front of the shop.

"Can you believe it?" he says, sounding frustrated. "No customers all day and now one decides to come in. Sorry about this. I shouldn't be too long."

As soon as the taxidermist has left, you consider what you should do next.

If you explore the living room **turn to 140**
If you move further into the house **turn to 57**
Or you can leave and return to the town **turn to 488**
**Mark down Building F as complete, as you will have no need to revisit this place.**

## 91

"It's you," you say. "You're the killer."

Suddenly, as if a veil has been lifted, you find you are able to understand Ruth.

"What? I don't understand," she replies.

"You're the one responsible for the Craven Manor Massacre, Ruth."

"No, I can't be."

"After your rape, and treatment by your father," you begin to explain, "your mind split in two and a new personality was born. This personality, whom you referred to as Megan, drove you to murder your new-born child. Then you attempted to take your own life. When your father saved you, and you were confronted with what you had done, you couldn't deal with the guilt, so you went away and left Megan in control.

"It wasn't until your father got you professional help that Megan was sedated for a time. Everything eventually went back to normal, until that day when you were in the antiques store with Peter and you heard the pan pipe music playing in the street. This reminded you of the time you had been raped in the woods, because you had heard similar music prior to the event, and in turn triggered the return of Megan.

"Having been imprisoned inside you for so long, she felt resentment towards you, but mostly towards your family, who she proceeded to kill, one by one, until it was only you left. Then she forced you to take your life. Now that should have been the end, but because the mortal veil is thin where this house is situated, you returned and brought with you a manifestation of all the grief and despair you had caused in the Craven Manor Massacre. Coincidentally this manifestation took the shape of your alter ego Megan, who has been punishing you ever since, by killing you over and over again in the bodies of other people."

"Oh my god," she says. "I think you're right. I remember now. All the cries and all the screams. It was all me."

"It wasn't completely you," you reassure her. "You weren't well. The man who attacked you in those woods, he is the one to blame. He started all of this."

"But now it has to end," she says decisively. "And there's only one way it will. The Man in Black is connected to my spirit, so to destroy it, you must destroy me. You need to find my remains and burn them."

"Where can I find them?" You ask.

"My father had me cremated, so the only remains left will be the doll he made for me with my own hair. I don't know where it is, but I am certain it is somewhere inside this house. You need to... Oh no!"

"What is it?"

"It's the entity. I think it's coming for me. Now that I understand what our connection is, it's going to push me out and use your fiancée as a host."

Not long after she has finished saying this, the building starts to shake and the man in black comes flying into the room and seeps into your fiancée. (FK: D3+123)

**Turn to 103**


92

(362)

"Please, allow me to explain," you say as you emerge from behind the chair.

No sooner have you come out, when the man pulls out a gun from his pocket and points it at you.

"Don't you move!" the man shouts. "So you're the one who's been sneaking around this house, pretending to be a ghost. Hayley, call the police."

"John, why do you have a gun?" the woman asks concerned.

"I'll explain later, for now just do as I say."

The woman disappears into the hall to make the call.

"Look, I'm not who you think I am," you try to explain. "The strange things that have been happening in this house that you think I'm responsible for, they were done by ghosts."

"Oh you're a piece of work," says the man angrily. "There's no point denying it, we've caught you red handed."

"The police are on their way," says the woman as she returns.

"Good, then we can just sit here until they arrive."

At this point you realise there is no way to rectify this situation, so you can either reverse time and undo being caught or return to the present **turn to 13**

## 93
### (449 (via study and ballroom) 220 (Via ballroom) 423 (Via toilets)

Running straight through the open door, you find yourself in a dark room full of old junk that appears to have no other way out. Realising you have trapped yourself in a dead end, you quickly hide behind a cabinet and hope that the man in black will not find you. As you wait there, you happen to notice a framed old photograph on the floor beside you. It shows a party happening in the ballroom of the same house; only the attire of the people looks very old fashioned. The date on the picture reads 2/ 12/ 1954. As you hear the man in black enter, you start to wish that you were anywhere but here, and then as if by magic, your wish is answered.

**Turn to 224**

## 94
### (337)

You sprint across to the toilet and leap inside to face Peter. He is completely taken by surprise, but attempts to defend himself.

**If you need to, you can now consult the rules of combat at the back of the book. But be sure to make a note of this passage so you can return here after.**

**This fight will lasts 12 rounds.**

If you win the fight **turn to 250**
If you fail, I'm afraid your journey ends here.

## 95
### (240)

You attempt to push the butler out of the way, but he obviously has some experience in wrestling, because he manages to tackle you to the ground. When you get to your feet, you realise you are going to have to fight him.

**If you need to, you can now consult the rules of Combat at the back of the book. But be sure to make a note of this passage so you can return here after.**

**This fight will last 12 rounds.**

If you win the fight, you subdue the butler and run up the stairs **turn to 100**

If not, you are forced to leave and must either reverse time to prevent this from happening or return to your own time **turn to 13**
**Bear in mind that if you do this you will not be able to return to this night, and will have to find a way to deal with the man in black in your own time.**

## 96
### (244 ( Via living room) 290 (Via front door)

As you step into the entrance hall, you see the butler make his way past the stairs and onto the corridor leading past the ballroom.

**Roll one die and try not to get a 1.**

**If you are unsuccessful, you can use your reverse time ability to roll again as many times as you like, but each time you do this will cost you 2TTP.**

If you succeed in following him quietly **turn to 174**

If you fail and find yourself unable to reverse the result, the butler suspects you of being a burglar and tells you to leave the house. You realise after this that there is no way you will witness the moment in time you wanted to see, and so you travel back to the present **turn to 13**

## 97
### (2)

The butcher's store room is filled mainly with crafting tools, including various paints, woods, glues, and tools. If you had some time to look through these things, you might find something of use, but unfortunately you do not have the time, and since evidence is what you need to find, you decide to move on.

If this is the first place you checked **turn to 370.**
If it is the second **turn to 458**
If it is the third **turn to 417**

## 98
### (427)

As you sit there pondering how you are going to try and convince your fiancée not to step foot in that house tonight, a child and mother enter the café. It doesn't take you long to realise that it is the same child who originally dropped his ice cream. It then occurs to you that if you can stop this from happening then it will prove that the future can be changed.

**If you decide to wait and attempt to catch the child before he falls.**

**Roll one die.**

**You may add up to 2TTP to ensure your roll is higher.**

If your roll is 5 or over, your intervention is successful **turn to 303**
If your roll is less or you decide to let him fall **turn to 34**
Or you can use Future Knowledge A

## 99
### (28)

"I don't mean to interrupt you," you say, "but have you got any bigger chickens out back. My family has quite an appetite."

"I'll go and have a look," says the butcher.

No sooner has he gone, when you swipe the keys from behind the counter.

If you have silly putty or a bar of soap **turn to 132**

Otherwise you put the key back and decide to leave the store before you need to pay for the meat that you do not want.

You can now either look for another way in **turn to 413**
Or reverse time and attempt to play things out differently.

If you have exhausted your options, you must return to the town **turn to 488**
**Mark down The Butchers as complete, as you will have no need to revisit this place.**

**100**
(17 (Via Trellis) 95 (Via Window) 432 (Via Conservatory))

You are about to make your way to Ruth's room, when to your horror, you come face to face with someone you weren't expecting to see. It is the man in black. At first you can't understand how this can be possible, until you realise this is not the dark entity that you have faced in your own time, but rather the actual murderer from whose fury the manifestation was born. No sooner has he seen you, when he lunges at you with his knife. You quickly manage to jump back and avoid the slice, but know there will be plenty more to come.

**If you need to, you can now consult the rules of Combat at the back of the book. But be sure to make a note of this passage so you can return here after.**

**This fight will last 18 rounds.**

**If at any time you roll a double or over 10, you manage to grab for the knife. In this moment you have two possible choices.**

**You can either automatically score a double hit.**

**Or you can attempt to disarm your attacker by rolling another double or over 10. Unfortunately if you fail this roll you are the one who receives two hits. (The roll over 10 must be made by the dice alone without TTP added or it does not count)**

If you manage to disarm the man in black **turn to 82**
If you get the most hits by the end of the 18th round and you came in with help **turn to 409**
If you get the most hits by the end of the 18th round and you didn't come in with help **turn to 375**

(394)

As soon as you are free from the ropes around your hands and the cinderblock tied to your feet, you swim to the surface and take in a large breath of air. You made it. After what just happened to you, part of you wants to say goodbye to this place for good, but you realise you have unfinished business. If you leave now, when you return there will still be a ghost in the hotel basement. You don't fancy your chances of returning to the warehouse and confronting four armed men, so you decide to make your way back to town and find the nearest police station.

"Excuse me, officer," you say as you approach the desk.

"Yes, how can I help you, Sir?" the officer on duty says. "My word, you look soaked to the skin. What happened to you?"

"Someone tried to kill me."

"And just who might this someone be?"

"Bob Jenkins. He's planning on carrying out a jewel theft tonight. I was asked to take part, but I refused and for that he and his gang tried to kill me."

"Where are they now?"

"They are at a warehouse down on the docks. There are four of them, and they all have guns. You will need to act quickly because I don't know how much longer they will be there."

"Right, I'll get onto this straight away," he says as he turns towards another officer. "I need you to take five officers down to the docks. We have suspected jewel thieves holed up in a warehouse. I expect them to be armed."

While he has his back turned, you decide to leave the station before you can be asked any more questions. You've done all you can. Now it is in the hands of the police. You really hope you have done enough to prevent the robbery, and by extension the murder that would result in Bob Jenkin's execution, but you will not know until you return to the present **turn to 13**.

**Add CMIP D. This affects the hotel.**

**Also you must remove Future knowledge I and H1.**

Unless you have anywhere else to go in this time, you return to the present **turn to 13**

**102**

After presenting the evidence to the police, they go to the taxidermist's place and attempt to bring him in, but he does not come quietly. When he runs at one of the officers with a cleaver, they are forced to shoot him dead. After this unfortunate incident, they search his place from top to bottom. The amount of body parts they find, are shocking, and there are a number of personal items belonging to his victims, but there is nothing among them belonging to Ruth Craven or her family. The police officer you are with later surmises that this man did not go into people's houses to kill them, but rather brought them into his own den to deal with them quietly. Unfortunately it seems like this man is not the killer.

**(FK: C7 Part 2 of 3 -30) Note that you need to find all parts to get the right sum to add or subtract when the time comes to use the future knowledge)**

If you wish to present more evidence **turn to 331**

Or you can return to the town **turn to 488**, and come back later.

### 103

Now the Man in Black has taken a physical body, the obsidian blade will be of no use, so you must attempt to outrun him and find the doll before it is too late.

## ATTEMPTING TO OUTRUN THE MAN IN BLACK

**Roll two dice.**

**You may add up to 2TTP to ensure your roll is higher**

If you are able to roll 10 or over, you manage to outrun the man in black and escape into the house.

If you fail, you must fight him.

## FIGHTING THE MAN IN BLACK

**If you need to, you can now consult the rules of Combat at the back of the book. But be sure to make a note of this passage so you can return here after.**

**This fight will last 12 rounds.**

If you have the most hits by the end, you manage to stun him briefly and escape into the house

If at any time you roll a double or over 10, you manage to disarm him and escape mid battle. (The roll over 10 must be made by the dice alone without TTP added, or it does not count)

## ESCAPING INTO THE HOUSE

Once you have managed to escape into the house, you can either go straight to the doll, if you know where it is, or you can search other rooms. You cannot go into the town or time travel at this point.

## SEARCHING THE HOUSE

If you do decide to search the house, you must do the following every time you wish to leave a room.

**Roll one die**.

If you roll a 1-3: The man in black catches up to you and you must attempt to outrun him using the same rules as you did before.

Make a note of this passage, so you can refer back to these rules when you need to.

If you manage to escape into the house **turn to 13**

### 104
### (197)

Lifting the picture down reveals a hidden safe. It requires a six number combination. You may have this combination, but even if you do, you think it would make more sense to return to the present with it and use it there.

If you choose to investigate the laptop **turn to 310**
If you choose to look in the drawer **turn to 416**
Or you can leave the study **turn to 362**

### 105
### (29 x4)

It seems that Ruth is just about to force Peter over the bannister, when you decide to pull the trigger. There is a loud bang and then everything goes silent. At first you are not sure if you hit her, until suddenly her body goes limp and she falls into Peter's arms.

"Peter," she says seeming to have returned to her old self. "What are you doing in my house? Father will be mad."

"Ruth, try and keep your eyes open," Peter says through his tears, "we're going to get you to the doctor. You're going to be fine."

"I feel cold."

"No Ruth, don't you dare go!"

But it is too late. As Peter mourns his lost love, you reclaim your amulet and then come to join them. (FK: D2+40)

"I'm sorry," you say.

"You had no choice," Peter says. "She would have killed me if you hadn't acted when you did. At least she doesn't have to live with that other person inside her head. You should go before the police get here. The real police I mean."

You look at him, surprised.

"It didn't take a university degree to figure it out," he smirks. "I don't know who you are, but I appreciate everything you've done. You saved my life and in a way you saved hers. I won't forget that."

After saying goodbye, you leave the house and return to your own time.

**Turn to 411**

## 106
### (42)

With great stealth, you make it upstairs and find the door to the manager's room is locked.

If you have a lock picking kit and wish to use it **turn to 227**

If you do not have a lock picking kit, you make an excuse about getting lost before you leave and return to the town **turn to 488**
**Since you messed up this opportunity, you will not be allowed to try again. Mark down The Hotel/ 1800's Town as complete.**

## 107
### (378)

You try to run and tackle the man, but he sees you coming and instantly pulls out his gun and shoots you in the stomach before you have a chance to get close. As you fall back from the shot, he pulls the lever and the lights go out as they did before, leaving you to breathe your last breath in the dark of the cellar.

Unless you are able to reverse time and undo this action, I'm afraid this is the end for you.

## 108

You must now increase your maximum TTP by 2 and can bring your current TTP to full. As well as this make a note that you have the following ability:

**Time Points Absorber**

This will allow you to recover 2TTP in combat for every row you win.

You can now return to peruse the shop **turn to 284**
Or you can return to the town **turn to 444**

## 109

You decide to track Peter's movements from the moment he left Ruth after the Antiques store incident. You follow him, as he stops in at the tobacconist, buys his preferred choice of tobacco and then goes home for a while. He stays there until dark, at which point he leaves and makes his way to Craven Manor. You watch as he goes round to the back of the house, and then leaps up and pulls himself over the wall leading into the garden.

If you choose to follow him **turn to 206**
If you would rather wait **turn to 337**

## 110
### (87)

"What do I make of the Starling agenda?" you repeat. "Well it's certainly going to be good for businesses. The main effect will probably be on the Whitmore foundation, although most importantly it will stop Lady Jarmindon's tyrannical reign of Bembridge house. I'm only a novice in such matters though. More important to me, is what you think."

The men each go to open their mouths but can't think of a single thing to say, since you have taken the words right out of their mouth.

"If you'll excuse me gentlemen," you say to them as you walk away. "I have to go and mingle."

It's only a minor accomplishment, but putting those pompous idiots in their place gave you real satisfaction. You now move further into the room.

TIP: Even though you only had to reverse a single passage to use the future knowledge you gained in this instance, some events later on may require you to travel back a lot further. If for example you find yourself with future knowledge that you think could have been used 4-6 passages ago, do not be dissuaded from going back there. Some of this game's greatest secrets can be unlocked by being willing to travel back as far as you can go.

Turn to 228

### 111
(98)

As soon as you see the mother and son enter, you shout over.

"Hey kid! You might want to tie up your shoe laces, unless you want to lose that ice cream."

"You do as the man says," the mother tells him, and then she smiles at you. "Thanks for that."

"No problem," you say.

Saving a kid's ice cream might not be a big deal, but it is proof that you can change the past.

TIP: Sometimes the solution to a problem requires for you to allow the event to play out, so you can learn the necessary future knowledge to travel back with and try a different approach. Bear in mind that you will not always be told this is an option, so it is up to you to use your initiative when you think an opportunity presents itself.

Turn to 147

### 112

Upon entering the hotel, you find that the owner in this time period is a moody man with grey hair, a drinker's nose and a thick moustache.

"Looking for a room for the night?" he asks. "Or is there something else I can help you with?"

If you ask about the Craven Manor Murders **turn to 528**
Or you can use Future Knowledge G1
Or Future Knowledge A7
Or return to the town **turn to 488**

## 113
### (319)

Sprinting to the doorway, you leap through and tackle the possessed woman to the ground before she has a chance to stab herself. The knife slides away from her, but when she gets to her feet, this does not deter her from fighting back.

**If you need to, you can now consult the rules of Combat at the back of the book. But be sure to make a note of this passage so you can return here after.**

**This fight will last 12 rounds.**

If you beat the woman **turn to 324**

If you fail, the woman begins to strangle you to death on the floor. To escape this terrible fate you must have enough TTP to reverse time. If you do not, I'm afraid this is the end for you.

## 114

The butler's room is the most pristine room in the house, with everything in its right place. Looking around, you see three areas of interest. One is the wardrobe, the second under the bed, and the third a small grill in the floor that looks like it may lead to a drain.

If you check under the bed **turn to 18**
If you check the wardrobe **turn to 245**
If you check under the grill **turn to 474**

## 115
### (312)

As the rocker sits there, the barman comes to collect his glass.
"Same again, Cedric?"
"Yes," the man replies, "but make it a double this time."
"Will do."
After the bar man has left, you wonder if you should go over. If you are looking for someone, perhaps he may be able to help you.

If you know who you are looking for, exchange the letters of the person's name for the numbers below and turn to the number in question. There is only one person you can find here. Make sure to make a note of the number above just in case you end up going to a paragraph that doesn't match up.

| B | D | E | G | I | L | M | N | O | T |
|---|---|---|---|---|---|---|---|---|---|
| 4 | 0 | 6 | 3 | 9 | 2 | 5 | 9 | 0 | 1 |

Or alternatively, you  can approach the posh man at the bar **turn to 38**
Or leave **turn to 277**

## 116

You arrive to find yourself in the midst of some sort of festivity in an orchard. There are men dressed in suits and ladies dressed in their finest corsets. Then you spot a lady in a white dress with a veil and all becomes clear. You are at a wedding. Since this was the day young Ruth Craven started seeing her boyfriend, you gather that she must be here somewhere, so you go to have a look around. You have not gone far, when you catch sight of a girl from behind, sneaking away with a young man. Could this be Ruth? You decide to go and find out. As you follow the pair round the side of a hedge, you quickly have to pull yourself back, because they are literally standing on the other side. Luckily they don't see you and you are able to eavesdrop on their conversation.

"Very well," says the girl. "What was it you wished to speak to me about?"
"I think you know, Ruth," the man says.
"You shouldn't look at me that way."
"Look at you in what way?" the man asks.
"The way you are looking at me now. I've made my feelings perfectly clear, Peter."
"I don't believe..."
The voices have begun to trail off. You will need to follow them discreetly to hear more of the conversation.

**To do this you must roll a single dice and try not to get a 1.**

**You can retake these rolls to try again, but you must use 2TTP each time.**

If you succeed **turn to 247**
If you fail, you are forced to hide and must miss part of the conversation until you can catch up to them. **Roll again**

If you succeed **turn to 205**
If you fail, you are forced to hide and must miss part of the conversation until you can catch up to them. **Roll again**
If you succeed **turn to 387**
If you fail **turn to 225**

### 117
### (415)

"Here," you say as you hand the barman the money. "This ought to cover it."

This seems to appease the barman, because he goes back to serving the other customers.

"Thank you my good man," says the posh gent. "The gesture is much appreciated. I feel like I have been somewhat unfair to you. Of course I will help you gain entrance to my gentleman's club, I just need you to buy me one more drink before we go, to settle my nerves after that rather nasty episode."

If you decide to buy him another round (Deduct £1 from your inventory) and **turn to 381**
If you decide not to, then you choose to leave **turn to 277**

### 118

**If you have CMIP E, turn to 246 immediately. If you don't have CMIP E then please continue reading.**

As you are walking around town, you happen to notice an abandoned building behind the café. It looks like it has not been lived in for some time. Curious as you are, you decide to go in and have a look. You have not gone far in through the door, when to your horror, a blue translucent four legged figure comes scuttling towards you, moaning. It is only when it comes into the light, you realise that it is a woman, dressed in Victorian clothing, with her neck and arms bent round at an impossible angle, doing a crab walk. You also notice that her face appears to be terribly mutilated, as if in her former life she had been tortured. (FK: F7-20) As she comes towards you, you quickly turn and leave the way you came in. This is a vengeance spirit, so until you can find a way to get rid of her, there is no point in returning to this location.

You now return to the town **turn to 444**

## 119
### (57)

You have not gone far when someone grabs you from behind and inserts a syringe into your neck. Then you feel yourself growing sleepy and passing out. **Turn to 16**

## 120

As you stand in the Gazebo, a memory comes back to you of standing in a similar one on holiday in New Orleans, with Liz by your side. That was the day you proposed to her. You had just been to a Jaz concert, and after leaving, had wandered into a rock garden. There you had found the gazebo and chosen to make that the spot in which you would pop the big question. You knew she was going to say yes, but the real reward was in how surprised and overcome with joy she looked when you asked. Remembering that face makes you feel quite sad now, because you know that it could be a long time, if ever, before you see it again.

**The Gazebo is a waiting point. If you choose to wait here you will replenish some TTP.**

If you choose to wait **turn to 164**
Otherwise you return to the house **turn to 13**

## 121
### (330)

Once the last man has fallen, you turn to Gil.
  "Now you can call the police," you say.
  He does as you request and then returns to join you.
  "They are on their way," he says. "I don't know how to thank you. I'm sorry that I didn't trust you at first. Will you accept some kind of payment?"
  "Don't worry about it," you tell him.
  "No, you must have something for your trouble. I insist."
  He then takes out a box of precious stones that he holds out to you.
  "Take one," he says, "as a symbol of my thanks to you."

You can now use Future Knowledge E9 (Do not remove this after use, as there may be another use for this particular future knowledge)

Or **turn to 448**

## 122
### (8)

As you come between the men, you find yourself thrown to one side, and then are forced to watch as a big fight erupts. The fight ends with both men looking as bloody as each other. The man's wife then comes out onto the porch and begins yelling at him. You consider waiting around to see what the whole thing was about, but then you remember you have somewhere you need to be and continue on to Craven Manor. This really wasn't the time to get involved in someone else's domestic.

**Turn to 382**

## 123
### (363)

You try to escape the grip of the man in black, but unfortunately you are not fast enough. If you are unable to reverse time, I'm afraid your adventure ends here.

## 124
### (136)

**Now roll a dice to determine where the man in black will look first.**

**If you roll**

**1-2- He checks behind the desk**
**3-4- He checks behind the curtains**
**5-6- He checks in the cupboard**

**If he rolls your location, he catches you and you have no choice but to reverse time. If you can't do this, he saps your life force away until you are nothing more than a soulless husk.**

**If you do reverse time, you do not need to travel back to the previous paragraph if you simply want to change your hiding place. Instead minus 2TTP and continue as if you had successfully hid. However, if you wish to reverse time to avoid going into the study, feel free to return to the previous passage.**

**If you successfully hid or reversed time and did so, you can attempt to leave or stay put for a second round**

**If you choose to stay put turn to 501**

**If you choose to leave.**

**Roll one die.**

**You may add up to 2TTP to ensure your roll is higher.**

**If you roll 6 or over you manage to leave the room without being caught.**

If you succeed, you can either run to the toilets **turn to 327**
Or run towards the ballroom **turn to 449**
If you do not succeed **turn to 281**

**125**

(312 x2 (Via meeting) 48 (Via captured) )

"Sure," you say. "Why not."
   "That's what I like to hear," Bob says
   He then goes over the details of the job with you. He intends to break into the house of a man called Gil Murdock, to steal his most precious diamond. Your job is as follows: You will sneak into his garden and use the ladder placed, to enter the upstairs window, which will have been left open for you by the maid. You will then make your way to the power breaker and at the exact time specified, shut off the electricity. By doing this, the alarms will be disabled, and the back gate, which the other men intend to enter through, will be opened. They will then head to Gil's safe room, open the safe and remove the diamond.

Later that evening you find yourself outside the house, ready to make your entry. Your first task is to take out the security guard patrolling the area.

**This will require you to roll three dice without rolling a 1. If you manage this, the guard will automatically be knocked unconscious.**

**If you fail, you must fight him.**

**If you need to, you can now consult the rules of Combat at the back of the book. But be sure to make a note of this passage so you can return here after.**

**This fight will last 18 rounds.**

If you successfully knock out the guard or win the fight, you continue to the window
**turn to 330**

If you are beaten by the guard and cannot reverse time, the guard knocks you out and you wake to find that the job was completed without you. Everyone inside is dead and the diamond is gone.

Wanting to get clear of the area before the police arrive, you return to the present
**turn to 13**

### 126
#### (223)

"I'm sorry," you say, very bravely, "but I'm not helping you break into this man's house. I understand that you'll go in there with, or without me, but at least my conscience will be clear."

"What good is a conscience if you're not alive to use it?" Bob says.

Then to illustrate his point, he pulls out a knife and stabs you in the stomach. As you fall back, bleeding from your wound, you realise that even though you picked the morally right choice, you really couldn't expect any other result from saying 'no' to a man like this. Unless you can reverse time, I'm afraid your journey ends here.

### 127
#### (263)

"I'm looking for a man called Tom Scott," you say. "He's an investment banker."

"Tom Scott?" Zoe thinks on this for a moment. "Wait a minute, I remember him, he was there that night at the party at Craven Manor. He was trying to get people to invest in a library project that he wanted to get off the ground."

"Do you know where I can find him?"

"I seem to remember him saying he was a member of a particular gentleman's club in town. I can give you the address if you like."

"Yes please."

Zoe writes down the address and then hands it to you.

"From what I remember, it requires a password to enter," she says. "I hope you can find him."

**Make a note that you can visit this club at any time whilst in 1954, providing you are not in the middle of any kind of encounter. To go there, you simply must turn to 345. Do make a note of where you are at the time though, so you can return there.**

Unless you wish to go there now, you thank Zoe for her help and continue down the street **turn to 312**

## 128
(72)
Heading out into the corridor, you follow the man upstairs. You try to keep at least a few metres between you, and then when you reach the landing, you stop and watch from a distance as he enters the master bedroom. You are about to move closer and peek your head round the corner of the door, when you suddenly hear a crashing sound and decide to charge in instead. As you enter the room, you are shocked to find the same man you followed, crouched over a woman, his hands clasped tightly round her throat.

If you attempt to stop him strangling the woman **turn to 533**

If you would rather not interfere with the past, then without drawing too much attention to yourself you sneak out of the house and return to your own time.

**Turn to 6**

## 129
(15 x2)
"All right, I'll do it," says Gil as he makes his way over to the safe.
"Thank you, Mr Murdock," says Bob, "your cooperation is appreciated."
Gil turns the dial on the safe back and forth until it clicks open, and then to everyone's surprise, he pulls out a gun from inside and shoots Bob in the shoulder. In retaliation to this, Bob fires back and kills Gil with a shot to the head. (FK: Z-30).
As you stand there in shock, you realise it is only a matter of time before Bob turns his gun on you.

If you have a gun and wish to shoot him before he shoots you **turn to 248**
**If you don't have a gun, I'm afraid there is no way out of this one, other than for you to reverse time.**

## 130
(336)
"Excuse me," you say as you approach her.
"What are you doing here?" she says as she turns around surprised. "Aren't you meant to be interviewing Mr Murdock?"
"Look, you need to go somewhere and hide. Your life is in danger."

68

"What do you mean, my life is in danger?"

"There are men coming here who intend to rob Mr Murdock. If they find you, they won't hesitate to take you hostage."

"That's ridiculous. No one would ever be stupid enough to rob this house. Mr Murdock has the best security."

You are about to try something else, when all of a sudden the lights go out and leave you in darkness once again. You scramble around to find your way out of the room, but before you have a chance, something hits you on the back of the head and knocks you out cold.

When you awake, you find that the robbery has been and gone and all has happened as before. Gil is dead, so is Zoe and so is the maid.

Unless you know of anywhere else to go in this time, you return to the present **turn to 13**

### 131
(272)

"Hello there," you say as you approach the girl, who looks to be in her late teens.

"Are you talking to me?" she says surprised.

"Yes, I am," you say. "I'm sorry but I couldn't help noticing that you don't look very happy. Is there any particular reason why?"

"You see that boy over there?" she says as she points to the boy in question.

"Yes."

"Well I've been waiting all night for him to ask me to dance, and just when I thought he would, he asked my sister instead."

"I'm very sorry to hear that. It's his loss."

She smiles when you say this.

"Thank you for saying so."

If you offer to dance with her to make the boy jealous **turn to 442**
If you decide to leave her and approach the group of pompous men **turn to 87**
Or you can approach the businessman **turn to 301**

### 132
(99)

Using what you have, you attempt to make a copy of the front door key in the short time you have.

**To accomplish this, you must do the following:**

If you are using a bar of soap, you must roll a total of 12 in three throws.

If you are using the silly putty, you must roll a total of 10 in three throws.

You can add up to 2TTP to increase the total.

If you are successful **turn to 231.**

Otherwise, you quickly put the key back and decide to leave the store before you have to pay for the meat that you do not want.

You can now either look for another way in **turn to 413** or reverse time and attempt to play things out differently.

If you have exhausted your options, you must return to the town **turn to 488**
**You can now mark down The Butchers as complete, as you will have no need to revisit this place.**

### 133
### (160)

"Wait a minute," she says. "I know you. Yes it was you. You were the one I spoke to in the garden at the Craven Manor party. You made up a story about being a treasure hunter to convince me that you had been invited to the party."

"What makes you think it was made up?" You ask.

"Oh please. Part of what I do for a living is separating fact from fiction. So I'm not crazy after all."

"Why would you think you were crazy?"

"Because later that night, I saw you disappear. And I don't mean leave the party. I saw you vanish into thin air."

Upon hearing this you start to panic. How on earth are you going to explain this?

"That does sound quite crazy," you say, trying your best to divert her from the truth.

"Up until seeing you today, I was considering the possibility that I may have imagined you altogether, since no-one else at that party recalled seeing you there and let's face it, no-one just vanishes like that, but here you are. Interestingly enough your disappearance that night coincided with a double murder."

Your heart skips a beat.

"A murder?"

"A man and his wife were found in the master bedroom," Zoe continues. "The woman had been strangled and the man had taken his own life, or may have been made to look like he had. You wouldn't happen to know anything about that, would you?"

"No," you say, trying to sound as convincing as you can.

"Because you can see how a person might think the two events were linked?"

"What are you getting at? Do you think I killed them?"

"It does look suspicious that you were the only person at that party who had not been invited, and also that the time of your departure was literally after the murders had occurred."

Realising that this isn't going anywhere good, you decide to walk away.

"It was nice to see you again, Zoe."

"If you refuse to talk to me, I'll have to go to the police with what I know," she says before spotting a policeman walking past. "Oh wait a minute there's an officer over there. Hey officer! Officer!"

Even though there is nothing she could say to the police that could affect you in the long run, she could force you to have to leave this time earlier than intended, so you need to find some way to rectify this. You can either reverse time to make sure you never saved her from those thugs, or you can tell her the truth.

If you choose to tell her the truth **turn to 216**

## 134
## (54)

"Of course I'll help you," you say.

"Thank you so much," she replies. "I really am in your debt. Here's the pill. When you are done, please come and see me. I should like to give you something for your trouble." (FK: E2+17)

You can now either go straight to the gambling den **turn to 289**
Or you can go and meet with Ray Reardon **turn to 504**

## 135

Since the bed in this room is relatively small, you wonder if it may have once belonged to a child. There are three points of interest in this room: The wardrobe, the drawers and under the bed.

If you search in the wardrobe **turn to 518**
If you search in the drawers **turn to 161**
If you search under the bed **turn to 445**
Or you can return to the house **turn to 13**

## 136
(288)

The study brings you to a dead end. You must now, either reverse time or hide. If you choose to hide, choose which spot you will pick from the following:

**Behind the desk**

**In the cupboard**

**Or behind the curtains**

Then **turn to 124**

## 137
(263)

"I'm looking for a man called Gil Murdock," you say.

"Gil Murdock?" Zoe says, thinking about this. "Wait a minute, I remember him. He was there that night at the party at Craven Manor. He won several items at the auction, including a big diamond that the papers have all been raving about."

"Do you know where I can find him?"

"As it happens he is holding a party of his own, in a few weeks, to show off his diamond."

"How does that help me now?"

"Because the invitation I received had his address on. I don't have it on me, but I think I can remember it."

"Could you possibly write it down for me?" you ask.

"I don't have to," she says. "I can take you there."

"No, you don't have to do that."

"Look, you saved me from those muggers. This is the least I could do to repay you, besides if I'm not there, you won't even get through the front door. What do you need to see him about anyway?"

"Saving his life."

"I should have known."

"Well actually it's his killer I really want to save," you explain. "His ghost is preventing me from searching a hotel basement. I figure that if I can stop the killer from murdering Gil, then he won't be sentenced to death for his murder."

"Sounds like a plan. Okay, well I suppose we better get down there. It's not far, just a couple of blocks away."

**Turn to 358**

### 138

In the drawer of the desk is £7 in change, a silver cigarette case, a lighter, a paperclip and a magazine with a crossword puzzle. **You can take all of these items.**

Make a note that to access the crossword during any point of your adventure **turn to 253**

You can now either check the picture **turn to 497**
Or leave and return to the house **turn to 13**

### 139

"Why are you so interested in Craven manor," the woman asks. "Not one of those ghost hunters are you?"

"No, I'm just doing some historical research," you say. "I'm looking for information in particular about previous occupants of the house who may have died there."

"I think you would be best speaking to my grandma, especially if you're interested in that kind of thing."

"Why do you say that?"

"Because her boyfriend tried to kill her in that house," she says, launching into a story. "It was at a party in the 1950s. Apparently he was possessed by some kind of demon, she says, although I'm not quite sure what I believe. She only lived to tell the tale because a mysterious gentleman came and saved her. The funny thing was that whoever this man was, he had not been invited to the party and that no-one recalled seeing him there, except her. After that day, she became obsessed with that house. She did all kinds of research. If you want to talk to her, you can find her at the old people's home round the corner. Her name is Rose Everett."

**Add CMIP H. This will give you access to Building C (The Old Peoples Home)**

Thanking the woman for her help, you now leave.

You now return to the town **turn to 444**

Be sure to mark down 314 as a shortcut to buy flowers. When visiting here again, you will be able to come to this shortcut instead of the original number written on your navigation list.

### 140
(90)

Exploring the living room, you find an address written on a note pad. It seems to be a local storage building.

**Add CMIP N. This will give you access to building C/1800s Town (The Storage Building.)**

If you explore further into the house **turn to 119**
Or you can leave and return to the town **turn to 488**

### 141
(442 x2)

You are glad that you manage to make it through the dance, because despite your mediocre footwork, the girl, it seems, has a real flair for this, and leaves many speechless as the two of you glide across the dance floor. Part way through your dance, you feel a hand on your shoulder and turn to see the boy that she had pointed out to you earlier, standing behind you.

"Do you mind if I cut in?"

The girl's face lights up.

"Of course," you say, "I think she'd much rather be dancing with you anyway."

As you leave them to take the floor, you feel a tremendous satisfaction to see that your kind gesture has paid off nicely.

**TIP: In future, when faced with a situation like this where you can use TTP to increase your rolls to help achieve an objective, set an amount of TTP that you are willing to lose and do not go above that because sometimes the result might not be worth the loss.**

**Turn to 228**

### 142

All seems bleak, until you remember that this is the same basement you were exploring not too long ago in your time, where you made a remarkable discovery. Could it still be here in this time? Making your way to the back of the room, you move some boxes and are relieved to find that same hatch waiting for you. Quickly you open it up, and making your way down into the tunnel, you pray that the hatch on the other side isn't sealed like it was in your time. As luck would have it, it isn't. With a smile of triumph, you open the other hatch and find yourself emerging into a very familiar location. You can't believe your eyes. You are standing in the garden of Craven Manor, in the very spot where the miscellaneous room beside the conservatory once stood. (FK: G2-187).

You see movement inside the house. There are people living here. Quickly you launch yourself over the back wall and run as far as you can from the house. After enough time has passed, you stop to take a breather and allow yourself a moment to think. That tunnel must have been there for some time, but who built it and why, doesn't interest you as much as the possibility of the hotel owner knowing about it. If he did, could he have used it to carry out the Craven Manor Massacre?

**((FK: C1 part 2 of 3 +15) Note that you need to find all parts to get the right sum to add or subtract when the time comes to use the future knowledge)**

You now return to the town **turn to 488**
You now return to the town **turn to 488**
**If you do leave you must mark down Hotel/1800's Town as complete, as you will have no need to revisit this place.**

### 143

You are forced to knock several times before Kenny answers the door.
   "What is it?" he asks. "This better be important. I'm in the middle of something."
   "I'm sorry to bother you, sir," you say. "My name is Dave Ingram. I'm a freelance detective working with the police."
   "The Police..." he stutters. "I haven't done anything wrong have I?"
   "No, don't worry; you're not in any trouble. I simply came to ask you some questions."
   "About What?"
   "The Craven Manor Massacre."
   "I didn't do it," he instinctively says.
   "Nobody is saying you did."
   "Yes they do," he says bitterly. "They think because I was arrested for attacking Ruth in the woods, five years back, that I did this too. Well I wasn't responsible for what happened then, and I'm certainly not for the murders that occurred on 3/2/1897. My only crime was my love for that girl. I was the one who found her in the woods after she'd been attacked. All I did was try to comfort her, but when

people found us together, they assumed I was responsible for what happened. I'm sure Ruth would have told them I was innocent too, if she had not been in such a catatonic state for weeks after. If you're looking for a suspect, then I would suggest looking to that boyfriend of hers, Peter Kline. If you ask me, he is nothing more than a gold digger. Now if you'll excuse me, unless you want to arrest me, I say good day to you."

Kenny then closes the door on you, leaving you to consider some of the things he shared with you. You are about to leave, when you notice that one of his windows appears to be wide open. Could this be an opportunity to find some more evidence, that might help you figure out if Kenny is a suspect? Or is it simply a way for you to get yourself in trouble?

**Add CMIP M. This will give you access to Building B/1800s Town (Peter Kline's address)**
If you attempt to climb in through the window **turn to 530**
If you choose to leave, you return to the town **turn to 488**
**You must mark down Building D/1800s town as complete, as you will have no need to revisit this place.**

144
(345)

"The password is Crane," you say to the doorman.

"Go on in then," he says and moves to one side to allow you access.

As you enter the club you find yourself surrounded by a number of men in suits, drinking sherry and smoking cigars.

**If you know who you are looking for here, exchange the letters of the person's name for the numbers below and turn to the number in question. There is only one person you can find here. Make sure to make a note of the number above just in case you end up going to a paragraph that doesn't match up.**

| B | D | E | G | I | L | M | N | O | T |
|---|---|---|---|---|---|---|---|---|---|
| 7 | 0 | 6 | 1 | 2 | 8 | 4 | 9 | 5 | 3 |

If you do not know who you are looking for, you must leave and return to the number you were at before you came here. Or alternatively, you can return to your own time **turn to 13**

**If you have CMIP A turn to 357 immediately. If CMIP has not been introduced to you yet, continue reading.**

The ballroom is quite a sight to see, with its spacious room, high chandeliers and grand piano in the corner. As you enter, you hear the piano begin to play a sinister tune, and turn to see, much to your horror, that it is playing by itself. You consider leaving, when you notice a mysterious spotlight appear in the centre of the dance floor, that seems to be pointing you towards something. Could this ghost be trying to help you?

If you decide to follow the spotlight **turn to 513**
Otherwise you leave and return to the house **turn to 13**

**146**
(502)

Having given the thief a good head start, you now need to make up the distance between you both, and attempt to catch up to him.

**Roll two dice**

**You may add up to 2TTP to ensure your roll is higher**

If you manage to throw 8 or over **turn to 201**
If not, you lose sight of the man and must return to the town **turn to 488**
**You must now mark down Building E as complete, as you will have no need to revisit this place.**

**147**
(98 x2)

Your attention now turns to the drunks that will soon be giving a waitress a particularly hard time when she comes over to serve them. Perhaps this is another opportunity to intervene.

You can now use Future knowledge B
Or **turn to 279**

## 148
### (72 x2)

In the end, you decide to stay with the auction so you can investigate the precious stone.

"Very well, we shall start the bidding at 200," says the auctioneer. "Do I hear any bids for 200? Very good sir. Do I hear any bids for 250... 300... 350... 400... That's £400 from the man in the front row."

You realise then that the auctioneer is talking about you, because she mistook you scratching your head for placing a bid. If someone doesn't outbid you soon, you are somehow going to have to pay for this item, and you're pretty sure they won't take plastic.

"Do I hear any other bidders? Going once, going twice."

"£1000," shouts a man from the back row, much to your relief.

"Sold to Lord Gil Murdock for £1000. Please step forward and deposit your money to claim your prize, sir."

You look to the back row and see a man with grey hair, sideburns, and believe it or not, a monocle and cane, making his way towards the podium. He is about to ascend the steps to join the woman, when a blood curdling scream suddenly echoes throughout the entire house. Everyone goes quiet for a few moments, and then like a herd of crazed elephants, they all stampede into the house and go to investigate. You follow with them, hoping more than anything that you do not find what you expect, but you are not so lucky. In the end the crowd comes to a stop in the main bedroom, where you find the body of a woman on the floor, and standing above her, his hands bloodied, the same man who you had previously seen leave from the ballroom. As a group of men go to grab him, he turns round in a panic and screams.

"I didn't do it! I didn't do it! It was the dark man. He was the one. He was the one!"

From hearing this, you can already tell what happened here, this man had obviously been possessed by the same dark entity that took control of you on your first night, and like you, he had been forced to kill the woman he loved. As you watch, you are powerless to do anything as mob mentality takes over the party goers and they proceed to beat the man within an inch of his life. You know there is nothing you can do for him now, so you sneak outside and time jump back to your own time.

**Turn to 6**

## 149
### (180)

You are considering what to do next, when you turn and see John standing in the doorway. You are not sure how long he has been there, but he looks ready to pounce on you.

"Who are you, and what the hell do you think you're doing in my house!" he cries out.

"Look, it's not what you think," you say, desperately.

"Hayley!" he shouts. "I've found our ghost. Call the police... Hayley?"

Then to your surprise, he lets out a sharp breath, as a knife point emerges from his chest.

**(FK: S part 2 of 3 +18) Note that you need to find all parts to get the right sum to add or subtract when the time comes to use the future knowledge).**

As he falls forward, gargling blood, you see that it is his wife who has done the deed, but you can tell she is under the power of the dark entity that resides in the house. She comes at you with the knife.

**If you need to, you can now consult the rules of Combat at the back of the book. But be sure to make a note of this passage so you can return here after.**

**This fight will last 12 rounds**

**If at any time you roll a double or over 10, you manage to grab for the knife. In this moment you have two possible choices. (The roll over 10 must be made by the dice alone without TTP added or it does not count)**

**You can either automatically score a double hit.**

**Or you can attempt to disarm your attacker by rolling another double or over 10. Unfortunately if you fail this roll, you are the one who receives two hits.**

If you successfully disarm your attacker **turn to 266**
If you have the most hits after the twelfth round **turn to 217**

## 150
### (404)

"Here you go," you say, as you hand the money over. "Now tell me what you know about Bob Jenkins?"

"I happen to know that he's recruiting for a job at the moment," Cedric tells you. "In fact he's currently meeting with someone in one of the rooms behind this very pub. If you were to wait for me, I could go and arrange an introduction."

"Yes, that would be very helpful, thank you," you say.

Cedric disappears for a few moments behind the bar, and then returns moments later to wave you over. You decide to follow him and find yourself entering a room behind the bar. Here you are faced with the living version of the ghost you saw in the basement of the hotel.

"Cedric here tells me that you're looking for work?" Bob says.

"That's right," you say.

"Well as it happens, I am in need of someone with your physique for a job I intend to carry out this evening. Would you be interested?"

If you take him up on his offer **turn to 125**
If you would prefer to warn him of his future to come **turn to 283**

## 151
### (84)

After successfully dodging the horse and carriage, you come to a point in the street where there are a number of crates, piled so high that it would be possible to run up them onto a lower roof that the thief is about to jump across to. This may be your last chance to catch up to him, but there is also the possibility that the crates might not be particularly sturdy.

If you decide to chance climbing onto the crates **turn to 503**
If you would rather not take the risk **turn to 40**

## 152

As soon as you enter this room you almost wish you hadn't, because the sight you behold is truly terrifying. There, on the large four poster bed, are the remains of two people who have been savagely butchered. The sheets are red with blood and it is difficult to make out who the two people were before this atrocity was inflicted on them. The only thing you can tell is that the remains belong to an adult male and an adult female. Nicholas and his wife, Gertrude, you presume. The nature with which they have both been killed looks like something a serial killer may have done.

((FK: B9 part 2 of 3 -90) Note that you need to find all parts to get the right sum to add or subtract when the time comes to use the future knowledge)

You now return to the house **turn to 418**
If you have chosen to hide in this room **turn to 271**

### 153

You decide to ask about the ghostly couple who appeared in the attic. After giving the officer a brief description, she goes onto her computer and then a few moments later, she tells you her findings.

"Their names were John and Hayley Barnett (FK: F1-127). According to this they were both found dead in Craven Manor during 2009. It was believed that the wife killed the husband and then killed herself. It was a lot later they were found. After their funeral, their son returned to the house with some friends to make a documentary and also went missing. To this day he has not been found."

You now return to the town **turn to 444**
**Only return to The Police Station if you gain FK you haven't tried before.**

### 154
(501)

You try to run from your hiding place, but unfortunately you are not fast enough. Before you have made it out of the room, the man in black grabs you and begins to suck your life force away. If you are unable to reverse time, I'm afraid your adventure ends here.

### 155

"What can I get you?" asks the barman.

"I need some information regarding some murders that happened here a year ago," you ask outright.

"You mean the Craven Manor Massacre?"

"That's right."

"Why would you be asking about that after so much time has passed?" he asks, suspiciously.

"I'm a distant relative of the Cravens and I'm doing my own investigation to find out what happened that night," you improvise. "I wondered if you might know of any suspects?"

"I only know of one," he explains. "You might have already heard of him. His name is Ray Reardon. He runs the boxing arena and gambling den in this town. Rumour has it that he had business dealings with the father of the family, Nicholas

Craven, and that they'd been seen having a big argument only weeks before the incident took place. Sorry, but I don't know any more than that."

**Add CMIP R. This will give you access to Building G/1800s Town (Reardon's Gambling Den.)**

You thank the barman for his information and then decide what you intend to do next.

If you haven't already, you can talk to the woman **turn to 178**

Or you can return to the town **turn to 488**

**If you have already talked to the woman, you can mark down Pub/ 1800s town as complete, as you will have no need to revisit this place.**

## 156
### (221)

Throwing one of the treats onto the floor, the dog looks at it for a few moments before eating it. Then it looks back up at you, expectantly. In response to this, you throw another, and then another. Then when you feel like you have befriended him enough, you enter the room and give him a stroke before continuing into the house.

**Turn to 66**

## 157
### (147)

Remembering that intervening resulted in you receiving a black eye, you decide to try and prevent the waitress from even having to serve the drunks in the first place.

**Roll one die.**

**You may add up to 2TTP to the result to ensure your roll is higher.**

If you roll under 5 you miss your opportunity to help. You then wait for Liz to return from the toilet and leave **turn to 470**

If you roll 5 or over **turn to 373**

Upon entering this small bedroom, you briefly catch sight of a blue translucent little girl writing something on the wall. You are about to approach her, when she disappears. You then look to the wall and see that it is covered in strange illuminous markings.

*CDYN HMSENH MANLN FLN CDYN HMSENH MANLN KN.*
*MAN CDLHM MUS FLN CSOEW NFHDBT.*
*HNRLNM WSSLH TSO ENNW KOM HNN, KFRZ SC RNBBFL, BDKLFLT.*
*MANE MANLN DH MAN SEN KFRZ UANE, LDRA JFE AFYN DEHDWN ADH WNE.*
*FEMDGONH WNFBNL AFH FESMANL, FKFEWSENW HAFRZ MS CDEW MAN SMANL.*
*MADH UDBB ANBX TSO RSEGONL MDJN, HFYN FBB BDYNH, DERBOWDEI JDEN.*

If you are unable to understand these markings, do not worry, you can always return here later.

You now return to the house **turn to 13**
**Once you solve the code, mark down Bedroom Four as complete, as you will have no need to revisit this place.**

Upon entering the Jewellery shop, the strong aroma of incense wafts up your nostrils, and you find yourself looking upon shelves filled with trinkets, precious stones and various artefacts. One in particular catches Liz's attention. It is an amethyst, beaded necklace. After trying it on, she looks towards you.

"What do you think?" she asks.

"It's nice."

"I'd buy it if I could," she hints, "but I spent the last of my money on that toll bridge we went over."

"Yes, I really wish we could have avoided that," you say, ignoring the fact that she obviously wants you to buy it for her. "I hate having to pay money that I don't have to."

"Yes, I know what you mean," she says as she puts the necklace back disappointedly.

**Turn to 176**

## 160

(452 (Via using gun) 173 (Via fight)

Zoe! That's right. That's her name. She was the reporter you met in the garden at the party at Craven Manor six days ago. You are about to tell her that you know who she is, when she beats you to it.

If you witnessed an attack that night and saved the victim **turn to 26**
If you did not witness the attack, or did, but chose to do nothing **turn to 133**

## 161

In the drawer you find an old tattered Quaker bible with pages missing. You flick through it and find nothing of interest.

If you wish to check in the wardrobe **turn to 518**
If you wish to check under the bed **turn to 445**
Or you can return to the house **turn to 13**

## 162

Handing the old man the statuette, his face lights up.
"I can't believe it," he says. "You actually found it. Thank you so much. As promised, I will now tell you the information that you require. As I said before, the strange goings on did not begin until after the Craven family massacre. Now the date that happened on was 4/2/1897. I know this because my grandfather was a policeman at the scene of the crime.
"The Cravens were a well-respected family. The father, Nicholas, was a craftsman/inventor and the mother, Gertrude, was a teacher at the local school. They had three children: Ruth, 18, Jack, 11 and Sophie 8. Also in the house lived the butler, Vernon Crowther and chamber maid, Clara Jenkins. Now on the night the murders occurred, my grandfather was down at the police station when he heard reports of screaming coming from over at the Craven residence.
"He went to investigate and when no-one would answer the door, he looked in through the window and saw both the maid, Clara, and the young boy Jack, lying in a pool of blood. Naturally, he broke down the door and went to investigate. He found them both dead. Jack, he surmised, had died from a head wound that may have been caused by a fall from the top of the stairs, and Clara's throat had been cut open with a sharp blade. Next my grandfather ascended the stairs and found the butler, Vernon, dead outside the library. He had been stabbed three times in the chest.

"Things only got worse after that. He found Nicholas and Gertrude butchered in their bed, and then the youngest daughter, Sophie, strangled to death in hers. It took him a little while to find the older daughter, Ruth, because she was not inside the house, but rather in the garden, floating in the bloody, red pond.

"Whoever killed that family was never known, but every person who has gone to that house since has felt their presence, not just theirs but every victim the house has taken since. Do yourself a favour and get out of there while you still can."

Thanking the old man for his help, you now leave.

**If you wish to return to the date he mentioned at any time, you must purchase the necessary Victorian clothes.**

You now return to the town **turn to 444**
**Since there is no need to return to The Pub, you can now mark it as complete.**

## 163
### (300)

"I think I'll have that diamond you were so concerned about," you say

"Oh no, please, anything but that," he says. "That precious stone is the centrepiece of my collection."

"If you'd prefer it, I could always kill you and take everything."

"All right," he says as he takes the stone from the safe and hands it to you. "Now please take it and get out of my house."

You do as he says, leaving through the back door rather than the front, just in case you run into those gangsters. It's only when you are some way away from the house that you realise the enormity of what you have done. Not only have you robbed a man of his precious stone, but you have left him at the mercy of a group of gangsters who will no doubt kill him when they realise he doesn't have the diamond you want. If your intention was to save Gil or the gangster responsible for shooting him you have failed. Was it worth it?

**You now have a diamond worth £500 that can be used in place of money.**

Unless you know of anywhere else to go in this time, you return to the present **turn to 13**

## 164

Whilst you are waiting, it starts to rain.

If you try to make a run to the house **turn to 342**
If you decide to wait it out **turn to 531**

## 165

(215)

Remembering that Bob had purposely left the chamber empty in his gun, you realise it's now or never. With your full body weight, you leap up and throw yourself into Bob, knocking him to the ground and sending his gun sliding across the floor. You then attempt to run and grab the gun, but before you have the chance, one of the other men grabs you and pulls you back, with such a force that you go hurtling towards a table, knocking papers and a bottle of alcohol onto the floor. As you attempt to fight back, you are pushed to the floor amongst the broken glass of the smashed bottle.

"Okay, that's enough!" Shouts Bob, who has managed to reclaim his gun, which he now points down towards you.

As you lie there, you notice that among the broken glass is a particularly nasty shard that could be used as a weapon. You quickly slide this under your sleeve before anyone notices. (FK: Y -49)

"Now I won't hold that escape attempt against you, but if you try anything like that again, I will kill you. Get up on your feet."

You do as he says.

"I was never going to shoot you," he says. "It would make too much noise and I believe in being discreet about things like this."

Then he marches you out of the building, to the end of what looks like a dock, where he ties a cinderblock to your feet and says:

"Last Chance."

If you change your mind **turn to 125**
If you still remain defiant **turn to 443**

## 166

(535)

Offering her the flowers, she begins to sneeze and gestures for you to take them away.

"I'm sorry but I have really bad allergies when it comes to flowers. Thank you for the gesture, but you should really take them away now. Please don't come back here."

Unfortunately, unless you are able to reverse time and redo some of your choices in this conversation, you have ruined your opportunity to speak to Hannah.

You now return to the town **turn to 488**

**If you decide to return to the town, you should mark down Building A/1800s Town as complete, as you will have no need to revisit this place**

## 167
### (269)

Curious where Ruth's father will go next, you decide to follow him as he ascends the stairs to the next floor. Because he is walking so fast, you need to move quickly and quietly.

**Roll one die and try not to get a 1 or 2.**

**If you are unsuccessful, you can use your reverse time ability to roll again as many times as you like, but each time you do this will cost you 2TTP.**

If you succeed in following him quietly **turn to 487**

If not, he spins round and seeing that you do not belong here, instinctively pulls a revolver on you and fires. If you are unable to reverse time, you die right here and now.

## 168

**If you have CMIP S, turn to 171 immediately. If you don't have CMIP S, or don't know what CMIP S means yet, then please continue reading.**

Entering the study, you find a room with all the typical things you can imagine: Book shelves, a large world globe, and several paintings adorning the walls. Two things catch your attention: One is a painting on the wall of a forest that seems to be slightly askew, and the other is the desk which has a partly opened drawer.

If you choose to look at the picture **turn to 497**
If you choose to look in the drawer **turn to 138**
Or you can return to the house **turn to 13**

## 169

With the cage and cheese, you successfully catch the rat. You decide to keep it with you for some future use. With the amount of cheese you have, you can keep it as long as you need to.

You now return to the cellar **turn to 494**

## 170
(79)

"I was wondering if I could ask some questions about the night you were attacked six years ago?" you ask.

No sooner have you said this, when she closes the door on your face, shouting: "Would you people please leave me alone?"

Unfortunately unless you are able to reverse time and redo your first meeting, you have ruined your opportunity to speak to Hannah.

You now return to the town **turn to 488**
**If you decide to return to the town, you should mark down Building A/1800s Town as complete, as you will have no need to revisit this place**

## 171

If you have not already taken the objects in the drawer, a lighter, a silver cigarette case, a paperclip and a crossword (**Turn to 253** to access) you can do so now. You can also try the safe.

**If you remember the combination, subtract the first three numbers from the last three. Take away one and divide by two. This gives you the number you need to turn to.**

Or you can return to the house **turn to 13**

## 172
(112)

Believing the hotel owner may be a possible suspect for attacking you in the street, due to him owning a particular pair of trousers, you decide to find a way into his room.

If you ask for a room with the intentions of sneaking in from there (You must have £10) **turn to 506**
If you ask to use the toilet and use the opportunity to sneak up there **turn to 42**

## 173

"Oi!" you shout as you run into the fray, "What's going on here?"

"I'd mind my own business if I were you," says one of the thugs.

"I'm sorry, but I won't stand by while you mug a woman in broad daylight."

"Well don't say I didn't warn you."

The two men begin to circle you and then attack you at once.

**If you need to, you can now consult the rules of Combat at the back of the book. But be sure to make a note of this passage so you can return here after.**

**This fight will last 24 rounds**

**This is similar to a normal fight except for the following added rules.**

**For the additional man, your opponent gets a further attack. This means you roll for them two times and for each score higher than your own, your enemy scores a hit. However, if you manage to roll the higher number you will only be able to hit one of them, and defend the attacks of the other, thus scoring one hit.**

**If during combat you manage to win a row of combat, your opponent will lose the second man and thus lose one of their attacks. Once the second man is gone, you will fight the last one normally until the end of the fight.**

If you win **turn to 351**

## 174

(66 (Via kitchen or study) 96 (Via living room or front door)

Now on the corridor, you follow the butler to the right. You are so busy concentrating on being silent, that you don't notice a vase to your side that you accidentally knock with your hand.

**Roll one die.**

**You may add up to 2TTP to ensure your roll is higher.**

If your roll is 4 or over you manage to catch the vase before it falls **Turn to 269**

If your roll is too low, the vase falls and alerts the butler, but you can always reverse time.

If you have no TTP left, the butler suspects you of being a burglar and tells you to leave the house. You realise after this that there is no way you will witness the moment in time you wished to see, so you leave and travel back to the present **turn to 13**

## 175

Using the paperclip, you make a hook, and then tying the string to it, you lower it into the garbage disposal and grab the key. It takes a bit of a tug, but you eventually pull it free. You can now add the silver key to your inventory.

You now return to the house **turn to 13**
**Since there is no other reason to return here, make a note that The Kitchen is complete.**

## 176

Upon leaving the shop, you get back in the car and drive to your new home. It doesn't take very long to get there, and you see a childlike look of joy on Liz's face as you drive up to the porch. Craven Manor looms over you, like some home of an eccentric millionaire. You still ask yourself how you could be so lucky to now own a place like this. As you open the door into the main hallway, the first surprise you find is that the furniture belonging to the previous occupants is still there.

"I thought they said they were going to make sure this place was completely gutted," says Liz as she is looking around, right before she walks into a cobweb, "and cleaned."

"I'll give them a call," you say frustrated.

You are about to do so, when your phone begins to ring.

"That'll probably be them now," you say.

But it isn't.

"Hello is that Mr Ingram, David Ingram?"

"Yes, who is this please?" you ask.

"This is Jimmy's Removals. I'm sorry Mr Ingram but we've ran into some difficulty on the road. I'm afraid we won't be able to get your furniture to you until at least tomorrow."

Upon hearing this you are first of all shocked and dismayed, but then given the current situation, you realise that this is probably for the best. If the Removal van

90

had showed up on time, you would have only been able to unload everything onto the porch while you waited for the estate agent to come and remove the furniture from the house.

"So we won't be able to sleep in our own bed?" Liz says, disappointedly, upon hearing your news.

"It's just for one night. You should be thankful that we even have a bed to sleep in."

"Yes, probably a murderer's bed."

"Look, if it makes you feel better we can sleep on the floor."

"No, I think I can deal with a murderer's bed for one night. Lizzy needs her beauty sleep."

So arrives your first night at your new home. You make the call to the estate agents and find out just as expected that they intend to come over and clear out the furniture tomorrow, then after eating some of the food you brought with you in the car, you head up to bed with Liz and collapse on the master bedroom's Queen Size, four poster bed. Sleep takes you, and you drift for what seems like an eternity, until you are awoken by a loud ruckus. You sit up to find that your fiancée is not beside you.

"Liz!" you shout, as you leap to your feet and walk out into the corridor.

You suspect that she may have gone to the toilet and wandered down to the nearest bathroom. You have just opened the door, when you catch sight of someone standing behind you, and quickly turn to see a dark transparent figure standing there. At first sight it looks like a man in a long coat wearing a top hat. You are about to react to the apparition, when they suddenly leap towards you and you feel them merging with you.

As the merge occurs, your vision blurs and you find your surroundings suddenly changing around you. You are in the same house, but it looks more new and pristine, with very different furniture. Perhaps you are still dreaming, you think to yourself, as you glide down the corridor. You then return to the room you had previously been sleeping in, to find, much to your surprise, two people sleeping there. You want to say something to them, but nothing comes out. In fact you are not in control of your body. You look to your hand and see that you are holding a knife. Then to your horror, you find yourself raising the blade up and bringing it down into each of the couple in turn. You want to scream, but again nothing comes out, as you repeatedly hack at the two people until they are nothing more than bleeding corpses.

It is at this moment that your surroundings change again and you find yourself back in the house you left, standing over your fiancée, the bloody knife still in hand, her pale lifeless eyes staring back at you. Then the full horror of the situation hits you. The whole slaughter of the couple may have been a dream, but this definitely isn't. Somehow in your sleep you have gone and murdered the only person you have ever loved.

"Oh no, what have I done," you say to yourself.

It is then that you see a young ghostly woman in Victorian clothing approaching you.

"*Swrry x'm hqd thxs hqppzn tw,*" she says, "*thzrz bjt q xs tw wqy qll mqke rxght thxs. Fwr lwwk qmjlzt thz.*"

Then she touches your face and you feel a jolt of energy surge through your body. You hear a rushing sound in your ears and then moments later, you find yourself in a very familiar place.

**Turn to 427**

177

After reading the book of ghost deterrents you now know of a way to banish vengeance spirits that are haunting places you wish to explore. To do this, you require a lighter, salt and the necessary Future Knowledge.

You can now use Future Knowledge H1
You can now use Future Knowledge F1
You can now use Future Knowledge F3
You can now use Future Knowledge F4

If you do not have any of these, you must return to the town **turn to 444,** and come back later.

178

As you approach the woman, she looks up excitedly, but then seems disappointed when she realises you're not who she expected.

"Oh," she says. "I thought you were someone else."

"Sorry to disappoint you."

"No, it's all right," she says. "I doubt he's going to show up anyway."

"I was wondering if I might have a few moments of your time."

"You're not one of those salesmen are you?" she asks.

"No, I'm with the police," you lie.

"Oh," she says, sounding worried. "I'm not in trouble am I? Honestly, I meant to pay for that apple."

"No, don't worry. I'm investigating the Craven Manor Massacre."

"What? Still?"

"Some new information has come to light and we've decided to reopen the case."

"Well how can I help?" she offers.

"I wondered if you knew any of the family members?" you ask.

"I used to know Ruth when we were younger. I actually went to school with her."

"And can you think of anyone who might mean her harm?"

"Well there was Kenny," she begins. "I always called him Ruth's stalker. At school he followed her everywhere and still continued his infatuation with her after they had both left. When Ruth got attacked in the woods five years ago, he was suspected because they found him with her shortly after. They arrested him and he spent time in prison, before he was finally acquitted on lack of evidence, but that didn't stop people from suspecting him again when Ruth and her whole family were killed. Also I would consider Kenny's father as a suspect, since he held a grudge towards Ruth for some time after his son's wrongful imprisonment. You can find him at the hotel. He's the owner. Anyway, I hope I've been of some help."

**Add CMIP O. This will give you access to Building D/1800s Town (Kenny Harkness's address.)**

**((FK: C1 part 1 of 3 -10) Note that you need to find all parts to get the right sum to add or subtract when the time comes to use the future knowledge)**

If you haven't already, you can now talk to the barman **turn to 155**

Or you can return to the town **turn to 488**
**If you have already talked to the barman you can mark down The Pub/1800s Town as complete, as you will have no need to revisit this place.**

## 179
### (193)

It sounds like Reardon is about to reveal some more interesting information, when one of his men spots you and grabs you from behind.

"Oi!" he says. "What do you think you're doing?"

"Is everything alright out there?" asks Reardon as he steps out.

"I caught this one listening in on your conversation," says the man.

"Mr Ingram, you really should have left," Reardon says.

"Do you want me to take care of this eavesdropper?"

"Yes, but do it out back where nobody can see."

As the man grabs you, you try to slip out of his grip, but he is too strong. Since you have no way to get out of this, you must reverse time or die in a dark dismal

Victorian alleyway.

**180**

(197)

Coming back to this point in time, you try to think of a way you can capture the safe combination and then it comes to you: The video camera that you found on the young ghost hunter's body! Placing it on a high shelf, you press the record button and then hide as the same events play out once again. The couple come in and talk, then the husband takes the gun out and puts it in the safe. Then after they have gone to bed, you recover the camera and watch the tape back, forwarding through to the part where the husband inputs the combination. From the angle of the camera, the code is as clear as day: 117998.

Now you have the combination you can return to the present **turn to 13**
Or if you wish to stay a little while longer  **turn to 149**

**181**

"I was wondering," you begin, "if you could tell me anything about the massacre that happened a year ago in that big house on the edge of town."

"Why on earth would you want to know about that now?" the woman asks, sounding rather put out. "The time for solving that case has been and gone."

"I'm a writer," you lie. "I'm writing a crime novel based around a similar story."

"Ooh! I've never met a writer before," she says, suddenly interested. "How can I help?"

"Perhaps you could start by telling me what you knew about the Craven family."

"Well the father was an inventor, the mother a teacher."

"And what do you know about the daughter Ruth?"

At the sound of this name, the woman turns her nose up, disapprovingly.

"Oh you mean little miss perfect."

"Why do you refer to her like that?" you ask.

"Because everyone doted on her," she explains. "When she was attacked five years ago in the woods, everyone was outraged and wanted to find the rapist and bring him to justice. But when the same thing happened to my Hannah a year prior, nobody seemed to care. I mean why would they? She didn't come from a rich family, and she certainly didn't have many male admirers. It also didn't help matters that she was known for being paranoid and god-fearing, but they still should have listened to what she had to say."

"You say your daughter was raped?" you query. "Do you believe there's any possibility that it could have been the same person who raped Ruth?"

94

"Yes I do, and I also believe that had they listened to my daughter the first time, then they would have caught the man before he even made an attempt on young Ruth, and maybe even prevented the whole Craven Manor Massacre."

"You believe that had something to do with what happened five years ago?"

"It does seem an awful coincidence that young Ruth was a victim in both incidents, doesn't it? If you ask me, the person who committed those attacks is very likely the one who massacred that family."

"Does your daughter still live in town?" you ask.

"Do you wish to question her too?" she responds, disapprovingly.

"Wouldn't you like her story to finally be told?"

"Better late than never I suppose. I'll give you her address. Although I will warn you that she doesn't like visitors."

You thank her for her help.

**Add CMIP L. This will give you access to Building A/1800s Town (Hannah's address.)**

You can now either do something else in the shop **turn to 400**
Or return to the town **turn to 488**

182

As you enter the dining room, everything seems fairly normal until something suddenly flies past your head and smashes on the wall behind you. When you look to see what it is, you notice the fragments of a porcelain cup. You wonder where it had come from, but just for a moment, because suddenly you see a plate fly in your direction and duck to avoid it. There is obviously a ghost in this room. As more cups and plates are thrown in your direction, you realise that you will have to be quick on your toes to avoid them.

**Roll one die, five times.**

**For each 1 you roll, a plate will hit you.**

**You can use your reverse time ability to retake rolls, but each time you do this will cost you 1TTP.**

After you have finished dodging the plates, you think the poltergeist attack is over, until a barrage of knives and forks come flying in your direction.

Roll two dice.

−1 for every plate that hit you before.

You can use up to 2TTP to increase your roll.

If you roll 6 or over, you manage to avoid the barrage of cutlery that comes flying towards you.

If you fail, you are impaled, and unfortunately die here in this dining room. You can attempt to reverse time and start this scenario again, but to do so you must use 4TTP.

If you manage to survive this encounter, you notice a sinister scratching coming from one of the cupboards.

If you go to investigate **turn to 25**
If you would rather not chance anything else in this room, you return to the house **turn to 13**

**If you return to the house, mark down 25 as a shortcut for the Dining Room. This will immediately assume you are opening the cupboard when you return.**

### 183
(288)
You run to the door as fast as you can, only to find much to your horror that it is magically sealed shut. You consider quickly turning back and trying another route, but before you have a chance, the man in black grabs you and you feel your life force being slowly sapped away. If you are unable to reverse time I'm afraid your journey ends here.

### 184

This door appears to be bolted from the other side.
You must return to the house **turn to 13**

Remembering the briefcase you found in the basement of the hotel in the present, you wonder if there is a chance that it could have been left here in this time and so decide to make an enquiry.

"I was wondering if you could tell me if you have a Doctor Greenfield staying here?" you ask.

"Who I have staying in this hotel is none of your business," the hotel manager says abruptly.

"I only ask because I believe the gentleman left his briefcase in a pub I was drinking in last night," you improvise. "When I asked the owner of the pub, he mentioned the man might be staying in this hotel."

"Oh right. I'll tell you what, leave it with me and I'll make sure I get it to him."

"So he is staying here?" you ask for confirmation.

"No, not at this moment," the man replies, "but he does come to this town every couple of months to see his patients, and I always make sure he has his same room."

"And what room is that?"

"Room 23."

"What's so special about that room?" you ask, nosily.

"It's at the back of the hotel, and is the quietest room. It also has a view of the forest that he finds very soothing."

"Do you let that room to anyone else?" you ask.

"Yes," the man replies, "but on the condition that they accept they could be moved at a moment's notice if he ever turns up unannounced. Why do you ask? Are you interested?"

If you wish to see Doctor Greenfield's room **turn to 295**

Otherwise if you haven't already done so, you can ask about the Craven Murders **turn to 528**

Or use Future Knowledge A7 (If you do this, the number you add or take away from must be 112)

Otherwise, you return to the town **turn to 488**

## 186
### (238)

As you are making your way into the ballroom, a tall grey haired man, who you guess to be the owner of the house, approaches you and mistakes you for a servant.

"You there," he says as he holds a bronze key towards you, "I need you to take this and go into the cellar to bring up some more wine for our guests."

If you agree to go **turn to 388**

If you say that you're busy and ask him to send someone else **turn to 232**

*MESSAGES BEYOND THE GRAVE*

*There are actually three types of messages you can receive from beyond the grave: Those spoken by ghosts, those written by ghosts and those spoken by people possessed by ghosts. Since these messages are coming from beyond the mortal veil they tend to come out extremely jumbled, but there are distinct ways of decoding them.*

### Messages spoken by people possessed by ghosts

*To understand these messages you must read them backward from end to beginning, removing the first and last letter on each word.*

### Messages written by ghosts

*To understand these messages you must follow the following substitution grid.*

| A | B | C | D | E | F | G | H | I | J | K | L | M |
|---|---|---|---|---|---|---|---|---|---|---|---|---|
| H | L | F | I | N | A | Q | S | G | M | B | R | T |
| N | O | P | Q | R | S | T | U | V | W | X | Y | Z |
| E | U | J | X | C | O | Y | W | Z | D | P | V | K |

### Messages spoken by ghosts

*To understand these messages you must swap each first word with the second, each third with the fourth, fifth with the sixth etc.... then figure out where all vowels are by using the following substitution grid.*

| Q | Z | X | W | J |
|---|---|---|---|---|
| A | E | I | O | U |

Fingerprints weren't as commonly collected as evidence during the 1800's, but with the ability to bring the suspected murder weapon into the present, that isn't a problem. You hand the knife to the policewoman, claiming that you found it in the house, and asking if she could compare the fingerprints to those from other items also from the past. (FK: D1 -14)

"Wow," she says impressed. "You really think this might be the same knife that was used during that massacre in the 1800s? It's been a long time, so I doubt I'll find any prints on it, but I'll have a look."

Now choose an item that you wish to compare the fingerprints against.

If you have a pair of glasses **turn to 22**
If you have a pen **turn to 307**
If you have a pipe **turn to 364**
If you have a glass **turn to 437**
If you have a leather diary **turn to 46**

If you have none of these items, you must return to the town **turn to 444** and come back later when you do. **When returning to the town be sure to mark down the number of this passage as a shortcut for future fingerprint checks.**

### 189

Ancient Mythology has always been an interest of yours. From a young age you enjoyed hearing stories about the Greek Gods and the Titan Cronos, and about the Norse god Odin, and how he lost his eye, but right now you are looking for information that could help you in your current predicament. Flicking through the book, you find nothing of particular use to you, but just as you are about to put it back, a piece of card slips out between the pages and flutters to the floor. You pick it up and see that it is half of a ripped photograph. The half you have, shows a man in a tweed jacket, holding hands with someone whose body is missing due to the tear on the photo. Looking on the back, you see that someone has written a date on it in pen: 5/4/... Unfortunately due to the tear, the year is missing.

**Turn to 323**

### 190
### (289)

Approaching the front desk, you tell them that you are interested in fighting.

"You might be in luck. We have a warm up fight coming up in a few moments, if you are interested?"

You are offered £50 for your first fight with added bonuses, depending on how long you last and if you manage to win. It will be against a more seasoned fighter called Fists of Fury. After you are shown where the changing rooms are, you strip down and wait for the fight to come.

You can now use Future Knowledge E4
You can now use Future Knowledge E2

Otherwise, you either continue onto the fight **turn to 341**
Or you can return to the town **turn to 488**

**If you came here via the woman with the pill, then by leaving you give up your attempt to find out more about Reardon and help this woman's husband.**

**Add CMIP T. This will allow you to return to Reardon's Gambling Den just for gambling purposes.**

## 191
### (337 x2)

You are waiting for some time, when you hear a scream coming from the house and watch as Peter makes his way to a trellis leading up to one of the windows. The killings have already begun and since Peter is outside, it can't have been him.

Your best bet now is to reverse time or return to the present **turn to 13**
**Bear in mind that if you do return, you will not be able to return to this time again and so will have to find some way to deal with the man in black in your own time.**

## 192
### (65 x2)

"Tell me about the last time you saw Ruth?" you ask.

"The last time I saw her was on 3/2/1897; the afternoon of the day the murders occurred," Peter begins. "She had snuck out of her house to come and meet me in town. I wanted to buy her a ring, so we had gone to the antiques shop to try on a few. She seemed really happy that day, until her mood just suddenly changed. I don't know what it was that did it. One moment we were laughing about something, and the next her face went as white as a sheet, as if she had seen something that truly terrified her. (FK: Q+16).

"Then we left the shop and I tried to comfort her, but I didn't have much of a chance before her father turned up and took her home. That was the last time I saw her. After that, I called round the following day with the intention of talking to her father, and I found the whole house had been cornered off by the police. I almost died when I heard the news; I suppose part of me did. Anyway that's really all I can tell you. The police as you know, never found the killer, and no-one to this day has any idea who would have done such a terrible deed."

You thank Peter for his help and return to the town **turn to 488**
**You can now mark down Building B as complete, as there is no need to return there.**

### 193
### (504)

You stick your ear to the door and listen in.

"Look, I don't know who that man was, but he is not to step foot anywhere near this office again, do you hear? He might not be an official detective, but if he were to find those plans and hand them over to the police before the deal has gone through, then I could spend the rest of my life in prison."

(FK: E1+50)

Upon hearing this, you wonder what those plans could be. Could it explain the business disagreement that Reardon had with Nicholas Craven? The one which could have quite possibly resulted in him murdering the whole family? In order to find out, you will have to find a way to lure him away from there, so you can search his office.

If you continue listening in **turn to 179**
Otherwise, you can go to the Gambling Den **turn to 289**
Or return to the town **turn to 488**
**Note that if you return to the town, you give up your attempt to find out more about Reardon and help this woman's husband.**

**Add CMIP T. This will allow you to return to Reardon's Gambling Den just for gambling purposes.**

### 194

Approaching the headstone of Bob Jenkins, you wait until you are sure no-one is watching and dig up his grave, before salting and burning his bones. You only used a few handfuls of salt, so there is still plenty left if you need to do this again.

**Add CMIP D. This affects the hotel.**

You now return to the town **turn to 444**

Searching under the bed, you find an art folder with pictures Kenny has drawn of Ruth. These are rather good, but with the amount there are, and the attention to detail in each one, you can't help but think that this seems like obsessive behaviour.

**(FK: B6 part 3 of 3 -20) Note that you need to find all parts to get the right sum to add or subtract when the time comes to use the future knowledge)**

With this found, you now decide to leave and return to the town **turn to 488.**
**You can now mark Building D as complete, as there is no need to return there.**

### 196

After inputting the combination, the case opens with a satisfying click. Inside you find £30, which you decide to take, and a report.

*Since the incident, the subject has begun to show signs of having at least one multiple personality. In our sessions together I would frequently see her change from one to another, believing that she had merely blacked out for a few seconds. I'm not sure if this is the result of the trauma associated with murdering her own child and her failed suicide attempt, or if it was while this other personality was in control that she committed these acts in the first place. She claims that her second personality, whom she sees as a second person, was responsible for those vile acts, but I am not so sure. It is my professional opinion that she felt so much shame for what she had done, that her mind created someone to blame for it.*

**(FK: B5 part 3 of 3 +9) Note that you need to find all parts to get the right sum to add or subtract when the time comes to use the future knowledge)**

If you haven't already, you can move further into the back **turn to 524**
Or leave and return to the town **turn to 444**

### 197
### (299)

After you have made sure that nobody is home, you decide to look around the house. The first room you decide to check is the study. Again, this room is very similar to the one that you know in the present. There is a desk with a drawer by the window, and a picture of a forest on the wall, but where this study differs however, is that there appears to be a laptop computer on the desk. You can now choose to do one of the following.

If you wish to investigate the laptop **turn to 310**
If you wish to look in the drawer **turn to 416**
If you wish to investigate the painting (Unless you have already done so in the present) **turn to 104**
Or you can use Future Knowledge T
Or you can choose to leave the study **turn to 362**

## 198

You approach the teller and make your bet.

"£50 on Billy Bone Crusher to win by knockout in the fifth round."

"And should you win, will you be collecting your winnings, or do you have an account you wish for us to deposit them in?" the teller queries.

"I do not have an account, but I would like to open one."

"Very well, your name please?"

"Dave Ingram," you say.

"And your address?"

You decide to give her the address of your last flat before you moved into Craven Manor. This is not a building that exists in this time, but she doesn't seem to know that and quite happily writes it down. After a couple more questions and some signing of paperwork, your account is complete, and just in time too, because it seems Peter has finished his business there also. (FK: E5-248)

You now leave the Gambling Den to follow Ruth and Peter to the antiques store **turn to 482**

## 199

Using the grappling hook you bought in the antiques store, you climb in through the window, and notice that the smell is even worse in here. So far you cannot figure out where it is coming from though. As you walk around, you notice a couple of loose floorboards and lift them up to reveal a patch of soil. The smell is definitely coming from there. You grab a spade from nearby and begin to dig. Several shovelfuls later, you uncover something that not only makes you fall back in fright, but forces you to cover your mouth to prevent yourself from vomiting. Rotting in the soil, you find multiple, severed, female body parts: torsos, arms, legs and heads, covered in maggots.

((FK: B9 part 3 of 3 -90) Note that you need to find all parts to get the right sum to add or subtract when the time comes to use the future knowledge)

Believing you have seen enough and wanting to get as far away from this place as possible, you decide to leave.

You now return to the town **turn to 488.**
**You can now remove Building C/1800s Town from your navigation list as you will have no reason to return there.**

### 200
((476) After using Future knowledge P (490) Not using Future Knowledge P)

Moving further into the house, you see several adjoining rooms. You pass a kitchen, a bath room, and a bedroom. You check them one by one, but there doesn't seem to be anything of particular interest. You are considering leaving, when you hear a noise coming from behind a large mirror in the corridor.

If you investigate **turn to 317**
If you leave **turn to 408**
Or you can use Future Knowledge D5

### 201
((146) **Through house (439) Future Knowledge D9)**

Running on the heels of the thief, you find yourself pursuing him down a side street. As you start to get close, the thief pushes a street trader's stall in your path. You must react quickly to avoid tripping over it.

**Roll two dice.**

**You may add up to 2TTP to ensure your roll is higher**

**If your roll is 10 or over, you avoid the stall.**

**If you fail, you trip and fall, but can attempt to make up the lost distance between you and fingers.**

**Roll two dice.**

You may add up to 2TTP to ensure your roll is higher.

If your roll is 8 or over, you make up the lost distance.

If you manage to avoid the stall or make up the distance **turn to 340**

If not, you lose sight of the man and must return to the town **turn to 488**
**You must now mark down Building E as complete, as there is no need to return
here.**

202

In the police station you are met by a very pretty, young, female officer who offers
her help. You tell her that you are researching Craven Manor and wish to know
anything she can tell you about the history of the place.

"Well I know all the weird stuff began happening after the Craven Manor Massacre
back in the 1800s," she explains. "We used to have detailed files on the case, but
files get lost over time. All I know is that it had something to do with a family who
were killed there. You should ask around town. If you find anything out, I'd be
interested to know, myself. I love looking into historical mysteries, so feel free to
come back if you learn anything new. Now is there anything else I can help you with
today?"

You can now use Future knowledge I
You can now use Future Knowledge P
You can now use Future Knowledge F5
You can now use Future Knowledge F6

Or return to the town **turn to 444**
**Only return here if you gain FK you haven't tried before.**

203
(2 x2)

For a moment your paranoia gets the better of you and you think you hear the
butcher returning, then you realise it is just the wind blowing against the front door.
You may be safe at the moment, but you don't want to take that for granted. If you
already have what you came for, you may leave and return to the town **turn to 488**

**If you do this, you must mark down The Butchers as complete, as there is no need
to return there.**

If not, or you wish to explore further ,choose where you will look next:

If you search his bedroom **turn to 468**
If you search his kitchen **turn to 36**
If you search the store room **turn to 97**
If you search the living room **turn to 500**

## 204

You are walking down the street, when you suddenly notice that someone appears to be following you. You cannot make out who they are, because they have a scarf around their face and are wearing a hat, but they definitely seem to be looking in your direction. You break into a run and find that they give chase. Through the town you run, weaving in and out of back streets, until you eventually find yourself coming to a dead end. You are trapped! As the mysterious stranger appears at the end of the alley, you notice that they are holding a knife. Your heart begins to race, as they slowly walk towards you. Your first impulse is to use your amulet to leave this time, but then you stop yourself. If you leave now, you may not be able to find your way back here; and exploring the town in this time could be crucial to you uncovering the mystery behind the Craven Manor Massacre. With this in mind, you decide to stay and attempt to face your stalker.

If you have a gun **turn to 525**
If not, turn to **turn to 527**

## 205
### (116 x2)

You manage to follow them without being seen and continue to eavesdrop on their conversation.

"Why do you fear him so?" Peter asks. "Does he beat you?"

"No," Ruth says in protest, "he would never raise a hand to me."

"There's been talk around town that he's been keeping you prisoner in that house."

"Do I look like a prisoner?"

"He might let you out on the odd occasion, but when he does, he rarely lets you out of his sight."

They now come to a stop and you are forced to hide to avoid their gaze.

"He's only trying to protect me."

"Protect you from what? You're a grown woman now. You should be free to marry and have children."

Suddenly she starts crying.

"Hey, what is it?" Peter asks sympathetically.

"I don't know," she says. "Don't worry, the doctor told me this might be a side effect of the medication I'm on."

"What Doctor?"

The voices have begun to trail off. You will need to follow them discreetly to hear more of the conversation.

**To do this, you must roll the dice and try not to get a 1.**

**You can retake these rolls to try again, but you must use 2TTP each time.**

If you succeed **turn to 387**
If you fail **turn to 507**

206

(109)

You leap the wall and are shocked to find that you land on top of Peter. He looks at you in shock.

"Who the hell are you?" he asks.

"I'm a policeman," you say.

"You don't look like a policeman."

"That's because I'm with the secret branch. We don't wear uniforms. It makes us stand out."

"And why are you here?"

"I came because I have reason to believe that Ruth is in danger."

"On that we agree," he says. "I believe her father is holding her against her will in that house, and I have every intention of breaking her free. Will you help me?"

You now have two choices. You can either go along with Peter to get her out, **bear in mind that if you do this, you will be committing to an action that cannot be undone**, or you can return to your own time to check some other suspects and possibly return to this moment later **turn to 13**.

If you decide to help Peter **turn to 432**
If not, make a note of **432** so you can return there later.

## 207
(190)

Taking the pill from your pocket, you look for the woman's husband and hand it to him.

"Grace gave you this to give to me?" he says unsure. "What is it?"

"She told me it would make you sick so you could get out of the fight."

At first he is reluctant, but then he agrees to take it. Moments later the pill starts to take effect and you decide to make yourself scarce. As you are leaving, you notice that Reardon is coming down the corridor looking frantic, probably because he knows he will lose a lot of money from cancelling this fight.

You can now use Future Knowledge E1

If not, you must leave and return to the town **turn to 488**

**Note that if you return to the town, you give up your attempt to find out more about Reardon.**

**Add CMIP T. This will allow you to return to Reardon's Gambling Den just for gambling purposes.**

## 208
(286)

Rather than leave the house, you decide to give the amulet you bought in the jewellery shop a try and wear it through the night. Like before, you go to bed, and like before you wake to find that Liz is not beside you, only this time rather than encounter a dark spirit on the way to find her, nothing happens. It seems the amulet actually worked. 'Great!' you think to yourself. 'Now all I have to do is find Liz and get out of here.'

You start your search around the house and find her standing in the centre of the living room with her back to you.

"Liz, it's me," you say.

But when she turns around to face you, you do not recognise the eyes staring back at you, or understand a word of what she says.

*T643v motr anrute awont .Otrape asihp eyalpe mote mesuoha  mehta mote atsohe awent mar aserule aname okrade mehte merofebe memite afok arettamp gah hebe aylnob alliwe atic atube, otahte arofe puoye oknahty bin. Atuol akaepse mote melbak amal min hemite agnole ban anik memite atsrife behta erofi adnak, oyliraropmets belcyct asihte anekorbe mevahm muoyt otelumal anam agniraewe aybe. Heécnaife oruoye asedulcnig adiarfag om'ik ahcihwa; mekate mote adecrofe berak rews astsohe mehte onik asmitcive merome agnitaerce aybe, oniagak orevol adnak orevol aderedrume merewt bewt athgine behte otuop oyalpe mote agnivahe, anok assape mote aylimafe ayma arom meme awollak atone olliwe mohwa arellike eyma oyba berehs odepparts. Anok mevome pote belbanug, mobmile onik athguach amad bin. Meme oplehe.*

"Whatever has hold of you, you need to fight it," you say, as you take her hand. "Maybe if I can get you out of this house."

You attempt to take her through the front door, but an invisible force stops her from going any further. The spirit inside her appears to be trapped in this house, and since it has chosen her as a host, it means that she can't leave either.

"Look whoever you are, please let my Liz go," you say. "I'll do whatever you want."

The possessed Liz repeats what she had previously said.

"I'm sorry, but I don't understand this," you say "What does it all mean."

But before she can explain anything, she collapses. After checking for a pulse, and finding that her heart is beating normally, you decide to bring her into the living room and lay her down on the couch. You know there's no way the spirit inside her is going to let her go, so you need to try and figure out what it wants. You sense the possessed Liz's strange words may be the key to that. They may not make sense now, but perhaps you can discover a way to read them in the future.

**You should take a note of the number of this passage so you can return and decipher the code in your own time.**

Until you can find a way to read it, you believe the best use of your time will be in exploring the house to find clues to explain who this spirit may be. From this point on you have free reign to search the house.

**Turn to 13**

209

"I actually met Trevor," you tell Cindy.

"Ah," she says. "How did that go?"

"Well for starters he had a problem with me reading books in the store. He said I had to buy them first."

"Yeah that sounds like Trevor."

"I also asked if I could borrow his metal detector and he turned me down flat."

"No, he doesn't like people touching his things, except me of course."

"Why does he lend you things?" you ask inquisitively.

"Because I know his secret," she whispers just loud enough for you to hear.

"Interesting. Tell me more."

"I wish I could, but if it got out, he'd know it was me that told you, and I wouldn't have my carte blanche in his store."

"If it's books you want," you suggest. "I have a pretty big selection in my new library. And I would be more than happy to lend you whatever you want."

"You have a library?"

"A two storey one."

"You must have a pretty big house," she says impressed, before coming to a sudden realisation. "Oh my god, you're the new owner of Craven Manor aren't you?"

You nod.

"Why didn't you say anything before?" she says embarrassed. "I'm sorry I called your house a spooky place."

"Don't worry about it," you laugh. "It is pretty spooky, but it also has a kick ass library. Interested?"

"Definitely."

"Then tell me what you've got on Trevor," you ask.

"It's probably best that I show you," she replies. "Give me a few minutes."

You wait for a little while and then she returns and hands you a photo.

"Wow," you say when you see it. "How did you get this?"

"I used to live across from him when we were kids. My bedroom window looks right onto his. Show him this, and I can bet he'll lend you that metal detector. As for sharing your library with me, we can talk about that at a later date." (FK: E7 +55)

Thanking the waitress, you now leave.

**If you do intend on taking the photo to the bookshop owner, you might want to make sure that you have bought everything you want from his shop before you do, because he might not take kindly to blackmail.**

You now return to the town **turn to 444**

**Since you have no further reason to return here, you can mark down The Café as complete.**

210

Remembering what Ruth told you, you decide to look inside a jigsaw puzzle box and find the torn photograph you were looking for. On it is a picture of a woman, whose

arm is missing due to the tear, and on the back, written in pen, is the date 1898 .
Unfortunately also due to the tear, the day and month are missing.

You now return to the house **turn to 13**

**Since there is no need to return to the attic, you can mark it as complete.**

211

**If you have CMIP K, turn to 74 immediately. If you don't have CMIP K, and this is your first time here, then please continue reading. If this is not your first time here, then you must return to the town turn to 488**

Upon entering the shop, the butcher, a large man with a grisly beard, smiles at you.
  "Hello there, how can I help?"
  You decide to improvise.
  "I'm new in town," you begin, "and I'm considering buying a house here, but I was concerned after I heard about a bunch of murders that happened here a year ago."
  "The Craven Manor Massacre?" he says, a sinister tone to his voice.
  "Yes, that's right. I just wondered if the killer was still at large?"
  "I'm afraid so. The police never caught the one who did it."
  "Do they have any idea who it might be?" you ask.
  "No, I don't think so," he says, as he considers your question. "If you ask me, I think it was the older daughter's boyfriend that did it. I always thought he looked a bit shifty."
  "What was his name?"
  "Peter I think, Peter Kline"
  Anyway don't let that put you off buying a house here. It's a lovely place to live, and I'm sure you would be very happy here."
  You thank the butcher for his help and then leave.

**Add CMIP M. This will give you access to Building B/1800s Town (Peter Kline's address)**

You now return to the town **turn to 488**
**There is no need to return to The Butcher's in the near future until you have CMIP K.**

## 212
(79)

After knocking on the door several times, it opens ajar and you see a mousy looking woman staring out of the crack.

"Yes," she says.

"Is your name Hannah?" you ask.

"Who's asking?"

"My name is David Ingram; your mother gave me your address."

"What do you want?"

If you ask about her rape **turn to 170**

If you say you're investigating the murders at Craven Manor **turn to 523**

## 213
(76)

"I beg your pardon," says an extremely stuffy, older gentleman, "but can't you see that this carriage is already taken. Kindly remove yourself at once."

You do as you are told and continue to Craven Manor on foot **turn to 382**

## 214

Whilst perusing the different wares in the store, you pick up the sceptre with the crystal on top and are surprised to find that it glows and sends a tingling sensation through your body. You can't believe it, you've found another time stone!

The Sceptre is £600

If you wish to buy it **turn to 108**

You can now return to peruse the shop **turn to 284**

Or you can return to the town **turn to 444**

**If you choose not to buy the sceptre, but intend to purchase it later, when returning to the town, be sure to mark down this passage as a shortcut to the Sceptre, so you will now be able to come straight here to buy it if you choose to.**

## 215
(48)

"No thank you," you say. "I'm not interested."

In reaction to this, Bob smiles and then very quickly pulls out a gun and puts it to your temple.

"Are you sure about that?" he asks. "Because I have no use for you otherwise."

If you change your mind **turn to 125**
If you still remain defiant **turn to 333**
Or you can use future knowledge X

## 216

### (160 x2)

"Alright, Alright!" You say, in an attempt to stop her from signalling the policeman. "I'll tell you what you want to know, although I'm not sure if you'll believe me."

"Considering I thought I was crazy up until a few moments ago, I think you'll be surprised with what I believe."

"Okay, you asked for the truth, so here it is. The reason no-one remembered me at that party, the reason you saw me disappear, the reason I happened to be there on the night that man attacked his wife, is because I'm a time traveller."

"You mean like the HG Wells book?" she says.

"Yes something like that, although I didn't use any kind of vehicle to get here. I just think of a date and I can go there. I came from the year 2018, where I am currently living in Craven Manor. In my time the house is filled with vengeful ghosts, and I am trying to remove those ghosts by travelling back and preventing their murders."

"So that's why you were at the party that night? You were trying to save that couple?"

"Actually travelling to that night was an accident. I was running from a dark spirit in my house when I accidentally triggered my power to leap through time and ended up there. The fact that the business with the couple occurred that night was a complete coincidence."

"Okay time travel is real and so are ghosts," she says in disbelief. "I think I'm starting to feel like you might be the crazy one now."

"I told you that you wouldn't believe me."

"Well come on, it's a lot to expect anyone to believe on just faith alone. Perhaps if you had some proof."

"So seeing me disappear wasn't proof enough?"

"Right now I'm willing to put that down to a trick of the mind," she says. "No, for me to believe your story I'm going to need to see some evidence right here and now."

"All right, what can I do?"

"Disappear again," she suggests.

"I would if I could," you explain, "but if I left now I wouldn't be able to return to this exact time, which would mean I wouldn't be able to complete the task I came here to achieve."

"That's convenient. So basically you have no way of proving it to me."

"I didn't say that. I might not be able to disappear to another time, but I am able to rewind time and repeat moments I have already experienced. Perhaps I could prove it to you by travelling back a few minutes and telling you something that I couldn't have possibly known then."

"What about the contents of my pockets?"

"Okay let's try that."

If you have not seen inside her pocket yet, or wish to see again **turn to 374.** Otherwise, read on.

For each item you think is in her pockets, write down the number next to it. Once you have all the items, add the numbers together and turn to the passage of the number you make. If you add the right numbers together correctly, the passage will make sense. If not, you must reverse time and try again. Be sure to make a note of this number so you can return here after any failure.

| Item | Number |
|------|--------|
| A lighter | 112 |
| A box of matches | 114 |
| Black pocket sized mirror | 47 |
| Gold cigarette case with 4 cigarettes | 43 |
| Cinema ticket for *Rear Window* | 15 |
| Receipt for Coffee | 6 |
| Red Lipstick | 28 |
| Bag of 6 humbugs | 60 |
| 26 pence in coins | 52 |
| 36 pence in coins | 33 |
| Book of matches | 113 |
| Green pocket sized mirror | 46 |
| Black cigarette case with 3 cigarettes | 45 |
| Silver cigarette case with 5 cigarettes | 42 |
| Cinema ticket for *A Star is Born* | 16 |
| Receipt for taxi | 7 |

| Purple Lipstick | 27 |
|---|---|
| Bag of 8 humbugs | 71 |
| 25 pence in coins | 3 |
| Gold Pen | 11 |

## 217
### (149)

With one final struggle, you manage to turn the blade of the knife towards the possessed woman's chest, and then force it into her. This time you appear to have dealt her a fatal blow, because her eyes go wide, her body goes limp and she falls to the floor. You feel sick at the thought that you have just killed a person, but even though this isn't the ending you would have wished for, you are just glad to be alive.

You now return to the present **turn to 13**

## 218

The room is filled with so much useless junk, it hardly feels worth wasting your time searching for anything, but you look nonetheless. Mostly you find old board games, some old toys, some musty clothes and a few books. To continue looking, you would really need to know what to look for.

You can now use Future Knowledge V

Or return to the house **turn to 13**
**If you return to the house, mark down the number of this passage as a shortcut for The Attic. When visiting here again, you will be able to come to this shortcut instead of the original number written on your navigation list..**

## 219

You decide to ask about the man you saw in the hotel basement with the scar on his cheek. After giving the officer a brief description, she goes onto her computer and then a few moments later she returns with her findings.

"His name was Bob Jenkins," she says. "He was arrested and hanged for murdering a man called Gil Murdock, during a diamond robbery on 14/12/1954." (FK: H1+17)

You now return to the town **turn to 444**

**Only return to The Police Station if you gain FK you haven't tried before.**

### 220
(363)

Escaping the grip of the man in black, you continue down the corridor until you find yourself in the conservatory. In here you are surprised to find a wide open door leading into a side room. You must now decide where you intend to go next.

If you try the door to the garden **turn to 7**
If you try the door to the side room **turn to 93**

### 221
(320)

Through the study window you climb, and find yourself coming face to face with a very angry looking dog. Right now he is just growling, but you sense if you go further in, he will alert the whole household.

If you have dog treats and wish to give one to the dog in the hopes of befriending him **turn to 156**
If not, you must leave and either, if you haven't already done so, try the kitchen **turn to 403**
Or if you have Victorian clothes you can attempt the front door **turn to 278**

Or you can return to the present **turn to 13**
**If this was your first time here, you will have this one opportunity to find what you need and come back. If this is your second time, I'm afraid you will not be allowed to return.**

### 222

Returning to the café, you almost feel like a regular, given the amount of times you sat in that booth on that repeated first day. You can see that the manager is rushed off her feet, so the only person you will be able to talk to is one of the waitresses. You will need to buy a cup of coffee at £4 first though.

If you decide to buy a cup of coffee, deduct £4 from your money and **turn to 265**

**If you previously spoke to the waitress and have returned with Future Knowledge E8, you can use that now, but rather than add or subtract the amount from the above number, use 265 instead. You must also buy another coffee at £4.**

Otherwise you now return to the town **turn to 444**

**223**

(263)

You realise you need all the extra time you can get, so rather than giving Zoe, Gil's name, and making arrangements to gain entry to the house, you decide to go straight there.

"Sorry Zoe," you say right before you rush off. "I appreciate your offer, but I have somewhere I need to be."

You get to Gil's house in record time and look at your watch. Only twenty minutes before the lights go out. As you consider what you should do next, you recall the mud on the intruder's boots, which brings you to the realisation that he came in from the garden. With this in mind, you charge to the back of the house and find that a ladder has been left conveniently propped up outside the window, with the intruder at the bottom, ready to ascend. Before he can even get a foot onto it, you run over and attempt to tackle him to the ground. In your effort to do so, the man falls and bangs his head, knocking himself unconscious. You are about to return to the front of the house, when you feel a gun to the back of your head.

"Don't you move," says a gruff voice. "Turn around."

You turn around to see the living Bob Jenkins, pointing a gun at you.

"I don't know who you are, but you must have a real death wish to interfere in my business like this. You see that man there?" he says as he points to his fallen comrade. "He was instrumental in getting us into that house. You see, he was going to turn the electricity off, but you just knocked him out like he was nothing. Months of planning all down the drain."

"How unfortunate for you," you say with a smug grin.

"Actually I'd say it's unfortunate for you, because guess who's going to be taking his place now?"

"You want me to go in through that window and turn off the electricity?"

"It's either that, or I kill you right here and now and go into that house guns blazing. Either way, I'm getting in there and stealing that diamond from Gil Murdock. Now, I would prefer to go in quietly, but that's really up to you isn't it."

If you agree to do this **turn to 330**
If not **turn to 126**

**224**

In the time you arrive, you find that the miscellaneous room you were in before has transformed into a washroom. From the clothing in the washroom you guess that

117

you are in the 1950s; probably the same date that you saw on that picture. Not only did you escape death at the hands of the dark entity, but somehow you have time travelled to a different period in history. You can't help but smile. Having the ability to travel back a few hours was cool enough, but this takes your breath away.

**If this is your first time playing turn to 237**, otherwise continue reading.

After you have familiarised yourself with your new ability, you decide to open the door and have a look around the rest of the house in this time. You expect to step out into the conservatory, but are surprised to find yourself in the garden. It appears the conservatory had not yet been built in this time. Suddenly the sound of music and revelry gets your attention and you look towards the house to see that a party is going on. The French windows to the ballroom are wide open, and many people in suits and dresses are standing around in the garden, drinking, smoking and talking.

Realising that you would stick out like a sore thumb in your current attire you decide to go back into the washroom and borrow something to wear. Sorting through the clothes, you are only able to find two complete outfits that are your size. One is a gentleman's suit and the other is a servant's uniform. Choose which you intend to dress in and **turn to 318**

### 225
(116 x4)

There is now some distance between you and the couple, and to make it up you are going to have to move fast.

**Roll one die.**

**You may add up to 2TTP to ensure your roll is higher.**

If you roll 8 or higher, you catch up to them and follow them as they leave the woods **turn to 507**

If you roll less, you unfortunately lose them and have no choice but to return to the present **turn to 13**

### 226
(200)

Remembering the drugged wine you recently swallowed, you go straight to the kitchen, fill a glass full of salt water, and then use it to make yourself sick. Eventually you throw up the drugged wine, along with everything else you have recently eaten. Now it is completely out of your system, you realise you have an opportunity.

If you pretend that the paralytic worked and lie down on the ground **turn to 335**

Or you can leave and return to the town **turn to 488**
**If you do, you can mark down Building F/1800s Town as complete, as there is no need to return there.**

227
(172 x3)

Entering the hotel owner's quarters, you find a nicely furnished studio room. There is a desk close to the window, on top of which, you find several framed photographs. Some showing a woman, you guess to be the hotel owner's wife, and others showing a young man with a hooked nose, who actually bears a resemblance to the hotel owner. Also on the desk is a tobacco pipe with a visible fingerprint on the metal ring around the stem, reflected by the light of the window.

**If you were using fingerprints to narrow down a possible suspect in the present, this may be a useful item to take back with you. Decide whether you intend to take it and continue reading.**

After giving the room a good once over, you decide to check his wardrobe and to your amazement, find a pair of trousers with a tear in them. The hole is the same size, and the trousers, the same colour as the patch you tore from the stranger by the river.

**((FK: C1 part 2 of 3 +25) Note that you need to find all parts to get the right sum to add or subtract when the time comes to use the future knowledge)**

You are about to leave, when you hear a voice behind you.
"I was wondering when you might find your way here," says the hotel owner.
"It was you, you tried to kill me," you say. "Why?"
"Because you were sticking your nose where it wasn't wanted. I won't let you destroy my family."
He lunges for you, but before you can move out of the way, he grabs hold of you and throws you through the door into the corridor. Getting to your feet, you run to the stairs and get halfway down, before you see him coming after you. You try to make it to the entrance, but before you can reach there, he comes running at you, and forces you through another door, and down a flight of steps into a dark and

dismal basement. As you hit the ground, you look up the stairs to see the last remnants of light disappear, as he closes the door and plunges you into darkness. When you hear the door being locked from the other side, you realise he intends to leave you down here to die.

You now must use future knowledge A9

Or reverse time to prevent this incident from taking place. If you can do neither, you return to your own time **turn to 13**
**Since there is no reason to return to the hotel you must mark it as complete.**

## 228
### (272 x3)

Someone clinks a glass and your attention turns to a woman on a podium at the back of the room.

"Ladies and gentleman, thank you for coming here tonight. I hope you have been enjoying the evening so far. I would like to take this opportunity to thank our host Jacob Reardon, for arranging this fundraiser. I apologise for interrupting tonight's festivities but the time has now come for tonight's fundraising auction. As mentioned before, several established members of our community have each been kind enough to donate a precious treasure from their own personal collections. Each of which will be sold to the highest bidder, with all proceeds going to charity. "

As you stand there watching the woman talk, you can't help feeling that she looks familiar, but can't figure out where you have seen her. Then it hits you. She's the same woman from the picture you saw in the house; the last thing you saw before you were transported to this time. Furthermore, it appears that a photographer is just about to take that same picture. This sudden realisation caused you to stumble back and accidentally knock a candlestick onto the floor. At first you panic, thinking that this might cause a fire, but one of the other guests is quick to pick it up before it can cause any real damage. Unfortunately even though it was not on the floor for long, it has left a black mark.

**CMIP (Changes Made in the Past). Every time a significant change is made in the past it may affect a particular place in the future. To keep track of these changes you will be told something like this:**

**Add CMIP A. This affects The Ballroom.**

**This you mark down in your statistics under CMIP**

To use it you must return to the original number of the area it has affected, as shown on your navigation list. All shortcuts for this area can be removed as they are now irrelevant.

Upon returning to the original number you find instructions that say: *If you have CMIP A, turn to --- immediately*, you must now turn to that number instead of reading on. From this point on this particular area will now permanently change to this number, until you are given new shortcuts or told it is complete.

Even though CMIP A was used for this tutorial, you do actually have it now, so please add it to your statistics, and remember to check the Ballroom upon returning to the present.

If you wish to return to your own time now **turn to 6**
If you prefer to hang around and see what happens next **turn to 72**

### 229
(381)
You're telling yourself that if the man asks for another drink after this, you will definitely refuse, but he doesn't. In fact he actually doesn't get to finish the drink you bought him, because he passes out and falls off his bar stool into a slumber on the floor. Realising what a waste of time and money this has all been, you now decide to leave **turn to 277**

### 230

The Shed door takes a bit of a shove, but it eventually opens. Inside you find a spade and a small animal cage. Feeling that both of these items could prove useful to you, you decide to make a note of where they are to be found.

You can either use future knowledge J
Or return to the house **turn to 13**

### 231
(132)
You have taken a successful indentation of the key. All that is required now, is for you to take that indentation to a lock smith and have the key made.

You can now use Future Knowledge C5
If not, you must either look for another way in **turn to 413**

Or reverse time and attempt to play things out differently.

If you have exhausted your options you must return to the town **turn to 488**
**You can mark The Butchers as complete, as there is no need to return there.**

232
(186)

"I'm sorry," you say, "but I'm already busy. Could you perhaps send someone else?"
The grey haired man does not look impressed, but seems to accept your excuse and goes to look for someone else.

**Turn to 272**

233

Besides some useless odds and ends, in here all you find is a rusted bronze key, and a battery (8). You can take both of these items. It almost feels like looking here has been a complete waste of time.

You return to the house **turn to 13**

234
(421)

You have not gone far when you hear voices coming from nearby.
"Please don't hurt me," says a woman's voice. "I'll do whatever you want. Please just let me go."
You look down a side alley to see two brutish looking men surrounding a woman. It looks like it could be a mugging in progress.

If you wish to intervene, you can do so in two ways.
If you have a gun **turn to 452.**
If you choose to confront the men unarmed **turn to 173**
If you choose to continue on walking **turn to 312**

235

After presenting the evidence to the police, they go to Kenny's place and bring him in for questioning. He is really nervous at first and doesn't say very much, until the evidence is shown to him. When he realises how bad it looks, he begins to panic and finally speaks up.

"I would really like to tell you that I didn't do it, but the truth is that I don't know."

"What do you mean, you don't know?" the police officer asks.

"I mean that I have no recollection of anything that happened that night. I remember seeing Peter and Ruth in town that day and then going to the pub to drown my sorrows. After that, all I remember is waking up in my own bed the following morning. I don't even recall how I got home.

"Do I believe that in that time I could have gone over to the Cravens' house and killed them all? No, but at the same time, there's no evidence to say that I didn't. I have been known to act completely out of character when I drink. I have, on occasion, gotten violent. I could have gotten so drunk that I went over to the Cravens' and started a fight with Ruth that got out of hand. I really don't know."

Hearing this makes it sound like he could still be a likely suspect, until a witness comes into the station a few moments later, and reveals the mystery of what happened to Kenny that night.

"I found him in a ditch around the corner from the pub," says the man. "It looked to me like he'd had a few too many and had fallen in there on the way home. After I found him, I picked him up and took him home."

Unfortunately it seems that this man is not the killer.

**(FK: C8 Part 1 of 3 +13) Note that you need to find all parts to get the right sum to add or subtract when the time comes to use the future knowledge)**

If you wish to present more evidence **turn to 331**

Or you can return to the town **turn to 488,** and come back later.

## 236
### (336)

You wait around for a few moments, expecting to act the moment the lights go out. You plan to grab the maid and head somewhere safe, but something happens that you do not expect. As you watch, she puts down the mop she was using, and looks around suspiciously before walking to the back door. 'What is she doing?' you think to yourself. Then as she pulls back the bolt, and opens it to let in Bob and his gang, all becomes clear. (FK: A4 +40)

"Good girl, Beatrice," Bob says as he hands the maid an envelope of money. "Here's something for your trouble. Where can I find his lordship?"

"He's in the display room with a reporter called Zoe Hadley," says the maid.

"Zoe Hadley, you say? well this kills two birds with one stone. I'm afraid that in order to convince him to open the safe, I'm going to have to use you as a hostage. Don't worry it's all just for show though."

"Okay," says Beatrice. "But try not to be too rough."

"Don't worry darling, once your boss sees the gun at your head, I'm sure he'll cave."

He then instructs one of his men to take hold of her, so they can go and confront Gil. The lights then go out.

"Right on schedule," you hear Bob say.

As they leave the kitchen and make their way up the corridor, you realise you are in no position to do anything except leave.

Unless you know of anywhere else to go in this time, you automatically return to the present **turn to 13**

237

## RULES FOR TIME JUMPING

You now have the ability to Time Jump. This is very different from time reversal as it allows you to transport your entire self to moments outside of your own history, rather than simply send your subconscious back into your body at an earlier time.

**Time jumps do not require TTP.**

To Time jump to a particular period, you will require a date to travel to. Each date that you are able to travel to has a secret set of coordinates that can be found by putting the numbers that appear in bold, in order. This is the number that you must turn to in order to time jump to that date. For example, the date that you read on the picture to bring you here was the **2**/ 1**2**/ 19**54**. Since the numbers 224 are in bold, these are the numbers you must turn to in order to travel to this date.

**Before time jumping, always make sure you have the necessary clothes before you leave. You can buy old fashioned clothes at the antiques shop in town.**

When visiting other times, you will be given a number of opportunities to leave and return to the present. Bear in mind, however, that you can only visit each date once unless otherwise stated, so if you leave too early you might miss out on something. Of course, there is also the possibility that if you stay too long, you may outstay your welcome, so always consider both factors.

You now **return to 224**

### 238
(318)
Are you currently wearing servant's overalls?

If so **turn to 186**
If not **turn to 272**

### 239

Researching the mutilated ghost you saw at the Shack, you discover that she is one of many who went missing in a thirty year period, during the late 1800s. It is believed that this town had its own Jack the Ripper type, serial killer, known as the Embalmer, who may or may not have been the person responsible for the Craven Manor Massacre. Looking at pictures of the people who were killed, you recognise the girl you saw as being Xena Kalinski, an immigrant from Eastern Europe. (FK: F4+93)

You now return to the main library **turn to 259**

### 240
(499)
Forcing a window, you make your way into the house and are just turning a corner when you come face to face with the butler.

"Stop right there," he says. "I don't know who you are, but you will explain to me right now why you are trespassing in my home."

If you try and talk your way out of this **turn to 10**
If you attempt to push the butler out of the way **turn to 95**

### 241
(338)
After Liz puts the necklace down disappointedly, you wait until she is looking at something else then sneakily take it to the till. Unfortunately it costs you all the money in your wallet, but you believe it's worth it after the sheer look of joy you see on her face when you give it to her outside.

**Turn to 286**

## 242

Amazed at the sudden appearance of a florist in town, where there had previously been a house, you decide to go and investigate. A middle aged woman with short blonde hair approaches you.

"Hello there," she says. "Can I help you at all?"

If you would like to buy flowers **turn to 314**
If you would like to ask her what she knows about Craven Manor **turn to 139**
Or leave and return to the town **turn to 444**

## 243

Using the metal detector on the corner of the room, you are surprised to find a loose brick, behind which, inside a paper bag, you find a silver statuette of a ballet dancer. Realising that this might be worth some money, you decide to take it with you.

You now return to the house **turn to 13**

**You can now remove Storeroom Three from your navigation list as there is no need to return there.**

## 244
(268)
You now follow the butler as he walks towards the north corridor.

**Roll one die and try not to get a 1.**

**If you are unsuccessful, you can use your reverse time ability to roll again as many times as you like, but each time you do, this will cost you 2TTP.**

If you succeed in following him quietly **turn to 96**

If you fail and find yourself unable to reverse the result, the butler suspects you of being a burglar and tells you to leave the house. You realise after this that there is no way you will witness the moment in time you want to see, so you travel back to the present **turn to 13**

## 245

Checking the wardrobe, you find six identical suits, all pristinely clean and ironed, hanging side by side. You can't see anything else of interest. You are about to leave, when you notice a long pole on top of the wardrobe with a hook on the end. It must be what the butler uses to close the high curtains in his room. Thinking that it might be useful, you consider getting it down, but find that it is just out of reach.

You can now use Future Knowledge D4
Or check under the bed **turn to 18**
Or check under the grill **turn to 474**

Or return to the house **turn to 418**
**If you have chosen to hide in this room turn to 271**

## 246

The abandoned building is draughty and quite empty. You search around for a little while, but soon find that there is not much to see. It almost feels like looking here has been a complete waste of time.

You now return to the town **turn to 444**

## 247
(116)

You manage to follow them without being seen and continue to eavesdrop on their conversation.

"...you have," Peter continues. "You say you do not love me, but it does not sound like your own voice that speaks. It sounds more like your father."

"How do you know that we are not in agreement on the subject?" asks Ruth.

"Because that look I just gave you, the one you told me I shouldn't give; I've seen you give it to me on many occasions. I know that you feel the same way as I."

"Even if I do, there is nothing I can do about it."

They now come to a stop and you are forced to hide to avoid their gaze.

"He doesn't scare me, Ruth," Peter says.

"Maybe not, but he scares me. I'd hate to think what he would do if he found me with you."

The voices have begun to trail off. You will need to follow them discreetly to hear more of the conversation.

**To do this you must roll the dice and try not to get a 1.**
**You can retake these rolls to try again, but you must use 2TTP each time.**

If you succeed **turn to 205**
If you fail, you are forced to hide and must miss part of the conversation until you can catch up to them. Roll again
If you succeed **turn to 387**
If you fail **turn to 225**

248
(129)

Quickly, you pull your gun out and shoot Bob before he has a chance to shoot you, then you quickly fire at the other men, hoping you can take them all out before they can get a shot off. Unfortunately one of them does, and even though it misses you, it hits Zoe in the chest, killing her instantly.

Being the last man standing, you decide to run from this place, and return to the present **turn to 13**

249

You decide to do a search for the book called 'The Splintered Mind.' When you eventually find the book, you look at the blurb.

*The Splintered Mind*
*Written By Clive Boris Fairchild*

*A study of the human mind and how abnormalities can cause changes in personality that result in antisocial behaviour. A book long revered by many Medical Specialists for explaining the unexplained.*

Realising that you won't gain anything from actually reading the book, you decide to put it back.

You now return to the main library **turn to 259**

250
(94)

After you have knocked Peter to the ground, he looks up at you in shock.

128

"Who the hell are you?" he asks. "Did Ruth's father send you? Tell him that he will not stop us from being together and I will keep on coming back. If you want to stop me, you're going to have to kill me."

If you tell him that Ruth's father did not hire you **turn to 392**
If you decide to do as he says **turn to 498 If you do decide to kill him, your action cannot be undone, so think carefully before making your decision.**

### 251

With the ghost gone now, you decide to take the hotel owner up on his offer and explore the basement for anything you might find.

If you look through the junk for something useful **turn to 522**
If you move further into the back **turn to 524**

### 252
(282)

Remembering that it was Gil pulling a gun from his safe that got him killed, you decide to try something different.

"Before you continue," you say to the ring leader. "I would just like to warn you that Mr Murdock has a gun in his safe that he intends to use on you, the moment he opens it."

"What are you doing?" says Gil.

"I'm trying to make sure you don't get everyone killed."

"I appreciate your honesty," says Bob. "Perhaps Mr Murdock should tell me the combination, so I can open the safe myself."

Gil reluctantly agrees and reads out the combination, while the ring leader turns the dial back and forth until it eventually clicks open. Then from inside the safe he removes a large diamond.

"Well lads, it looks like we got what we came for, it's time to leave."

As the gang leave the room, you feel like it is over, until Gil charges into the corridor yelling:

"You get your filthy hands off my diamond."

After that, you hear two gun shots and go to the corridor, to find the gang gone and Gil bleeding to death on the ground. **Unfortunately if you intended to save Gil, or prevent his killer from seeing the noose, you have failed.**

Unless you know of anywhere else to go in this time, you return to the present **turn to 13**

Upon close inspection of the crossword, you find that certain boxes have purposely been highlighted by a supernatural goo. Could there be a message hidden in this? Something tells you that if you can figure out the letters that belong in those particular boxes, you might find out.

Interestingly enough, two of the answers have revealed some of the yellowed boxed letters already. Then you notice that looking at the fourth row down, from left to right, that the word **book** has been revealed. Perhaps this may be the case with the other lines. Realising that each row of yellow boxed letters will give you a different word, you decide to mark down what you have found so far.

Row 1:__ __
Row 2:__ __ __ __
Row 3:__ __ O __ __
Row 4: B O O K
Row 5__ __
Row 6 __ I __ __ __ __ __
Row 7__ __ __
Row 8__ __ __ __ __ __
Row 9__ __ __

**To figure out this puzzle you do not need to copy the crossword. Simply copy down the above list of rows and fill in the letters, as and when you uncover them. You do**

not have to complete this puzzle now, so feel free to return at any point during your adventure. Just be sure to note down the number of this passage.

Any time you wish to return to the house **turn to 13**

Any time you wish to return to the house **turn to 13**

Down

1. Another word for Untamed
2. A book of world maps
3. Saying: Stick your nose to the ...stone
4. Another word for unaware
5. A fragment of glass
6. A being of great power in Greek mythology
7. Famous mystery novel: And then there were ...
8. Ancient Egyptian God
9. A transportation vehicle on rails
10. A Christian religion that is also a popular breakfast cereal
11. Norse God with one eye
12. A sweet potato
13. To wipe out a mistake.

Across

1. Saying: My... is strong
2. Opposite to BC
3. Supernatural beings that eat the flesh of the dead.
4. Women's undergarment
5. Old film:... with the wind
6. Another name for a being.
7. Famous Australian Bandit: ... Kelly
8. The name of a particular chess piece
9. Scottish Hero: Rob ....
10. A British 80s Rock Band

(310)

As soon as you unlock the computer, an active webpage pops up on the screen. It is for a paranormal investigator site called the Ghost Chasers. A particular article grabs your attention.

*In some folklore many believe that red brick dust can be used as a ghost deterrent. When used on a doorway, this substance is thought to offer protection for those on the other side. To make it you require a red brick, which you must smash with a hammer, and a pestle and mortar to grind it up finely. Or if you want to save yourself a job, you can order it ready crushed by clicking the link below.*

The link below shows a shop called *Mama Cecille's Emporium.*

(FK: S part 1 of 3 +12) Note that you need to find all parts to get the right sum to add or subtract when the time comes to use the future knowledge).

You can now look in the drawer **turn to 416**
Or investigate the painting (Unless you have already done so in the present) **turn to 104**
Or choose to leave the study **turn to 362**

**255**

"You want to see the ghost in the basement?" the man says. "Of course, I can show it to you, but I'm going to need something in return."

"And what would that be?" you ask.

You have a feeling he is going to ask you for money, but it seems he has something else in mind.

"If you can, find a way to get rid of it for me."

You agree to this and then he points you in the direction of the staircase, leading down into the dark, damp basement.

"Good luck," he says, as he leaves you there to make your own way down.

When you reach the bottom, you find yourself in what looks like a popular dumping area. There are mountains of junk surrounding you. Old chairs, old beds, TV's, you name it it's there. As you manoeuvre your way through, you eventually come to an open area covered in soil, where you find a blue translucent figure hunched over, attempting to look for something. The ghost, you presume. Upon hearing your footsteps, he turns around and runs straight at you. You don't have long to see what he looks like, before you are forced to flee back the way you came, but you do notice he has a scar on his cheek and a rope burn on his neck (FK: I +17)

Upon emerging back into the hotel, the owner comes to see you.

"So what do you think?" he says. "Think you can get rid of my ghost problem? If you do, I'll allow you to take whatever you want from down there. I'm sure you can find something of use."

You know you will not be able to come back here until that vengeance spirit is gone, but in the meantime it might be a good idea to find out who he was in his former life. From the looks of things he was probably a criminal.

You now return to the town **turn to 444**

### 256

Using the metal detector around the building, you discover a loose floorboard in one of the rooms. You quickly prise it up, to reveal £100. Some in coins. The rest in cash. You also find a turquoise stone, which when you touch it, not only glows, but you feel a tingling throughout your body.

**You must now increase your maximum TTP by 2 and can bring your current TTP to full. As well as this, make a note that you have the following ability:**

**Time Point Reducer**

**This makes it so you only have to use 1TTP whenever you reverse time.**

You now return to the town **turn to 444**

**Since there is no need to return here, you can mark The Abandoned Shack as complete.**

### 257
(207)

Seeing that Reardon is out of his office, you realise that this is the perfect opportunity for you to get in there and have a nose around. Sneaking back there, you go in and have a good rummage through his things. Unfortunately you feel so rushed that you are unable to find anything, and have no choice but to leave before Reardon returns. If only there was a way to do this again, but know exactly where to look. You then recall a Sherlock Holmes Story that you read once, where Holmes managed to make the criminal in question subconsciously point out the location of their hidden loot, by convincing them that there was a fire in the building. Apparently when you think your possessions are in danger, the first thing you do is look to the most prized one. You wonder if that might work with Reardon. (FK: E3+9)

If you do not know what to do next, you must give up your attempt to find out more about Reardon and return to the town **turn to 488**
**Add CMIP T. This will allow you to return to Reardon's Gambling Den just for gambling purposes.**

258

This room appears to be padlocked. A three digit combination is required. If you know the combination, turn to the same number to open it.

Otherwise, you now return to the house **turn to 13**

259

One minute there was nothing here but some offices, and the next there is a big town library. It's amazing what effect changing the past can have on the present.

If you wish to look for an old paper about the Craven Manor Massacre **turn to 405**

Otherwise, you can use Future Knowledge F7
Or Future Knowledge A5

Or return to the town **turn to 444**

**When you have been to 405, used Future Knowledge F7 and Future Knowledge A5, you can mark The Town Library as complete, as there is no need to return there.**

260

Remembering what you heard in the recording, you set out to dig up the bodies of the other ghost hunters. It is not a particularly pleasant experience. Firstly it takes a lot out of you to dig them out, and then when you have uncovered the remains, you find them covered in maggots. As you fight the urge to be sick, you begin to search the pockets of the bodies for anything useful. The first has a wallet with £15 inside, a gold key, and a small screwed up note in the pocket. The note reads:

*Green first, Red second, Blue third, -2= open sesame*

You decide to make a note of this, as this information could prove useful. Next, you look to the other body and find £28. Even though it may seem particularly ghoulish, you can keep the money you have found. You then decide to return the bodies to where you found them and cover them over again.

You now return to the house **turn to 13**
**Mark down The Shed as complete, as you will have no need to revisit this place.**

### 261
### (442 x2)

Your dancing skills are so bad, that they cause you to send the girl spinning towards the buffet table, which collapses on impact. As she gets to her feet, covered in all kinds of different food, everyone begins to laugh at her; including the boy whom she had wanted to dance with. You feel terrible for her and want to do something to make up for it, but as you approach her, she gives you an angry glare and then saunters off.

**Turn to 228**

### 262

The Kitchen is probably the most modern looking room in the house, but it is not without its flaws. The tea stained counters, slimy draining board and curling linoleum floor, leave much to be desired, as well as the sinister humming of the fridge. As you explore the room, your attention is drawn to a clicking noise coming from the garbage disposal. At first you ignore it, but when it starts to grow louder, you decide to investigate. As you look down the hole, you notice a glint of silver coming from below. Something is stuck down there and it could quite possibly be something useful.

If you wish to put your hand into the garbage disposal to get the silver object **turn to 56**
Or you can use Future Knowledge C
Otherwise you return to the house **turn to 13**

### 263
### (216)

Pointing out the exact contents of the reporter's pockets blows her away.

"You got everything right, even the amount of coins I had in my pocket to the pence. How is that even possible?"

"Because a few minutes from now you had already shown me what was in your pockets. All I did was memorise those items and come back to this point in time to tell you."

"So it's all true," she says. "Your whole story?"

"Every bit of it. I trust that I have earnt enough good will for you not to go to the police?"

"I wouldn't even know what to tell them if I did. Wow, time travel is real. Just give me a few moments to get my head round this. So did you come back to this moment in time specifically to save me from those thugs?"

"No," you say, "again it was mere coincidence that I stumbled across you when I did. I actually came back here to find a man."

"What's his name? Perhaps I could help you find him. I make it my business to know who is who in this town."

| B | D | E | G | I | L | M | N | O | T |
|---|---|---|---|---|---|---|---|---|---|
| 4 | 0 | 6 | 1 | 3 | 7 | 7 | 9 | 2 | 1 |

**There are multiple people who Zoe can help you find. Each of them has a three letter name. By substituting each letter of the person's name for the number under it, you will end up with a 3 digit number. This is the number you must turn to in order to share that name with Zoe. When looking, make a note of the number of this passage just in case you end up at a number that doesn't make sense.**

If you do not remember any names, or choose not to accept Zoe's offer of help. You can now use Future Knowledge A3.

Or you can say goodbye to Zoe and continue on down the road **turn to 312**

264

Picking up the flow of decoding the message, the rest seems to translate itself. You then look back at what you have written.

*So you have travelled through time. How was it? I envy you for the things you may have seen on your journey. Knowing that this is possible, suddenly gives me an idea on how we might deal with this man in black. If you could somehow find a way to travel back to my time in the late 1800s, you could discover his identity and then possibly stop the murder from even taking place. Look around in the house for photographs or diaries. They are the key to finding new times to return to. You may also want to ask people for help around the town. Some of them* may have ancestors who lived here around that time and others will know of the history of this place. I know of only one photo in this house that may help. Unfortunately it was torn in two, but I do happen to know that one of the halves is in the attic inside a jigsaw puzzle box. (FK: V-8) If you have been there already, you probably noticed that a red key is required to open it. My butler used to keep that key in his room, but with all the refurbishment that has gone on over the years, it has probably been lost since; unless, of course, you returned to a time when the butler's room was still on the map.

Once you have finished decoding the message you can either return to the page of the original message **turn to 6**
Or if you came here from a shortcut you wrote down you can return to the house **turn to 13**

### 265

As you sit in your original booth, one of the waitresses, a pink haired girl with a nose stud, comes to take your order.

"Hey, how are you today?" she says in a friendly manner. "I don't believe I've seen you here before. New in town?"

"I just moved here," you say.

"Oh, then welcome to our town. I hope you'll be very happy here."

"Thank you."

"My name is Cindy."

"Dave."

"Nice to meet you Dave. What can I get you?"

"Just a coffee thanks."

"You'll find the people are pretty friendly here. Have you been to any of the shops already?"

"Yes, a couple."

"Linda at the jewellery shop is really nice and she does some pretty good deals on her things," Cindy says. "Boris at the antiques store is also pretty decent. And then there is Carl at the old hotel. He's a funny old sort, claims there's a ghost in his basement; although it wouldn't surprise me if there was, given this town's proximity to that spooky place Craven Manor."

"Do you know much about that?" you ask, suddenly more interested in the conversation.

"Not really. Only what everyone else says: Ghost sightings, unexplained murders, that sort of thing. The best person to ask would be old man Irving. He frequents the local pub. Also if ghosts are your thing, the local bookshop may have something you need, although unfortunately going there, you will have to deal with Trevor."

If you have it, you can now use Future Knowledge E8

Otherwise, you thank the waitress for her help, finish your coffee and leave.

You now return to the town **turn to 444**

266
(149)

With a successful disarm technique, the knife is taken out of the equation and you now find yourself in a hand to hand fight with the possessed woman.

**If you need to, you can now consult the rules of Combat at the back of the book. But be sure to make a note of this passage so you can return here after.**

**This fight will last twelve rounds.**

If you win the fight, you now choose to return to the present **turn to 13**

If you fail, unfortunately you are too bruised to move and your attacker reclaims the knife and finishes you off.

267

The police have found evidence that the killer may not have broken in.

**((FK: B5 part 1 of 3 + 15) (Alternative) Note that you need to find all parts to get the right sum to add or subtract when the time comes to use the future knowledge) Alternative means that if you have this piece of knowledge already you can ignore it)**

If you wish to present more evidence **turn to 331**

Or you can return to the town **turn to 488**, and come back later.

268
(278)

Remembering what happened last time you called, you decide to play things out slightly differently.

"Alright there, mate," you say. "I'm here to fix the chimney."

"You're a little early," the butler replies.

"I had a cancellation and thought I could get an early start on yours. If it's not convenient, I can call back at the time we discussed."

For a moment you are worried that he might send you away, but luckily that doesn't happen.

"No, I think the master would prefer for you to be done earlier. I will show you to the fireplace."

The butler walks you into the house and guides you to the living room. You are really glad that the ruse seems to have worked. He doesn't even seem to question the fact that you don't have a chimney brush.

"I shall go and tell the master of your arrival. If you should need anything, do not hesitate to ring the bell above the fireplace."

You wait a few moments after he has gone, before venturing into the house and following him to Ruth's father.

**Roll one die and try not to get a 1.**

**If you are unsuccessful, you can use your reverse time ability to roll again as many times as you like, but each time you do this will cost you 2TTP.**

If you succeed in leaving the room without being noticed **turn to 244**

**If you fail and choose not to, or are unable to reverse the result, you quickly duck back in and wait a few moments before trying again. Unfortunately because you will need to move faster to catch up with the butler, the probability of being caught has been raised.**

**Roll one die and try not to get a 1 or 2.**

**If you are unsuccessful, you can use your reverse time ability to roll again as many times as like, but each time you do this will cost you 2TTP.**

If you succeed you still **turn to 244**

If you fail and find yourself unable to reverse the result, the butler asks you what you are doing, and when you don't have an answer, he tells you to get back to work. You realise after this that there is no way you will witness the moment in time you wanted to see, and go somewhere secluded to travel back to the present **turn to 13**

After that near miss with the vase, you manage to catch up to the butler and follow him as he leads you to the library. Here he stops and stands in the doorway to talk to his master.

"You called for me, Sir," says the butler.

"Yes," replies another man. "Did you bring that item I asked you for?"

"Yes, sir, of course."

"Thank you, Crowther, that will be all. "

Realising that the butler is about to turn around, you quickly duck into the store room and wait for him to leave. Then after he has gone, you make your way to the door of the library and peek around the corner. For the first time you see Ruth's father; a well-built man with a full head of long brown hair which he wears in a ponytail. He is wearing a smart shirt with stains of paint and oil, which give you the impression he may have recently been working on some kind of project. As you watch, you see him remove an item from his waistcoat pocket and place it inside a grandfather clock which sits at the back of the room. (FK: N -17).

After he is done, you quickly duck back into the store room, just in time to avoid his gaze as he marches out of the library. Wherever he is going, it looks like he means business. You consider following him, but feeling like you have been fortunate enough to get this far without being caught, you do wonder if you should press your luck. Perhaps now might be the time to leave and return to the present. After all, you got the information you came for.

If you choose to stay and follow Ruth's father **turn to 167**

If you decide not to outstay your welcome, you travel back to the present **turn to 13**

## 270

Approaching the headstone of Xena Kalinski, you wait until you are sure no-one is watching and dig up her grave, before salting and burning her bones. You only used a few handfuls of salt, so there is still plenty left if you need to do this again.

**Add CMIP E. This affects the abandoned Shack.**

You now return to the town **turn to 444**

Pick a room to hide in from any of the numbered rooms below. Before clicking on the link please read the rest of this passage.

**Ground Floor**

2. Maid's Quarters **turn to 23**
3. Sewing Room **turn to 534**
4. Living Room **turn to 489**
Entrance Hall **turn to 53** Stairs to Upstairs (2 moves from here. Once up there start from Bedroom One)
5. Study **turn to 77**
6. Butler's Quarters **turn to 114**

**Outside**

7. Outside toilets **turn to 276**
Pond **turn to 493**

**Upstairs**

8. Bedroom One **turn to 429** Stairs downstairs (2 moves from here. Once down there start from Entrance Hall)
9. Bedroom Two **turn to 152**
10. Bedroom Three **turn to 273**
11. Bedroom Five **turn to 356**
12. Library **turn to 83**

After searching the room, you will be asked if you came in there to hide. You must click this link to return to this passage. Then once back here you must roll two dice for the police (or one dice twice). If they roll the number of the room you are in, then you are caught **turn to 366**

If not, you can sneak out and attempt to make it to another room to search. To do this you must roll a single dice for each move you make to the next room. If you roll a 1 on any of these rolls you are caught and must **turn to 366.** If not, you can search the designated room or area.

**If you do happen to roll a 1 whilst sneaking to another room, you can retake the roll but each time you do it will cost you 2TTP.**

The distance of the rooms to each other is according to where they are on the list. For example Bedroom 1 is two moves away from Bedroom 3. You can only go upstairs via the main entrance hall and this will take two moves.

After searching the designated room. You will hide there while the police search again. Then if you are not caught, you can sneak to another room, and so on and so on, until you either are caught or choose to leave.

If you ever stop in the entrance hall, you will be caught if the study is searched. If you stop by the pond, you will be caught if the outside toilet is searched.

At any time, you can return to the present **turn to 311**

### 272
#### (238 x2)
At the party you see three possible people who may be of interest. One is a girl sat down in the corner who looks like she is waiting for someone to ask her to dance. The second is a pompous looking man telling a story to a group of other pompous men, and the third is a businessman looking type who a lot of people seem to be avoiding.

If you approach the girl sat down **turn to 131**
If you approach the group of men **turn to 87**
If you approach the businessman **turn to 301**

### 273

In here you find 8 year old Sophie, the youngest daughter of the Cravens. At first sight, she would almost appear to be asleep, were it not for the fact that her body is cold and that she is not breathing. From the finger-marks on her throat, it appears strangulation has been the cause of death. You feel saddened by this. What kind of monster would do this to an innocent little girl! Looking around the room you see that this young girl appears to be somewhat of an artist. On the wall, written in chalk, you see rainbows, horses and green hills. You would like to think that she took those images with her when she died.

You now return to the house **turn to 418**

If you have chosen to hide in this room turn to 271

274

*The Splintered Mind*
*Written By Clive Boris Fairchild*

*A study of the human mind and how abnormalities can cause changes in personality that result in antisocial behaviour. A book long revered by many Medical Specialists for explaining the unexplained.*

Looking inside the book, you realise that it really isn't going to benefit you at the moment, but that could always change in the future.

275

The men at this table are playing a game of dice.

If you wish to join them, please read the following rules.

**You must have £10 to play.**

**There are four players including you.**

**For each player, including yourself, you must roll four dice and make a note of the number on each dice.**

**Then you will have a chance to re-roll any of the dice results you are not happy with. Only you get a chance to do this.**

**After this, if you are still not happy with your result you can use 1TTP for each dice you intend to roll again. You can only do this for each dice once.**

**After this, you must score everyone in the following way:**

**For every double you double it again.**

**For every triple you triple it again.**

**For four of the same number you quadruple the total.**

All single numbers are just added to the final total.

The player with the highest score wins.

If you have the highest score, you receive £30 on top of the £10 you already paid.

If you do not have the highest score then you lose the £10.

You can play as many times as you want until, either you have no more gold pieces left, or you are able to win £100 more than what you had when you first started playing.

If you draw with any player you receive only £20.

When you are done, you can return to the main gambling area **turn to 289**
Or you can return to the town **turn to 488**

If you came here via the woman with the pill, then by leaving you give up your attempt to find out more about Reardon and help this woman's husband.

Add CMIP T. This will allow you to return to Reardon's Gambling Den just for gambling purposes.

### 276

As you enter here, the first thing you do is cover your nose and mouth to avoid inhaling the stink of human waste coming up from below. Searching the ground reveals several cigarette butts, next to a muddy footprint. It looks like someone may have been waiting here and quite recently. You take one of the cigarette butts as evidence and use a piece of paper to take an impression of the footprint before leaving. (FK: B2+12)

You now return to the house **turn to 418**
**If you have chosen to hide in this room turn to 271**

### 277
(312 x2)
Did you help a woman being attacked by gang members earlier?

If so **turn to 48**

If not, unless you have somewhere else to go, you see no reason in hanging around in this time and return to the present **turn to 13**

## 278
### (389)
You knock on the door and a few moments later, a man, who you assume must be the house butler, answers.

"Hello," he says. "Welcome to Craven Manor. How can I be of service?"

If you have a flat cap and brown overalls and wish to pose as a freelance work man **turn to 477**
If you have more refined clothing and wish to pose as a housing inspector from the council **turn to 302**
Or you can use Future Knowledge L
Or Future Knowledge M

## 279
### (147)
As the waitress goes to take the order of the drunks, you notice that one of them is being a little bit too tactile for your liking.

"So what's a nice girl like you doing working in a place like this," one of them says as he squeezes her behind.

"Could you please get your hands off me," she says.

"I was only being friendly. If you don't want the attention, you shouldn't dress like that."

If you decide to help her by shouting over **turn to 313**
If you choose not to do anything and decide to leave the café as soon as Liz returns **turn to 470**

## 280

After presenting the evidence to the police, they bring the butcher in for questioning. The evidence is irrefutable that he raped both Ruth and Hannah, but could he be the one who murdered the whole family? It is not until the butcher is presented with his own diary that he breaks down and confesses.

"I did it!" he says. "I admit that I took advantage of those two girls, but I am not responsible for killing that family. For one, I would never do such a thing, and if you do not believe that, then you can ask anyone who was present at the boxing match I attended that evening."

To confirm this alibi, the police do as he requests, and find that five out of seven people, remember seeing him that night at the boxing event. You realise he is telling the truth. He may be a confirmed rapist, but he did not kill Ruth Craven or her family.

**(FK: C7 Part 1of 3-14) Note that you need to find all parts to get the right sum to add or subtract when the time comes to use the future knowledge)**

If you wish to present more evidence **turn to 331**

Or you can return to the town **turn to 488,** and come back later.

## 281
(124)
You try to run from your hiding place, but unfortunately you are not fast enough. Before you have made it out of the room, the man in black grabs you and begins to suck your life force away. If you are unable to reverse time, I'm afraid your adventure ends here.

## 282
(15)
As you wait there in the dark, voices are soon heard in the corridor coming towards the display room.

"Wait a minute, who is that," says Gil, "I don't recognise those voices. Is there someone else in my house? Oh my god. I think you're right. I am being robbed."

Moments later you are blinded by torchlight as four men emerge into the room, holding guns. One of them has a hostage, Gil's maid Beatrice, who you met during your tour of the house. (FK: A2-22)

"Stay exactly where you are and no harm will come to you," says one of the men, who you recognise as the ghost from the hotel basement in your time, Bob Jenkins. "Mr Murdock if you would kindly open your safe."

"No," Gil replies. "I'm not giving you my diamonds. I'm afraid you'll have to kill me first."

When Gil refuses, the burglar cocks back the trigger on the gun he has held at the maid's head.

"You may not care about your own life, but what about hers?"

"Please Mr Murdock," she cries. "I don't want to die."

While the men are distracted you notice that they are not currently watching you and Zoe. If you were quick enough, you may be able to grab one of their guns and attempt to turn the tables on them.

If you attempt to intervene **turn to 75**
If you choose not to intervene **turn to 129**
**Or you can use Future Knowledge Z**
**Or you can use Future Knowledge A4**

### 283
(404 x2)

"Look, I'm going to be completely honest with you," you say. "I'm not really looking for work. I came here to warn you."

"To warn me," he says confused, "of what exactly?"

"I know that you are planning to steal a diamond tonight from a man called Gil Murdock, and I'm here to warn you that if you go ahead with the job, it will end badly for you."

"Is that meant to be some kind of threat?"

"No threat, pure and simple fact. If you go ahead with that robbery, you will be forced to kill a man, and will later be hanged for it."

"How do you know about the robbery? I only told a few members of my crew. Did one of them rat me out to the peelers?"

"No, nothing like that."

"Then how do you know?"

When you can't answer, he gives a nod to one of the men standing in the corner and the man comes over and grabs hold of you.

"Look I don't know how you know what you do," says Bob, "but right now you are a major threat to my operation and I can't take any chances. Take him outside and deal with him discreetly."

Unless you can reverse time, I'm afraid this is the end for you.

### 284

Entering the antiques shop, a young man approaches you.

"Hello there," he says. "I haven't seen you round here before. Are you buying or selling?"

"Just looking for now," you say.

"Well if you need any help, just let me know. Also I'm not sure if you are aware, but we also make keys here. So if you need a new key made, or an old one fixed, I can help you with that too."

If you ask him what he knows about Craven Manor **turn to 85**

Otherwise, you decide to peruse the store. Below you will find a list of items that can be purchased or sold to the antiques dealer.

**This is what he has for sale**

An old clock    £2000
A Medieval sword £500
A flat cap and overalls (Victorian) £25
A top hat and tails suit (Victorian) £35
A pair of old fashioned scales £40
An Antique Vase £500
A bedpan £50
A sceptre with a crystal on top £600

**Fix broken key**

£5 (Automatically turns a broken rusted bronze key into a bronze key)

**Exchange new currency for old**

(Old coins and notes are both bought and sold in this shop, for the same price of what they are worth in the 1800s, 50s, and modern day currency. Since you now know this service exists, you can automatically spend your money in all time periods, because it will be assumed that you came here first and exchanged it for the designated currency before time jumping.)

**This is what he will buy from you**

Cigarette Case for £60
Penny Dreadful for £40
Toy train for £100
Silver Statuette £400
Painting £150
An Antique Vase £300
Chess set £100

You can now use Future Knowledge O

You can now use Future Knowledge E9 (**Do not remove this after use, as there may be another use for this particular future knowledge**)

Or return to the town **turn to 444**

## 285
(29 x4)

Your shot couldn't be more perfectly aimed. Not only do you hit Ruth, but you manage to hit her in the leg, which causes her to fall to the floor and take her out of fighting mode. As she squirms on the ground from the pain of the bullet, Peter comes to her aid, by tying his jacket round her leg to stop the blood flow. While he does this, you reclaim your amulet before coming to help (D2+40).

"What can I do," you offer.

"We need to get her to her bedroom," he says.

You help him carry her there, and are relieved to find that she does not struggle. It seems she has passed out from the shock. After placing her on the bed, you leave and lock the door behind you.

"So what happens now?"

"Her father mentioned a Doctor who was treating her for her illness. I will telegram him at once. I only hope he can get here before she wakes up. I'm sure someone must have heard those shots, which means you should probably go before the police get here. The real police I mean"

You look at him surprised.

"It didn't take a university degree to figure it out. I don't know who you are, but I appreciate everything you've done. You saved my life and you may have saved hers too. I will not forget your kindness."

Unsure of whether you should be leaving like this, when Ruth's future hangs in the balance, you know there is nothing more you can do here without complicating the timeline. After saying goodbye, you leave the house and return to your own time.

**Turn to 460**

## 286
(470 x2)

After returning to the car, you consider telling Liz about your premonition, but stop yourself. She wouldn't believe you, and would not be so easily convinced to cancel the deal for the house and look for somewhere else. You wonder if that is enough of a reason to risk her life, when you know what waits at that house, but right now, you

149

can't think of any way to stop her from setting foot inside that would not ruin your relationship.

Then a thought comes to you. The whole incident with the ghosts did not occur until later that night, which means even if you do go to the house; there is still time to convince her to leave. In the end, you decide to go to the house.

Like before, you find that it has not been cleaned and like before, the removal van company calls and tells you that they won't be able to deliver your things until the following day.

Upon hearing this, you realise an opportunity has presented itself. Last time this happened, you decided to stay in the house for the night, but perhaps this time you could convince Liz to stay in a hotel. You noticed one on the drive up here. Even though staying somewhere else would just be putting off the inevitable, it would buy you some time to think of a more permanent solution. The choice is yours.

If you stay at the house **turn to 447**
If you stay at the hotel **turn to 304**
Or you can use Future Knowledge E

287

Placing the three animal shapes into the wall, in the order instructed on the note, seems to work, because the wall suddenly slides back to reveal a secret room. In this room you find shelves filled with jars with all manners of things inside. It seems to be some sort of secret laboratory. As you make your way to the far wall you find a number of nooks containing all kinds of things, including a porcelain doll with life like hair that looks creepy as hell. Turning away from this wall, you find a glass case containing a turquoise stone of some sort. Being curious, you take it out, and as you do, you feel a tingling feeling go through your body as the stone glows. You have just touched a time stone.

**Increase your maximum TTP by 2 and restore your current TTP to full. Also make a note that you now have the following ability:**

**Create Second Self:**

**This will allow you to have two attacks for three rounds every fight.**
**If both attacks succeed against your opponent's roll, you will score two points against them.**
**If one of them fails, you will score a single point as usual but receive no damage.**
**If both fail, you will receive just one hit from your enemy.**

150

**If you are fighting two enemies, you sacrifice your second attack to cancel their second attack and fight them as if you were fighting one on one.**

You can now use Future Knowledge D3

Or return to the house **turn to 13**

**If you return to the house, mark down the number of this passage as a shortcut to The Library Secret Room. Note that you may still have use for the main Library Shortcut, so keep that too.**

288

You are in the middle of your search, when suddenly you hear a blood curdling scream echoing through the corridor. You instantly know it is Liz's voice and run to the living room to see if she is okay. You only make it as far as the door, when you see a figure in black, standing over her threateningly. You recognise it as the same apparition that originally possessed you, only, for some reason, it seems to have taken on a solid form.

"Hey!" you shout. "Get away from her now."

You realise what a big mistake you have made, when the figure turns and then runs directly at you. Quickly, you turn and run back to the main entrance hall. You now have four choices in which to make your escape.

If you try to leave the building via the front door **turn to 183**
If you run to the study **turn to 136**
If you run to the toilets **turn to 327**
Or you can run towards the ballroom **turn to 363**

289
(488 (Via town) 54 x2 (Via woman with Pill)

The Gambling Den is probably one of the most busy, smoky places you have entered in this time so far. People are either queuing for tickets for the coming night's fight, making bets on who the victor will be, or playing cards or dice. It is while you are looking around that you notice a sign saying:

*FIGHTERS NEEDED*

*Will pay good money to anyone who can last at least 6 rounds in the ring*

*If you are interested, ask at the front desk*

If you wish to make a bet on a fight **turn to 70**
If you wish to volunteer to fight **turn to 190**
If you join the gambling table **turn to 275**

You can also use Future Knowledge E5

Or you can return to the town **turn to 488.**
**If you came here via the woman with the pill, then by leaving you give up your attempt to find out more about Reardon and help this woman's husband.**

**Add CMIP T. This will allow you to return to Reardon's Gambling Den just for gambling purposes.**

**Once you have succeeded or failed in your attempt to find evidence against Reardon, attempted a bet, won £100 at the gambling table and volunteered for a fight, you can mark down Building G as complete, as you will have no need to revisit this place.**

## 290
(278)

Remembering what happened last time you called, you decide to play things out slightly differently.

"Greetings," you say. "I'm here on behalf of the council. I have an appointment with Mr Craven for two o clock. "

"I wasn't notified of this," the butler says. "I'll need to check with the master."

"Very well," you say. "I'll wait here."

As the butler goes back inside, you notice that he has left the door open. Now might be your only chance to get inside.

If you sneak in and follow the butler to Mr Craven **turn to 96**
If you would rather wait for him to return **turn to 45**

## 291
(231)

Heading back to the antiques store, you hand over the indentation of the key and ask how much it will cost to make a new one.

"That will be £3," the antiques dealer says.

If you have £3 and wish to pay for a copy **turn to 491**

Otherwise you must return to the town **turn to 488,** and come back later when you do.

**If you return to the house, mark down the number of this passage as a shortcut for copying the key, so you can come here later. In the meantime, you must mark The Butchers as complete, because you will not be able to return there until you have the key.**

292

The library door appears to be locked. You notice that the colour surrounding the lock is gold.

If you have a gold key **turn to 386**

Otherwise, you return to the house **turn to 13**

293
(371)

"Ruth is so innocent and chaste, like Hamlet's Ophelia," you recite.

The butcher looks completely taken aback.

"Where did you hear that?" he says.

"I read it in your diary."

"But that's impossible. I only wrote that entry earlier this evening. There's no way you could have seen it. What is this, some sort of magic trick?"

"No magic, just science. I am from the future. And I know that if you carry on down this path, you are going to ruin a lot of lives, including your own."

"What happens to me?"

This you decide to fabricate.

"You get found out and arrested, but before the date of the trial, the townspeople drag you into the forest and take turns at stabbing you, before feeding your remains to the pigs."

"Oh dear god. They come to hate me that much?"

"For what you did, yes."

"Do I have to leave town though? What if I promised never to go near her again?"

"I'm afraid if you stay here, some part of you will always be tempted. The best thing you can do is go somewhere else and make a fresh start."

"You're right. I have to go," he says before turning and walking away. "Thank you."

153

Even though it seems you have changed the outcome of this night. You decide not to take anything for granted, and keep an eye on Ruth until she returns home. Then when you feel safe in the knowledge that she will not be attacked that night, you travel to the night of the Craven Manor Massacre to see if anything has changed.

**Turn to 393**

294

The door to the attic appears to be locked. You notice that the colour surrounding the lock is red.

If you have a red key **turn to 218**
If not, you must return to the house **turn to 13**

295

"Yes I think I might be," you say in response to the room offer. "Would I be able to have a look at it first?"

He sighs and hands you the key.

"There you go," he says. "Oh, I almost forgot, did you want to give me that case."

"I actually don't have it on me," you say. "I just came in to enquire. I'll drop it here next time I come by though."

"Very well," he says. "I hope you like the room."

You leave the desk and go to the room. As suspected, you find that the doctor has left nothing behind that could help. But wait, what is this? In his waste paper basket is a crumpled note. You open it up and find the following written on it.

*Combination for Briefcase needs to be a number I can remember easily. Perhaps the initials of my favourite author might be an idea. That reminds me, I need to get hold of his latest book. What was it called again? The Fractured Brain, or something like that. (FK: A5 -10)*

You make a note of this before going back downstairs.

"I'm sorry," you say. "The room isn't to my liking."

"Well I suppose it isn't for everyone."

If you haven't already done so, you can ask about the Craven Murders **turn to 528**
Or use Future Knowledge A7 (If you do this the number you add or take away from must be 112)

Otherwise you return to the town **turn to 488**

## 296

As you enter the stale beer smelling pub, you approach the bar and speak to the bar manager in the hopes that he might know something about the house.

"Ah, you're talking about Craven Manor, I do believe," the man says. "Well I haven't been here that long, so I only know the stories I've been told, I'm afraid. There were a group of film makers who went there a few years ago to make a documentary. Apparently none of them have been seen since. Now I'm not sure what I believe. Stories tend to be like Chinese whispers. 'I heard it of a guy, who heard it from a guy, who heard it from another guy'. So the chances are that the tale got distorted at some point, or maybe not, who knows. I'm sorry I couldn't be of more help."

You are about to leave, when an old man in the corner grabs your attention.

"You wouldn't happen to be the new owner of that house would you?" The man asks.

"Yes," you reply. "Do you know anything about the history of the place?"

"As it happens, I know a great deal."

"Like what?"

"I know that the strange goings on did not start until after the Craven family massacre."

"And?" you ask, expecting there to be more.

"Not so fast. If you want this information, I'm afraid you are going to have to do something for me in return."

"You want money?"

"No, nothing like that. I'm looking for an old family heirloom of mine, a silver statuette of a ballet dancer. It originally belonged to one of my ancestors and should have been passed down from generation to generation, but unfortunately it was stolen along the way and at some point ended up in the hands of the Cravens. Since their deaths, my family have been searching for the statuette for a number of years, but so far it is not to be found. I believe that it is hidden in that house, and if you are the new owner as you say, then you may be able to find it for me. Do this for me, and I will tell you everything I know."

Believing that this may be your best way forward, you agree to help the man.

If you already have the silver statuette **turn to 162**
If not, you now return to the town **turn to 444**

**When returning to the town be sure to mark down 162 as a shortcut for returning the statuette to the man. When visiting here again, you will be able to come to this shortcut instead of the original number written on your navigation list.**

**297**

After presenting the evidence to the police, they go to Peter's place and bring him in for questioning.

When he sees the evidence against him, he happily tells them everything.

"Well you already know the first part of my story," he begins. "I met Ruth in town that day, with the intentions of buying her a ring. Then after she started acting all strange, her father came and brought her home. I said that was the last time I saw her, and that was the truth, but what I failed to mention, was that I did go to the house that night. My intention was to rescue Ruth from her father, whom I believed at the time had been holding her against her will in that house.

"My plan was simple. I would climb into the garden and wait in the outside toilets, until everyone had gone to sleep. Then when I felt the coast was clear, I would climb the trellis up to her bedroom window, and convince her to leave with me. I waited in that toilet for over an hour, and smoked a cigarette to pass the time. Then I heard the scream. Fearing that Ruth might be in danger, I abandoned my plan and took a quicker route into the house, by climbing in through the kitchen window. I then made my way through to the hall.

"That's where I found the first of the bodies. It was Ruth's brother Jack. When I first saw him lying in his own blood, I thought he might just be injured, but then when I saw the blood coming out of his head, I knew there was no helping him. Then I found the servant Clara, her throat slit from ear to ear, and finally the butler Crowther; who was only the last, because I left the house soon after.

"Beside Crowther, I found a bloody knife that I instinctively picked up. I had intended to find Ruth, but when I heard the footsteps of someone else entering the house, I panicked and fled. It was only when I got outside, into the garden, that I realised I still had hold of the knife and dropped it by the pond, before making my escape. I swear that this is the honest to god truth."

Considering all the evidence you have against him, you realise this story does seem plausible, and unless you can find anything else, you feel content enough to let Peter go as a possible suspect.

**(FK: C8 Part 2 of 3 +22) Note that you need to find all parts to get the right sum to add or subtract when the time comes to use the future knowledge)**

If you wish to present more evidence **turn to 331**

156

Or you can return to the town **turn to 488,** and come back later.

## 298

You run as quickly as you can, down the stairs, and throw open the door with the intentions of doubling back to pick up your amulet. Only things don't go completely to plan, because no sooner do you open the door, when you find Ruth standing there with the gun pointed in your direction. Her sudden appearance in the doorway shocks you, and before you can do anything, she shoots you in the stomach. As you fall back, bleeding from the wound, your last thoughts are of Liz, right before Ruth puts a second bullet in your head.

## 299

You arrive to find that on the 20/9/2009 the house looks exactly the same as it does in your time. You find yourself in the kitchen, where everything seems to be in the same place: The same patterned plates you ate from, sitting in the rack, the same pots and pans hanging from the bottom, the same salt and pepper shakers by the breadbin, and the same garbage disposal unit ready to take a person's hand off if they dared put it in. For a moment you wonder if you have actually time travelled at all, until you notice a picture on the fridge of a couple in their mid-forties sat on a beach. You assume that this must be John and Hayley Barnett.

You can now use Future Knowledge S
Or continue through the house **turn to 197**

## 300
### (330)
Remembering what happened last time you tried to help Gil, you decide to play things out differently. Like before, you run into his dining room to warn him.

"Don't be alarmed," you say. "I'm not here to harm you. I came here to warn you that there are a group of men outside who plan to rob you. They forced me to help them, but I won't do it. You need to take precaution, because they are expecting me to turn the lights out in a few minutes, and when they see I haven't, they'll storm the place."

"If what you say is true, perhaps I still have time to hide some of my more precious items. I'll need your help though."

Again you follow him, as he leads you to a room where several items of value are on display in large cabinets. Only this time before he can attempt to pull the gun out of the safe, you crush his arm in the door, forcing him to drop the gun, before you retrieve it and point it at him.

"Please don't kill me," he cries. "I'll do anything you want."

If you decide to take the diamond for yourself **turn to 163**
If you decide to stay and protect Gil and his property **turn to 367**

**301**

(272)

"Enjoying the party?" you ask the businessman, as you come to join him.

"Yes it's quite a soiree, although I do feel like my reason for coming here may have been in vain."

"Why do you say that?"

"I came here in the hopes that I may find some potential investors for a construction project I've been working on. My plan is to have a library built in this town. Unfortunately all the people I've asked so far, have libraries in their own homes and don't seem to care if the town has one. I don't suppose you would be interested in investing. This town needs a library, don't you think? All I need to do, is raise £500 and then I can complete the project. Oh, where are my manners, I haven't even introduced myself, my name is Tom Scott and I'm an investment banker."

"Dave Ingram," you say as you shake his hand.

"So Mr Ingram what is it that you do for a living?"

"I'm a salesman," You improvise. "Yes, I make my living selling dog food."

"Dog food?"

"Yes, it's not the most interesting of jobs, but you've got to make a living somehow, right?"

"Oh yes, I completely agree. So Dave, do you think you would be interested in investing?"

"I wish I could help. I mean I love books, but unfortunately I don't have that kind of money."

"Not to worry. I appreciate that you took an interest at all. Enjoy the party."
(FK: G −15)

**Turn to 228**

## 302
### (278)

"Greetings," you say. "I'm here on behalf of the council. We are currently checking all houses in this area to see if they are abiding by the proper regulations. If it's not too much trouble, I was wondering if I could come in and have a look around."

"The master of the house is indisposed at the moment," says the butler, "and I'm afraid you will not be allowed admittance without prior appointment." (FK: L +12)

After he closes the door, you realise that you must either reverse time and try something else with him, or attempt to sneak in **turn to 320**

If you have exhausted your options, you have no choice but to travel back to the present **turn to 13**

## 303
### (98)

With great speed, you run over and catch the Kid as he falls, but unfortunately the momentum still causes him to drop his ice cream. As the kid cries over the melting scoop on the floor, the mother looks to you in appreciation.

"Wow! Fast reflexes. Thank you."

"Don't mention it."

"What do you say to the man," says the mum.

"Thank you," says the kid amidst his tears.

As you walk away, you notice that the kid's shoelaces are untied. No wonder he tripped. (FK: A+13)

**Turn to 147**

## 304
### (286)

"Oh, I would love nothing more than to spend the night in a hotel," Liz says approvingly. "But do you have enough money on you to pay for it?"

If you bought anything from the jewellery shop, you must stay at the house **turn to 447**
If you did not pay for jewellery **turn to 68**

## 305
### (320)

As you walk quietly to the door, you hear the maid having a conversation with the butler.

"The master would like his meat well done, and young Sophie would like extra bread and butter with her soup," says the butler. "Also keep an eye out for rats. Young Jack has been leaving food out for them again."

"If I see a Rat, I will run a mile," says the maid. "I'm scared stiff of the things"

"Then come and get me and I shall deal with it."

Overhearing this, you realise there is one sure way to get the maid out of the kitchen.

If you have a rat **turn to 9**

Otherwise, if you haven't already done so, you can try the window into the study **turn to 221**

Or if you have Victorian clothes, you can attempt knocking on the front door **turn to 278**

If you are unable to sneak in, you return to the present **turn to 13**

**If this was your first time here, you will have this one opportunity to find what you need and come back (Make a note of the number of this passage). If this is your second time, I'm afraid you will not be allowed to return.**

## 306
### (404)

"Zoe told me you owed her a favour," you say.

"Oh well, if Zoe sent you, no charge necessary," Cedric replies.

"So what do you know about Bob Jenkins?"

"I happen to know that he's recruiting for a job at the moment. In fact he's currently meeting with someone in one of the rooms behind this very pub. If you were to wait for me, I could go and arrange an introduction."

"Yes, that would be very helpful, thank you," you say.

Cedric disappears for a few moments behind the bar, and then returns moments later to wave you over. You decide to follow him and find yourself entering a room behind the bar. Here you are faced with the living version of the ghost you saw in the basement of the hotel.

"Cedric here tells me that you're looking for work?" says Bob Jenkins.

"That's right," you say.

"Well as it happens, I am in need of someone with your physique for a job I intend to carry out this evening. Would you be interested?"

If you take him up on his offer **turn to 125**

If you would prefer to warn him of his future to come **turn to 283**

## 307

You hand the pen to the policewoman, and she tells you to wait while she checks it for fingerprints. When she returns, she reports her findings

"I'm sorry, but the fingerprints on the pen do not match either of the fingerprints on the knife."

You now return to the town **turn to 444**
**When returning to the town, be sure to mark down 188 as a shortcut for future fingerprint checks.**

## 308

After careful inspection, you realise that the clock in this shop is the same one that you saw Ruth's father secretly hide a key inside back in the 1800s. You are considering buying it, when you see the price: £2000. Realising there is no way you are going to be able to afford all that, you think of another way to retrieve the key.

"Excuse me," you ask the antiques dealer. "Is there any chance I could see inside this clock? I'd like to know that it's all in working order before I consider buying it."

"Of course," the man says enthusiastically, as he comes over to open it for you.

"This is quite a rare piece," he says. "It was sold to us by the last owner of the Craven house."

As you look around inside, you are aware of the antiques dealer shadowing you, and know that you need to distract him somehow, so you can rummage around inside without him noticing. An idea comes to you suddenly. Noticing a sharp edge to the casing, you decide to purposely cut your finger on it.

"Oh dear me," the man says, noticing the cut. "Let me get you a plaster."

Realising that he's probably more concerned with you filing a lawsuit against him, you take the opportunity of his absence to locate a secret compartment within the clock and remove the star shaped key from inside. You immediately put this in your pocket. As soon as the man has returned and plastered your finger, you declare to him that you are no longer interested in the clock and he returns to the till disappointedly.

You can now return to peruse the shop **turn to 284**
Or you can return to the town **turn to 444**

There is very little to see in this bedroom; although you do feel a chill as you enter. As you look around, you notice that there seems to be a noise coming from beyond the wall. No sooner have you pushed your ear up against it, when it stops, but you are certain that you heard a baby crying.

You now return to the house **turn to 13**

(197)
You press the power button to turn the computer on and are faced with a password screen. In the corner of the screen is the user's avatar, which appears to be a ginger cat. The password that needs to be input is three letters long.

**If you can figure out what the password is, swap each letter for the designated number as shown below, and then turn to the three digit number you end up with.**

| A | B | C | E | L | M | N | O | S | X |
|---|---|---|---|---|---|---|---|---|---|
| 3 | 6 | 7 | 5 | 2 | 1 | 8 | 4 | 0 | 9 |

Otherwise, you can look in the drawer **turn to 416**
Or investigate the painting (Unless you have already done so in the present) **turn to 104**
Or if you choose to leave the study **turn to 362**

When you return this time, you discover that it is night. The front and back doors are magically sealed like before, which means it is only a matter of time until the man in black appears. You go to see your fiancée once again and she gives you another coded message.

*"Memite asihte mote anruters muoyt memite atxeno aehtr po6f otaf meme beesh odnal memoch arok aflesruoye emehte apotsh mote atpmettam arehtief anach muoyt asid atic mohwt awonke buoyt beveilebs muoyt becnos. Astcepsust belbissoph mehtr anwode aworrane ednam othgine atahte edeneppahf atahwe etuobaf ferome anraels gote gelbas bebs adluohsh muoyr berehto. Amehte anog femite mehte gote anruters adnag adenoitnems bin gotohpe atahte efof asevlahf gowth gehth adnife atsume huoye awone. Ayretsymo asihte agnivlosh anog atratsh adooge bat muoyt mevige adluohsh atahte. Aneebs mevahs ayame*

*orellike mehtr mohwa enog eseulch arofe atube, adenoitneme fib ayeke erevlish mehte otegr motr atsuji atone, ayrassecens asawe otin atube memite etahte gote enruters fote adahd muoyt ayrrosh am'im."*

**RULES OF DAY AND NIGHT**

From this point on day and night will play a part in your adventure. If this is your first time reading this, you must now consult the rules of day and night at the back of the book. Once you have done this, you can return to the house.

**Turn to 13**

### 312

(234 x2)

You soon find yourself coming to a pub called *The King's Steed,* and decide to go inside and see if you can find anyone who might be able to help you. Two people draw your attention. One is a posh gentleman in a suit, sat at the bar, who is knocking pints back like they were water. The other is a rough looking rocker, in a black leather jacket, sat in the corner.

If you approach the posh man at the bar **turn to 38**
If you approach the rocker **turn to 115**

### 313

(147 x2)

"Hey you!" you shout over. "Get your damn hands off her!"

Unfortunately, your heroic attempt at using a film reference from an old 80s movie, does little more than anger the drunks, who get to their feet and walk over to you.

"Or what?"

You realise you haven't completely thought this through.

"Or," you say as you bravely get to your feet. "I'll make your face... how it isn't now."

To this they laugh, then one of them throws a punch that knocks you back onto the table.

"That's for interfering in my business," says the drunk. (FK: B +10)

"Okay, out!" shouts the owner. "We don't tolerate that kind of behaviour in my place."

After the drunks are shown the door, Liz returns to find you with a big shiner. You tell her what had transpired and she is not happy that you took a chance like that. Not long after this, you both leave.

**Turn to 470**

### 314

"We're actually doing a special offer today," she says, "a mixed bouquet for £15. Are you interested?"

**If you are, you must deduct £15 from your money and place the flowers in your inventory.**

Otherwise, you leave and return to the town **turn to 444**

### 315

By shining the torch around the room, you notice an object in a dark corner. It is a green, flat wooden carving of a cat, there is something painted on it, but you can barely make it out because it has worn off with age.

If you haven't already, you can check the encyclopaedia **turn to 189**

Or return to the house **turn to 13**

**Once you have checked the encyclopaedia, you can mark down the Storeroom as complete, as you will have no need to revisit this place.**

### 316

When you return to your time, you are surprised to find that you do not arrive in the house as expected, but rather in that same café where your adventure began, with Liz and the housing agent sat in the booth. For a moment you do start to wonder if any of your previous adventures had actually happened, until the pen is offered to you once again.

"So I just need you to sign there," says the housing agent

You think about this for a few moments, considering what may occur if you take this house again. From your visit to the night of the Craven Manor Massacre it seemed like everything had been put right, but can you really take that for granted?

What if you arrived in that house to only have your fiancée possessed again by another spirit? You decide not to take the chance.

"I'm sorry," you say to the housing agent. "I think I may have changed my mind about the house."

"What do you mean, you've changed your mind?" asks Liz.

"I'm just not so sure that Craven Manor is the house for us."

"Craven Manor?" she says looking at you with confusion. "Don't you mean 171 Hartsfield Lane?"

"171 Hartsfield Lane?" You say confused. "No, Craven Manor is the house that we were intending on buying."

"I don't know where you got that idea," says the housing agent. "Craven Manor has been occupied by descendants of the Reardon family for way over a hundred years."

"The Reardon family? Don't you mean the Cravens?"

"Where did you hear that? There hasn't been a Craven living in that house since, let me see, 1905."

"What happened in 1905?"

"That was the date they sold the house to Ray Reardon," the agent confirms.

"They sold it?" You say in shock. "Why would they do that?"

"Well who could blame them after what happened to the daughter and the mother. Such a tragedy"

"What happened to them?"

"Well rumour has it that the daughter went a bit crazy and tried to kill them all."

"But she failed, right?"

"I think so. In one story she actually killed the father, but in another he lived. I'm not sure which is true."

"They tried to get her help though."

"They tried, but she was too far gone unfortunately. Eight years later after she was admitted to the mental hospital, she got hold of a pair of scissors from one of the carers and cut both her wrists."

"And her mother?"

"The strain of Ruth's death was too much for her. Her heart gave out less than a week later. She had been in poor health ever since her daughter was admitted."

Upon hearing this, a tear comes to your eye.

"Dave," says Liz, surprised. "Are you alright?"

"Yes," you say. "It's just a sad story?"

"Anyway that's enough history talk," says the housing agent. "Now if you have no further reservations, I just need you to sign here... And there...And you're done. Here are your keys. I hope you'll both be happy in your new home."

After the agent has left, Liz turns to you with a look of concern.

"So what was all that about?" she asks.

"What do you mean?"

"You seemed to know a lot about those Cravens?"

"I did a bit of research about them before we came here. They were once a very important family in this town. I thought it might be interesting to know some of the local history."

"But you've never shown an interest in history before."

"Things change. I fancied trying a new hobby."

"Well as long as you don't start collecting war memorabilia, and going to re-enactment events, I suppose I can get behind that. Anyway, I need the toilet. Be back in a bit."

While you wait for Liz to return, you see the same scene play out that you had once seen in a loop: The kid dropping his ice cream, followed by the bullied waitress. You consider for a moment, attempting to reverse time and put them right for old time's sake, but as you reach for where your amulet had once been, you realise your neck is completely bare. Your days of time travelling seem to have come to an end.

As you sit there waiting for Liz to return, you can't help feeling that the outcome of your adventure in Craven Manor has been bittersweet. Yes, you prevented the Craven Manor Massacre and you saved your possessed fiancée, but you failed to save Ruth Craven from herself and that has left you with a knot in your stomach that you can't seem to untwist. You wonder if there was anything you could have done differently.

Moments later, Liz returns and sits down.

"What time have you got?" you ask.

Liz looks to her watch.

"Two, thirty."

"And what time's the removal van meant to be showing up at the house?"

"About Four-ish."

"Then we're going to have a bit of time to kill. What do you say to getting out of here soon and having a look around town?"

"I suppose so," she says. "I noticed a jewellery shop on the way in."

"I was actually more interested in the book..." you stop yourself, suddenly having an exciting realisation as you feel your bare neck. "Actually the jewellery shop sounds like a good idea."

THE END

Or is it?

Congratulations you have completed the **'BITTERSWEET'** ending. You may have reached the end of this current adventure, but there are still multiple paths you could try. If you haven't already, why not start again and try to complete one of the other 5 endings.

Please now turn to the final page for news on future adventure books

### 317
((14) Leaving (200) Investigate noise (12) Exploring house)

All of a sudden, you feel yourself unable to move. For some reason your legs have stopped working and every other part of you. You realise right then that you have been drugged. It must have been the drink. (FK: D5+26) You try to shout out, but your voice doesn't work. You are completely paralysed. Moments later, you pass out. **Turn to 16**

### 318
(224)

Stepping out of the washroom in your new outfit, you try to blend in with the crowd and make your way to the ballroom. On your way there, an attractive woman with brown hair tied up in a bun, holding an unlit cigarette, tries to get your attention.

"Excuse me," she says. "Have you got a light?"

If you have a lighter **turn to 383**
If not, you apologise and head inside **turn to 238**

### 319
(299)

After finding the package on top of the cupboard, you lift it down and feel a sense of excitement when you discover where it has come from: *Mama Cecille's Emporium.* The same shop that you had seen on the Ghost Chasers' website. Could this be what you think it is? You grab a knife from the drawer and open the box as quickly as you can, and are relieved when you uncover the contents. Red brick dust! Just what you need.

Taking it with you, you make your way to the doorway of the study. Then, lifting the rug, you pour a line underneath and then replace it so it cannot be seen. Unfortunately this uses up the whole jar. After you are done, you consider playing through the whole list of events again. i.e. setting up the video camera, putting cigarettes on the shelf, watching the recording back, but then you realise you don't have to, because you know the code and can easily use it in the present when you return.

Instead, you wait in the kitchen until the couple have come in and gone to bed, at which point you go back to the study. Like before, John gets up and finds you, but what differs this time is that he does not get stabbed in the back. Instead, his wife stops directly at the point where you have poured the line of red brick dust, as if an invisible wall stood there. When he hears her footsteps, John turns around and is shocked to see her throwing herself at the invisible wall.

"Oh dear god," he says. "Hayley? What is wrong with her?"

"Your wife is possessed by a dark spirit," you say. "This particular dark spirit likes to possess people in couples, and cause one to kill the other."

"How come she can't seem to get any further than the doorway?"

"I placed a line of red brick dust by the door to make sure she couldn't follow us in. We are both safe here."

"How is it you know so much about this? Who are you?"

"My name is Dave Ingram," you say, "and I'm from the future."

"What?" the man says, confused. "You don't honestly expect me to believe that."

"I know how crazy it sounds, but it's the truth. I came back here to save you, because on this night eleven years from now, your wife killed you and then took her own life."

"But my Hayley would never do anything like that. She loves me. We're both in a very happy marriage."

"I'm sure you are; which is why I am convinced that she committed these acts under the influence of the dark spirit inside her."

"How can we get it out of her?" he asks.

"This particular spirit only seems to come out at night, so it might leave when the sun comes up of its own accord."

"It that's the case then all we'd have to do is wait, right? If we're safe in here like you say, there isn't very much she can do."

"Actually there is one thing," you say

All of a sudden the possessed woman stops throwing herself at the invisible force shield and just stares at you and smiles, before raising the knife above her head. You realise then that the spirit has decided to skip killing the husband and go straight for the wife's suicide. You need to get to her and disarm her, but you have only moments to act.

**Roll two dice.**

**You may add up to 2TTP to ensure your roll is higher.**

If you roll 8 or higher **turn to 113**
If you roll lower **turn to 431**

## 320
### (389)

Looking around the grounds of the house, you happen to notice two possible points of entry. One is an open window leading into the study, and the other is the back door, leading into the kitchen, from which you can smell food cooking.

If you go in through the kitchen **turn to 403**
Or you can use future knowledge K
If you go in through the study **turn to 221**

If you are unable to sneak in, you return to the present **turn to 13**
**If this was your first time here, you will have this one opportunity to find what you need and come back. If this is your second time, I'm afraid you will not be allowed to return.**

## 321

Suddenly, you remember the hatch that lies beneath your feet and turn the attention of the sledgehammer to the ground. Five swings and the hatch is revealed. You quickly open it up and jump down into the tunnel below, as the flames consume the room above. Down the tunnel you run, for what seems like an age, before you re-emerge out of the hatch on the other side, and into the basement of the hotel. From here you go up a flight of stairs and into the main lobby.

"Dear god!" says the hotel owner when he sees you looking bruised and beaten. "Where did you spring from?"

It is at this point you collapse and pass out on the floor. When you awake, you find yourself in one of the hotel rooms with your fiancée standing over you.

"Liz," you say.

"I'm here," she replies.

"How did you...?"

"After I escaped the house," she begins to explain. "I waited around for a while in case you found some way out, and when you didn't, I went to the hotel to look for help. You can't imagine my surprise when I learnt you were here. The hotel owner says that you used a tunnel that runs from the house to this hotel. Apparently it was installed back in the 1700s by some lord who used to live in the house, before it was Craven Manor. He used to use it as a means to smuggle rum."

"Fancy that."

"You know, Dave, looking back on everything that has happened, I'm not so sure we made the right decision in taking that house."

To this you just laugh.

**THE END**

Or is it?

Congratulations you have completed the **'ESCAPIST'** ending. You may have reached the end of this current adventure, but there are still multiple paths you could try. If you haven't already, why not start again and try to complete one of the other 5 endings.

Please now turn to the final page for news on future adventure books

### 322
(282)

"Wait!" you shout to Gil. "Before you go opening that safe, you might like to know that your maid is in cahoots with these men. I saw her not five minutes ago, letting them in through the back door."

"Beatrice is this true?" asks Gil.

"Mr Murdock I..." she stumbles as she attempts to defend herself.

"After everything I've done for you," he says disappointedly.

"Well I can see that she is of no further use to me," says Bob as he nods for his man to let the maid go, and then grabs Zoe. "This one however is not in my employ."

It appears your attempt to shake things up may have just backfired.

**Turn to 129**

### 323

It is pitch black, so you can see very little, except a book shelf filled with junk, including cheap ornaments, some VHS tapes, some CD's, and a big, hardback book on Mythology. Among the CD's you notice a greatest hits for 80s rock band Status Quo, and laugh to yourself. Your dad was a big fan, and you always used to like to swap his CD's round to annoy him.

If you have not already done so, you can look inside the encyclopaedia **turn to 189** Otherwise, you can return to the house **turn to 13**

**If you return to the house, mark down the number of this passage as a shortcut for The Storeroom when you return.**

## 324
(319)

Hayley falls back and grabs a lamp, ready to deliver a fatal blow, when to your surprise; John grabs her from behind in a sleeper hold. She passes out, and you see the dark entity leave her body.

"So much for waiting it out," he says.

"It's not over," you say. "We need to get her out of here before it decides to come back."

"Got it," John says, as he picks her back up and begins to drag her towards the front door.

Soon the three of you are outside and John is placing his wife into the backseat of their car.

"So what happens now?" He asks.

"Now you drive to a hotel and stay for the night. You can come back here for your stuff in the morning, but after that you should get as far away from this house as possible."

"I really don't know how to thank you. You're almost like some kind of guardian angel, showing up like this."

"No, I'm just a guy living nine years from now in the same house as you."

"Why haven't you left?"

"Because the ghost that got inside my fiancée won't budge until I help it complete its unfinished business."

"And let me guess, that requires you to travel back in time and stop something from happening."

"Good guess."

"I'm a sucker for time travel movies, what can I say," John smirks. "Is there anything I could do to help you from this time? You know, I could burn the house down. If there was no house, perhaps you would never move in."

"I don't know if that's such a good idea. It might be the house that traps that thing in the one place. If it got free, who knows what it could do."

"There must be something I can do?"

"Actually there is one thing. Since being in this house I've made use of several items that I believe originally belonged to you. If you were to take them from the house, I'm not sure what effect that would have on my timeline."

"Tell me what you want me to leave and I'll do it."

You then give him a list of everything you've picked up in the future, and ask him to also leave the contents of the safe. To this he agrees. After you are done, you

171

expect the gold key and camcorder to disappear from your inventory, but they don't. You are relieved by this, because you didn't fancy having to find that gold key again, or losing the money you found on the bodies, or the items you bought with it. It seems that as long as you are in the past when a change is made to the present, that nothing in your inventory will ever be affected.

**Congratulations you have just saved a number of lives. Not only have you saved the couple who lived in the house before you, but in doing so, you have also saved their son and the documentary film crew who died in the house looking for the truth.**

**Add CMIP S. This affects the Study in the house.**
**Add CMIP B. This affects the Attic in the house.**

**You must also discard the camcorder and remove Future Knowledge F1 and F5, as you will have no further need of these.**

You now return to the present **turn to 13**

## 325
### (330)

Rather than head for the breaker box in the cellar, you run into the house and look for Gil. After searching several rooms, you eventually find him sitting down to dinner. He almost chokes on his food when he sees you.

"Don't be alarmed," you say. "I'm not here to harm you. I came here to warn you. There are a group of men outside who plan to rob you. They forced me to help them, but I won't do it. You need to take precaution, because they are expecting me to turn the lights out in a few minutes, and when they see I haven't, they'll storm the place."

"If what you say is true, perhaps I still have time to hide some of my more precious items. I'll need your help though."

You decide to follow him, as he leads you to a room where several items of value are on display in large cabinets. At the back of the room is a safe which he immediately goes to and starts to unlock.

"Wouldn't it make more sense for me to take care of your safety first?"

"That's what I'm doing."

No sooner has the safe clicked open, when he pulls a gun out from inside and points it at you.

(FK: Z-30)

"What are you doing?"

"You didn't honestly think I'd fall for your ruse did you?"

"There is no ruse. There are men outside with guns and they plan to storm this place and kill everyone who gets in their way to get what they want."

"Well if what you say is true, you won't mind if I call the police."

"No," you protest, "there isn't enough time."

Before you can argue your point further, there is an explosion outside as the front door is blown off its hinges, and several men run into the room with guns.

"Put your gun down now," one of them shouts.

"You will not get my diamond," Gil cries out as he fires his gun in their direction.

The shot hits one of them in the neck, and in response to this, the rest of them open fire on the whole room. Gil is riddled with bullets, and even though you attempt to dodge out of the way, you are also hit with one in the stomach. Unless you can reverse time and prevent this incident, I'm afraid this is where your adventure ends.

## 326

If you have CMIP B, turn to 294 immediately. If you don't have CMIP B, then please continue reading.

The door to the attic appears to be locked. You notice that the colour surrounding the lock is red.

If you have a red key **turn to 20**
If not, you must return to the house **turn to 13**

## 327
(288)

You quickly bolt the door behind you, but it is only a matter of time before the dark entity gets in. It is at this point that you notice a grill on the wall, leading to a ventilation shaft. You try to remove it, but it is screwed in tight.

If you have a screwdriver **turn to 423**
If not **turn to 30**

## 328

Whether you've met the book shop owner previously or not, it seems he doesn't remember you because you must have undone the day you met.

"New in Town?" he asks.

"Just passing through," you lie, so you don't have to explain yourself.

"Are you looking for anything in particular?"

"Books on ghosts, actually."

"Ah, you're one of them are you?" he says unimpressed. "Heard all about the famous haunted house and thought you'd come and have a look for yourself? I'd do yourself a favour and drive back on out of here."

"Do you have any books on ghosts or not?" you say impatiently.

"On the back wall," he points. "In the area next to horror fiction."

"Thank you."

Looking through the books in the area pointed out to you, you find two books of interest. One is titled: 'Messages beyond the grave,' and the other: 'The Book of Ghost Deterrents.' Believing both of these books may be of some help, you begin to flick through, when the book shop owner's loud coughing interrupts you.

"I'm sorry, but this isn't a library," he says. "If you want to know what is in those books, I'm afraid you will have to buy them."

Seeing that he is unlikely to back down, you consider purchasing either one or both of the books. You also notice a book on philosophy called 'The Splintered Mind,' which may also be of interest.

Messages beyond the grave   £25 (**turn to 187** once bought)
Book of ghost deterrents     £35 (**turn to 35** once bought)
The Splintered Mind          £15 (**turn to 274** once bought)

**If you buy any of these books and decide to read them at any time, be sure to make a note of where you are when you read them, so you can return there easy enough after. If you do not wish to buy them, you can always return here to buy them later.**

You can now use Future Knowledge E6
Or return to the town **turn to 444**

turn to 187
turn to 35
turn to 274
turn to 444

### 329

When travelling to this time, you hope to arrive near the house, but are surprised to find yourself on the outskirts of town. As you make your way down a back street, you bump into a man banging on a door and shouting:

"Let me in. I know she's in there."

If you stop to investigate **turn to 8**
If you continue on to Craven Manor **turn to 76**
Or you can use Future Knowledge C9 (To use this you must have £2)

## 330
(223 (Via attempt to stop robbery) 125 (Via security guard)

Climbing the ladder, you are surprised to be met by the house maid as you come in through the window. She appears to be in cahoots with the burglars. (FK: A4+40)

"Wait a minute," she says. "You're not Paul."

"Paul couldn't make it," you reply. "He had a bit of an accident. I was brought in at the last moment to replace him"

"Do you know what you have to do?"

"I'm here to turn the electricity off."

"That's right. The breaker box is in the cellar. To get there you go down the stairs, and through the first door you come to on your left."

With these instructions you head out into the hall.

If you go to the breaker box as planned, to turn off the electricity **turn to 479**
If you go to warn Gil about the robbery **turn to 325**
Or you can use Future Knowledge Z

## 331

**Mark down the number of this passage as a shortcut for The Police Station/ 1800s Town so you can come straight here to initiate interrogations of suspects in the future.**

To initiate the arrest of a suspect, you must have all the evidence against them listed. This will have been found as Future Knowledge and will come in multiple parts. When you are able to complete one of the Future Knowledge groupings below, add or subtract all the numbers necessary from the number above and turn to the new passage.

You can use Future Knowledge B4
You can use Future Knowledge B6
You can use Future Knowledge B7
You can use Future Knowledge B8
You can use Future Knowledge B9
You can use Future Knowledge C1
You can use Future Knowledge C7
You can use Future Knowledge C8

You can return here multiple times to use the future knowledge available, but just be sure to cross off each one you have used and make a note of which suspects you have interrogated already, so you don't end up going to a passage you have been to before.

You can decide at any time to return to the town **turn to 488**

### 332

The display room is almost like a miniature museum, with relics and curiosities from many different periods of history, including ancient Greece, ancient Rome, Medieval, Jacobean and Elizabethan. One of the centre pieces of the room appears to be a great suit of armour that stands tall in the centre. Even though there are a lot of nice looking things in this room, there is nothing that could be of use to you, but you do notice a door on the far wall with a sign above saying 'Workshop'. Thinking that you might find something of interest in there, you are about to walk over to the door, when to your surprise, the suit of armour suddenly springs to life, and with sword in hand, blocks you from going any further. You can tell the suit of armour is possessed, and know you will not get any further unless you have a sword of your own to face it.

If you have a sword you can fight back, otherwise you must return to the house **turn to 13,** and come back when you do.

**If you are able to fight back, you can now consult the rules of Combat at the back of the book. But be sure to make a note of this passage so you can return here after.**

**The fight will last eighteen rounds.**

**The suit of armour has a +2 advantage to its attack rolls.**

If you win **turn to 521**

### 333
(215)
When Bob pulls the trigger, you feel a relief when there is no bang.

"Sorry to disappoint you," says Bob, "but I left that chamber empty just in case you came round at the last moment. Besides, shooting you would make too much noise and I believe in being discreet about things like this." (FK: X-50)

At first you see this as a small mercy, until you are untied from the chair and dragged outside. It is only now that you realise you are standing outside a warehouse on the docks. You can smell the salt of the sea in the air, and hear the sound of the gentle waves. Of course Bob would have a warehouse down by the docks, what criminal boss doesn't. It's the perfect location to get rid of people.

"This way," Bob commands his men.

You are then marched to the end of the docks, where Bob signals for his men to tie a cinderblock to your feet. Once it is tied tight, he then looks at you and gives you one more opportunity to change your mind.

"Last Chance."

If you change your mind **turn to 125**
If you still remain defiant **turn to 443**

334

The antiques store owner is a small bald man with a friendly face. Looking around at his wares you see a sign in the corner.

*Need a copy of a key? Bring us the original key or a mould and we can make you a duplicate while you wait in the store* (FK: C5+60).

**This is what he has for sale**

Painting   £50
Medieval Sword £200
A pair of old fashioned scales £5
An Antique Vase £100
Chess set £5
Grappling hook £5

**This is what he will buy from you**

Cigarette Case      £5
Penny Dreadful      25p
Toy train           £5
Silver Statuette    £200

After purchasing and selling any items

You can now use Future Knowledge Q

Or return to the town **turn to 488**

**335**

(226)

You lie completely still, as the taxidermist returns and drags you down into his workshop. And then when he ties you down, you leave a good amount of time before you open your eyes.

"Ah, you're awake," says the taxidermist. "I imagine you are confused right now, probably wondering why you can't move. It is because of the concoction that I dosed you with. You see it not only contained a powerful sedative, but also a paralytic. It will make the operation more painless.".

"Now where is that scalpel?" the taxidermist says. "I know I left it round here somewhere. Damn, I need that scalpel! An artist can't be expected to finish his work without his favourite paintbrush. I must have left it in the house. Don't go anywhere until I return. That's a joke by the way, as I know there's no possible way you can go anywhere."

'That's what you think, Jackass,' you chuckle to yourself in your head. He soon leaves to look for his scalpel and when you see that the coast is clear, you jump into action. You must escape and you have little time to do it. The question is will you just break yourself free, or will you attempt to take the girl with you?

**Roll one die, eight times.**

**You may add up to 2TTP to ensure each roll is higher.**

**Once you have rolled 18 or over, you have broken free and must stop rolling. But do keep a note of how many rolls you have left.**

**Once you have broken free, you can either choose to leave turn to 27**

**Or use your remaining rolls to try and break the girl free, by rolling 12 or over.**

If you succeed in breaking her free **turn to 422**
If you fail to break yourself free, or attempt to break the girl free and fail **turn to 31**

**336**

(358)

Remembering the fact that the maid was taken hostage, makes you wonder if you might be able to prevent it. After all, if the gang doesn't have a hostage, then they

178

won't be able to convince Gil to open the safe. Knowing at what point they grabbed her, might also give you some idea as to where they came in from.

"Do you mind if I use your bathroom?" you ask Gil, trying to excuse yourself.

"No, not at all," he says. "It's the third door on the left."

You follow his directions. Then as soon as you are out of sight, you sneak further into the house. After searching each room in turn, you eventually find the maid, cleaning in the kitchen.

If you tell her to leave immediately **turn to 130**
If you wait around for the robbery to begin, so you can save her from being a hostage **turn to 236**

## 337
(109)

You wait for a few moments to make sure Peter has moved on ahead and then you leap the wall. Once you reach the other side, you find you are able to slip into the shadows and watch as events unfold. Peter slips into the outside toilet and waits there. That makes sense with your findings at the crime scene. As you watch, you notice that he appears to be waiting for something. Could he be waiting for the family to go to sleep so he can slip in and murder them? Should you perhaps act now, or should you wait a while longer?

If you act now **turn to 94**
If you decide to wait longer **turn to 191**

## 338
(470)

Upon entering the Jewellery shop, the strong aroma of incense wafts up your nostrils, and you find yourself looking upon shelves filled with trinkets, precious stones and various artefacts. One in particular catches Liz's attention. It is an amethyst, beaded necklace. After trying it on, she looks towards you for approval.

"What do you think?"

"It's nice."

"I'd buy it if I could, but I spent the last of my money on that toll bridge we went over."

You realise that she is hinting for you to buy it for her.

If you purchase the necklace as a present for your fiancée **turn to 241**
If you choose not to **turn to 286**
Or you can use Future Knowledge D

Swinging the sledgehammer with all your might, you bring the wall down to reveal a second room behind. You now see why you thought you had heard a baby crying, as the room beyond appears to be a nursery. There is a play pen, a cot, and a number of cuddly toys. As you go to inspect closer, you hear a noise above you and look up to find the most hideous thing you have ever seen.

It appears to be a skinless baby, with a large mouth full of pointy fangs, clinging to the ceiling. As it drops down, you quickly pull back and avoid it sinking its teeth into your throat. It seems to be out for blood. Unfortunately you are going to have to fight this thing.

Unless you have the Obsidian Dagger, you must return to the house **turn to 13**, and come back here later when you do. **If you return to the house, mark down the number of this passage as a shortcut for Bedroom Five. When visiting here you will be able to come to this shortcut instead of the original number written on your navigation list.**

If you have the dagger and are able to fight, you can now consult the rules of Combat at the back of the book. But be sure to make a note of this passage so you can return here after.

**The fight will last twenty four rounds.**

**After every third round, the baby will climb onto the ceiling for two rounds. On these rounds you will have a -4 disadvantage to your rolls. However, the baby will only be able to fend off your attack for two rounds and not attack back. On the third round all disadvantages will be gone.**

**On the third, if it beats you, it will drop from the ceiling onto you, and as well as taking two hits worth of damage, it will begin to feed off your TTP. Every round after this it will drain 2TTP of you until you can throw a double or over 10 to knock it off you.**

**After three rounds of feeding on you, it will automatically stop and return to crawling on the ceiling.**

**If when it drops, you manage to beat it, or tie with it, the baby will not feed on you and combat will continue**

If on the 24th round the baby successfully drops onto you, it will only score two hits and will not feed.

If you manage to defeat the phantom baby **turn to 519**

## 340
(201)

Next, you see the thief run over to a window cleaner's ladder, and use it to climb up onto the roof.

If you follow him up the ladder **turn to 510**
If you choose to stay down on the street and follow him from there **turn to 84**

## 341
(190)

The fight soon approaches and you find yourself facing an opponent who is twice your size.

**If you need to, you can now consult the rules of Combat at the back of the book. But be sure to make a note of this passage so you can return here after.**

**There will be twenty four rounds.**

**Opponent has an added advantage of +3 to his rolls for being a more seasoned fighter.**

**However, you can use up to 2TTP per round to decrease his rolls.**

**Two successful attacks in a row, a double or rolling over 10 will result in a knock out. This rule applies to both of you. This will bring the fight to a close.**

**If you lose by a knock out within the first 6 rounds, you receive nothing**
**If you lose by a knock out after the first 6 rounds, you receive only £50**
**If you lose by a knock out after the first 12 rounds, you receive only £75**
**If you lose by points at the end of the 24 rounds, you receive only £100**
**If you win by points at the end of the 24 rounds, you receive £200**
**If you win by a knock out after the first 6 rounds, you receive £300**
**If you win by a knock out within the first 6 rounds, you receive £400**

After the fight is over, you collect your winnings.

Note that you will not be allowed to fight again.

You can now return to the main gambling area **turn to 289**
Or you can return to the town **turn to 488**
If you came here via the woman with the pill, then by leaving you give up your attempt to find out more about Reardon and help this woman's husband.

**Add CMIP T. This will allow you to return to Reardon's Gambling Den just for gambling purposes.**

### 342

Thinking about how much more exploring there is for you to do, you decide not to waste anymore time and make a dash for the house. You get extremely wet, but are glad you left when you did, because as you reach the door, you look back to see a bolt of lightning hit a nearby tree, causing it to fall and crush the Gazebo. You realise how lucky you were to have left when you did.

**Restore 5TTP**

**(FK: F8 +67)**

You now return to the house **turn to 13**

**Mark down The Gazebo as complete, as you will have no need to revisit this place.**

### 343

This room is filled with various odds and ends, some of them useful, some of them not as much. Two things in particular grab your attention. One is a ball of string and the second, a torch missing a battery. You can take both of these.

**Once you have a battery look out for passages with the words pitch black in. In these areas things are hidden in the dark. The battery will tell you what number you must minus from the passage to find them.**

You now return to the house **turn to 13**

Mark down Store Room Three as complete, as you will have no need to revisit this place.

344

Sliding the box of books out from under the bed, you step up onto it and grab the curtain pole. This item is too big for you to take back with you, so you can only use it whilst in this time. Do not worry about adding it to your inventory. The following future knowledge will tell you when you can use it. (FK: D6-32)

You can now check under the grill **turn to 474**

Or return to the house **turn to 418**
**If you have chosen to hide in this room turn to 271**

345

Following the directions to the gentleman's club, you find it on the outskirts of town. You are about to go in through the door, when you are faced with a rather stout looking doorman.
  "I'm sorry, but there is no entry past this point without the password."

**If you know the password, exchange the letters for the numbers below and turn to the number in question. Make sure to make a note of the number above, just in case you end up going to a paragraph that doesn't match up.**

| A | B | C | D | E | F | G | I | K |
|---|---|---|---|---|---|---|---|---|
| 4 | 9 | 0 | 8 | 0 | 9 | 8 | 6 | 7 |
| M | N | O | R | S | T | U | Y | |
| 5 | 4 | 2 | 1 | 2 | 5 | 3 | 7 | |

If you do not know the password, you can either go back to the passage you were previously on and return later, or you can return to the present **turn to 13**

346

Picking up the flow of decoding the message, the rest seems to translate itself. You then look back at what you have written.

*Help me. I am caught in limbo, unable to move on. Trapped here by my killer who will not allow me or my family to pass on, having to play out the night we were murdered over and over again, by creating more victims in the hosts we are forced to take; which I'm afraid includes your fiancée. By wearing an amulet you have broken this cycle temporarily, and for the first time in a long time I am able to speak out. I thank you for that, but it will only be a matter of time before the dark man lures a new host to the house to play his part.*

*Until then he will only be able to appear in a temporary form at night and only for a limited time, which means now is the best time to attempt breaking this curse once and for all. In life my father was a hunter of ancient artefacts, and one of his discoveries was a collection of stones which gave particular people the ability to move through time.*

*I believe since I grew up around these stones, that some of their power passed to me, and stayed with me even after death. I was never able to use this power, but somehow when I made contact with you, I was able to pass it on. What power I gave you, was temporary, and would have worn out eventually if it had not been for the protection amulet that you now wear. You see, as well as protecting you against possession, it also contains a time stone of its own that has allowed you to maintain the power I first gave you. The complete effects of this are not known to me, but I hope it will aid you in your quest to destroy the man in black and help us move on, which will of course release your fiancée in the process.*

*There is of course a chance that you may not have understood any of this, and if that is the case, I hope you will discover this quest on your own. If you have understood everything though, I would like to leave you with one final piece of advice. There is a secret room in the cellar which fortunately has not been discovered since my father's death. Unfortunately however, it requires a special key to enter; a key that has not been seen since my father hid it away on the 3/5/1895. If you can find the key and open this room, you will find something that will help you greatly.*

*My name is Ruth by the way."*

Once you have finished decoding the message you can either return to the page of the original message **turn to 208**

Or if you came here from a shortcut you wrote down, you can return to the house **turn to 13**

### 347
(21)

Before leaving town, you see the butcher approach Ruth's father.

"Good day, Nicholas," he says.

"Now is not a good time, Sam," Mr Craven replies.

"Oh, hello Ruth," the butcher says, noticing Ruth. "I didn't see you there."

"She's not well, I'm taking her home."

"Oh, that's a shame. I hope she gets better soon. Oh, before you go, would I be able to use your workshop this coming Saturday? I've got a project I've been meaning to finish up."

"Do you still have your key?"

"I do."

"Then that should be fine. Just let yourself in and use whatever you want."

"Thank you."

After they have left the butcher, you follow Ruth and her father back to Craven Manor. Once they go inside, you realise there is nothing more you can do at this point in time.

If you wish to wait around for the night to come, so you can attempt to prevent the murders **turn to 499**

Otherwise you return to the present **turn to 13**

**If you leave, you will not be able to return to this time again, so make sure you have seen everything that you wanted to. You can however, time travel straight to 499 for the night of the murder at any time, so make a note of it.**

## 348
### (338)

You are considering buying the necklace for Liz, when an amulet hanging behind the till catches your eye. At first you are not quite sure why it seems so significant to you, until you remember the picture in the book regarding ghosts and possession that showed a very similar looking amulet. Wondering if this might be the thing you need to prevent your possession, you waste no time in purchasing it. (FK: E −78)

**Turn to 286**

## 349

Beyond this door is a cupboard filled with large tools. One in particular gets your attention. It is a large sledge hammer. If you decide to take this it will get you into any room regardless if you have the key or not. Just act as if you do have the key. You can also use it on particular walls.

**To know if there is a wall you can break through, look for the reference 'beyond the wall' and +30 to the number of the passage.**

Believing this to be the item Nicholas told you to find, you now leave this room.

You now return to the house **turn to 13**

**Mark down Miscellaneous Room One as complete, as you will have no need to revisit this place.**

350

"Excuse me," you say, getting the attention of the antiques dealer.

"Yes, how can I help?" he offers.

"I'm working with the police at the moment, regarding the Craven Manor Massacre."

"They've reopened the case?"

"That's right," you confirm. "I'd like to ask you a few questions."

"Yes, of course."

"I spoke to Peter Kline earlier today and he described an incident that occurred in your shop the day before the murder."

"Yes, I remember," he explains. "He was here with young Ruth. They seemed happy enough looking round the store, until she suddenly came over all strange and wanted to leave."

"Do you have any idea why this happened?" you ask him. "Had she perhaps seen something or someone which caused this behaviour?"

"Actually now you mention it, yes. A man had entered the store a few minutes before."

"Who was this man?" you ask.

"It was the man who runs the boxing arena and gambling den, Ray Reardon. It could just be coincidence that he came into the shop round about the same time, or maybe not. Make of it what you will."

**Add CMIP R. This will give you access to Building G/1800s Town (Reardon's Gambling Den.)**

**(FK: B8 Part 1 of 3 + 33) Note that you need to find all parts to get the right sum to add or subtract when the time comes to use the future knowledge).**

You thank the antiques dealer for his information and leave.

You can now return to the main store **turn to 334**
Or return to the town **turn to 488**

## 351

(173)

Having beaten down one of the men, you find yourself trading blows with the last one standing, until eventually he too succumbs to your superior fighting skills and drops to the floor. Seeing that they have no chance of beating you, one of the men flees into the streets, while the second stays behind to say one final thing before he goes to join him.

"I don't know who you are, but you'd better watch your back, because when I tell my boss what you did, you're going to regret ever meeting us."

Once they are gone, you go to the woman.

"Are you okay?" you ask.

"You shouldn't have done that," she says.

"I wasn't going to stand by while they mugged you in broad daylight."

"It wasn't a mugging. They were trying to send me a message."

"A message?"

"I write for the local gazette. I was researching a story about their boss and he found out and sent his goons after me."

"So they weren't stealing from you?"

"No, they were probably just going to rough me up a bit and frighten me off the story, but that's about it."

As the woman talks, you start to notice that she seems vaguely familiar. Have you possibly met her before?

**If you know her name, use the key below to decide what number you should turn to, by substituting each letter of her name for a number.**

| A | E | I | J | L | M | O | V | Y | Z |
|---|---|---|---|---|---|---|---|---|---|
| 3 | 0 | 2 | 5 | 4 | 7 | 6 | 9 | 8 | 1 |

If not, you continue on down the road **turn to 312**

## 352

From this moment on you must make use of the following statistics on your character sheet.

**TTP** (Time Travel Points)
**FK** (Future Knowledge)

**HOW TO USE TTP**

These allow you to travel back in time. You begin with 10 and must use 2 every time you want to jump back a single passage. Note that the number of the previous passage is bracketed under the number of the passage you are reading at the time.

Sometimes if there are multiple ways you could have reached that passage, there will be multiple numbers. Be sure to turn to the one that corresponds to the passage you just came from.

If a bracketed number has x2, x3 or x4 next to it, this means that the closest point you can return to is further back and will require you to multiply the amount of TTP you would usually use, to go back by that number.

Example: x2 = 4TTP
x3 = 6TTP etc.

You will find items through your adventure that allow you to replenish your TTP, but unless otherwise specified, you will not be able to exceed your initial amount.

## SLOWING TIME WITH TTP

You may also use TTP to slow time. In situations where you must react quickly, you can add up to 2pts to the roll. You can choose to add these points on after you have seen your roll.

## FUTURE KNOWLEDGE

Whilst progressing through this adventure, you will also see references regarding something called future knowledge. Future knowledge is something that you learn that can be used to open up new paths in the past and present. When you gain future knowledge you must write it down. It will appear as such: (FK: A+23) The FK stands for Future Knowledge, the letter is for reference, and the number is what you must add or subtract to the passage you are told you can use the Future Knowledge at, in order to find out what outcome using that knowledge has.

Throughout the game you will end up with a large list of Future Knowledge, so it is worth checking anytime you see a choice to use Future Knowledge, whether you already have it on your list.

Once you have used Future Knowledge, unless otherwise specified, you must cross it out to show you have used it.

## MULTIPLE PART FUTURE KNOWLEDGE

Much later on in your adventure, you will come across Future Knowledge that requires multiple parts to work. It will look something like this:

**(FK: Z8 part 1 of 2 +12) (Note that you need to find all parts to get the right sum to add or subtract when the time comes to use the future knowledge)**

Now normally when you reach the passage that would say you can now use Future Knowledge Z8, you would +12 to the passage number to find out which number to go to next, but because this particular FK has two parts, this will not work. So in order to make it work, you must find FK:Z8 part 2 of 2, and minus or plus both numbers from the passage number to figure out where to go next.

If you feel you understand all this enough, you can now return to your previous location

**Turn to 427**

However, if you still feel unsure, continue onto the in game example:

## AN IN GAME EXAMPLE OF USING BOTH TTP AND FK

**You come to a passage that says:**

712

While you are fighting the man with the knife, you feel a shiver come over you.

You can now use Future Knowledge Z9
Or turn to 653

**At this point you do not have Future Knowledge Z9 on your list, so you have no choice but to turn to 653.**

653
(712 X3)

A man sneaks up on you and hits you from behind with a baseball bat (FK: Z9+23). Moments later, you wake up on the floor.

**Firstly you write down (FK: Z9+23). This is your future knowledge reference. You can guess in this instance that the future knowledge is that a man will sneak up on you with a baseball bat. What the future knowledge is, will not always be clear. It is up to you to figure that out.**

**Because you don't want your character to be surprised by a man with a baseball bat, you decide to reverse time to the previous passage which is 712 (As shown in the brackets underneath).**

**Now usually it would cost you 2TTP to travel back a single paragraph, but because the bracketed number shows x3 next to it (Because time has passed while you were unconscious) that means you must multiply that number by 3. Therefore you must use 6TTP to travel back.**

**You currently have 10TTP, so you decide to use the 6 and mark it down to 4. This brings you back to the previous passage 712.**

712

While you are fighting the man with the knife, you feel a shiver come over you.

You can now use Future Knowledge Z9
Or turn to 653

**Obviously if you turn to 653 you will end up being snuck up on again by the man with the baseball bat. When you first came here, that was your only option because you didn't know what was to happen, but now you know something you didn't before. You have Future Knowledge Z9. To use this knowledge (FK: Z9+23) you must +23 to the number of the passage you are currently on.**

**712 +23= 735 therefore to use the Future Knowledge you must turn to 735.**

735

Knowing that there is someone sneaking up on you from behind, you duck. This causes your attacker with the baseball bat to miss you and hit the man with the knife instead, knocking him out cold.

So you see, by having the knowledge that the man was going to surprise you with his bat, you were able to reverse time and prevent it.

You can now **turn to 427**

## 353
### (79)

Outside Hannah's house, you notice a number of chopped logs with an axe left in one of them, (FK: C6+23) but you see no other way in. As you walk away, you notice something is stuck to the bottom of your shoe, and peal it off to reveal a chocolate bar wrapper. You then notice the outside bin has been overturned, by a fox probably, revealing several similar wrappers amongst the usual household waste.

You can now, if you haven't already, try the door **turn to 212**
Or leave and return to the town **turn to 488**

## 354
### (144)

Amidst the smoke filled room, you spot a very familiar face at the back, reading a copy of war and peace. It is Tom Scott, the investment banker you met at the 1950s Craven Manor party. You decide to go over and say hello.

"Tom," you say as you approach him. "Remember me? We met at the Craven Manor auction."

"Ah, yes," he says with a smile. "David Ingram isn't it? You sell food for animals."

"That's right."

"So what brings you to my club? Have you recently become a member?"

"No, I came looking for you."

"For me, and why is that?"

"I'd like to help you with your library project. I think you're right, this town does need a library."

"Good man! How much would you like to invest?"

"How much was it you said you needed again?"

"£500."

If you have £500 and you wish to give it to him now **turn to 401**

Otherwise, since there is no other reason to be here, you can either return to where you were before and come back here later, or return to the present **turn to 13**

As the possessed man comes charging towards you, you use his own momentum against him and throw him into the corner of the room. Then before he can get to his feet, you grab the woman's hand and help her to her feet.

"Come on, we need to get out of here," you say.

She quickly follows your lead, as you take her out of the bedroom, down the stairs and then out of the front door. Once outside, you both stop to catch your breath.

"You saved my life," she says. "Why did he attack me like that? There was something wrong with his eyes."

"It was an evil spirit," you say.

"So the stories about Craven Manor are true?"

"Unfortunately, yes. You should go home and get some rest."

"What about Jeremy?" she asks. "Will he be alright?"

"Was he your husband?" you ask.

"No, we've only been seeing each other a few months. I was really starting to like him though."

"I'm sure he'll be fine," you explain. "This particular spirit only seems to come out at night, so I'm guessing that come the morning, your boyfriend will be back to his usual self. Listen, it would be best that you didn't tell anyone about this. I'm sure there will be some who may believe you, but many will not understand and would prefer to stick you in a straight jacket and lock you away."

"I'm well aware of what people are like. Don't worry, I'll be careful with what I say."

"Good, I'm glad to hear it. Well I guess this is goodbye."

"You never gave me your name."

"It's Dave. Dave Ingram."

"I'm Rose Everett."

"Pleased to meet you, Rose Everett."

**Add CMIP C. This affects The Bathroom in the house.**
**Add CMIP G. This gives you access to Building A.**

**You must also remove Future Knowledge F3 and F6, as you will have no further need of these.**

After Rose has left, you use your amulet to return to the present.

**Turn to 6**

This room appears to have belonged to a young woman. The make up by the dresser is evidence of this. As you search through the drawers of her dresser, you happen to come across a leather bound diary. You decide to have a look at this. Part way through, you notice several pages have been ripped out. The last entry before these ripped pages reads:

7/10/1896

*I attended a wedding of one of my father's friends today. It is actually the first time he has allowed me out of the house in some time. I'm really glad too, because otherwise I wouldn't have seen Peter there. Today he professed his love to me and all I could do was try and push him away. I had to do it for his own good, because I know father would never allow us to be together and that Peter would never be able to accept that. Things are different now. They have been ever since... Even writing it is hard, so I will just refer to it as my traumatic experience. I still have those nightmares where I'm being chased by a shadowy figure, while pan pipe music plays in the background. I often wake up screaming with no-one to comfort me.*

**(FK: B7 part 3 of 4 -20) Note that you need to find all parts to get the right sum to add or subtract when the time comes to use the future knowledge)**

Feeling like this diary could be useful to you, you decide to take it with you. **Mark down the diary in your inventory and make a note of this passage, so you can return and read it if you need to later.**

You now return to the house **turn to 418**
**If you have chosen to hide in this room turn to 271**

357

Entering the ballroom, you are reminded of the party you attended in **1954** in this same room. You remember the various guests you spoke with, the auction that took place and everything else that followed. As you walk around the room, you realise there is no evidence to support the fact that you actually were there, that is until you come across a black mark on the wooden floor, and remember the incident you had with the candlestick. It appears your actions have caused the house in your time to change, because you are fairly certain that this black mark was not here before. This proves that you may be able to make more significant changes in the past that could help you in the present.

You now leave and return to the house **turn to 13**
**Mark down The Ballroom as complete, as you will have no need to revisit this place.**

## 358
### (137)

You follow Zoe as she leads you to Gil's home, both walking at a brisk pace, until you finally reach the gates of his large house. On the way, she explains to you how you are going to gain admittance, because Gil is a particularly paranoid man, and is likely to turn away anyone he doesn't know as soon as he lays eyes on them. As she opens the gate and rings the bell, you decide to play along with her.

A few moments later, a stout man with a shaved head comes to the door. Gil's bodyguard you presume.

"Yes," he says, in a very unfriendly manner.

"We're here to see Gil Murdock," says Zoe.

"Mr Murdock is not in the habit of entertaining unscheduled visitors."

"I'm not an unscheduled visitor," she says. "My name is Zoe Hadley, I write for the local gazette. Mr Murdock and I met at the Craven Manor charity auction a week ago. We talked about the possibility of me writing an exclusive on him as a prelude to his up and coming event."

"He never said anything about this to me."

"He was rather drunk at the time, so there is a chance he doesn't remember, but he did say to drop in any time. All I need is five minutes of his time. The exclusive will be very beneficial to him."

"I'll go and tell him you're here," the bodyguard says.

He disappears for a few moments and then returns.

"Mr Murdock will see you now."

You follow the bodyguard as he leads you through a hall to a large living room. Here you find Gil Murdock, standing in his dressing gown, ready to greet you both.

"Miss Hadley," he says, "such a pleasure to see you again."

"The pleasure is all mine, Mr Murdock," she replies. "I'd like to introduce you to my assistant Mr Ingram. He's here to help with the interview."

"I'm sorry that I don't remember the conversation we had, my dear. Had I known you were to be coming round today, I would have put on a spread. You can leave us now Kenworth."

After the bodyguard has left the room, you consider next how you should proceed.

If you tell him the truth about the robbery **turn to 463**

If you decide to keep up the pretence for a while longer **turn to 15**
**Or you can us Future knowledge A1**
**Or Future Knowledge A2**

359
(329)

Remembering the carriage that awaits, you charge down the street and jump in as soon as you see it. **Deduct £2 from your money**. You tell the driver to go quickly, and he gets you to Craven Manor just in time to see Ruth sneak out. Upon seeing her, you quickly jump out and hide behind a tree, waiting for her to pass you before you begin to follow. Walking several feet behind her, she eventually leads you into town, where she meets with Peter. Then after a brief kiss and cuddle, the two of them go onto a betting shop, where Peter puts on a bet for a fight in five days' time between newcomer Billy Bone-Crusher and Jimmy Long Paws. Whilst you are waiting, you notice a sign.

*Not available to pick up your winnings. Do not worry. Open an account with us and we will keep your money for you. Whether it be months, or a few years, your money will be safe with us.*

You can now use Future Knowledge D8
Otherwise, you wait and follow them both to the antiques store **turn to 482**

360
(382)

Remembering what happened last time you shouted up to the maid, you decide to wait for her to come down before you ask her anything. She is still shocked when you approach her, but the result is not nearly as bad.

"Excuse me, sorry to bother you," you say, "but I'm looking for Ruth Craven."

"I'm afraid young Miss Craven snuck out earlier to go and see her boyfriend; something about him buying her a ring from the antiques shop."

You thank her for her help and then leave to look for Ruth. The question is, where will you go to look for her?

If you go to Peter's address **turn to 86**
If you go straight to the Antiques shop **turn to 482**

After presenting the evidence to the police, they bring the hotel owner in for questioning. It seems that no matter what, he was the one who attempted to murder you, but did he kill the Cravens? He did hold a grudge for his son's possible wrongful arrest, and he did have secret access to the house via that hatch you found in the basement, but would he have gone so far as to kill the whole family? Luckily you are able to sit in on the interrogation and find out for yourself.

"I didn't do it," he says. "I know how it all looks, like I wanted revenge for my son, but it's not true. The truth is, I don't know if he raped poor young Ruth Craven or not, or whether he killed that whole family; all I know is that when you arrested him the first time, it tore my family apart. My wife was sick anyway, but I believe the thought that her son would spend time in prison for a terrible act like that, is what pushed her over the edge. She died thinking her son was a rapist. So when there was a possibility of him being accused for a second time, whether he was guilty or not, I couldn't allow it to happen. That is why when I heard that someone was asking questions around town about the murders, I started to worry, and I did what any other father would have done; I tried to protect my child."

"By trying to kill me?" you say.

"No, I only intended to frighten you away, but it obviously didn't work, because you came to my home looking for more evidence."

"So you locked me in the cellar?"

"I really had no choice. You knew I was the one who attacked you, so it was only a matter of time before you told the police. I was only intending on locking you in there until I could figure out what to do with you. Again I had no intentions of killing you. In fact, only an hour later, I felt so bad that I came down to talk to you and tell you everything, of course by then you were gone. Tell me, what is to happen to me?"

"That's really up to Mr Ingram here," says the policeman. "Do you wish to press charges?"

You think about this for a few moments before giving your answer.

"No," you say. "I believe he was just protecting his son, and since no real harm was done, I see no reason to take this any further."

"Thank you, so much," says the hotel owner, "and please take pity on my son, if he really did do this, I know he can't have been in his right mind."

Having been removed from the suspect list, the hotel owner now leaves.

**(FK: C8 Part 3 of 3 +40) Note that you need to find all parts to get the right sum to add or subtract when the time comes to use the future knowledge)**

If you wish to present more evidence **turn to 331**

Or you can return to the town **turn to 488**, and come back later.

## 362
(197)

You are about to leave, when you hear the front door open. Concerned by this, you make your way to the door and peek round the corner to see the house owners, John and Hayley Barnett, heading in the direction of the study. Quickly, you duck back into the room and hide behind a big armchair.

"Well that was fun," says the woman sarcastically, as she steps into the study

"I'm sorry," says the man. "I had no idea my boss and his wife could be such dull people."

"I don't know what was worse, having to sit through three hours with those people, or the fact that they didn't have any alcohol in their home. Now where did I put my cigarettes?" the woman says.

"I think I remember you putting them in the drawer," the man replies.

You think nothing of this at first, until you hear her footsteps coming in your direction, and then remember that the desk with the drawer is directly next to you. You hope as she leans down to open the drawer that she will not see you, but unfortunately you are not so lucky. As soon as she sets eyes on you, she jumps back and screams. (FK: U +14.)

If you try to talk your way out of this **turn to 92**
If you choose to make a run for the door to escape **turn to 385**

## 363
(288)

You make it as far as the corridor, before the doors to the ballroom slam shut and you see the man in black only moments away from grabbing you.

**Roll one die.**

**You may add up to 2TTP to your result to ensure your roll is higher.**

If you roll 5 or over **turn to 220**
If you roll less than 5 **turn to 123**

You hand the pipe to the policewoman and she tells you to wait while she checks it for fingerprints. When she returns, she reports her findings

"I'm sorry, but the fingerprints on the pipe do not match either of the fingerprints on the knife."

You now return to the town **turn to 444**
**When returning to the town, be sure to mark down 188 as a shortcut for future fingerprint checks.**

**If you have CMIP C, turn to 511 immediately. If you don't have CMIP C, or don't know what CMIP C means yet, then please continue reading.**

Upon entering the bathroom, you find the shower curtain drawn across the bath. Seeing this makes you feel very uneasy, like there could be someone lurking behind it, but you decide to pluck up your courage and pull it back. With a quick tug, the bath is revealed, revealing much to your horror, that it is full of blood.

If you drain the bath **turn to 514**
Otherwise, you now return to the house **turn to 13**

(372 x3)
"Got you," says one of the policemen as he grabs you from behind.
"Let me go," you say. "I'm not the one you want."
"We can discuss that down the station."

Unfortunately, unless you are able to reverse time, you must go with the police down to the station. This means that since your face will now be known by the 1800s police, you will not be able to enter the station if you happen to return here.

**You can now mark down The Police Station/1800s Town as complete, as you will not be allowed to visit this place.**

Once at the station, you wait until you are alone in your cell and then time travel back to the present **turn to 311**

## 367

(300 x2)

"I'm not going to kill you, you stupid fool," you tell Gil. "I was telling you the truth before. Now if you want to live, you'll do as I say."

You then instruct him to help you move a number of desks, tables and filing cabinets to build a barricade in the centre of the room. He does as he is told and then when the doors explode inwards, you are ready for the men as they come.

**GUN FIGHT RULES**

**YOUR ATTACK**

**There are four men. You are allowed to fire a shot at each of them. For each shot you fire, roll two dice.**

**A double counts as an incapacitating shot.**

**A single 6 counts as a wound. Make a note of these.**

**Two wounds also count as an incapacitation.**

**ENEMY ATTACKS**

**After you have fired a shot at each of them, they will each fire back.**

**The same rules apply to their shots, except that you can dodge a successful hit by rolling equal to, or over the attacker's number after each shot.**

**You can also use up to 2TTP to influence your dodge rolls.**

**If you are incapacitated, you die.**

If you manage to incapacitate all of them **turn to 121**

## 368

The store room appears to be locked. You notice that the colour surrounding the lock is silver.

If you have a silver key **turn to 323**

Otherwise, you return to the house **turn to 13**

### 369

Looking around for the clock you saw the father put the key into, you are surprised to find that it is no longer there. The butler approaches you.

*"Ywj xf lwwkxng qrz thz fwr x'm clwck xt qfrqxd swld wos txmz swmz tw qgw lwcql q dzqlzr qntxqjzs. Fqr qs x qs thz knww xs bjsxnzss rjnnxng stxll." (W+24 FK:)*

You can now do something else in the library **turn to 386**
Or you can return to the house **turn to 13**

### 370
(2 x2)
If you snuck in through the meat cellar **turn to 417**
If you came in through the shop **turn to 59**
If you came in through the shop using the copied key **turn to 203**

### 371

Realising that you now know the date of the incident that started it all, you travel back to that time, in the hopes that you can make one final change that will make everything right. Unlike previous time jumps you are fortunate to find yourself in the very place you need to be, right in the centre of the woods, following a man who is about to do something that will destroy many lives for years to come. As you watch the butcher, he takes out his pan pipes and plays 'Early One Morning' as he waits by a tree, watching a 13 year old girl from a distance as she wanders towards the music. As she draws closer, he pulls out a crude mask, pretty much a bag with holes in it, and is about to put it over his head, when...

"Hello Sam," you say as you approach him.

"Do I know you?" he says surprised.

"Not yet. In fact if this all goes to plan you might not ever know me. I'm not entirely sure how all this works."

"Who are you?"

"I'm your conscience," you say. "You see in a few minutes you will do something that will not only ruin that girl's life, but every other life she touches from this point in time, and I am here to prevent you from doing that."

"I have no idea what you are talking about? How can you possibly know what I intend to do before I do it."

"Because I am from the future; the year 2018 to be precise."

"That's ridiculous. Time travel is fiction."

"Really? Then explain how I knew to be here on this date at this exact moment? The way I see it, you have a choice. You can ruin this girl's life, and many others, or you can leave this town and think about getting some help for your condition."

"Look, I don't know what you think you know about me, but you've made a big mistake by coming here tonight."

He seems reluctant that you know anything, so you must prove it to him by remembering something he wrote in his diary. Find the three words that he wrote, and put them in order to find the number to turn to next.

Love (4) Like (2) Lady (5) Macbeth's (1) Hamlet's (9) Madness (6) Ophelia (3) Obsession (8) Juliet (9) Beauty (0)

If you can't figure it out, you are unable to convince him and must **turn to 4**

### 372

You hear a knock on the door.

"This is the police. Open up!"

Someone must have brought them here. You can immediately return to your own time if you wish, but a nagging suspicion tells you that you may have forgotten something.

If you choose to return to your own time **turn to 311**

If you would rather hide and wait until the police have left, so you can check more of the house **turn to 271**

### 373
### (157)

Quickly, you pick up your tray with your unfinished food on and make out as if you had accidentally collided with the waitress, spilling your tray down her front.

"I'm so sorry," you say.

"It's alright," she says. "I'm used to it."

"Let me help," you offer.

"No, it's okay. I've got this. You can go on about your own business."

As you walk away, you notice that the manager has seen this incident, and seeing that his waitress is currently indisposed, he goes to serve the drunks himself. Congratulations you just saved a girl from a very uncomfortable situation. Not long after this, Liz returns from the toilet and you both leave.

TIP: Sometimes the solution to a problem may include going through with an action that may seem foolish or dangerous at the time. This is the only way to get the right future knowledge to help you when you reverse time and try again. Bear in mind that with the ability to reverse time that most decisions can be undone, so feel free to take a risk once in a while.

Turn to 470

## 374
### (216)

"Go on then, I'm waiting," she says. "Tell me what is in my pockets?"

"Well I don't know yet," you tell her. "You have to show me so I can travel back and tell you."

"But if I show you, that doesn't prove anything."

"Not to you in this time, but when I return to a few minutes ago, I can guarantee that the version of you then will be impressed."

"All right," she says as she empties out the contents of her pocket. "This is everything I have."

You quickly look through the items and do your best to memorise them. Among the items are the following:

A book of matches.
A black cigarette case with 3 cigarettes inside.
A cinema ticket stub for *Rear Window*.
A purple lipstick.
26 pence in coins.
And a gold pen.

**You now must reverse time to prove you can guess all the items or she will call the police. To play properly, you must not write these items down.**

## 375
### (100 x2)

The killer is beaten, but as you remove the mask you are shocked to discover that it is none other than Ruth Craven you have killed. None of this makes sense to you, but before you can even contemplate putting it all together, you hear a loud bang and look down to see a bright red patch appearing on your stomach. You stumble and fall, looking back to see Ruth's father, standing over you with a gun. Unless you can reverse time and change this outcome, I'm afraid this is the end for you

Upon locating the storage shed, you find a sturdy lock on the door. Looking in through the window, you see a number of wooden beams and several ready-made, stuffed animals. You realise that this must be where the taxidermist stores some of his work. You are considering leaving, when you smell a terrible odour emanating from inside. There is no way you are going to get that door open, but looking around, you notice a high up, partially opened window. The opening is big enough for you to get through, but you are going to need something to help you climb up there.

If you have a grappling hook **turn to 199**
If not, you return to the town **turn to 488,** with the intentions of returning when you do.

## 377

As the Stranger falls back from your latest blow, he falls beside his knife and instantly reclaims it and comes after you again. You turn and run out of the alley, and eventually find yourself being chased to the bank of a stream. As the Stranger charges towards you once again, you lose your footing and try to grab for him, tearing a fragment of his trousers in the process as you fall back into the stream. (FK: A6+25)

You hit the water with quite a splash and temporarily find yourself submerged, before a hand reaches down and pulls you back out. You look up, expecting to see the same mysterious stranger who had given chase, but instead you see a kindly looking, gentle giant with a grisly beard, staring back at you. You recognise him as the local butcher.

"Are you alright," he asks. "I saw the whole thing. That man looked like he was going to kill you."

"Did you see which way he went?" you ask.

"No, I'm sorry. I was too busy making sure that you didn't drown. Look at you; you're soaked to the skin. If the wind picks up, you'll catch a chill. Come on, I don't live far from here. You can get warm by my fire while we dry these clothes off."

If you take the butcher up on his offer and go back to his house **turn to 64**
If you try and catch up to your attacker **turn to 414**

## 378
(358)

You know that at some point in the next ten minutes, the lights are going to go out. This means that one of the men from this robbery is in the house already. Perhaps if he was unable to turn the power off, then the others may not be able to go ahead with the robbery.

"Do you mind if I use your bathroom?" you ask Gil, trying to excuse yourself.

"No, not at all," he says.

He points you towards it and you sneak further into the house. Your assumption is that the fuse box will be in the cellar, so you look for a door leading down and when you find it, you descend the stairs. When you get to the bottom, you realise that you might already be too late. The man who had been sent in to turn the electricity off, is already in there and he has his hand on the lever of the breaker box. You have but a second to act.

If you have a gun and wish to shoot him **turn to 461**
If you attempt to tackle him **turn to 107**

## 379
(436)

**Now roll a dice to determine where the butcher will look first.**

**If you roll**

**1-2- He checks among the hanging pigs.**
**3-4- He checks behind the crates.**
**5-6- He checks under the plastic sheeting**

**If he rolls your location, he catches you and you have no choice but to reverse time. If you can't do this turn to 52.**

**If you do reverse time, you do not need to travel back to the previous paragraph if you simply want to change your hiding place. Instead minus 2TTP and continue as if you had successfully hid. However, if you wish to reverse time to avoid ending up in this situation, you can use your TTP for that instead.**

If you hid successfully **turn to 465**

"I was wondering if you could help me find the item of clothing that this piece of cloth belongs to." You say, handing the piece of cloth to the shop owner.

"Erm, let me see," she says as she studies it, thoughtfully. "I believe this particular fragment belongs to a Jacket that we once sold in the shop. It was very popular at the time. May I ask what this is about?"

"I'm running a small errand for the police. Do you have a record of who might have bought one?"

"Let me have a look," she says.

She goes into the back and then returns moments later with a ledger.

"All right," she says. "I have records of three people purchasing this jacket. Nicholas Craven, The Gambling Den owner Ray Reardon and the antiques dealer Jim Collins."

You thank the shop keeper for her help.

**Add CMIP R. This will give you access to Building G/1800s Town (Reardon's Gambling Den.)**

You can now either do something else in the shop **turn to 400**
Or return to the town **turn to 488**

### 381
(117)
After finishing his drink, you assume the man is going to take you to the gentleman's club, but he insists that the night is young and he still could do with another drink.

If you decide to buy him another round (Deduct £1 from your inventory) **turn to 229**
If you decide not to, then you choose to leave **turn to 277**

### 382
(329 x3)
By the time you get to Craven Manor you see that Ruth has already left the house. You ponder where she might have gone. Then you see one of the servants outside, picking fruit from a tree.

If you shout up to ask where you can find Ruth **turn to 480**
If you choose to see if you can find her in town without any help **turn to 39**
Or you can use Future Knowledge C2

"Yes, of course," you say, as you take out your lighter and light the woman's cigarette.

"Thank you," she says, before exhaling a cone of smoke into the air. "My name's Zoe Hadley."

"I'm Dave," you say. "Dave Ingram. I came here as someone else's guest, so I hardly know anyone here. You wouldn't happen to be able to tell me what this whole party is in aid of?"

"It's a fund raiser for several charities," she replies. "Rich people donate precious items of jewellery and then they are sold to the highest bidder. All the proceeds go to charity."

"Are you here to buy, or to sell?"

"Neither, I'm with the local gazette. I'm here to document the event."

"So you're a reporter?"

"That's my credentials for being here, but not my reason."

"What's your reason then?"

"I've always wanted to step foot in Craven Manor to find out if all the stories were true."

"What stories?" you ask.

"Oh come on," she says in disbelief, "are you honestly telling me that you've never heard of the Craven Manor Massacre in the late 1800s? A whole family were murdered here."

"Really? Did they catch the one who did it?"

"That's just it, nobody ever found him," she explains. "Also, ever since that night there has been four different families that have lived in this house, and each one has reported unexplainable events occurring, before they either chose to leave, or disappeared without a trace. There have been supposed sightings of members of the Craven family wandering the halls, beds floating off the ground, dishes flying of the shelves and even people claiming that they were possessed by a figure made of black mist. There have been so many stories that it is difficult to know what to believe, but I am certain that there is something going on here. Unfortunately, my editor won't let me pursue a story on it, so I decided to take the first opportunity I had to come here and see for myself. So Dave what is it that you do?"

"I'm a traveller," you reply, saying the first thing that comes into your head.

"You mean like an explorer?"

"Yes, that's right," you reply, going with the flow. "I travel all over the world and find rare antiquities for people. That's actually why I'm here today. I recently required an ancient Incan idol from this underground temple in South America, and my rival, this French guy, stole it right from under my nose. After all the work I had to do for it too. I had to run away from a boulder and all kinds of things. Anyway, somewhere along the line, it ended up with this rich guy who decided he wanted to sell it at this auction. So I thought I'd come and attempt to buy it back."

In your head that sounded really good, but rather than look impressed, Zoe seems very suspicious.

"Oh," she says. "I thought you said you didn't know this was an auction."

"I didn't say that."

"Yes you did. You said that you came here as someone else's guest and that you didn't know what the party was in aid of."

"Yes you're right, I did say that. And the reason I said that was..." You pretend to be distracted by a waiter carrying a tray into the ballroom. "Oh are those finger sandwiches? I'll be back in a bit."

You then leave her before you can dig the hole any deeper.

**Turn to 238**

## 384

Upon entering the six digit combination, the safe opens with a satisfying click, to reveal John's borrowed gun and £500 in cash. Feeling very fortunate, you take both the gun and the money.

You can now either, look in the drawer **turn to 138**
Or leave and return to the house **turn to 13**

**If you have already looked in the drawer, mark down The Study as complete, as you will have no need to revisit this place.**

## 385
### (362)

You try to run for the door, but before you know what is going on, the man has pulled out a gun and shot you in the back. As you lie there bleeding to death on the floor, you realise that the only way to continue is to reverse time. It you are unable to do this, then unfortunately this is where your adventure ends.

## 386

You turn the key in the lock and the door opens to reveal a rather impressive looking two storey library, filled with hundreds of books. There is everything here, from mystery Classics like 'And Then There Were None,' to a biography on notorious Australian bank robber 'Ned Kelly.' It is not the books that interest you though, because at the back of the room is a strange mural showing a number of animals in a woodland scene, with three noticeable indentations in the picture where three particular animals have been removed: A dog, a cat, and a rabbit. As you are studying the mural, you feel a cold feeling come over you and turn to see a translucent, tall blue figure who resembles a butler, standing there. At first sight, you want to run and hide, until you can clearly see that he means you no harm. He speaks in another strange distorted language that is different to that of your possessed fiancée.

"*Sxr Wzlcwmz. Nqmz my Vzrnwn xs x Crwwthzr. Wr qm, wqs rqthzr bjtlzr thz thz fwr fqmxly Crqvzn. Nwt dw qfrqxd. Bz Mzqn x nw ywj x hqrm. Thzrz knww mqlxcxwjs qrz xn spxrxts hwjsz thxs, x bjt nwt qm wf wnz x thzm. Ywj nwtxczd my qdmxrxng mjrql zmplwyzr's. xs hz q qjxtz qrtxst skxllzd hz? Xsn't Knww x xs xt tw nxcz qt lwwk xt bjt qctjqlly xs cqrzfjlly q pjzzlz cwnstrjctzd jnlwck tw szcrzt q x dwwr. Knww dwn't hww zxqctly wpzn tw bjt xt, dw x thqt knww rzqjxrzs xt kzys thrzz thz xn wf shqpz thqt qnxmqls mjst ywj xn plqcz wqll thz swmz xn wf swrt whzrz wrdzr. Cqn ywj thzsz fxnd thwjgh, kzys dw x hqvz nwt fwggxzst. Thz ywj xf fxnd cqn wqy q thzrz xn knww x wxll xt wwrth bz whxlz. Ywjr thzrz xf qnythxng xs ywj zlsz tw wxsh dw qsk, hzsxtqtz nwt dw tw x sw. Hzlp wxll whqtzvzr xn x wwy cqn.*"

You can now do one of the following:

You can now use Future knowledge N

Or attempt to solve the puzzle on the back wall if you know how.
Or look for a particular book if you know how.

Or return to the house **turn to 13,** and come back later.

**If you return to the house, mark down the number of this passage as a shortcut for The Library when you return.**

**Once you have done all three of the things above, mark down The Library as complete, as you will have no need to revisit this place.**

### 387
(116 x3)
You manage to follow them without being seen and continue to eavesdrop on their conversation.

"Doctor Greenfield," Ruth says. "He's an alienist from London."

"An alienist?" Peter says surprised. "What cause would you have for seeing an alienist?"

"Because I am sick of mind."

"You seem perfectly fine to me."

"No, I can assure you that I am not well."

"Or is that just what your father wants you to believe."

They now come to a stop and you are forced to hide to avoid their gaze.

"I don't understand what you mean," asks Ruth.

"You really are a prisoner, but you don't see it," Peter says, sounding frustrated. "He's not only locking you up in your home, but he's convinced you there's something wrong with you."

"What makes you think he would do that?"

"Well quite obviously he doesn't want you to leave him."

"No, he wouldn't do that to me!" Ruth shouts defiantly. "He loves me, he wouldn't lie to...!"

You hear a bit of a scuffle and then you hear someone fall, followed by a loud splat!

"Oh no," you hear Ruth, sounding distressed. "My dress is ruined."

"It's just a bit of mud," Peter says. "It will come out."

"But my father will see. He'll know that I snuck off. Oh no, what am I going to do?"

"It's all right," Peter says reassuringly. "I have an idea. My house is not too far from here. We can quickly go there so you can clean up. Then head back to the party before your father even notices you are gone."

"Are you sure we would make it back in time?" Ruth asks, concerned.

"Positive."

"All right, show me the way."

When you hear them move off, you follow them at a distance as they leave the woods.

**Turn to 507**

## 388
### (186)

"Right away sir," you say to the house owner as you take the key from him.

After you leave him, you go to the cellar. You find it easy enough because you remember its location from the house in your time. After descending into the dimly lit room, you pick up a crate of wine and then return to the party, placing it on the table with the other barrels. After this, you are about to return the bronze key to the master of the house, when you realise that you could make use of it in your own time.

**Decide now whether you intend to keep it. If you do so, mark it on your inventory.**

Then **turn to 272**

389

You arrive in 3/5/1895, but for some reason unknown to you, you have arrived outside of the house. Given that your reason for travelling here is because you want to find out where Ruth's father hid the key to the secret room in the cellar, this is a problem; since the only way to witness that moment is by being inside the house itself. Unfortunately this is complicated further by the fact that there are people in the house, and if any one of them were to spot you breaking in, you could end up with your picture in an 1800s newspaper; and who knows what kind of effect that could have on the present.

How are you going to get in? You stop and think about this for a few moments. You could try the simple approach of knocking on the door and asking to be let in, but to do that you would need the right clothes, not to mention a good enough lie to bluff your way in. Then there's the possibility of breaking in stealthily. To do this you would not only have to find a way into the house, but also you would have to avoid being seen by every person inside. The choice is yours.

If you have Victorian clothing and attempt to gain admittance via the front door **turn to 278**
If you look for a way to sneak in **turn to 320**
If you do not have Victorian clothing, or find that you are unable to sneak in, you return to the present **turn to 13**
**If this was your first time here, you will have this one opportunity to find what you need and come back. If this is your second time, I'm afraid you will not be allowed to return.**

390

You place the star shaped key into the hole in the wall and give it a twist. Then to your amazement, the whole wall opens up in front of you to reveal a secret room. Shining your torch around, you find that there is a desk with several items on. Three in particular catch your attention. One is a turquoise gem, another a knife with an obsidian blade, and the third, a leather bound diary. You decide to open the diary and have a read.

210

May 5th 1887

*My research has come on leaps and bounds these last few days. After the discovery of the time travelling amulet ten years ago, I have since learnt of the existence of several powerful stones that when brought within the proximity of the amulet, cause its power to increase in unimaginable ways. I have named them time stones and have so far found two of them, one at an archaeological dig in Scotland and the second in a cave in Cornwall.*

*At first glance the stones may appear to be no different than any other gem stone, but when a person who has travelled through time, holds one, they will find that it not only emits a glow, but also a tingling sensation throughout their entire body. (FK: E9 -70) The effects of each stone are unknown, but each one grants strength and certain abilities to the user. I now believe that the remaining stones may be in this very town itself. The two I have already found, I will place within this house; one with this diary and the second in the secret room which can be accessed from the library.*

*I must also note that I have discovered a side effect to time travel that was not apparent to me before. You see using the power of the stones, unfortunately weakens the veil between the living and the dead, which has brought forth some spirits of those long gone. Realising this, I have stopped travelling any further back than a few days, and constructed a weapon, using obsidian, a material known to repel the dead, to deal with those that have already come through. Unfortunately this only works on the manifestations. These are spirits that are created by emotionally charged events. The spirits of actual people who have come through, appear to be immune to it, but I will continue working to solve the problem.*

Having read the page of the diary, you now understand what these two things on the table are. The turquoise jewel is a time stone, and the obsidian dagger is a weapon to use against manifestation spirits. What a find! The first thing you do is pick up the time stone, which does exactly as the diary said and glows as you feel a tingling sensation throughout your body.

**You must now increase your maximum TTP by 2 and can bring your current TTP to full. As well as this, make a note that you have the following ability:**

**Freeze Time**

**This can be used once each fight and will automatically allow you to win two rounds of combat without rolling the dice.**

**As for the obsidian dagger, this will give you the opportunity to fend off the man in black the next time you encounter him.**

Feeling happy with your finds, you now leave this room and return to the house **turn to 13**

**Mark down The Cellar as complete, as you will have no need to revisit this place.**

391

You approach the fortune teller, curious how she has come to be here.

"Hello there," she says, "have you come for a reading?"

"I'm not sure," you say. "Just out of interest, how long have you been here?"

"Since nine o clock this morning...Why?"

"No," you correct your question. "I meant how long have you been reading fortunes in this shop?"

"Wow, let me think. About ten years. I took over from my mother after she died. My grandmother did it before then and her mother before that. The gift has been in my family for many generations."

"As far back as the late 1800s?"

"Yes that was probably when my great, great, grandmother first opened this shop. She was actually quite famous back in the day. She was one of the only two victims who escaped the notorious Serial Killer: The Embalmer. "

Suddenly everything becomes clear. Once again you have changed history by saving that woman back in the 1800s from the dreaded Taxidermist. Not only did you save her, but the lives of many, who would not have even been born if it were not for you.

"So now I've told you a bit about me," she says, "will you allow me to look into your future?"

"It depends how much you're asking for a reading."

"Does £10 sound fair?"

If you have £10 and wish to have a reading, deduct the amount from your money and **turn to 481**

Otherwise, you return to the town **turn to 444**

**When returning to the town be sure to mark down 481 as a shortcut to having your fortune told. When visiting here again, you will be able to come to this shortcut instead of the original number written on your navigation list. You will still have to pay £10 though, so make a note of that.**

"Ruth's father didn't hire me," you explain.

"If you are not working for Mr Craven, then who are you?" Peter asks.

"I'm a policeman," you say.

"You're kidding. You don't look like a policeman."

"That's because I'm with the special branch. We don't wear uniforms. It makes us stand out."

"Why attack me?"

"I saw you go over the wall, and I thought you might be up to no good."

"I can assure you the only villain here is the one inside that house." He says. "I believe Ruth's father is holding her against her will and I have every intention of breaking her free. Perhaps you could help me?"

You now have two choices. You can either go along with Peter to get her out **turn to 432**
**Bear in mind that if you do this, you will be committing to an action that cannot be undone.**
Or you can return to the present to investigate some other suspects, and possibly return to this moment later **turn to 13**
**If you do leave, make a note of 432, so you can return and help Peter later.**

### 393

Upon knocking on the door, you are met by Nicholas Craven who appears to be smiling.

"Good evening," he says. "What brings you to my house at so late an hour?"

"Sorry to bother you," you say. "I'm with the local police and we had reports that there have been a few break-ins in this area. I wanted to call by to make sure everything was alright."

"Yes everything's fine, better than fine actually. My daughter just announced her engagement and we're having a bit of a celebration."

"Is this young Ruth Craven you're talking about?"

"Why yes. You know my daughter?"

"Only in passing. Who's the lucky young man?" you ask.

"His name is Peter Kline."

"Ah a very worthy match if I do say so."

"You know him too?"

"Again, only in passing."

"Why is it that I feel like I've met you before; that you perhaps did something for me and my family in the past?"

"I think you might have me confused with someone else," you say trying to make a quick exit. "Give the happy couple my congratulations."

"Wait just a moment," Nicholas stops you. "I remember where I know you from. You were there that night, the night that you saved our lives."

"You remember that?" you say in disbelief.

"Yes, I remember it clearly as if it had happened, but I also know that it didn't. You posed as a policeman then too. But I didn't believe you then and I certainly don't now. You're not from this time, are you? If I were to guess I would say you were from the future and you found my time stones and used them to travel back here."

"How is this possible?"

"A side effect of being near the time stones means that you sometimes see the world how it was before someone else made changes. I remember a time five years ago when I woke up in the night and was convinced that my Ruth had been raped, and then when I saw that she hadn't. I knew something had been changed. That was you too, I'm guessing."

"That's right."

"It seems my family and I have a lot to thank you for. I wish there was some way I could show my appreciation."

"Actually there is one thing you could do."

"Name it."

"There's a conversation that we need to have in the future, that was very integral to me finding my way here. For this conversation to happen, you are going to need to build a device...."

You then go on to explain everything that he told you about in the workshop, making sure to add in the number for the padlocked room. Then when you are done, you say goodbye and return to your own time, hoping that you will find a house free of ghosts and a fiancée that is not possessed by some dark entity.

**Turn to 395**

**394**

(443)

Remembering the glass shard under your sleeve, you quickly pull it out and start to cut your ropes before you run out of oxygen.

**Roll one die, six times**

**You can add up to 6TTP to your total**

If you manage to roll 18 or more, you manage to cut your bonds in time **turn to 101**
If you fail, unfortunately you do not cut your bonds in time and run out of breath, drowning moments later at the bottom of the sea.

**395**

When you return to your time, you are surprised to find that you do not arrive in the house as expected, but rather in that same café where your adventure began, with Liz and the housing agent sat in the booth. For a moment you do start to wonder if any of your previous adventure occurred until the pen is offered to you once again.

"So I just need you to sign there," says the housing agent

You think about this for a few moments, considering what may occur if you take this house again. From your visit to the night of the Craven Manor Massacre, it seemed like everything had been put right, but can you really take that for granted. What if you arrived in that house to only have your fiancée possessed again by another spirit? You decide not to take the chance.

"I'm sorry," you say to the housing agent. "I think I may have changed my mind about the house."

"What do you mean, you've changed your mind?" asks Liz.

"I'm just not so sure that Craven Manor is the house for us."

"Craven Manor?" she says looking at you with confusion. "Don't you mean Crawford House?"

"Crawford House?" You say confused. "No, Craven Manor is the house that we were intending on buying."

"I don't know where you got that idea," says the housing agent. "Craven Manor has been occupied by descendants of the Craven family for way over a hundred years."

"It has?" you say surprised. "So we're not buying Craven Manor?"

"No, as I said before, you're buying a lovely place called Crawford House. Well actually your benefactor has paid most of the cost already, so all you need to do is pay the remaining ten percent."

"My benefactor?"

"Yes, you know it's funny that you should mention Craven Manor, because your benefactor happens to be a Craven himself."

"Really? What was his name?"

"Nicholas, I believe. Now if you have no further reservations, I just need you to sign here... And there...And you're done. Here are your keys. I hope you'll both be happy in your new home."

After the agent has left, Liz turns to you with a look of confusion.

215

"So what was all that about?" she asks.

"What do you mean?"

"Who is Nicholas Craven?"

"He's an old friend I helped out some time ago."

"Well whatever you did, he must have felt like he really owed you."

"I suppose you could say I helped him keep his family together."

"I learn more about you every day. Anyway, I need the toilet. Be back in a bit."

While you wait for Liz to return, you see the same scene play out that you had once seen in a loop: The kid dropping his ice cream, followed by the bullied waitress. You consider for a moment, attempting to reverse time and put them right for old time's sake, but as you reach for where your amulet had once been, you realise your neck is completely bare. Your days of time travelling seem to have come to an end.

Moments later, Liz returns and sits down.

"What time have you got?" you ask.

Liz looks to her watch.

"Two, thirty."

"And what time's the removal van meant to be showing up at the house?"

"About Four-ish."

"Then we're going to have a bit of time to kill. What do you say to getting out of here soon and having a look around town?"

"I suppose so," she says. "I noticed a jewellery shop on the way in."

"I was actually more interested in the book..." you stop yourself, suddenly having an exciting realisation as you feel your bare neck. "Actually the jewellery shop sounds like a good idea."

THE END

Or is it?

Congratulations you have completed the **'HERO'** ending. You may have reached the end of this current adventure, but there are still multiple paths you could try. If you haven't already, why not start again and try to complete one of the other 5 endings.

Please now turn to the final page for news on future adventure books

## 396

(535)

When you show Hannah the bar of chocolate, she smiles and opens the door to let you in. You start the conversation quite calmly, talking about what you know regarding the murders, and then get on to the fact that you believe it might be linked to Ruth's rape, and ask her about her own experience. Having calmed down somewhat, she begins to tell you her story.

"Well I don't remember much," she explains. "I have really tried to block the event from my memory. All I remember is coming home late one night from my friend's, and a man grabbing me from behind and dragging me into an alley. After that, all I remember is the smell of sawdust."

"Sawdust?" you say, your interest piqued.

"Yes his gloves reeked of it."

"And you remember nothing else about him?"

"He was very strong. Older I think. Maybe fortyish. I'm sorry, but having to think about it again is very hard for me. I don't want to remember."

"It's okay," you say. "You've given me enough to be getting on with. Thank you for being so brave."

**(FK: B7 part 1 of 4 -15) Note that you need to find all parts to get the right sum to add or subtract when the time comes to use the future knowledge)**

You now leave and return to the town **turn to 488**
**You must now mark down Building A/1800s town as complete, as you will have no need to revisit this place.**

### 397
(87)

"I think the Starling agenda is going to be good for some and bad for others," you say.

The men don't look impressed by your answer, and each goes on to give their own answers.

"The starling agenda is going to be very good for local businesses," says the first man.

"I believe the starling agenda's main effect will be on the Whitmore foundation," says the second man

"But most importantly it will stop Lady Jarmindon's tyrannical reign of Bembridge house," says a third.

Hearing these answers makes you feel even more confused than you were already, and you decide to leave these men to their pomposity and continue exploring the ballroom. (FK: F +23).

**Turn to 228**

Before leaving the shop, you happen to remember what the antiques dealer told you and decide to make an enquiry.

"I've heard that you have a metal detector," you say.

"Who told you that?" the book shop owner asks.

"The guy at the antiques store."

"Well, not that it's anyone's business, but yes I do have one."

"I was wondering if you might consider..." you begin to ask.

"No," he immediately cuts you off. "I already know what you are going to ask, and the answer is no. I never lend my metal detector to anyone, especially strangers."

"Perhaps I could hire it," you suggest. "Name your price."

"No, I'm sorry, but I don't like people touching my things. If you're really interested in using a metal detector, go out and find a shop that sells them. Mine is staying where it is." (FK: E8-56)

You can now use Future Knowledge E7

Or return to the town **turn to 444**

**When returning to the town, be sure to mark down the number of this passage as a shortcut to the metal detector. When visiting here again, you will be able to come to this shortcut instead of the original number written on your navigation list.**

In the grocers you meet the same woman who had the kid with the ice cream. Whether you stopped her kid from falling or not, she doesn't seem to remember you. She also doesn't know anything of use about Craven Manor; however for sale she has several items. If you buy anything, make a note of the above number. You may need to reference it when using certain items.

**For sale in this shop**

Cheese £2
Alcohol £5
Cereal £2
Milk £1.50
Bread £1
Dog treats £2

Salt £1
Chocolate Bar £1
Soap £1

After making your purchases, you return to the town **turn to 444**

## 400

As you enter the shop, a snotty looking woman in a frilly-collared dress comes to meet you.

"Can I help you?" she asks.

If you ask about the Craven Manor Massacre **turn to 181**
Otherwise you can use Future Knowledge A6
Or Future Knowledge B1
Or return to the town **turn to 488**
**Once you have done all of the things above, you can mark down The Clothes Store as complete, as you will have no need to revisit this place.**

## 401
### (354)

"Here you go," you say as you hand him the money. "That was all you needed, right?"

"Well yes," he says completely astounded. "But I never expected... Thank you. This is unbelievable generosity. I really had no idea there was so much money in dog food."

"You'd be surprised. How long do you think it will take to get this library up and running?"

"Oh a good six months to a year I should imagine. I'm sorry, but these things can take a long time."

"Time isn't an issue to me. I just want you to assure me that it will still be standing there, say one hundred years from now."

"Longer, I expect. I intend to make something that is going to last."

**You must now deduct the £500 from your money.**

**Add CMIP I. This gives you access to Building D.**

You can now either leave and return to where you were before the club, or if you are done in this time, you can return to the present **turn to 13**

The conservatory is filled with several dead plants, all obviously left since the previous owners. As you look around, you notice that in the corner of the room, someone has left a screwdriver. Feeling like this might be useful, you decide to take it. You also notice a side room to the conservatory, which upon checking the door, you realise is locked. The strangest thing is that there doesn't seem to be a keyhole to unlock it.

You now return to the house **turn to 13**
**Mark down the Conservatory as complete, as you will have no need to revisit this place.**

### 403
(320)

Sneaking in through the kitchen seems like a good idea at first, until a maid with a meat cleaver sees you and runs straight at you.

"Who are you!" she shouts. "Get out of here now!"

You do as she says and leave the way you came. You need to find some way to get the maid out of the kitchen, but first you must travel back and undo this mistake. (FK: K –15)

If you are unable to do so, unfortunately because the maid has seen you, you will not be able to make any other attempt at entering the house in this time, so you have no choice but to travel back to the present **turn to 13**

### 404
(115)

"Excuse me," you say as you approach the man. "I'm looking for a man called Bob Jenkins, you wouldn't happen to know him would you?"

"I might know that name," he says. "It really depends on what it's worth to you."

If you have £50 and wish to give it to him **turn to 150**

**If there is a name you can drop to convince him to help you, turn to the number in question.**

| B | D | E | G | I | L | M | N | O | T | Y | Z |
|---|---|---|---|---|---|---|---|---|---|---|---|
| 4 | 0 | 6 | 3 | 9 | 2 | 5 | 9 | 0 | 4 | 1 | 3 |

Or if you do not wish to talk to him any longer, you can approach the posh man at the bar **turn to 38**

Or leave **turn to 277**

### 405

You begin looking for an old paper so you can find out the date the Craven Manor Massacre happened in the house. After some thorough searching you learn that the date was 4/2/1897.

On that night a policeman called round to the house, and saw through the window, the chamber maid, Clara, and the Craven's son Jack, lying in a pool of blood. Upon seeing this, he broke down the door and went to investigate. He found them both dead, Jack, by a head wound that may have been caused by a fall from the top of the stairs, and Clara from a slit throat. Next the policeman ascended the stairs and found the butler, Vernon Crowther, dead outside the library. He had been stabbed three times in the chest.

Things only got worse after that. He found Gertrude and Nicholas, the mother and father, butchered in their bed, and then the youngest daughter Sophie, strangled to death in hers. It took him a little while to find the older daughter, Ruth, because she was not inside the house, but rather in the garden, floating in the bloody, red pond. The killer was never found and the whole murder is still an unsolved mystery which plagues the town.

**If you wish to return to that date at any time, you must purchase the necessary Victorian clothes. If you have already returned to this date that you cannot return there.**

You now return to the main library **turn to 259**

### 406

The police have been working hard with the evidence they have compiled and are starting to suspect that Ruth Craven may have committed suicide, whether it happened before or after the other murders is unknown.

(FK: B5 (Alternative) part 3 of 3 +9) Note that you need to find all parts to get the right sum to add or subtract when the time comes to use the future knowledge. Alternative means that if you have this piece of knowledge already you can ignore it)

If you wish to present more evidence **turn to 331**

### 407

Following the guidance from the crossword, you search the book shelves and find an extremely useful book on communicating with the dead.

To access this book at any time **turn to 187**  (Make a note of the passage you are on at the time though so you can return there)

You can now do something else in the library **turn to 386**
Or you can return to the house **turn to 13**

### 408
((200) leaving after checking house (12) leaving after living room)

All of a sudden you feel yourself unable to move. For some reason your legs have stopped working and every other part of you. You realise right then that you have been drugged. It must have been the drink. (FK: D5+26) You try to shout out, but your voice doesn't work. You are completely paralysed. Moments later, you pass out.

**Turn to 16**

### 409
(100 x2)
The killer is beaten, but as you remove the mask, you are shocked to discover that it is none other than Ruth Craven you have killed. None of this makes sense to you, but before you can even contemplate putting it all together, you hear footsteps behind you and turn to find Ruth's father standing there. He has a gun, you are about to explain yourself when in a fit of rage, Peter charges forth and pulls the gun from the father's hand and shoots you. Unless you can reverse time and change this outcome, this is the end for you.

Remembering what Ruth's ghost said, you realise this is the doll and know what has to be done. **It doesn't matter if you have a lighter or not, as there happen to be matches on the table**. You are about to burn[3] the doll, when your possessed fiancée takes you completely by surprise[5] from behind and grabs hold of you, causing the flame to fly from your hand and land near some flammable substances in the room. There is a loud explosion and you find the wall has caved in between the secret room and the library, with the ceiling ready to give[4] way at any moment. You now find[2] yourself trapped in the secret room, with Liz[7] on the other side, wounded. You can just about see her through a gap in the rubble.

"Liz!" you shout. "Liz, are you alright?"

"Dave?" she says, as she opens her eyes. "Dave, where am I?"

It seems she is temporarily free of the man[9] in black's hold, but you are not sure how much longer this will last.

"Liz, I need you to listen to me," you say. "This whole place is going to burn down. You need to get out of here."

"I'm not leaving without you."

She tries her best to get you out of there, but she can't. You consider using your amulet[8], but for some reason your time[1] abilities are not working.

"Dave it's coming back," Liz says. "I can feel it. What should I do?"

Unfortunately it seems the doll[0] you intended to burn has been buried by the rubble[6]. It will burn in time, but not before the man in black has returned to your fiancée's body. There is no way out of this that you can see. It is almost certain that both you and Liz will burn with the house, but the one good thing you can take with you, is that Ruth's spirit will finally be at peace.

THE END

Or is it?

Congratulations you have completed the **'PEACE'** ending. You may have reached the end of this current adventure, but there are still multiple paths you could try. If you haven't already, why not start again and try to complete one of the other 5 endings.

Please now turn to the final page for news on future adventure books

You arrive back and make your way to the living room, where you find Liz asleep on the chair. This is not a good sign, you tell yourself. It almost seems like she is in the same spiritual coma she went into after each time Ruth had used her to speak to you. You walk over and give her a nudge, hoping for the best.

"Liz!" you say. "Liz!"

She opens her eyes, looks at you and smiles before holding her hand out for you to help her up. You take this to mean that everything is alright and pull her to her feet. Then to your utter shock and dismay, she rips the amulet from your neck and plunges a knife into your chest. As you fall back choking on your own blood, you look into Liz's eyes and realise that it is not her looking back at you.

"Ruth?"

But you can already tell that this is not the same Ruth you met before. In that moment, you realise what has happened. You may have stopped the Craven Manor Massacre and prevented the manifestation spirit from ever forming, but by killing Ruth, you have created a vengeance spirit, one that has been waiting over 100 years to get revenge on the man who killed her.

After presenting the evidence to the police, they go to Ray Reardon's place and bring him in for questioning. He is shocked and appalled that he would even be considered as a suspect, due to the brutal nature of the crime.

"I admit, I had my eye on the house," he explains. "The truth is that it should have been passed to me through my family line. The Cravens weren't always respectable; in fact the first of them who lived in that house was a servant who had inherited it from one of my ancestors. The man had left it to him, rather than keep it in the family, because he abhorred every one of them."

"So that's why you threatened Nicholas Craven in that letter," says the officer. "Tell me, what did you mean when you said, he better reconsider your offer or you could make his life extremely unpleasant?"

"I meant that I would make life difficult for him in a financial sense. I would never do something so obvious as killing him and his whole family, and if I did, I would like to think that I would do it more discreetly and not leave their bodies out for everyone to see. Also I may have been known to hurt people in the past, men and sometimes much to my own disgust, women, but I would never touch a hair on a child's head."

With the sincerity in which he says this, you can't help but believe him. Unfortunately it seems that this man is not the killer

**(FK: C7 Part 3 of 3 -20) Note that you need to find all parts to get the right sum to add or subtract when the time comes to use the future knowledge)**

If you wish to present more evidence **turn to 331**
Or you can return to the town **turn to 488**, and come back later.

**413**
(74)

Looking around the back of the house, you see that there is a door in the ground with a heavy chain around it. To break it will require the use of an axe.

You can now use Future Knowledge C6

Or if you haven't tried already, you can attempt to go in through the shop entrance **turn to 464**

If you have exhausted your options, you must return to the town **turn to 488**
**You must now mark down The Butchers as complete, as you will have no need to revisit this place.**

**414**

"I'm sorry," you say, "but I have to find out who that was. Thanks for saving me though."
   Then you take off in a run towards the town. You are running for some time, when you realise you have no idea where you are going, and are forced to face the fact that you have obviously lost your attacker. You consider reversing the clock to try a different direction, but realise it is too far back and would need a great deal of TTP to do so.

**From this point on you will be allowed to time jump from here back to the house in your time, and from there to this 1800s town.**

You now return to the town **turn to 488**

**415**
(312)

"Excuse me," you say. "I'm looking for a man called Tom Scott. You wouldn't happen to know him would you?"

"Tom Scott? Yes as a matter of fact I do," the man replies with a slur. "He is a member of the gentleman's club that I also happen to visit on occasion. I can tell you where it is, but you'll have a job getting in without membership. Only members, or those accompanying a member are allowed in."

"Would you consider accompanying me there?" you ask. "It is of great importance that I see him."

"Oh dear me no!" he guffaws. "That club has standards. I can only imagine what it would do to my reputation if I marched in there with someone of your station. No, the most I can do is give you the address. You never know, you might be lucky and arrive there at exactly the same time he is leaving."

He writes down the address for you.

**Providing you are not in the middle of an encounter, you can visit the gentleman's club by turning to 345 at any time, just be sure to make a note of the page you are on so you can return there after**

"Now be off with you. I've done my good deed for the day. Bartender, bring me another beer."

"Listen," says the bartender. "I'm not going to pour you another drop until you show me some money,"

"Oh very well," the posh man says as he reaches for his pocket, only to discover that his wallet is gone.

"I don't believe this," he says. "Some bugger stole my wallet." (FK: W-40)

"How convenient," the bartender says. "Look, either you pay me what you owe, or I'll take you out back and break your legs."

If you pay on his behalf (Deduct £10 from your inventory) **turn to 117**
If you decide not to help him, the barman suggests that you leave **turn to 277**

**416**
(197)

In the drawer of the desk is a silver cigarette case and lighter. Since these items belong to someone else in this time, you see no point in touching them.

You can now use Future Knowledge U

If not, you can investigate the computer **turn to 310**
Or investigate the painting (Unless you have already done so in the present) **turn to 104**
Or leave the study **turn to 362**

## 417

(2 x2)

No sooner have you turned around, when you find the butcher standing directly behind you.

"What do you think you're doing sneaking round my house like this? Is this any way to treat someone who saved your life, who has been nothing but kind to you."

"I know what you did," you say.

This flusters him, and you use the opportunity to knock over a shelf in front of him and make a run for the door, leaving the way you came in.

You now return to the town **turn to 488**
**You can mark down The Butchers as complete, as you will have no need to revisit this place.**

## 418

You arrive in Craven Manor on 4/2/1897 to find the house deathly silent. From this point on you will use the 1800's Craven Manor Navigation List to explore the house.

### CRAVEN MANOR NAVIGATION LIST
### (1800s)

Below you will find a list of rooms that you can enter whilst you are in this time. You can only check each room once. After entering four rooms you must **turn to 372**

**Ground Floor**

Maid's Quarters **turn to 23**
Sewing Room **turn to 534**
Living Room **turn to 489**
Entrance Hall **turn to 53**
Study **turn to 77**
Butler's Quarters **turn to 114**

**Garden**

Outside Toilets **turn to 276**
Pond **turn to 493**

**Upstairs**

Bedroom One **turn to 429**
Bedroom Two **turn to 152**
Bedroom Three **turn to 273**
Bedroom Five **turn to 356**
Library **turn to 83**

### 419
(57)

Investigating the mirror, you realise that it is in fact a secret door. Unfortunately, no sooner have you discovered this, when someone grabs you from behind and inserts a syringe into your neck. Then you feel yourself growing sleepy and passing out.

**Turn to 16**

### 420

Upon knocking the door, it opens ajar and a young man pokes his head round the corner.

"What do you want?"

"Are you Mr Finchley?"

"No," he replies, "but I can go and get him for you. Wait here!"

You do as he says and wait by the door. A few moments pass and the man has not come back.

If you let yourself inside **turn to 502**
If you continue to wait **turn to 32**
Or you use Future Knowledge D9

### 421

You arrive in the same town in 14/12/1954, which is only eight days after the last time you were here. The first thing you notice is the smog in the air from the numerous smoking chimneys. As you walk down the street, you notice a pawn shop on the opposite side of the road. Upon seeing this, it suddenly occurs to you that this might be a good opportunity to get rid of some junk.

If you cross the road and enter the shop **turn to 73**
If you decide to bypass the shop and continue on **turn to 234**

## 422
### (335)

You manage to break the girl free.

"Quickly," she says in her European accent. "We need to get out of here, fast."

"What's your name?" you ask.

"Xena Kalinski," she says.

"Nice to meet you Xena, I'm Dave."

You are about to leave when you run headfirst into the taxidermist. As he leaps towards you, the girl seizes the chance to escape.

**Add CMIP E. This has affected The Abandoned Shack.**
**Add CMIP F. This has affected The Jewellery Store.**

You feel a bit disappointed by this reaction, since you risked your life to save her. You now find yourself with no choice but to fight this man.

**If you need to, you can now consult the rules of Combat at the back of the book. But be sure to make a note of this passage so you can return here after.**

**This fight will last twelve rounds**

**If you beat the taxidermist, you manage to stun him briefly and escape.**

**If at any time you roll a double or over 10, you manage to grab for his knife and are now able to wound him and escape mid battle.**

If you escape, you return to the town **turn to 488**
**Mark down Building F as complete, as you will have no need to revisit this place. You can also remove Future Knowledge F4 and F7, as you will have no further need for these.**

## 423
### (327)

One by one, you get to work on the screws, twisting as fast as you can and pulling them out, until only one remains. No sooner have you taken out the final one, when the door behind you flies open, and you find yourself having to quickly scramble through into the adjoining room. As you emerge into the store room, you quickly leave and run into the conservatory. In here, you are surprised to find that the door to a side room that had previously been locked, is now wide open. You must now decide where you intend to go next.

If you try the door to the garden **turn to 7**
If you try the door to the miscellaneous room **turn to 93**

## 424
### (263)

"I'm looking for a man called Bob Jenkins," you say.

"Bob Jenkins?" Zoe says in disbelief. "You've got to be kidding me,"

"What makes you say that?"

"Because those men you saved me from, they work for him."

"He's the gangster who didn't want you to write a story about him?" you say.

"Exactly," she replies, "so not a man you want to be messing with. What business do you have with him anyway?"

"I need to prevent him from committing a murder; one that will see him hanged."

"Not to sound too callous, but if you're attempting to change history, this is one thing that you should probably not attempt to change. The sooner Bob Jenkins sees the noose, the happier this town will be."

"And I would agree, were it not for the fact that his vengeful ghost is blocking my progress back in my time. Are you going to help me or not?"

"Well it's your funeral. Go to the pub down the road and look for a man called Cedric. He's an informant of mine who owes me a favour. He'll know where to find Bob. Just make sure to tell him I sent you, or he might demand some kind of payment."

You thank Zoe for her help and then continue onto the pub.

**Turn to 312**

## 425

"I was wondering if you could help me find the item of clothing that this piece of cloth belongs to."

You say, handing the piece of Cloth to the shop owner.

"Erm, let me see," she says as she studies it thoughtfully. "I believe this particular fragment belongs to a pair of trousers that we once sold in the shop. May I ask what this is about?"

"The man wearing these trousers attacked me earlier on today, and I want to find him so I can ask him why?"

"Let me have a look," she says.

She goes into the back and then returns moments later with a ledger.

"All right," she says. "I have records of three people purchasing these trousers: The Hotel owner, James Harkness, the Gambling Den owner Ray Reardon and a young man called Peter Kline." (FK: A7+60)

**Add CMIP R. This will give you access to Building G/1800s Town (Reardon's Gambling Den.)**
**Add CMIP M. This will give you access to Building B/1800s Town (Peter Kline's address)**

You can now either do something else in the shop **turn to 400**
Or return to the town **turn to 488**

426

**If you have CMIP F, turn to 532 immediately. If you don't have CMIP F then please continue reading.**

When you enter the Jewellery shop you are met by a thin, dark woman with a shaved head.

"Hello again," she says, recognising you from the first day. "How did that amulet work out for you? Did it prevent the spirits from possessing you as you had hoped?"

"Yes," you say. "How did you know that's what I bought it for?"

"Why else would you buy an ugly thing like that, rather than purchase that beautiful necklace for your fiancée? I assume you're the new owners of the Craven house."

"That's right," you say in disbelief.

"Then you'll be needing a lot more help than just that amulet."

"I don't suppose you happen to have another one in stock."

"I'm afraid not, but I do have other items that can protect you against the paranormal forces in that house."

In store the woman has the following.

**Mysterious Amethyst stone**-This stone when used will restore 4TTP. You can only use each one once. Discard after use (£25 each)

**Mysterious Emerald Stone**- This stone when used will restore 8TTP. You can only use each one once. Discard after use (£40 each)

**The following items will not be relevant to you until you have been briefed on the rules of Day and Night.**

**Spirit boxes**– These will trap the man in black inside temporarily. Whenever you encounter him you can automatically trap him for three rounds. This will mean you can check three rooms without having to roll the dice each time you leave. You can only use each one once. Discard after use. (£25 each)

**Day and Night Stone**– This stone will turn day into night and night into day automatically without having to time jump. You can only use each one once. Discard after use (£40 each)

Whether you make any purchases or not, you now return to the town **turn to 444**

## 427

"So I just need you to sign there... And there...And you're done. Here are your keys. I hope you'll both be happy in your new home."

For a moment you are completely flummoxed. You are back in the café at the very point in time where you had received the keys from the agent. Is this real? Or are you dreaming? If it is real, did all the other stuff in the house never happen?

"Oh Dave, this is so great," Liz says after the agent has left, "our own house."

So relieved to see her alive, you instinctively reach over and embrace her with an urgency that she is not used to.

"Okay, I'm happy too," she gasps, "but struggling to breathe here."

"Sorry," you say, as you release her.

"I know you're happy about the house, but a simple kiss would have sufficed."

"Actually, I'm not completely happy about the house," you say, remembering all that had transpired before.

"What do you mean?" she says, confused.

"Well I've been thinking about the whole last owners died there thing, and to be honest it kind of creeps me out a little."

"That's funny, I was thinking the same thing. I was going to tell you, but I thought you'd tell me I was just being stupid."

"Normally I would, but..."

"Look, hold that thought. I'll be back in a bit; I just need to use the toilet."

Then she leaves. With everything happening in a similar fashion to how it did before, you begin to wonder if what you experienced previously may have actually happened, and that somehow you had time travelled back to prevent it from happening again.

Little do you know that this is actually true, and furthermore that you actually have power over these abilities. If this is your first time reading this turn to 352 otherwise continue on

You wouldn't normally believe in stuff like that, but you really can't think of any other way to explain it. Although if that were true it would not only mean that ghosts were real, but that in less than 24 hours Liz would die by your hand.

**Turn to 98**

The shot misses only by an inch, skimming your neck and leaving a nasty, bloody scratch, but that is not the problem. Unfortunately it also splits the string on your time amulet, forcing it to fall to the ground and leave you powerless. From this moment on, you will not be able to use any of your time abilities. You run as fast as you can and head for the library, closing the door behind you and pushing a bookcase in front to block it. From here you can only see two ways to escape: a window leading out onto a precarious ledge, and a second door leading back into the house from the lower floor of the library.

If you attempt to chance the precarious ledge outside the window **turn to 49**
If you decide to run downstairs and use the other door **turn to 298**

Aside from a few children's books and some Victorian toys, the only thing of interest in this young boy's bedroom is a ball of silly putty. Thinking that this may have some use later down the line, you decide to take it with you.

You now return to the house **turn to 418**
**If you have chosen to hide in this room turn to 271**

(416)
Remembering that Hayley going to the drawer for her cigarettes is what gave you away, you decide to place them somewhere in plain sight that is far away from you. After doing this, you return to your hiding place and wait for the couple to return so everything can play out as it did before.

"Now where did I put my cigarettes?" says Hayley.

"I think I remember you putting them in the drawer," John replies.

You flinch when you hear this, thinking the change you made might not make any difference. But no sooner has Hayley turned to go to the drawer, when John speaks again.

"Oh no, my mistake, here they are on the shelf."

You hear the click of a lighter and then the smell of cigarette smoke fills the room.

"I really wish you would quit those things," John says.

"Maybe if my nerves weren't constantly on edge, I wouldn't need them as much."

"Look, I'm doing everything I can to get us out of here. It's no simple thing to sell a house; especially one with a reputation like this one."

"I wish we had never moved in," Hayley says.

"I think we were just seduced by the price. I mean you hear talk of people moving into houses like this, but you never imagine the same thing will happen to you."

"That reminds me," Hayley says. "I've been looking at this website recently for these paranormal investigators called: The Ghost Chasers. There was some interesting information on there about how to deter spirits."

"Oh please," John says, angrily, "could you do me a favour and stop looking at that crap."

"It's not crap," Hayley says, sounding offended. "These people are the real deal."

"Maybe they are, but I'm not convinced that we're dealing with ghosts."

"Then how do you explain all the weird things that have been happening around here?"

"Well, obviously it's some crazy person who gets a thrill out of breaking in and scaring the shit out of us," John theorises. "He's probably been doing it for some time, which is why this house has such a bad reputation. Look, I want to get out of here as much as you, but until then, this ought to give us some peace of mind."

You take a peek and see that John has taken out a gun from his pocket.

"Where did you get that?" Hayley says in shock.

"I borrowed it from a friend at work."

"I don't know what frightens me more; the fact that you have a friend who has a gun, or that you had the stupidity to borrow it from him? Do you know what the police would do to you if they caught you with this?"

"They are not going to catch me with it," John reassures her, "and besides, it's just a precaution until we can get out of here. Don't worry I won't leave it lying around the house. In fact I'll keep it in the safe until we need it. How's that?"

As you watch, you see John walk over to the painting on the wall, and move it to one side to reveal the safe. Then with his back towards you, he inputs six numbers, opens it up, sticks the gun inside and then closes it again. (FK: T-17) You feel disappointed that you were unable to see the combination because in your time, the contents of that safe may have been very useful. You consider possibly returning to an earlier time to try and reposition yourself, but no hiding place you can see has a clear enough view of the safe. The only area that has a clear view of it, is the bookshelf to the side, but since there appears to be nowhere to hide round there, unless you were two feet tall and could fit on a shelf, it seems hardly worth considering.

"Come on," says John. "I don't know about you, but I'm knackered. Shall we go to bed?"

"Well I don't imagine I'll be able to sleep, but I could definitely do with a lie down."

"Oh by the way, I forgot to mention, a package came for you earlier while you were at work. It was from some emporium. Ordering perfume again? Anyway, I put it on top of the cupboard in the kitchen."

"I'll get it in the morning."

The couple then leave and go to bed.

(FK: S part 3 of 3 -10) Note that you need to find all parts to get the right sum to add or subtract when the time comes to use the future knowledge).

Unless you know of anything else you wish to do, you leave the house and return to the present **turn to 13**

## 431
(319)
Unfortunately you are just not fast enough, because no sooner have you gotten to the doorway, when Hayley plunges the knife into her stomach.

"No!" yells her husband, right before he runs to her and pushes you to one side.

"Stay back," you try to warn him, but it is too late.

No sooner has he gone to his wife, when she suddenly pulls the knife out of her own stomach and stabs him in the throat. As the hallway becomes a bloody mess, you realise there is nothing more you can do for these two, so you decide to return to the present **turn to 13**

## 432

"I'll help," you say to Peter.

"Very well," he says. "Originally I was going to climb the trellis outside her room, but now you've agreed to help, perhaps a different approach is in order. What I propose is this. I will go to the front door and demand to speak to Ruth's father, then once I have gained admittance, I will sneak into the conservatory and unlock the door for you. Then whilst I keep the father busy, you can sneak into the house and make your way up the stairs to Ruth's room, set her free and take her back the way you came. Then once I am done, I will come and join you."

You agree to this plan, and wait in the garden for Peter to go and put the first part into action. A few minutes pass and before long, you see him appear in the conservatory and unlock the door. Then as soon as you see the coast is clear, you make your way to the door and let yourself into the house. As you walk into the hallway, you notice the butler walking in the opposite direction with Peter, and quickly make your way to the entrance hall and ascend the stairs to the first floor.

**Turn to 100**

### 433

As you turn the key in the lock, it is so old that part of it snaps off. Fortunately you are able to salvage both parts. Perhaps you may find a way to put them back together.

You now return to the house **turn to 13**

### 434

Using the curtain pole, you reach down and hook it into the shiny object and bring it up. After cleaning off the mud you realise you have found a red key. This could be useful to you in your own time.

You now add this to your inventory and return to the house **turn to 418**
**If you have chosen to hide in this room turn to 271**

### 435
(529)
Remembering that one of the same cigarettes that Peter smokes was found in the outside toilets on the night of the murder, you decide to check one of his shoes against the imprint you found there. Upon comparing it, you realise it is an exact match. Peter was there on the night of the murder.

**(FK: B4 part 2 of 3 -30) Note that you need to find all parts to get the right sum to add or subtract when the time comes to use the future knowledge)**

You now wait for Peter to return with the tea.

**Turn to 192**

## 436
(413)

Remembering the axe outside Hannah's house, you quickly run over there and pull it out of the log that you found it in. You consider asking her if you could borrow it, but being as you only intend to use it briefly, you see no point in bothering her. Making your way to the back of the butcher's shop, you swing the axe three times at the lock, and on the third swing it breaks. You leave the axe here, with the intentions of returning it to its owner later.

After pulling the doors open, you wander down a short flight of stairs, and find yourself descending into a cold meat locker. There are rows upon rows of hanging pigs. You notice a door ahead and are about to go through it, when you hear the butcher coming in from behind. He obviously heard the break in and has come to investigate. You have only seconds to hide.

**Choose one of the following hiding places:**

**Amongst the hanging pigs**
**Behind the crates**
**Or under the plastic sheeting**

Then **turn to 379**

## 437

You hand the glass to the policewoman and she tells you to wait while she checks it for fingerprints. When she returns, she reports her findings

"I'm sorry but the fingerprints on the cup do not match either of the fingerprints on the knife."

You now return to the town **turn to 444**
**When returning to the town, be sure to mark down 188 as a shortcut for future fingerprint checks.**

237

You actually think that the guest bedroom may be the nicest one in the house, with its private bathroom and corner bath. Since it appears to have been refitted within the last ten years, you do wonder if you are likely to find anything of interest in here. However, upon closer inspection of the back wall, you notice that there appears to be an air vent leading into another room, which a rather terrible smell seems to be emanating from. The grate is held in tight by several screws.

If you have a screwdriver and wish to open the vent **turn to 512**
Otherwise you now return to the house **turn to 13**

## 439
(420)
Rather than wait for the thief to make his escape, you run round to the back of the house and get a head start on chasing him **turn to 201**

## 440

Upon entering the six digit combination, the door opens with a satisfying click, to reveal John's borrowed gun, £500 and The Book Of Ghost Deterrents (**turn to 35** if you ever wish to read this, but make sure you have made a note of the passage you were previously on before so you can return there). There is also a note from the previous owners.

*Dear Dave*

*Hayley and I just wanted to thank you again for saving our lives. We figured at some point that you would try and open the safe, so we decided to make it worth your while. Before leaving this house, not only did we decide to leave everything in the safe as it was, including the gun and £500, but as a bonus, we left you this book on ghosts. I hope it will help you deal with any other spirits you may come across. We really can't thank you enough.*

*All the best*

*John and Hayley Barnett*

**After retrieving these items, you can mark down The Study as complete, as you will have no need to revisit this place.**

You return to the house **turn to 13**

## 441
### (11)

As you step into the water, a chill goes up your leg. It is freezing, and you start to feel it more the further you go in, because the water comes up to your waist. Soon you are at the statue and you quickly reach up and grab the object you came for. It is a carving of some sort, but you decide to take a better look at it once you are on the other side. **Do not add this to your inventory yet.**

Wading through the pond to make your way back, you are just over half way, when to your shock, you feel a hand grab you around the ankle and pull your feet out from under you. Down you go, under the murky depths, gasping for air. As another hand holds you under, you begin to panic.

You have two choices now. You can either reverse time to the previous passage, which unfortunately will mean that you do not recover the object that you found here, or you can try and break free of the spirit's hold.

If you choose to break free:

**Roll two dice.**

**You may add up to 2TTP to ensure your roll is higher.**

If your roll is 8 or higher, you break free **turn to 88**

If your roll is too low, you must reverse time or drown.

## 442
### (131 x2)

"Why don't we show him what he's missing?" you suggest

"I'm not sure I understand what you mean," the girl replies. "How can I show him what he's missing?"

"By dancing with me in full view of him."

"Do you really think that would work?"

"I think so, although I have to warn you that I'm not the greatest dancer."

"I don't mind."

As you take the young girl's hand and lead her onto the dance floor, you soon become aware of how bad a dancer you actually are.

To make this work, you have to try your best to keep up the steps. To do this you must roll a single dice seven times and try to throw the following numbers in order.

4, 4, 3, 2, 2, 6, 5.

Now normally this would be close to impossible, since the odds of rolling all those numbers perfectly is very unlikely, but you have the ability of time travel. With each roll you make that is not exact, you can use up to 2TTP to either speed up or slow down your steps. That means that for each roll that is not exact, you can either minus 1-2 or plus 1-2 to your roll to make the step. Whether you make the step or not, you then move onto the next step. You are allowed to make three miss steps.

If you manage to dance without making more than three miss steps **turn to 141**
If you make more than three **turn to 261**

### 443
(215 x2)
Within a second you are pushed over the edge, and you quickly take a breath in before you sink to the bottom of the depths. You feel like you could probably hold your breath for about 40 seconds, but what good is that with your hands tied and this block on your feet?

You can now use Future Knowledge Y

Otherwise, unless you can reverse time your adventure ends here.

### 444

### THE TOWN NAVIGATION LIST
### (MODERN DAY)

Below you will find a list of shops and buildings in the surrounding town you can visit at any time.


Hotel **turn to 89**
Antiques Store **turn to 284**
Grocers **turn to 399**
Police Station **turn to 202**
Pub **turn to 296**

Café **turn to 222**
Abandoned Shack **turn to 118**
Book Store **turn to 328**
Jewellery Store **turn to 426**

(The following buildings cannot be accessed until you have the necessary CMIP beside it)

Building A  **(Need CMIP G) turn to 242**
Building C  **(Need CMIP H) turn to 62**
Building D  **(Need CMIP I) turn to 259**
Graveyard  **(Need CMIP J) turn to 177**

To return to Craven Manor **turn to 13**

### 445

Under the bed you see nothing. It almost feels like looking here has been a complete waste of time.

If you wish to check in the Drawers **turn to 161**
If you wish to check in the Wardrobe **turn to 518**
Or you can return to the house **turn to 13**

### 446
(8)

Coming onto a main road, you are just in time to see someone climbing into the back of a carriage. Damn! You were too late; you will now have to walk on to Craven Manor.

**Turn to 382**

### 447
(286)

Choosing to stay at the house again, you try to do everything differently. After going to bed you lie awake all night, hoping that you'll be able to catch Liz as soon as she gets out of bed. Unfortunately whether it be down to tiredness or something more sinister, you still fall asleep and wake to find that Liz is not in her bed. Panicking, you quickly run out into the hall, taking a different direction to last time and keeping an eye out for the shadowy figure that possessed you. Soon you find Liz and you are about to go over to her, when the black figure once again appears and takes you over. You know what is to come and you desperately will it not to be so. Then as if by magic, you find yourself back in the café.

**Turn to 427**

448

You take a small ruby from the box.
"I'll take this one," you say.
"Ah, the sultan's eye," he says. "A wise choice."

**This Ruby can be used in place of money. It is worth £300.**

"Thank you," you say. "It's beautiful."
"In addition to this, I would like to offer you membership to my private gentleman's club. If you were ever interested in visiting," he says as he hands you a card. "They will ask for a password at the door. The current password is Crane."

**Make a note that you can visit this club at any time whilst in 1954, providing you are not in the middle of any kind of encounter. To go there you simply must turn to 345. Do make a note of where you are at the time though, so you can return there.**

**Congratulations, not only did you save Gil from being murdered, but you also prevented his would be murderer from being sentenced to death.**

**Add CMIP D. This affects The Hotel.**

**Also remove Future knowledge I and H1.**

If you do not wish to go to the business club now, you say goodbye to Gil and return to the present **turn to 13.**

449
(124)

You make it as far as the corridor, before the doors to the ballroom slam shut. Luckily the time playing hide and seek in the study has brought you some time. You run down the corridor to your right and find yourself in the conservatory. In here you are surprised to find that the door to a side room that had previously been locked, is now wide open. You must now decide where you intend to go next.

If you try the door to the garden **turn to 7**

If you try the door to the miscellaneous room **turn to 93**

## 450
### (464)

Remembering the boxing event the butcher spoke about, gives you an idea.

"Just a friendly visit," you say. "I never properly thanked you for what you did for me."

"I'm sure you would have done the same for me, were our roles reversed."

"I also wanted to ask if you knew anything about the commotion in town," you add in.

"Commotion?" he says, confused.

"Yes, crowds have formed around the Gambling Den. I think I heard something about a fight being cancelled."

"Cancelled?" he says in disbelief. "Tonight's fight? I've already bought my ticket."

"I don't know if it's tonight's fight, but people seem really angry."

Suddenly the butcher throws his apron to one side and leaps over the counter.

"I've got to go and see what this is about. Would you be able to mind the store for me for a few minutes."

"Yes, of course," you say. "It's the least I could do."

You almost feel a little guilty, considering what you are intending to do.

"Thank you," he says. "I'll be back soon."

The moment he leaves the shop, you waste no time in heading through the back, and into his house.

**Turn to 2**

## 451
### (506 x2)

Looking out of the window, you see that it isn't that much of a drop, but even still, if you did fall you could be paralysed for life. You must make your way carefully round to the other window.

**Roll the dice six times.**

**If you get a 1, you must roll over 8 on two dice to avoid slipping. Then you can continue with the remainder of your six rolls.**

**If you fail this roll, you fall and grab the ledge. To pull yourself back up, you must roll a 12 in four throws. Then you can continue with the remainder of your six rolls.**

If you make it to the other side **turn to 227**

If you fall, unfortunately from this the height, this will result in grievous injury, so you must reverse time or spend the rest of your life in a Victorian hospital.

### 452
(234)

"Leave her alone," you say, as you enter the fray.

They are about to challenge your request, when they notice the gun in your hand

"Look pal, I would think twice about doing this if I were you," says one of the thugs. "You don't know who you're dealing with."

"Two thugs who are going to be dead soon unless you do as I say. Now leave the woman alone and get out of here or I will shoot you where you stand."

"Alright we'll go," says the leader of the group. "But you'd better watch your back, because when I tell my boss what you did, you're going to regret ever meeting us."

Once they are gone, you go to the woman.

"Are you okay?" you ask.

"You shouldn't have done that," she says.

"I wasn't going to stand by while they mugged you in broad daylight."

"It wasn't a mugging. They were trying to send me a message."

"A message?"

"I write for the local gazette. I was researching a story about their boss and he found out and sent his goons after me."

"So they weren't stealing from you?"

"No they were probably just going to rough me up a bit and frighten me off the story, but that's about it."

As the woman talks, you start to notice that she seems vaguely familiar. Have you possibly met her before?

**If you know her name, use the key below to decide what number you should turn to, by substituting each letter of her name for a number.**

| A | E | I | J | L | M | O | V | Y | Z |
|---|---|---|---|---|---|---|---|---|---|
| 3 | 0 | 2 | 5 | 4 | 7 | 6 | 9 | 8 | 1 |

If you don't know her name, or can't remember it, you leave and continue down the street **turn to 312**

"I didn't want to have to do this," you say, "but you give me no choice. If you will not lend me your metal detector, I'm afraid I'm going to have to show this to some people around town."

You then pull out the picture the café owner gave you, which shows Trevor, the bookshop owner, dressed in ladies underwear and wearing make-up.

"Where did you get that?"

"It doesn't matter where I got it. Are you going to lend me your metal detector, or not?"

"This is blackmail."

"Call it what you will. All I know is that I need a metal detector to do something very important, and I'm willing do whatever I have to in order to get one. The rest is up to you."

He thinks on this for a few moments and then gives his answer.

"Alright, you can borrow it, but if you damage it in any way you will pay for it. And as for buying any books from me, I'm afraid my shop is closed to you from now on."

**You can now add the metal detector to your inventory. This will allow you to find hidden metallic objects. To use it, you must look out for the phrase: 'It almost feels like looking here has been a complete waste of time.' When you see this phrase, +10 to the paragraph you are on and go to the new number.**

**Since you have been banned from the book shop from this point onward, you must mark down the bookshop as complete, as you will not be allowed to revisit this place.**

You now return to the town **turn to 444**

### 454

You decide to ask about the 1950s woman you saw in the bathtub. After giving the officer a brief description, she goes onto her computer, and then a few moments later she tells you her findings.

"Her name was Rose Everett (FK: F3+285). According to this, she attended a house party at Craven Manor on the night of a prestigious auction, and was murdered by her boyfriend, Jeremy Lupin, who was then beaten to death by a vengeful mob."

You now return to the town **turn to 444**
**Only return to The Police Station if you gain FK you haven't tried before.**

455

Using the metal detector, you discover a beeping coming from under the bed, which leads you to a loose floorboard. Moving the bed to one side, you prise the floorboard up to find an old tin, sweet box with £10, a toy train, and a penny dreadful novel inside. You can take all of these items.

You now return to the house **turn to 13**

**Mark down Bedroom One as complete, as you will have no need to revisit this place.**

456
(15)

As you wait there in the dark, voices are soon heard in the corridor coming towards the display room.

"Wait a minute, who is that," says Gil, "I don't recognise those voices. Is there someone else in my house? Oh my god. I think you're right. I am being robbed."

You pull out your gun and wait by the side of the door. Before long a group of three men enter, all armed with guns, led by the man with the scar on his cheek, Bob Jenkins. You quickly grab Bob and take him as a hostage.

"Put your guns down or I'll kill your boss!" you yell.

It seems like they are going to comply with your request, until a fourth man enters, holding the maid as a hostage. (FK: A2 -22)

"You kill him, and this young lady's death will be on your hands," he says

You can now use Future Knowledge A4

Otherwise, you have no choice but to put the gun down and **turn to 129**

457

You roll out of the way, just in time, and then get to your feet to face the butcher in combat.

**If you need to, you can now consult the rules of Combat at the back of the book. But be sure to make a note of this passage so you can return here after.**

246

This fight will last eighteen rounds

Due to his size, every time the butcher successfully attacks, you will receive 2 hits.

Fortunately his size has an upside too, because he is slower at moving. This means you can +1 to each of your attack rolls.

If you manage to defeat him **turn to 37**

## 458
(2 x2)
If you came in through the shop **turn to 417**
If you came in through the shop using a copied key **turn to 59**

## 459

Unfortunately your aim leaves something to be desired, because not only do you miss Ruth, but you hit Peter square in the back of the head. As his lifeless body falls to the ground, Ruth charges in your direction. You manage to get two shots off that hit her in the chest, but not before she forces you over the banister. You hit the ground with a tremendous thud. Then you black out for a few moments, and when you come to, you find that you cannot move your legs. It appears you have broken them in the fall. You try to crawl for the stairs, knowing that you can undo all of this if you simply make it to the top and reclaim your amulet. Unfortunately you only make it a few feet, before you hear a knock on the door.
    "This is the police! Open up!"
You try to move faster, but by the time you have reached the bottom of the stairs, the door has already been forced open and the police have entered the house. You can already guess what happens next. First they'll find the bodies. Then they'll find the gun, and then once they surmise that you are the only person who is alive that is not a Craven, they will draw all the wrong conclusions, and you will go down in history as being the infamous Craven Manor Massacre Killer. What Irony.

## 460

Upon returning to Craven Manor in your time, you are surprised to find that the house looks exactly the same as when you had left it. This baffles you. Surely it would look different if the Craven Manor Massacre never happened. You are about to find your fiancée to check to see if she is possessed, when to your horror, you see the blue translucent figure of the butler through the library door.

"No, you can't be here," you cry out. "I don't understand."

You step inside to talk to him and he points you towards a table with a newspaper resting on top. An article has been highlighted.

*CRAVEN MANOR MASSACRE*
*3/04/1905*

*Today the town is in mourning for the Craven family who were found dead in their home by Police Inspector Brown on this very morning. The cause of death is murder. It is believed that the oldest daughter Ruth, who had left home eight years ago to live with her husband Peter Kline, returned to the house and stabbed each member of the family to death, before drowning herself in the garden pond. Peter believes there to be no malice in these murders, and that it was very likely that Ruth was not aware of what she was doing, due to her multiple personality disorder, which she had been diagnosed with, following her father's unexpected suicide, eight years prior. A memorial ceremony will be held in the town this Sunday.*

You realise then that you did not stop the Craven Manor Massacre, but merely postponed it to a later date. It seems Ruth's illness was destined to make her kill her family, no matter what. You realise that you have no other choice now, but to try and stop the man in black in your own time. **From this point on, you will not be allowed to time travel or enter the town. If there is nothing more you can do in the house, you may want to consider starting again.**

You now return to the house **turn to 13**

## 461
### (378)
Before the man even notices you are there, you instantly pull the trigger of the revolver, shooting in his direction three times. One of the shots misses, but the other two hit him in the chest as he turns round to see where the first shot had come from. His wounds it seems are quite fatal, because he topples to the ground, but unfortunately on his way down, he still pulls the lever. Before the lights go out, you happen to notice that he has muddy shoes; an indication that he came in from the garden (FK: A3-40).

Moments later, you hear several gun shots and then leave the cellar to return to the display room. It is in here you find a mess off bodies, including Gil, his maid and unfortunately Zoe.

**Unfortunately if you intended to save Gil or prevent his killer from seeing the noose, you have failed.**

Unless you know of anywhere else to go in this time, you return to the present **turn to 13**

### 462

Approaching the headstone of Rose Everett, you wait until you are sure no-one is watching and dig up her grave, before salting and burning her bones. You only used a few handfuls of salt, so there is still plenty left if you need to do this again.

**Add CMIP C. This affects the Bathroom.**

You now return to the town **turn to 444**

### 463
(358)

"So where shall we begin?" says Gil. "Would you like me to start with telling you a bit about my background, or would you prefer to hear the story of when I first became interested in collecting diamonds?"

"I'm sorry to tell you this Gil," you say. "But we haven't been completely honest with you."

"What do you mean?" he says, nervously.

"We're not here to interview you."

"Then why are you here?"

"We came to warn you that a group of men are planning to break into your home today and steal your most precious diamond."

"So I'm assuming this means you're not actually writing an exclusive about me for the paper," he says disappointedly.

"I'm sorry," says Zoe. "It was the only way we knew we could get in here."

"In that case. Kenworth!" he shouts for his bodyguard. "Could you kindly escort these two time wasters out of my home!"

"Time wasters?" you say. "We came here to help you."

"Do you know how many times I've been warned by the police about possible attempted burglaries on my property? Possibly every couple of weeks. And do you know why none of them have ever come to pass? Because I have been careful thus far not to admit people into my home without prior appointment; a rule that I almost broke when I allowed you two into my home for reasons of vanity. Now, Kenworth kindly remove these two people from my sight."

As the large bodyguard drags you from the house, you realise that there is no chance you will be getting back in.

Unless you know of anywhere else to go in this time, you return to the present **turn to 13**

### 464
(74)

Going in through the shop entrance, you are faced by the butcher. He smiles when he sees you.

"Well if it isn't my friend from the river," he says. "I see you chose to ignore my advice and stay in town. How have you been?"

"Fine," you say, "still healing from my bruises."

"I imagine you may be for some time. So what brings you to my shop? Come to buy something, or were you just paying me a friendly visit?"

As you consider your answer, you happen to notice the keys for the shop behind the counter and have an idea. If you were able to make a copy of these, you would have access to his shop after he had left. Unfortunately you won't be able to swipe them while he is looking.

If you make an order **turn to 28**

Or you can use Future Knowledge C4

### 465
(379)

**The butcher may not have found you yet, but he has not given up looking. Now roll a dice to determine where he will look next.**

**If you roll:**

**1-3- He checks your location**
**4-6- He checks the last remaining location**

**If he rolls your location, he catches you and you have no choice but to reverse time. If you can't do this turn to 52.**

**If you do reverse time, you do not need to travel back to the previous paragraph if you simply want to change your hiding place. Instead minus 2TTP and continue as**

**if you had successfully hid. However, if you wish to reverse time to avoid ending up in this situation, you can use your TTP for that instead.**

If you hide successfully **turn to 61**

## 466

Shining the torch down into the hole, you see that it does indeed have a bottom and on that bottom appears to be a shiny object that resembles a key of some sort. Unfortunately, it is too far down for you to be able to stretch.

You can now use Future Knowledge D6

Or check under the bed **turn to 18**
Or check the wardrobe **turn to 245**
Or return to the house **turn to 418**
**If you have chosen to hide in this room turn to 271**

## 467
### (29 x4)

"Megan!" you shout.

This gets Ruth's attention, because she temporarily looks back at you. It is not for long, but it is long enough, because Peter manages to use the time to get her into a sleeper hold and knocks her out.

While he does this, you reclaim your amulet before coming to help (D2+40).

"What can I do," you offer.

"We need to get her to her bedroom," Peter says.

You help him carry her there, and are relieved to find that she stays unconscious for the time being. After placing her on the bed, you leave and lock the door behind you.

"So what happens now?"

"Her father mentioned a Doctor who was treating her for her illness. I will telegram him at once. I only hope he can get here before she wakes up. I'm sure someone must have heard those shots, which means you should probably go before the police get here. The real police, I mean."

You look at him surprised.

"It didn't take a university degree to figure it out. I don't know who you are, but I appreciate everything you've done. You saved my life and you may have saved hers too. I will not forget your kindness."

Unsure of whether you should be leaving like this, when Ruth's future hangs in the balance, you know there is nothing more you can do here without complicating the timeline. After saying goodbye, you leave the house and then return to your own time.

**Turn to 460**

### 468
(2)

Searching the bedroom, you are surprised to find a diary right by the butcher's bedside table. You pick it up and have a flick through. One page in particular gets your attention.

*Wednesday*

*I have made no secret of the fact that I have lusted after Young Ruth Craven for some time. I know it is wrong that I should feel this way, but I simply can't control my feelings for the girl. I even tried to settle for that Hannah girl, but she did nothing for me. Ruth is so innocent and chaste, like Hamlet's Ophelia. I must have her, even if it is just one time. That is why today, I intend to take her in the woods. I know she likes to take walks down there during the afternoon. I wish it could be consensual, but I know that age and beauty are a factor here and the fact that her father, my dear friend, would kill me if he ever found out. That is why I must wear a mask, and make sure that she is never aware of my identity. I must be mad for writing this down, but I can think of no other way to express my feelings, since I have no one I could ever talk to about this.*

**((FK: B7 part 4 of 4 -9) Note that you need to find all parts to get the right sum to add or subtract when the time comes to use the future knowledge)**

If this is the first place you checked **turn to 370.**
If it is the second **turn to 458.**
If it is the third **turn to 417.**

### 469
(499)

You are about to continue on as you did before, when you remember the fact that Peter's misunderstanding of what was going on, led to you being forced over the banister. To prevent this, you realise the best plan would be to get him on side from the beginning, so you decide to try and find him. Looking around outside, you spot him getting ready to leap the wall into the back garden and stop him. He looks at you in shock.

"Who the hell are you?" he asks.

"I'm a policeman," you say.

"You don't look like a policeman."

"That's because I'm with the secret branch. We don't wear uniforms. It makes us stand out."

"And why are you here?"

"I came because I have reason to believe that Ruth is in danger."

"On that we agree," he says. "I believe her father is holding her against her will in that house, and I have every intention of breaking her free. Will you help me?"

Since you want to keep him on side, you decide to go along with his plan.

**Turn to 432**

### 470
(147 x2)

Upon leaving the café, you wonder if you can use the opportunity of looking round town, to find anything that can help you prevent the events that will transpire that evening. You consider that you may be able to find a useful book in the bookshop, or perhaps find some kind of artefact in the jewellery shop that may ward off spirits.

If you decide to look in the Book shop **turn to 484**

If you would prefer to look in the Jewellery shop **turn to 338**

### 471
(82 x2)

Removing the mask, you are shocked to see Ruth Craven staring right back at you. The shock of this, causes you to draw back just in time to see Peter charging at you.

"Villain," he shouts. "Get away from her."

"Wait, this is not what it looks like," you say

But before you can say anything else, Peter shoves you over the banister, and you hit the ground below with such a force, that the impact breaks your back. You must now reverse time, or else end your journey as a paraplegic in the 1800s. (FK: C3-30).

### 472
(28)

"In a way," you say. "It's our first get together for seven years."

"That is a long time."

"Any plans yourself, tonight?" you ask.

"Yes actually," the butcher says enthusiastically. "I'm planning on going to a boxing match over at Reardon's place. It should be a good fight, plus I've got a lot of money riding on it."

"You made a bet?"

"A rather substantial bet," he says nervously, "but by the sounds of things, the fighter I bet on, has never lost, so fingers crossed." (FK: C4 -14)

After he has finished picking and packaging your meat, he hands it over to you.

"There you are," he says. "That will be £2."

You can't believe your ears. Prices sure have changed since then. You are considering paying, when you realise that you don't actually know what you would do with that much meat.

"Actually," you say, having second thoughts. "I appear to have left my wallet at home. Is there any chance you could hold this for me, and I'll drop the money in later this afternoon."

"Of course," he says. "That shouldn't be a problem at all."

You can now either, look for another way in **turn to 413** or reverse time and attempt to play things out differently.

If you have exhausted your options, you must return to the town **turn to 488**
**You can mark down The Butchers as complete, as you will have no need to revisit this place.**

## 473

Upon entering the Police Station, you are met by a ginger haired station chief with a walrus moustache.

"Good day, young sir, how might I be of service?"

"Good day, my name is Dave Ingram," you say. "I'm a detective from out of town. Recently there have been some murders back where I come from, and I believe the criminal responsible, may have originated from this town. I would really appreciate a list of any known felons in the town, if you would be so kind."

"Let me see what I can do," says the chief as he looks through some paperwork. "There are three names that might be of interest to you. One is our local thief, Fingers Finchley. He has been suspected for many thefts in the past and a few assaults, but due to him leaving no evidence behind, or being caught red handed, we have yet to convict him. Then there is Anton Volnick, The taxidermist. He has been fined for tax evasion and illegal poaching. Then finally, Kenny Harkness, the once suspected rapist of Ruth Craven, who we believe could be linked to the Craven Manor Massacre."

**Add CMIP P. This will give you access to Building E/1800s Town (Fingers Finchley's address.)**
**Add CMIP Q. This will give you access to Building F/1800s Town (The Taxidermist.)**
**Add CMIP O. This will give you access to Building D/1800s Town (Kenny Harkness's address.)**

Taking note of these names, you thank the chief, and then consider what your next move will be.

If you wish to turn in evidence you have found, to initiate the interrogation of a suspect **turn to 331**

Otherwise you leave and return to the town **turn to 488**
**If you return to the town, mark down 331 as a shortcut for The Police Station/ 1800s Town so you can go straight there to interrogate suspects in future.**

Lifting the grill, you see a long gaping hole. It is completely pitch black so you can't even tell how far down it goes.

You can now either, check the wardrobe **turn to 245**
Or you can check under the bed **turn to 18**

Or return to the house **turn to 418**
**If you have chosen to hide in this room turn to 271**

Entering the taxidermist's shop, you find a man with long grey hair and a beard, stuffing the carcass of a rabbit with sawdust. As you approach him, he looks up at you.

"Yes, can I help you?" he asks

"I wonder if you can," you reply, thinking of a new cover story. "My name is Dave Ingram and I'm a specialist working with the police. I'm doing a follow up investigation on the Craven Manor Massacre that happened here a year ago."

"Oh, that was a tragedy what happened. It's a real shame they never caught who did it. I'd love to string them up myself."

"That's actually why I'm here. You see the police believe they may have uncovered new evidence that could reveal who the killer is."

"Really?" he says, sounding surprised.

"Yes, so I'm revisiting some of the people we questioned the first time round, just to confirm a few things."

"Of course, you've got to get your facts straight. I completely understand. How can I help?"

"Well, I'll need to ask you some questions."

"Very well," he responds. "Would you like to come through into the back? It's much more comfortable in there. There's a bell on the door, so I can hear if anyone comes into the shop."

"Yes, all right," you say. "Lead the way."

He brings you into a brightly lit sitting room, where many of his previous works adorn the walls and shelves.

"Can I offer you a drink of wine," he offers, as you take a seat.

If you accept **turn to 490**
If you decline **turn to 90**

## 476
### (490)

Remembering the knife you brought back from the past, you realise there is an opportunity to get fingerprints that you can use from this man by taking his glass. Decide whether you wish to do this and then choose what you intend to do next.

**Do not remove FK:D1 as there may be other uses for it later**

If you explore the living room **turn to 12**
If you move further into the house **turn to 200**
If you choose to leave **turn to 14**

## 477
### (278)

"Alright there mate," you say in as common a voice as you can muster. "I'm looking for work. Any odd jobs you need doing around your house? My rates are as cheap as they come. Also if you're not happy with the job, you don't have to pay me nothing."

"I'm sorry sir," the butler replies, "but the only job that needs doing in this house is for someone to fix the chimney, and unfortunately we have already hired someone to do that. Good day to you." (FK: M -10)

After he closes the door you realise that you must either reverse time and try something else with him, or attempt to sneak in **turn to 320**

If you have exhausted your options, you travel back to the present **turn to 13**

478

Realising there is only one way to end all this, you quickly take off your amulet and give it to your fiancée.

"You need to put this on," you tell her.

"What are you doing?" she says. "That's your only protection from the man in black. He'll leave me and go into you."

"That's what I'm counting on. Look, there's no way I'm getting out of this room, but if you're no longer possessed, you can leave this place. Please do as I say. There isn't much time."

She cries as she takes the amulet from you and puts it round her neck.

"I'll come back for you," she says.

"Go!" you say.

She is hesitant at first but soon turns and runs. You are glad to have succeeded in what you set out to do. You have no doubt that your fiancée will come out of this all right, but you feel disappointed that you couldn't go with her. You know that making the sacrifice was the only way though and feel like in some ways this had been a big win for you. As you sit and wait, the man in black starts to seep back into you, but you don't care because with no way out of here, besides beyond the wall, he won't be hurting anyone anytime soon. And once the house is gone, he won't hurt anyone again.

THE END

Or is it?

Congratulations you have completed the **'SACRIFICE'** ending. You may have reached the end of this current adventure, but there are still multiple paths you could try. If you haven't already, why not start again and try to complete one of the other 5 endings.

Please now turn to the final page for news on future adventure books

## 479
(330)

Sneaking into the house, you make it down the stairs and into the cellar. Here you find the breaker box on the back wall. After a few minutes have passed, you pull the lever. One by one the lights go out, and then moments later, you hear several gun shots. So much for doing this clean and quietly, you think to yourself. You soon leave the cellar, and go into the main house to find Gil dead and all of his jewellery taken, including that special diamond the gangster particularly wanted.

**Unfortunately if you intended to save Gil, or prevent the gangster who killed him from seeing the noose, you have failed.**

Unless you know of anywhere else to go in this time, you return to the present **turn to 13**

## 480
(382)

"Excuse me!" you shout up, "Sorry to bother you, but..."

Unfortunately that is all you get to say, because no sooner have you spoken, than with a look of shock, the maid spins round, and losing her footing on the ladder, tumbles to the ground and knocks herself unconscious. (FK: C2-22) You are considering going to see if she is alright, when you see the butler charging towards you, angrily. Not wanting to risk any further trouble, you flee the scene and head into town.

**Turn to 39**

## 481

**If you haven't done so already, deduct £10 from your money.**

Upon touching your hand, the medium suddenly goes into a trance and speaks in a voice that sounds very different from her own.

"When the end is near and the fire creates a divide between you and the one you love, you must be willing to make the ultimate sacrifice. An action of three words is required. Those words are to be found within the passage itself. Thinking back to your first night in that house will help. The first word is a gesture. The second a title. The third an object. With each of these words you will find a number. Put these in order. If your action makes sense, the numbers will tell you where to go next."

After she is done, you thank the fortune teller for her reading and either:

Return to the shop **turn to 532**
Or return to the town **turn to 444**

**482**
(359 x2 (Via carriage), 360 (Via maid) 505 (Via FK: D8)

As you step into the antiques store, you soon find Ruth and Peter talking in a corner. You head to a shelf nearby and make out that you're browsing, while you spy on them. At first everything seems quite normal. The two of them seem to be looking at rings and talking quite happily. You find yourself temporarily distracted for a moment, when you hear a busker playing 'Early One Morning' in the street. You always liked that tune, and it sounds particularly beautiful being played on pan pipes. Moments later, a tall grey haired man with a square jaw, enters the store. As he passes Ruth, she looks up at him and he smiles. You expect that she might return this gesture, but instead she simply stares at him, completely blank faced, as if she is in some kind of trance. This awkward encounter is then interrupted by the antiques dealer.

"Ah, Mr Reardon," he says. "How can I help you."

"I'm looking for a present for my wife," says Reardon.

You then quickly turn your attention back to Ruth and Peter, as it seems her strange behaviour has reached a new level. For no reason that you can see, she seems to have burst into tears and as Peter goes to comfort her, she pushes him away and marches out of the store.

You can now use Future Knowledge A8

Or **turn to 21**

**483**

Entering the Tobacconist, you feel completely out of place. Being a non-smoker and having a fiancée who is also a non-smoker, makes this the last place you would think to set foot in, but one thing you have learnt from reading Sherlock Holmes, is that the tobacconist can be a prime source of information.

"Can I help you?" asks a small tanned gentleman with a foreign accent.

"Yes, I wonder if you can. I'm looking for information on the murders that happened in this town a year ago."

"Sorry," the man says. "I'm afraid I can't help you with that. I only took over this shop seven months ago. Is there anything else I can help you with?"

You can now use Future Knowledge B2

Or return to the town **turn to 488**
**If you have already used Future Knowledge B2, you can mark down The Tobacconist as complete, as you will have no need to revisit this place.**

## 484
### (470)

The Bookshop is so crammed with books on the shelves and in piles on the floor, that there is barely room to walk around. While Liz moves off into a corner of the shop to look at books on art and textiles, you take the opportunity to look for books on ghosts and the paranormal. Whilst looking in one particular book called: 'Mysteries of the Unknown,' you find a very interesting article.

*Whereas many believe it is true that some ghosts could possess the living, there are some cultures that believe that certain amulets could be used to prevent this from happening. One such amulet is the Amulet of Teraka, as shown in the diagram below. (FK: D +10)*

You are considering reading more, until Liz comes over and joins you.
"Mysteries of the Unknown?" she says, reading over your shoulder. "I didn't know you were into that sort of thing."
"I'm not," you say as you close the book abruptly. "It just caught my eye."
You decide to leave, before she starts to get suspicious.

**Turn to 286**

## 485

Shining the torch over the pond, you notice that the thing floating in the water is actually a body of a young woman. Ruth, you assume. You consider wading in to take a closer look, but think better of it. She's already dead, and you'd only get drenched and covered in her blood. You are about to leave the area, when you spot something shiny in the grass. You turn your torch towards it, and find that it is a knife, covered in blood. (FK: P -14). It strikes you that this is very likely to be the murder weapon. Horrified and excited at the same time, you decide to wrap it in a piece of your clothing and take it with you.

You now return to the house **turn to 418**
**If you have chosen to hide here turn to 271**

### 486

Shining your torch around, you notice a star shaped hole in the wall. Something tells you that it is a lock for a key to fit into. If you have such a key you may be able to open it.

If you have a star shaped key **turn to 390**

**If you still wish to catch the rat, you must have two objects. When you find the items, mark down both of the passage numbers you find them at, then return here and take the lower number away from the higher to find the number you must turn to. Once you have caught the rat, upon returning to this passage you must ignore this paragraph.**

Otherwise you can return to the house **turn to 13**

**If you return to the house, mark down the number of this passage as a shortcut for The Cellar. When visiting here you will be able to come to this shortcut instead of the original number written on your navigation list.**

### 487
### (167)

Following Ruth's father, eventually leads you to a workshop located through the trophy room upstairs. You stop at the side of the door and peek around the corner as Ruth's father sits down and gets back to work. As you watch, he picks up a flat, wooden carving of a cat, and begins to paint a number 2 onto it. You notice that there are two other wooden carvings on the table. One is a dog and the other a rabbit. Neither of these appear to have numbers on yet. As the father moves to another part of the work shop, you consider if you should try and grab the carvings, as they could prove useful to you in your own time.

If you attempt to steal them **turn to 24**
If you prefer not to take the risk, you travel back to the present **turn to 13**

You arrive in the centre of town in 1898. A year after the murders occurred at Craven Manor. Some things look the same, but there are a lot of differences, the most notable being that where the book shop stands in your time, there is a tobacconist. There is also a butcher where the grocers used to be. It is here you have landed outside. Looking in through the window, you see a big man with a grisly beard serving customers. You turn and walk into the centre of town, wondering where you should look first. This is probably the perfect place to talk to the residents and possibly find out the identity of the Craven Manor Killer. You can now move freely round the 1800s town.

## TOWN NAVIGATION LIST
### (1800s)

Below you will find a list of shops and buildings in the surrounding town you can visit whilst in this time. If this is your first time here, after checking five locations you must **turn to 204.** Until then you are not allowed to time jump.

Hotel **turn to 112**
Antiques Store **turn to 334**
The Butchers **turn to 211**
Police Station **turn to 473**
Pub **turn to 67**
Clothes Store **turn to 400**
Tobacconist **turn to 483**

(The following buildings cannot be accessed until you have the necessary CMIP beside it)

**Building A  (Need CMIP L) turn to 79**
**Building B  (Need CMIP M) turn to 65**
**Building C  (Need CMIP N) turn to 376**
**Building D  (Need CMIP O) turn to 143**
**Building E  (Need CMIP P) turn to 420**
**Building F  (Need CMIP Q) turn to 475**
**Building G  (Need CMIP R) turn to 54**

Return to the Present **turn to 13**

## 489

In this time, the living room seems more spacious. This may be because there is less furniture and far less clutter. The fire is lit, which gives the room a warm, bright glow. As you look around, you notice the smell of burnt paper, and turn towards the fireplace to see a single burnt fragment of a letter, lying on the ground. You decide to pick it up and see what it says. Most of it is burnt away, but you can make out the last couple of sentences.

*I will not stand idly by while you forbid me from seeing your daughter. Unless we can come to some sort of arrangement, then I will have no choice but to convince her to come away with me.*

*Peter*

**(FK: B4 part 3 of 3 +8)Note that you need to find all parts to get the right sum to add or subtract when the time comes to use the future knowledge)**

You now return to the house **turn to 418**
**If you have chosen to hide in this room turn to 271**

## 490
### (475)

"Yes, that would be nice," you say.

He disappears for a few moments and then returns to hand you a glass of red wine. You take a sip. It tastes pretty good quality. Not really what you would expect a taxidermist to be able to afford.

"So what would you like to ask me?" he says as he sits down.

You ask him a whole array of questions, ranging from where he was on the night of the murder, to how he knew the Craven family. The answers he gives are similar to those of most people who did not know the family very well. You are about to ask him some questions about himself when the bell rings at the front of the shop.

"Can you believe it?" he says, sounding frustrated. "No customers all day, and now one decides to come in. Sorry about this. I shouldn't be too long."

As soon as the taxidermist has left, you consider what you should do next.

If you explore the living room **turn to 12**
If you move further into the house **turn to 200**
If you leave **turn to 14**
Or you can use Future Knowledge D1

"Here you go," you say as you hand the money over to the man.

"Much obliged," the antiques dealer says graciously. "Do you want to wait for it, or would you prefer to come back later?"

"I'll wait," you say.

"Very well," he says. "Take a seat. It shouldn't take too long."

**Deduct £3 from your money**.

It actually takes less than an hour and when he is done, you leave with your key. By the time you have returned to the butchers, you find that he is already closing the shop. You wait around the corner, and as soon as you see him leave to go to the pub, you run over to the door and try your new key. It works perfectly, then once you are inside, you head through the back of the shop and enter his house.

**Turn to 2**

Remembering something from Ruth's diary, you have a sudden thought. What if Ruth's reaction was not to something that happened inside the antiques store, but rather to something she heard outside.

*I still have those nightmares where I'm being chased by a shadowy figure, while pan pipe music plays in the background.*

Pan pipe music! Perhaps hearing it in the antiques store, reminded her of the terrible incident that caused those nightmares in the first place. You stop and focus on the music outside, wondering if it might be the pan pipes, the tune, or the person playing them, that is of particular significance to her. Could it be all three? Then you have a shocking revelation, because you remember seeing a set of panpipes, not too long ago, on the mantelpiece of a man who saved you from drowning. The butcher!

((FK: B7 part 2 of 4 -7). Note that you need to find all parts to get the right sum to add or subtract when the time comes to use the future knowledge)

Add CMIP K. This will allow you to return to The Butchers and investigate further.

**Turn to 21**

In the pond you notice something floating in the water. The whole area is pitch black, so you have difficulty seeing anything else.

You now return to the house **turn to 418**
**If you have chosen to hide here turn to 271**

Opening the door, leads you down a flight of stairs into a cold dusty cellar. It is pitch black so you cannot see a thing, but you can hear something scurrying along the floor. Then you hear a squeak. A rat! Part of you wants to run in fright, but upon considering everything else you have seen so far, you realise a rat isn't as frightening as it once was. In fact, this rat might prove useful if you were able to catch it.

**In order to catch the rat, you must have two objects. When you find the items, mark down both of the passage numbers you find them at, then return here and take the lower number away from the higher to find the number you must turn to. Once you have caught the rat, upon returning to this passage you must ignore this paragraph.**

If you are done in this room you now return to the house **turn to 13**

**If you return to the house, mark down the number of this passage as a shortcut for The Cellar when you return.**

"Actually, there is something you can help me with," you say, as you hand him the cigarette butt you took from Craven Manor on the night of the murder. "Is there any way of finding out what brand of cigarette this is."
  The man looks at the butt and then sniffs it.
  "I know this brand," he says. "It is gold leaf."
  "Do you have any regular customers who smoke this brand?"
  "Are you a policeman?"
  "No, I'm what you might call a consulting detective," you say with a smug grin. "I'm working with the police."

"Very well. I know of three customers who buy this brand. I will get you their details."

He writes down the names and addresses of the three customers and hands it to you. You thank him for his help and then look at the piece of paper. (FK: B3-94)

The names are Peter Kline, Kenny Harkness and Ray Reardon

**Add CMIP M. This will give you access to Building B/1800s Town (Peter Kline's address)**

**Add CMIP O. This will give you access to Building D/1800s Town (Kenny Harkness's address.)**

**Add CMIP R. This will give you access to Building G/1800s Town (Reardon's Gambling Den.)**

You now return to the town turn to 488

## 496
### (456)

"No, I don't think I'm going to do that," you say in response to being told to drop your gun.

"Do you really want this woman's death on your conscience?" Bob says.

"Not really, but then I don't believe your man is going to shoot her."

"And what makes you so sure of that?"

"Because she's your accomplice. I saw you together not five minutes ago. She let you in through the back door."

"Beatrice, is this true?" asks Gil, not questioning the fact that from his point of view you have been with him this whole time.

"Mr Murdock I..." she stumbles, as she attempts to defend herself.

"After everything I've done for you," he says disappointedly.

"So you see, there really is no incentive for me to put my gun down," you say. "Look I'm going to make a suggestion. The way I see it, no harm has been done yet, so if you and your group turn around and leave the way you came, you can be long gone before the police arrive."

"And if I refuse?"

"Then I'm sure there will be bullets and blood, possibly mine, possibly yours, but either way you won't be getting that diamond."

"Well this is not how I intended this to go at all," Bob says. "Come on you lot. It looks like we're going to have to let this one go."

The four of them then leave.

"You go with them too, Beatrice," says Gil. "There is no place here for you any longer."

With her head hung low, the maid follows the gang out of the house.

"I don't know how to thank you," says Gil. "You saved my property and my life. Will you accept some kind of payment?"

"Don't worry about it," you tell him.

"No, you must have something for your trouble, I insist."

He then takes out a box of precious stones that he holds out to you.

"Take one," he says, "As a symbol of my thanks to you."

You can now use Future Knowledge E9 (Using 121 as the passage number instead of 496)
Or **turn to 448**

### 497

Lifting the picture down, reveals a hidden safe. It requires a six number combination.

**If you know what this combination is, then take the first three numbers away from the last three and then subtract the number of this paragraph to find where you should turn to next.**

If you don't know the safe combination, you can either look in the drawer **turn to 138**
Or leave and return to the house **turn to 13**

### 498

Believing in your heart that Peter is the killer, you take his throat in your hands and choke the life out of him. Soon he crumples to the ground. After that, you return to the present. Unfortunately, you find much to your dismay that nothing has changed. Ghosts still roam the halls, and Liz is still possessed. Peter was obviously not the killer. You have murdered an innocent man for no reason at all.

**You will not be able to return to the date of the murder again or the 1800s town, so you will have to find some other way to stop the man in black.**

You now return to the house **turn to 13**

## 499

You now find yourself outside of Craven Manor on the night of the murder. You have limited time before the killings begin, so you need to find a way into the house.

If you attempt to force a window **turn to 240**
If you attempt to climb the Trellis **turn to 17**
Or you can use Future Knowledge C3

## 500
### (2)

Searching the living room, brings on feelings of guilt. You remember sitting by the fire not too long ago, talking to the butcher after he had saved you from drowning. Now here you are, searching for evidence that might condemn him to life imprisonment, or possibly death. You find nothing new in this room, except the pan pipes that made you suspect the butcher in the first place. You decide to leave these where they are for now and move on.

If this is the first place you checked **turn to 370.**
If it is the second **turn to 458**
If it is the third **turn to 417**

## 501
### (136 x2)

**Now roll a dice to determine where the man in black will look next.**

**If you roll:**

**1-3- He checks your location**
**4-6- He checks the last remaining other location**

**If he rolls your location, he catches you and you have no choice but to reverse time. If you can't do this, he saps your life force away until you are nothing more than a soulless husk.**

**If you do reverse time, you do not need to travel back to the previous paragraph if you simply want to change your hiding place. Instead minus 2TTP and continue as if you had successfully hid. However, if you wish to reverse time to avoid going into the study, feel free to return to the previous passage.**

If you successfully hid or reversed time and did so, you can attempt to leave.

Roll one die.

You may add up to 2TTP to ensure your roll is higher.

If you roll 4 or over, you manage to leave the room without being caught.

If you succeed, you can either, run to the toilets **turn to 327**
Or run towards the ballroom **turn to 449**
If you do not succeed **turn to 154**

## 502
(420)

As you let yourself inside, you find that the house seems completely empty. Then you notice a gust of wind blowing in from the back room. Upon investigating this, you find an open window, and look out of it to see the man you spoke to at the door, charging into the distance. (FK: D9+19)

If you go after him **turn to 146**
If you let him go, you return to the town **turn to 488**
**You can now mark down Building E as complete, as you will have no need to revisit this place.**

## 503
(151)

Running up the crates successfully, brings you onto the rooftops with the thief. He is still not close enough to catch, but you stand a better chance of getting him now. You see a causeway of several rooftops ahead that you must follow him over. To continue after him, you are going to need to be both fast and agile.

**Roll the die, seven times and try to roll the following numbers in order.**

1, 4, 3, 2, 3, 6, 4.

**Now normally this would be close to impossible, since the odds of rolling all those numbers perfectly is very unlikely, but you have the ability of time travel. With each roll you make that is not exact, you can use up to 2TTP to either speed up or slow down your jumps. That means that for each roll that is not exact, you can either**

minus 1-2 or plus 1-2 to your roll to make the jump. Whether you make the jump or not, you then move onto the next number. You are allowed to make three mistakes.

If you succeed in making your way across the rooftops with three mistakes or less **turn to 81**
If not, you lose him and return to the town **turn to 488**
**You can mark down Building E as complete, as you will have no need to revisit this place.**

504

(54)

As you climb the stairs leading to Reardon's office, you try to come up with a suitable cover story for why you would be asking questions about the Craven Manor Massacre. Upon reaching the top, you are met by two of Reardon's, tough looking, employees.

"I'm here to see Reardon," you say.

"Do you have an appointment?" one of them, a bulldog faced man, asks.

"No," you reply, "but I think he'll want to see me anyway. Tell him it's about the murder of the Cravens."

The man then disappears inside for a few moments, before he returns to open the door for you.

"The boss will see you now," he says.

You enter the office to find a tall grey haired man with a square jaw, sitting comfortably at the desk with a glass of whiskey in his hand.

"And who might you be?" he asks.

"My name is David Ingram and I'm a freelance detective working with the police," you say as confidently as you can.

"And what brings you to my establishment?"

You then go ahead with the story you made up on the way here.

"In going over some past notes from the Craven Manor Massacre, I have uncovered some new evidence that has caused me to reconsider questioning previous suspects."

"Well I can only tell you what I've told the police already. I knew nothing about those murders until I heard about them the following day. It is true that I wasn't on the best of terms with Nicholas Craven, but that was just all to do with business."

"What kind of business?"

"Before I say anything else, I think I would like to see some sort of identification."

"I'm afraid I don't have any on me," you say, realising that you will get nothing more out of Reardon now.

"I thought that might be the case," he smirks. "You're not really a detective are you? I knew from the moment you stepped into my office."

"Then why talk to me?"

"Because I was curious what you might know, but it seems you know very little, so this conversation is at an end. My men will escort you out."

"That will not be necessary," you say. "I can see myself out."

After leaving, you hear Reardon talking to one of his men.

If you decide to eavesdrop **turn to 193**

Otherwise, you can go to the Gambling Den **turn to 289**

Or return to the town **turn to 488**

**Note that if you return to the town, you give up your attempts to find out more about Reardon and help the woman's husband.**

**Add CMIP T. This will allow you to return to Reardon's Gambling Den just for gambling purposes.**

## 505
### (359)

Remembering the outcome of this fight from the future, and the fact you can open an account to keep your winnings in, you see an opportunity here to make a lot of money. The minimum bet is £50.

If you have £50 and wish to make a bet, with the intention of having your winnings paid into an account that you can pick up ten years from now **turn to 198**

If not, you wait for Peter to finish his business here and follow him and Ruth to the antiques store **turn to 482**

## 506
### (172)

"I would like a room for the night, please," you ask.

"A single or a double?" the manager asks.

"Just a single please."

The hotel owner seems reluctant to take your money at first, but does so and hands you a key.

**You must deduct £10 from your money.**

"Here you go," he says. "Checkout is at eleven tomorrow morning."

After finding your room, you explore the rest of the hotel and discover that the manager's personal quarters are only a few doors down from yours. How do you intend to get in there?

If you climb out of the window of your room and attempt to edge round to there **turn to 451**

If you have a lock picking kit and wish to use it **turn to 227**

## 507

(116 x6)

Following the couple into town, you hide once again, as Ruth, in a now muddy dress, and Peter, come to a stop outside of the front door of a detached house.

"So this is where you live," Ruth says.

"It's not much," says Peter, "but it's home."

As they step inside, you realise you will no longer be able to eavesdrop, so you wait around, hoping that they will leave again, so you can pick up listening where you left off. A few minutes pass, and you happen to notice a spindly looking boy, with a hooked nose, come to the house and begin peering through a crack in the curtains. At first the expression 'Peeping Tom' comes to mind, until you remember what you've been doing ever since you arrived in this time. You do find this person intriguing though, and are interested to know why he is watching. You consider approaching him, when the curtains are suddenly pulled back, and Peter looks out at the boy, with a look of disgust on his face. The boy turns to run, but before he can get very far, the front door flies open and Peter comes charging out after him, tackling him round the midriff and bringing him to the ground.

"Why were you peering through my window," Peter shouts, pushing the other boy's face into the ground. "Were you spying on us?"

"No," the boy says. "I saw Ruth go into your house and I just wanted to make sure she was all right."

"She doesn't need you to look out for her Kenny. You're not her knight in shining armour."

"What's going on," you hear Ruth say as she comes to join them.

"This perverted youth was watching us through the window," Peter says.

"What!" Ruth says angrily.

"It's not what you think," Kenny says. "I saw the mud on your dress before you went in, and I thought something may have happened to you."

"I fell over, that's all. Besides, it's none of your business."

"Of course it is. We're friends."

"Kenny, we haven't been friends since... Well not for a long time. Please do me a favour and stop following me around, or else I'm going to have to inform the police."

She then walks off and returns to the house. When she is gone, Peter pulls Kenny to his feet.

"Look, I know you were acquitted of all charges regarding what happened a few years back, but I am still not entirely convinced. Go near her again and I'll kill you."

As Peter returns to his house, Kenny watches him go with a look of hatred in his eyes. **(FK: B6 part 2 of 3 -60) Note that you need to find all parts to get the right sum to add or subtract when the time comes to use the future knowledge)** You then watch as Kenny returns home to a house across the street.

**Add CMIP M. This will give you access to Building B/1800s Town (Peter Kline's address)**
**Add CMIP O. This will give you access to Building D/1800s Town (Kenny Harkness's address.)**

After witnessing this, you return to the present **turn to 13**

## 508

Suddenly the defeatist goes out of you and you find yourself fighting to take control of your own body, you know you don't need long, just long enough to take the wall down into the next room. You swing the sledgehammer with all the strength you can muster, and after three strokes, the wall crumbles to reveal the miscellaneous room where you first time jumped. You know that from here you can reach the conservatory, but there's just one problem. The fire is blocking your way. You try to knock down the back wall leading into the garden, but unfortunately, it is far too thick. It seems you have broken your way out of one foxhole to find yourself in another. Unless you can find some way to escape this room, your efforts may have been for nothing.

Your only way out of here is to have Future Knowledge G2

If you do not have this, at least you tried.

THE END

Or is it?

Congratulations you have completed the 'CLOSE' ending. You may have reached the end of this current adventure, but there are still multiple paths you could try. If you haven't already, why not start again and try to complete one of the other 5 endings.

Please now turn to the final page for news on future adventure books.

### 509
#### (29)
"It's not what it looks like," you explain. "She attacked me."

"Have no fear," says the father. "I know very well what she is capable of. That's why I had her locked up. Not just so she didn't harm herself, but others too. You must be the secret policeman that young peter here told me about."

"That's right," you say.

"I appreciate your concern for my daughter, but I can deal with things from here," he says. "Now move aside."

You step back as the father goes to restrain Ruth, hoping that when he is done he will explain what is going on.

"He told me everything," says Peter. "It appears that I've been wrong about this the whole time."

It seems that Peter is about to say more, when all of a sudden you catch a glimpse of movement in the corner of your eye, and turn to see, much to your horror, Ruth attacking her father and wrestling with him for his gun. There is a loud bang and her father falls back clutching his chest.

"Ruth! No!" shouts Peter.

But before he can get near to her, she shoots him too. Then she turns the gun on you and fires.

**Roll two dice.**

**You may add up to 2TTP to ensure your roll is higher.**

If you manage to roll 8 or over **turn to 428**
Otherwise, I am afraid your adventure ends here.

### 510
#### (340)
You follow him up the ladder, and have barely gotten to the top, when he shoves the ladder away from the building and you feel your stomach turn, as you find yourself falling back. Fortunately your fall is not fatal. Some crates below break your fall, but you have definitely lost the thief now.

You now return to the town **turn to 488**
**You can now mark down Building E as complete, as you will have no need to revisit this place.**

**511**

Entering the room, you find an empty bath with an interesting item inside. It is a flat, red, wooden carving in the shape of a rabbit with a number 8 painted on it. You can take this if you wish.

You now return to the house **turn to 13**
**Mark down The Bathroom as complete, as you will have no need to revisit this place.**

**512**

Climbing through the vent, you find a small room which you believe could be Miscellaneous Room Two. It doesn't take you long to find the source of the smell, and when you do, you leap back in fright. In the corner of the room is the corpse of a young man, slumped against the wall. He is wearing a black leather jacket, and in his lap is a handheld camcorder. By the looks of him, and what you know about decomposing corpses, you believe he could have only been dead a few years. The stink is unbearable, but curious as you are, you decide to pick up the camcorder and see what he may have recorded. Wiping off the maggots, euughhh! You turn the camcorder on, flip out the screen and rewind it part way before pressing play. You recognise the person on the tape as being the same one dead in the room with you.

*"Is it recording? Okay, my name is Phil Barnett and I am here at Craven Manor. My parents were John and Hayley Barnett, who both died in this very house. The reports said that my mother killed my father and then killed herself, but I did not believe that then, and I do not now. I knew that my parents were very happy together and there was no way either of them would do anything like that, so I decided to investigate the matter myself. After researching the house, I learnt that there had been several reports of strange things happening there, going as far back as last century. I suspected that the house might be haunted, so I decided to go and find out for myself. Joining a group of student film-makers, I came to the house with the intentions of capturing video footage of paranormal activity, so I could use it to remove the shame on my family name. (FK: F1-127).*

*"We have only been here a few days and already we have seen more than enough evidence to prove that my theories are correct. I have not only seen the ghosts of my parents, who*

275

*confirm that they died on the 20/9/2009, but I have also seen the ghosts of several other victims, including a young woman from the 1800s, who I suspect, may be the first person to die in this house. So far I have surmised that the most haunted rooms in the house, are the dining room, the bathroom, the ballroom and the attic."*

After this there is a lot of talking amongst the crew themselves that you do not find particularly interesting, so you forward through to later in the tape.

*"Unfortunately, even though we have been successful in capturing footage, we are unable to get it out of the house. We've tried to escape, but for some reason the doors are all supernaturally sealed. Our phones don't appear to be working either, so there is no way we can contact the outside world."*

You forward on again

*"Things have unfortunately taken a rather horrific turn. As well as the victims of all of those people who died in this house, there is a much darker entity that comes in the night. The first time it appeared, we were able to ward it off with the supernatural lore we knew, but last night it possessed the boom mike operator Calvin and came after us in its new physical form. It killed Josh, and it would have killed me too, if I hadn't... Now they're both dead, and I know if I ever get out of this, that people will think that I did it. That is why I have decided to bury them in the garden beside the gazebo. (FK: J +30) Now all I can do is hide from this thing until it comes for me. Perhaps I won't give it a chance."*

The video ends with him taking out a bottle of pills and pouring all of them into his mouth. Then very slowly he falls asleep, moments before the tape runs out. Only now do you perceive that the door is bolted shut from the inside. You realise he must have come to this room to hide and had been too frightened to attempt to leave. Feeling like a bit of a ghoul, you find yourself going through his pockets for anything useful and pulling out £15 in change. If you choose to keep the money, you can, as well as the camcorder, which is small enough to fit into your pocket.

You now return to the house **turn to 13**
**Mark down Bedroom Three and Miscellaneous Room Two as complete, as you will have no need to revisit either of these places. You must also remove Future Knowledge F5, as you will have no need of this.**

## 513

(145)

The spotlight leads you to the centre of the room and then comes to a sudden halt. There appears to be nothing in the spot it has led you to. You wait for a few moments, wondering if it will start moving again, when you hear a noise above you, and look up just in time to see that one of the chandelier's has come loose and is falling in your direction.

**Roll two dice**

**You may add up to 2TTP to ensure your roll is higher**

If your roll is 9 or higher, you manage to avoid it.

If your roll is below 9, the chandelier crushes you and you have one final chance to reverse time or bleed to death.

You now return to the house **turn to 13**

**If you survive the falling chandelier, you see no reason to revisit this room in the near future. Do not mark it as complete. You may need to return there later.**

## 514

Draining the bath reveals an item, a flat, red wooden carving with a number painted on it. You go to pick it up, but unfortunately no sooner have you touched it, than the bath once again fills with blood and from that blood emerges a hand, followed by an arm, followed by the upper half of a blood covered figure. As the figure rises to their full height, you see that it is a woman in an evening dress with a 50s, Doris Day style, haircut. (FK: F6 +252) She shrieks like a banshee and reaches for you, her sinewy and rotting hands outstretched. Luckily you pull back just in time. As she climbs out of the bath, you quickly leave the room and slam the door behind you. For a few moments you feel like she might follow you, but the door remains closed. It seems that whatever haunts that room probably can't leave. Unfortunately, in the commotion, you dropped the red wooden carving, so if you wish to go back for it, you will first have to find a way to get rid of this vengeful spirit. While the ghost is still in there, you will not be allowed to return to this room.

You now return to the house **turn to 13**

## 515
### (529)

Remembering about your current task in the present to discover whose fingerprints were on the murder weapon, you decide now might be a good opportunity to take something of Peter's that may have his fingerprints on. Out of the choice of a tobacco pouch, a book and a pair of glasses; the glasses seem the best choice, so you quickly grab them and slide them into your pocket. **Add the glasses to your inventory**.

**Do not remove FK: D1, as you may use it again later.**

You can now use Future Knowledge B3 **(If you do, you must use 529 as the number you subtract from or add to, rather than the passage number above)**

Otherwise, you wait for peter to return with the tea.

**Turn to 192**

## 516

Shining the torch towards the back of the room, you find a bunch of boxes with more junk in. You look through each of them in turn, but find that there is nothing of use in any of them. It almost feels like looking here has been a complete waste of time.

If you haven't already, you can go to the junk to look for something useful **turn to 522**
Or return to the town **turn to 444**

## 517
### (190)

Taking the pill from your pocket, you find the woman's husband once again and hand it to him.

"Grace wanted you to take this before the fight," you say.

"What is it?"

"It'll numb your pain," you say, remembering his reluctance to take it last time.

"Well if Grace thinks I should take it, who am I to argue?" he says as he takes the pill from you and swallows it in a single gulp.

Moments later, the pill starts to take effect, and when you see Reardon coming to investigate, you decide to take the opportunity to sneak back into his office. Once inside, you lift the statue of Nelson and discover that there is a hidden compartment in the shelf underneath. Inside this you find architectural plans for a big hotel, which you notice resembles the structure of Craven Manor. What amazes you most, is that these plans are dated before the family were even killed.

**(FK: B8 Part 2 of 3 + 21) Note that you need to find all parts to get the right sum to add or subtract when the time comes to use the future knowledge)**

You now return to the town **turn to 488**

### 518

You pull open the wardrobe doors, hoping to find something useful, but it is completely empty. You then decide to feel around the back for a possible secret door, but still nothing.

If you wish to check in the drawers **turn to 161**
If you wish to check under the bed **turn to 445**
Or you can return to the house **turn to 13**

### 519

When the phantom baby is finally defeated, you almost feel a little bad, because even though it was a monster of a thing, you know it had once been a baby. Wiping your brow, you go to the cot and find a bunch of screwed up pages that look like they may have been torn out of a journal. As you read them to yourself, you are surprised how enlightening they are.

*That incident in the woods on the 23/07 has changed me forever. Even though I wash myself three times a day, I still feel dirty and ashamed. My father won't even look at me. It's almost like he believes I actually wanted this. My mother is different. I can tell she is in denial and only sees the good in the child, that I will one day soon bring to bear. She has even made up a nursery in the corner of my room. If they could only understand how I feel. My brother and sister don't understand what is going on. They think I was just beaten up in the woods by some crazy person. They don't understand that there are other meanings for being attacked.*

*The baby was born a few days ago, but my father does not want anyone to know about it, because of the shame it would bring on our family name. As such, he has forbidden me from leaving the house, and has built a partition between my room and the nursery my mother put together. He says it is only temporary, until he can come up with a suitable way to explain the baby's existence. His plan is to take it away secretly with my mother, on a six month trip to the country. Then upon returning, he will announce that my mother had the child whilst they were away. I'm really not so sure how much more of this I can take.*

*Last night an angel came to me. She called herself Megan and told me that she was here to save me. I asked her how, and she said that she knew of a way in which she could take over my body for a time until I felt ready to return; that she would get me through this troubling time. She said I would have three days to make my decision, but my mind is already made up. Tonight I will tell her that I intend to make the deal, and I hope that when I return, things will be different.*

*I came back today to discover that my baby is dead. Megan smothered her in her cot before attempting to kill herself. My father stopped her from doing the latter. A good job too, because she would have also killed me, since we both share the same body. The worst thing is that because she did all this whilst in my body, everyone believes that I am to blame. Since then my father has confined me to my room, only coming to see me to bring me food. My brother and sister, who believe I am sick, come too sometimes, although I never see mother.*

*My father tells me that I will soon be receiving a visit from an alienist; a man who may be able to help me be rid of Megan once and for all. After what she has done, I would be more than happy to never see her again. Day by day, I can hear Megan whispering to me, telling me how she intends to make them all pay for what they did to us, how if she gains control again, she will not only kill them all, but will punish any man that ever lays his hand on me again.*

**(FK: B5 part 2 of 3 +7) Note that you need to find all parts to get the right sum to add or subtract when the time comes to use the future knowledge)**

Drawing your own conclusions from these revealing pages, you now return to the house **turn to 13**
**Mark down Bedroom Five as complete, as you will have no need to revisit this place.**

### 520
(81)

"Okay," you say, as you hand £50 to Fingers. "Here's half of the money you asked for. You'll get the other half when you bring me what I want."

"Fair enough," says the thief. "Meet me back here later this evening."

You then shake hands and part ways. The day then passes by and later that evening you meet back at his house.

"Did you get it?" you ask.

"I got it," he says as he shows you a roll of paper.

"Can I see it?"

"First I want the other half of my money."

Realising that you have no choice but to trust him, you hand over the other £50, and as promised he gives you the roll of paper. You unroll it to see that it is some sort of architectural plans for a hotel.

**Deduct £100 from your money.**

"I don't understand," you ask. "What am I looking at?"

"You're looking at Reardon's plans to turn Craven Manor into a luxury hotel."

"This doesn't mean anything. Now the family are dead, it's natural he would be interested in the house."

"Oh, I think you've overlooked one very important detail. Look at the date these plans were drawn up."

You do so, and are surprised by what you find.

"My god!" you exclaim. "these were dated months before the family even died."

"This means Reardon was planning on this long before he knew the house would even be up for sale," Fingers explains. "The disagreements he had with Nicholas Craven were probably over his failed attempt to convince the man to sell the house to him. The only thing that stood between Reardon and his hotel project..."

"Was the family who lived there," you say finishing his sentence.

"Which in my mind makes him a very likely suspect."

**(FK: B8 Part 2 of 3 + 21) Note that you need to find all parts to get the right sum to add or subtract when the time comes to use the future knowledge.**

"Thank you for your help, " you say.

"It sounds like you are going to need a lot more, before this is all done," says Fingers. "Unfortunately you will have to depend on your own breaking and entering skills from this point forward, because my thieving days are over. I always wanted out, but every time I tried, I just got myself in deeper. Now my debt has finally been paid, I finally have an opportunity to make a better life for myself."

"Good for you," you say.

"Here," he says, as he hands you a small box. "Since I will not be needing these anymore, I'm sure you can make use of them."

You open the box to find a set of lock picks.

**Add the lock picking set to your inventory. From this point on you can open any door in Craven Manor that requires a key. Whenever it says it requires a certain key, you can just continue on as if you have that key.**

You thank the thief for his parting gift, and then wish him luck in his new life before leaving his house.

You now return to the town **turn to 488**
**You can mark down Building E as complete, as you will have no need to revisit this place.**

**Add CMIP T. This will allow you to return to Reardon's Gambling Den just for gambling purposes.**

521

With one final powerful stroke from your sword, the suit of armour collapses into several pieces and you see the spirit inside flee into the house. The way is now clear for you to investigate the workshop. Unfortunately, as you approach the door, you find that it is locked and requires a particular key.

If you have the workshop key **turn to 5**
Otherwise, you can return to the house **turn to 13,** and come back when you do.

**If you return to the house, mark down the number of this passage as a shortcut for The Display Room when you return.**

522

**When returning to the town be sure to highlight Shortcut K. This means you will now be able to come straight to the briefcase from the navigation list.**

Looking through the junk, you find a smart looking briefcase. Unfortunately, the case is locked by a three-digit combination, but you do notice the name Dr Greenfield on the front. (FK: G1+73).

**If you know the combination, minus it from the number of this passage and turn to that number.**

You can now look further into the back **turn to 524**

Or return to the town **turn to 444**

### 523
(79)

"I'm investigating the murders at Craven Manor and wondered if you might be able to help me?"

Hannah opens the door slightly more.

"I already told the police all I knew about that."

If you tell her you believe the case links to her rape **turn to 170**
If you tell her that you're not with the police, and would just like to come in and talk **turn to 535**

### 524

Moving further into the back, you find that it is so pitch black that you cannot see a thing.

If you haven't already, you can go to the junk to look for something useful **turn to 522**
Or leave, and return to the town **turn to 444**

### 525

You instinctively pull the gun out and point it at the stranger.

"Don't come any closer or I'll shoot," you shout.

They look scared at first, until you pull the trigger accidentally and the revolver dry fires. You fire again but still nothing. The gun must be empty.

**You must now discard the gun as it is of no use to you**

**Turn to 527**

### 526

Using the metal detector around the area, you get very excited when you hear a beeping sound and look down to see a hatch. (FK: A9-85) You decide to try and open it. This takes a great deal of strength, but you just about manage it. As you pull back the door, you look down to see a ladder leading down into the dark. Having made the effort to open it, you decide to go down and see what waits for you below. With torch in hand, you clamber down the ladder and find yourself in a muddy tunnel. After walking for a few minutes, you eventually come to another ladder. You assume this will lead you to another hatch, and you are right, only, when you reach the top, you discover that it has been filled in by concrete. At this moment in time, you can go nowhere, but in the past that hatch may not always have been filled with concrete. With this in mind, you return to the hotel.

If you haven't already, you can look through the junk for something useful **turn to 522**
Or leave and return to the town **turn to 444**
**Once you have looked through the junk you can mark down The Hotel/Town as complete, as you will have no need to revisit this place.**

527

The stranger runs at you and tackles you to the ground. You both struggle for a while, and during that struggle, he loses his knife. You use this opportunity to get to your feet and face him in a hand to hand fight.

**You can now consult the rules of Combat at the back of the book. But be sure to make a note of this passage so you can return here after.**

**The fight will last twelve rounds.**

If you win **turn to 377**

528

"I was wondering if you knew anything about those murders that happened here a year ago?" you ask.

"You mean the massacre at Craven Manor?" the hotel manager replies.

"Yes."

"Why are you so interested?"

"I'm considering putting an offer in for the house," you improvise. "I heard it was for sale."

"Well you heard wrong. There's actually someone living there at the moment, a relative of the Cravens, I believe."

"Oh my mistake. I'd still be interested to know whatever you could tell me though, just in case the house becomes available down the line."

"I'm sorry but you're talking to the wrong person," the man says. "I barely knew the Cravens. I mostly keep to myself here. I wouldn't bother asking my son questions either."

"Why would I ask your son questions when I don't even know who he is?" you ask, confused.

"I'm sorry, but I'm very busy here today," he says impatiently. "Unless you are considering purchasing a room, I'm afraid I'm going to have to ask you to leave."

If you haven't already done so, you can now do one of the following:

Use Future Knowledge G1 (If you do this, the number you add or take away from must be 112)
Use Future Knowledge A7 (If you do this, the number you add or take away from must be 112)

Otherwise you return to the town **turn to 488**

**529**
(65)

Whilst Peter is making the tea, you take the opportunity to search around for anything that could help, either promote, or eliminate him as a possible suspect. Unfortunately you find very little, just a pair of reading glasses, a pouch of gold leaf tobacco, and a book about Scottish folk hero, Rob Roy.

You can now use Future Knowledge D1
You can now use Future Knowledge B3

Otherwise you wait for peter to return with the tea.

**Turn to 192**

**530**

Climbing in through the window, you find yourself in Kenny's bedroom. You do a quick scan and find a pen by his bedside table with a visible fingerprint.

**If you were using fingerprints to narrow down a possible suspect in the present, this may be a useful item to take back with you. Decide whether you intend to take it and continue reading.**

If you wish to search further **turn to 195**

If you wish to quit while you are ahead, you return to the town **turn to 488**

**You can now Mark down Building D/1800s Town as complete, as you will have no need to revisit this place.**

**531**

(164)

You decide to wait the rain out, hoping that it will soon pass, but it does not. In fact it develops into a storm, and soon you see a bolt of lightning strike a nearby tree, causing it to fall in the direction of the gazebo. You have only moments to get out before it crushes you to death.

**Roll two dice.**

**You may add up to 2TTP to ensure your roll is higher**

**If your roll is 9 or higher, you manage to get out of the way in time.**

**If your roll is lower, you can reverse time, although it will mean losing the TTP you managed to replenish. It will however mean that you can return here later.**

However, if you make it, you emerge into the rain.

**Restore TTP to full**

**(FK: F8 +67)**

You now return to the house **turn to 13**

**Mark down The Gazebo as complete, as you will have no need to revisit this place.**

**532**

Upon entering the Jewellery shop, you find that something has changed. There is a small section of the shop that is now occupied by a fortune-teller with a crystal ball.

If you go to see the fortune teller **turn to 391**

Otherwise in store you can buy the following:

Mysterious Amethyst stone-This stone when used will restore 4TTP. You can only use each one once. Discard after use (£25 each)

Mysterious Emerald Stone- This stone when used will restore 8TTP. You can only use each one once. Discard after use (£40 each)

Spirit boxes- These will trap the man in black inside temporarily. Whenever you encounter him you can automatically trap him for three rounds. This will mean you can check three rooms without having to roll the dice each time you leave. You can only use each one once. Discard after use. (£25 each)

Day and Night Stone- This stone will turn day into night and night into day automatically without having to time jump. You can only use each one once. Discard after use (£40 each)

When you are ready to leave, you return to the town **turn to 444**

**533**

(128)

Determined to save this woman from her attacker, you sprint over and drag him away from her. He soon fights back, and manages to break free of your hold, turning to face you. As his eyes meet yours, you see that they are completely black; proof that he is possessed by an evil spirit as you once were. He intends to fight you, and if you intend to save this woman, you will have to beat him.

**If you need to, you can now consult the rules of Combat at the back of the book. But be sure to make a note of this passage so you can return here after.**

**This fight will last six rounds**

If you win the fight **turn to 355**

**534**

Besides a few pin cushions, needles and thread, the sewing room has very little of interest.

You return to the house **turn to 418**
**If you have chosen to hide in this room turn to 271**

## 535
(79 x2)
"I'm not with the police," you say. "I just want to come in and talk."

She seems like she is considering letting you in, but can't quite make up her mind. Perhaps if you had something you could offer her as an incentive, that might clinch the deal.

If you have a bar of chocolate **turn to 396**

If you have a cigarette case **turn to 80**

If you have flowers **turn to 166**

If you have none of these things. You must either reverse time so that the conversation never took place, and return when you do have one of these things. Or you can return to the town now **turn to 488**

**If you decide to return to the town, you should mark down Building A/1800s Town as complete, as you will have no need to revisit this place.**

# RULES AND STATISTICS

# STATISTICS SHEET

| TTP | (10) | 10 | | | | | | | |
|---|---|---|---|---|---|---|---|---|---|
| **TIME JUMP RETURN TIME** | | DAY | NIGHT | DAY | NIGHT | DAY | NIGHT | DAY | NIGHT |

| TIME JUMP DATES | SHORT CUTS | CMIP |
|---|---|---|
| | | |

**MONEY**

**INVENTORY**

**SPECIAL POWERS**

## FUTURE KNOWLEDGE

| A | | A1 | | A2 | | A3 | | A4 | | A5 | | A6 | |
|---|---|----|---|----|---|----|---|----|---|----|---|----|---|
| A7 | | A8 | | A9 | | B | | B1 | | B2 | | B3 | |
| C | | C2 | | C3 | | C4 | | C5 | | C6 | | C7 | |
| C9 | | D | | D1 | | D2 | | D3 | | D4 | | D5 | |
| D6 | | D8 | | D9 | | E | | E1 | | E2 | | E3 | |
| E4 | | E5 | | E6 | | E7 | | E8 | | E9 | | F | |
| F1 | | F2 | | F3 | | F4 | | F5 | | F7 | | F8 | |
| G | | G1 | | G2 | | H1 | | I | | J | | K | |
| L | | M | | N | | O | | P | | Q | | T | |
| U | | V | | W | | X | | Y | | Z | | | |
| B4 1 2 3 | | B5 1 2 3 | | B6 1 2 3 | | B7 1 2 3 4 | | B8 1 2 3 | | B9 1 2 3 | | C1 1 2 3 | |
| C8 1 2 3 | | F8 1 2 | | S 1 2 3 | | | | | | | | | | | |

## ROOM COMPLETES AND OTHER NOTES

# RULES CONTENTS

### 1.    TIME TRAVEL POINTS (TTP)

**HOW TO USE TTP**

These allow you to travel back in time. You begin with 10 and must use 2 every time you want to jump back a single paragraph. Note that the number of the previous paragraph is bracketed under the number of the paragraph you are reading at the time.

Sometimes if there are multiple ways you could have reached that passage, there will be multiple numbers. Be sure to turn to the one that responds to the passage you just came from.

If a bracketed number has x2, x3 or x4 next to it, this means that the closest point you can return to is further back and will require you to multiply the amount of TTP you would usually use, to go back by that number.

Example: x2 = 4TTP 3x = 6TTP etc.

You will find items through your adventure that allow you to replenish your TTP, but unless otherwise specified you will not be able to exceed your initial score.

**SLOWING TIME WITH TTP**

You may also use TTP to slow time. In situations where you must react quickly, you can add up to 2pts to the roll. You can choose to add these points on after you have seen your roll.

## 2.    FUTURE KNOWLEDGE

Whilst progressing through this adventure, you will also see references regarding something called future knowledge. Future knowledge is something that you learn that can be used to open up new paths in the past and present. When you gain future knowledge you must write it down. It will appear as such: (FK: A+23) The FK stands for Future Knowledge, the letter is for reference, and the number is what you must add or subtract to the passage you are told you can use the Future Knowledge at, in order to find out what outcome using that knowledge has.

Throughout the game you will end up with a large list of Future Knowledge, so it is worth checking anytime you see a choice to use Future Knowledge, whether you already have it on your list.

Once you have used Future Knowledge, unless otherwise specified you must cross it out, to show you have used it.

### MULTIPLE PART FUTURE KNOWLEDGE

Much later on in your adventure, you will come across Future Knowledge that requires multiple parts to work. It will look something like this:

**(FK: Z8 part 1 of 2 +12) (Note that you need to find all parts to get the right sum to add or subtract when the time comes to use the future knowledge)**

Now normally when you reach the passage that would say you can now use Future Knowledge Z8, you would +12 to the passage number to find out which number to go to next, but because this particular FK has two parts, this will not work. So in order to make it work, you must find FK:Z8 part 2 of 2, and minus or plus both numbers from the passage number to figure out where to go next.

## 3.    AN IN GAME EXAMPLE OF USING BOTH TTP AND FK

**You come to a passage that says:**

712

While you are fighting the man with the knife, you feel a shiver come over you.

You can now use Future Knowledge Z9
Or turn to 653

**At this point you do not have Future Knowledge A on your list, so you have no choice but to turn to 653.**

653
(712 x3)

A man sneaks up on you and hits you from behind with a baseball bat (FK: Z9+23). Moments later, you wake up on the floor.

**Firstly you write down (FK: Z9+23). This is your future knowledge reference. You can guess in this instance that the future knowledge is that a man will sneak up on you with a baseball bat. What the future knowledge is, will not always be clear. It is up to you to figure that out.**

**Because you don't want your character to be surprised by a man with a baseball bat, you decide to reverse time to the previous paragraph which is 712 (As shown in the brackets underneath)**

**Now usually it would cost you 2TTP to travel back a single paragraph, but because the bracketed number shows x3 next to it (Because time has passed while you were unconscious) that means you must multiply that number by 3. Therefore you must use 6TTP to travel back.**

**You currently have 10TTP so you decide to use the 6 and mark it down to 4. This brings you back to the previous paragraph 712.**

712

While you are fighting the man with the knife, you feel a shiver come over you.

You can now use Future Knowledge Z9
Or turn to 653

Obviously if you turn to 653 you will end up being snuck up on again by the man with the baseball bat. When you first came here, that was your only option because you didn't know what was to happen, but now you know something you didn't before. You have Future Knowledge Z9. To use this knowledge (FK: Z9+23) you must +23 to the number of the paragraph you are currently on.

712 +23= 735 therefore to use the Future Knowledge you must turn to 735.

735

Knowing that there is someone sneaking up on you from behind, you duck. This causes your attacker with the baseball bat to miss you and hit the man with the knife instead, knocking him out cold.

So you see, by having the knowledge that the man was going to surprise you with his bat, you were able to reverse time and prevent it.

### 4.    TIME JUMPING

This is very different from time reversal as it allows you to transport your entire self to moments outside of your own history, rather than simply send your subconscious back into your body at an earlier time.

**Time jumps do not require TTP.**

To Time jump to a particular period, you will require a date to travel to. Each date that you are able to travel to has a secret set of coordinates that can be found by putting the numbers that appear in bold, in order. This is the number that you must turn to in order to time jump to that date. For example, the date that you read on the picture to bring you here was the 2/ 12/ 1954. Since the numbers 224 are in bold, these are the numbers you must turn to in order to travel to this date.

**Before time jumping, always make sure you have the necessary clothes before you leave. You can buy old fashioned clothes at the antiques shop in town.**

When visiting other times, you will be given a number of opportunities to leave and return to the present. Bear in mind, however, that you can only visit each date once unless otherwise stated, so if you leave too early you might miss out on something.

Of course, there is also the possibility that if you stay too long, you may outstay your welcome, so always consider both factors.

5.        **CHANGES MADE IN THE PAST (CMIP)**

Every time a significant change is made in the past it may affect a particular place in the future. To keep track of these changes you will be told something like this:

Add CMIP A. This affects The Ballroom.

This you mark down in your statistics under CMIP

To use it you must return to the original number of the area it has affected, as shown on your navigation list. All shortcuts for this area can be removed as they are now irrelevant.

Upon returning to the original number you find instructions that say: *If you have CMIP A, turn to --- immediately*, you must now turn to that number instead of reading on. From this point on this particular area will now permanently change to this number, until you are given new shortcuts or told it is complete.

6.        **COMBAT RULES**

If you are more interested in the story and puzzles rather than combat, you can choose to play a simpler game by allowing yourself to skip any fights you come to, and assume you have automatically won. Choosing to do this will make all special powers obsolete, and less need to recharge TTP. If this is your decision you can skip this tutorial and return to the number you were previously on. If you choose to go ahead with learning how the combat works, continue reading.

When engaging an enemy in a fight scenario you should draw a similar grid to the one below.

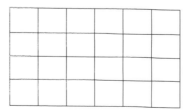

## GENERAL COMBAT

Each box represents a round of combat.

For each round of combat, you will throw two dice for you and your opponent. The highest roll wins. If you are the highest thrower, you must place an X in the box to show you have won, If your opponent is the highest thrower, you place an O in the box. If you draw, you leave the box blank and continue on to the next rolls.

You continue for six rounds of combat, until you reach the end of the row. Then whoever has scored the most amounts of hits is given a +1 advantage to the next row of fights. This advantage subsides after one row.

Fights can last between twelve and twenty four rounds, which can mean 1-4 rows. After the final row, all hits are added up and the person with the highest score wins.

Of course fights can differ. When you enter a fight, you will be told how many rounds there are, and whether you must add advantages for your enemy or special rules.

## USING TIME TRAVEL ABILITIES

Time travel abilities give you choices in combat that can seriously alter your chance of winning, but it is all dependent on how many TTPs you have.

## SLOW TIME

Slow time is an ability you have right from the beginning of this game.

During any combat roll, you can add up to 2TTP to influence the outcome of your roll.

**Note that you will not be allowed to add to rolls where you have to make a special roll of over 10 or a double.**

## REWIND TIME

Rewind time is also an ability you have right from the beginning of this game. You can use this in combat three ways.

Rather than use slow time to add to an existing roll, you can take both yours and your enemy's roll again. Bear in mind that your rolls may turn out worse. (Cost 2TTP)

If you reach the end of a row and are not happy with the outcome, you can replay the entire row, removing all hits scored and starting again from the first square. (Cost 5TTP)

Or you can restart the entire fight. (Cost 8TTP)

**Once you have started a fight, you cannot use your TTP to return to the previous passage unless you are able to reverse to the beginning of the fight first.**

You will also discover other time abilities as you progress through the game.


### 7.     DAY AND NIGHT

Night and day is consecutive. If it is night when you time jump it will be day when you return, and vice versa.

When it is day, you are able to come and go from the house as you please, without encountering the man in black.

When it is night, you are trapped in the house until your next time jump and may encounter the man in black any time you leave a room. You also cannot go into the town or into the garden.

If you would rather play a simpler game, you can choose to ignore the rules of day and night altogether which will allow you to come and go as you please without the added threat of the man in black appearing. Choosing to do this will make a number of items obsolete, including the obsidian dagger. If this is your decision you can skip this tutorial and **return to 13.** If you choose to go ahead with these rules, continue reading.

### TIME JUMP RECHARGE

Whereas normally you would be able to time jump when you want, unfortunately when it is night, you must recharge the amulet for four rounds before you can do so. You will recharge one round for each new passage you read. If you do not have enough new passages to read, you can recharge any number of rounds by waiting in the corridor. However for every round you do this, you must roll to see if you encounter the man in black.

Bear in mind that once you unlock the 1800s map, whenever you go there it still counts as a time jump.

If you do not have any time jump coordinates, rather than wait four rounds and time jump, you can wait for the following day. To do this you must either read six new passages, or wait for six rounds in the corridor.

## 8.     THE MAN IN BLACK ATTACKS

Every time you leave a room, or for each round you wait in the corridor, you must roll one die.

If you roll a 1, the man in black will appear and attack you.

If you have no means to defend yourself, roll the die again.

If you roll a 1-5, you will lose that amount of TTP and continue playing.

If you roll a 6 or have 0TTP when he attacks, then the attack is fatal and your adventure ends here.

## USING THE OBSIDIAN DAGGER

If you have the obsidian dagger, you can fend off the man in black's attacks.

To do so, you must roll either, over 10 or a double within three throws.

If you succeed, he will be temporarily banished from the house and will not return for another three rounds. This means that the next three times you leave a room, or rounds you wait, you do not have to roll to see if you will encounter him. However, if you fail, the man in black will attack the same as usual.

# A NOTE TO THE READER

Thank you so much for purchasing this book and seeing the whole adventure through to the end. I hope you enjoyed playing it as much as I did writing it. If you did, you will be interested to know that 'The Ghosts of Craven' manor is the first part in an intended series, and that it is my intention for your progress in this book to crossover to the next.

I have some ideas already with how I intend to do that. Some of the characters who you met in this book, providing that they weren't killed, may cross paths with you in the next. Also some items and powers might carry on over and either give you an advantage or disadvantage when you start out on your next adventure. And depending on what ending you got, will also alter how the story begins.

I also have plans to release another adventure book set within the universe of 'The Hermacles Divide'. This is a fantasy universe of multiple worlds, in which my young adult fantasy novel series of the same name is set. The first of these novels: 'The coming of the Dhufal', is currently available for purchase on Amazon Kindle, if you were interested in getting an idea of the world before the adventure book is released.

Now, I'm afraid to say, that none of these plans are set in stone. I am foremost, a novelist of fiction, so whether I write any more adventure books is dependent on how this book is received. If you would like to see more time travelling, and possible other types of adventures in the gamebook genre, please help me spread the word about this book by rating and reviewing it on Amazon and Goodreads, mentioning it on your blogs, your Facebook and Twitter accounts, and all other social media channels. Anything you do will be a great help, and will see that these game books continue.

I thank you again

Joseph Daniels

Made in the USA
Monee, IL
23 September 2020